The Rylerran Gateway

Mark Ian Kendrick

iUniverse, Inc.
New York   Bloomington

The Rylerran Gateway

Copyright © 2008 by Mark Ian Kendrick

All rights reserved. No part of this book may be used or reproduced by any means, graphic, electronic, or mechanical, including photocopying, recording, taping or by any information storage retrieval system without the written permission of the publisher except in the case of brief quotations embodied in critical articles and reviews.

This is a work of fiction. All of the characters, names, incidents, organizations, and dialogue in this novel are either the products of the author's imagination or are used fictitiously.

iUniverse books may be ordered through booksellers or by contacting:

iUniverse
1663 Liberty Drive
Bloomington, IN 47403
www.iuniverse.com
1-800-Authors (1-800-288-4677)

Because of the dynamic nature of the Internet, any Web addresses or links contained in this book may have changed since publication and may no longer be valid. The views expressed in this work are solely those of the author and do not necessarily reflect the views of the publisher, and the publisher hereby disclaims any responsibility for them.

ISBN: 978-0-595-52625-3 (pbk)
ISBN: 978-0-595-62677-9 (ebk)

Printed in the United States of America

TABLE OF CONTENTS

Prologue	vii
Part I	1
Part II	131
Part III	345
Epilogue	415
People, Places and Things	419

Prologue

S'Hith, H'Tor and G'San, all of the 2nd Telkan Science Inquiry Team, ran as fast as their two primary legs could carry them. Dodging low bush branches and trying to avoid the projectiles the Kelna'ack raiders were firing at them, they followed the narrow, barely perceptible dirt trail in the gathering darkness. The nearby nebula hadn't yet risen to fill the night with its even sky glow. No matter. The Telkan weren't bred on this uninhabited world, but rather were interlopers, as were the Kelna'ack.

G'San, who was in the lead, activated the display on the device he held tightly in one of his hands. The cavern, which held the recently discovered gateway, was slightly over eighty metyons away. The brush still obscured their view of the slight rise that marked the entrance to the cavern. His voice rang out a full two octaves higher than normal due to the stress of the chase. "This way!" His companions re-doubled their efforts, even lowering their secondary legs in a futile attempt to accelerate their race to the cavern. Those legs weren't built for such speed or to bear their full weight as they had tens of thousands of years ago, but the instinct to use them still lay in their genes when danger arose.

All four of H'Tor's lungs were working overtime. His nostrils flared in an attempt to draw in more air. "I can't make it," he hissed.

"You can, clansmate," G'San told him. "It's just a bit further."

H'Tor summoned all his strength and pressed on. Moments later the foliage gave way to a clearing in front of the cave.

Another whine rang through the leaves and branches behind them. A round found its mark, striking G'San's shoulder with its poisonous potassium-sulphur mixture. It penetrated cleanly through his clothing and flesh, then struck the stone in front of him. It ricocheted somewhere within the cavern's entrance. The marksman couldn't have known he had made a hit since the tormentors were still dozens of metyons behind them through thick undergrowth.

G'San's first reaction was anger. They had run so far into the brush and had finally arrived at the cavern only to be shot just at that moment. He knew the Kelna'ack weren't interested in killing their quarry in a fast merciful way, but rather relished the slow painful death of their highly feared chemically powered and laden projectiles. But the searing pain of the projectile replaced his anger. G'San stifled his normal reaction to roar out loud. He slumped against the cavern entrance. He attempted to hold himself up, but the pain was already overwhelming. S'Hith and H'Tor quickly grabbed him and pulled him upright. G'San's backpack strap dug unto his armpit as they did so.

They knew the way. They had to enter the cavern then travel down the right wing where their investigation team had found the ancient tunnel. The tunnel was inside a large, highly polished rectangular stone made by an unknown race for an, at first, unknown purpose.

Only recently had they culled its mystery from the remote past. After the iridescent disc-shaped devices were discovered in a nearby cubbyhole, it quickly became obvious that the tunnel-like structure was a transportation device, a gateway into another quantum dimension. Very little else was known about the gateway. It seemed to belong to their universe, yet it didn't have all the properties objects normally possessed. It was powered by a means completely elusive to the Telkan scientists who analyzed it. It allowed one to emerge into a place nearly identical to their own, yet somehow different. Not enough study had been brought to bear to fully understand where just yet. The other scientists working on that mystery were now dead from Kelna'ack weapons fire only minyons before.

Now only these three knew of the mysterious tunnel's existence. The rest of their investigation team at the camp were either dead by now or would be shortly. For what reason? Sport. The Kelna'ack were nothing more than marauding sport killers. They hunted their Telkan quarry whenever they came across them. Once they killed everyone they would burn anything they found. Not interested in Telkan technology, the Kelna'ack wanted nothing except bragging rights for the kill. It defied logic that a spacefaring race could be so bloodthirsty. But it was a reality. Thousands of Telkans had died by their hands over the last four decanes.

The Kelna'ack hadn't claimed the star system or this world. Indeed there had been no reports of Kelna'ack venturing this far from their known hunting quadrants. These marauders must have followed the recent re-supply ship's ion trail to the surface of this planet. Once Telkan ships went sublight they left such a trail in space. Even the solar winds in this system couldn't erase it quickly enough.

The three scientists now gathered in the cavern had had only a few minyons warning. They had all been together in Lab Building C when B'nir triggered the warning klaxon from across the encampment. They had gathered the scant belongings they happened to have with them and raced toward the cavern's shelter once they realized that Kelna'ack were upon them.

They had run as quickly as they could away from the research post, hearing the death roars of their comrades, the sickening sound of weapons fire, a small explosion, then just the wind in their tiny ears as they ran deeper and deeper into the brush.

Knowing they would be hunted down until they were dead, they took the only alternative they could. Get to the cavern that held the tunnel. Go through the tunnel and emerge here, yet not here. Perhaps they could simply hold out in the alternate world for a day, maybe even two, until the Kelna'ack left. No one liked the idea. The plan was crazy, but in G'San's backpack were the disc devices. At least no Kelna'ack would be able to follow them across. He had the only ones known to exist.

S'Hith was much younger than either H'Tor or G'San. He had yet to shed his second skin. For that he had endured much derision about his youth by the older scientists, especially from G'San. But it was S'Hith who was carefully pulling G'San along the corridor now. He may have gotten a lot of grief from his elder, but G'San was the smartest of all the team members. Smart and true. Two Telkan traits S'Hith found appealing. Traits he wanted to declare for himself at his Third Shedding, which was the declaration rite all adults celebrated.

Telkan eyes could function quite well in near-darkness, although they required some photons to see. They didn't dare switch on the string of lights they had earlier strung along the ceiling of the corridor. That would simply give the raiders easy access to them. H'Tor quickly pulled out a flat phosphorescent band from his backpack and pressed the adhesive side against his broad forehead. He pulled out another and pressed it against S'Hith's. Now, with an even greenish-white illumination above their eyes, they could more quickly make their way to the inner chamber. The chamber where the strange rock with the tunnel in it had lain for untold centremes before they accidentally discovered it.

The narrow corridor walls opened up to the chamber much more quickly this time. They had never rushed to make it here before.

G'San's breath was labored now. The pain in his shoulder had spread downward. His right secondary leg was useless now. He could barely feel it and couldn't move it anymore. He hissed. "The discs… each… gets one." Each ragged breath felt as if it was responsible for spreading the pain.

H'Tor tore open his pack and placed a disc into S'Hith's hand. He pressed another one into G'San's still-working hand. The third he held in his own hand.

A distinct noise came from the dark corridor behind them. The three ceased all movement to listen. Their ears were tiny but tuned to a broad frequency range. Nearly imperceptible vibrations told them the murderers were on their way. Footsteps echoed faintly. One set. Two. Three. Now four. Four against three, and no weapons with which to defend themselves.

They had performed only two tests on the strange tunnel they had discovered. Those tests, which B'nir had volunteered for, proved the device led to a world much colder than this world. It was in the midst of an ice age. They weren't dressed for that climate. Yet, it was that or die a painful death. After holding out as long as they could and then returning, they might find a working communications computer. With it they could send a signal to the satellite they had in orbit in hope of being rescued later on. That is, if the satellite was still in orbit. It was a stretch to be sure, but G'San who was a quick thinker had worked out the scenario in his head even before they had left the research building.

G'San passed out. His body slumped as if lifeless. S'Hith let go of him and was immediately blinded by the bright lights they had strung up. Their tormentors must have found the on switch! It took several secyons for both S'Hith and H'Tor eyes to adjust. The sounds of the footsteps were hurried, frantic. The scientists were being hunted. Sensors must have told the killers where their quarry was located.

H'Tor pointed to G'San's primary legs. "We'll pull him across," he hissed as quietly as he could. H'Tor placed his hands beneath G'San's shoulders.

S'Hith obeyed and grabbed G'San's legs. Just as he stood up, the sound of a weapon being discharged rang out in the corridor behind him.

S'Hith couldn't believe the searing pain he felt. He dropped G'San's legs and placed his hand over an open wound in his chest. The Kelna'ack weapon had pierced him from back to front, passing through his body, just as it had G'San's. The same projectile had pierced H'Tor's left secondary leg, too. The pain wasn't enough for him to let go of G'San's shoulders, but it made him hesitate.

"S'Hith! Go. Now! I can pull G'San across myself," H'Tor ordered.

S'Hith bent down slightly and literally threw himself into the tunnel. Once he reached the middle of it he instantly disappeared from view. H'Tor dragged the totally limp body of his colleague through. They slowly disappeared across the shimmering barrier inside the mysterious tunnel. There was no sound, no indication anything had activated. In a silent instant, they simply disappeared from one quantum universe and emerged into another

PART I

Chapter 1

The city of Tokaias on Andakar sprawled along the northwestern shore of Koehkelko bay near the foothills of the Patoria Mountains. The bay was an almost perfect three-quarter circle. The city was the hub of Andakar culture, was its business center, and had the largest spaceport on the planet. Due to its protected location at the interior of the bay, Tokaias had many cruise ship docks, which served thousands of tourists throughout the year. Being so close to the equator gave its denizens nearly thirteen and a half hours of sunlight and darkness each day.

Tokaias's scattered public buildings displayed striking classic Roman architecture. Citizenship Hall, built in this enduring style, was one of the more impressive buildings in the southeast part of the city. Situated two blocks east of the downtown administrative center building, the hall was where all persons, native born or not, who reached 29 Andakar years of age became Citizens. That is, of course, if they had passed the Citizenship Exam. The extra requirement for nonNates was they had to be naturalized.

The hall's front façade was massive. Twenty-nine steps led up to an outer entryway. Six Ionic columns stood two stories high and overshadowed tall, elaborately carved boshwood doors at the front entrance. The building was clad with milky-red marble from a quarry in the foothills of the Frontside mountain range some thirty kilometers to the south. The dehumidifiers inside the hall were running at nearly full capacity. The outside air was already thick with humidity although it was still two weeks before the normal beginning of Haze Days, the hottest days of the year.

Two rows of uniformed men and women from the Andakar Space Navy filed in to the ceremony room from side entrances. Although the military was still considered new, it had already become a tradition for a detachment to accompany the proclamation of new Citizens. Their formal uniforms and regimented formation made a notable embellishment to what otherwise could have been a boring procedure.

One row of fifteen men and women formed to the left side of the audience, another to the right side, taking their places along the outer aisles.

One of the military men, Lieutenant Commander Darreth James-Po stood next to his buddy, another Lieutenant Commander named Rehl Takaramyus. This was Darreth's second time attending these proceedings. The first time was for his own citizenship ceremony nearly a year ago. This time was because his name came next on the roster.

Several men stood on the slightly raised platform at the front of the room. One was Kalder Pent, Tokaias's City Manager. However, the most dominating person was Darreth's father, Siloy James-Po, the Provincial Manager of Siaron province and Chief Council of the eleven provinces. Despite being well into his fifties, Siloy had a muscular chest and a lion's mane of mostly dark, slightly long hair. The overall impression of the man with his trim waistline yet imposing stance was of a proud lion. He would be giving a short speech to the participants before leaving for his next appointment. Standing next to the two men was the New Citizens department head.

Darreth hadn't taken note of the people in the audience yet since their own ranks had just halted, turned to face the seated crowd, then came to parade rest. His attention was immediately diverted to a man in the second row not more than three meters away. Darreth's buddy Rehl was to his right. Rehl saw Darreth's eyes immediately lock onto the figure in the audience. The look on Darreth's face wasn't difficult to read. He'd seen it before.

"Cute, huh?" Rehl asked in a whisper just loud enough for Darreth to hear. He knew he shouldn't be speaking at all, but couldn't help himself.

"No kidding," Darreth replied in the same whisper, still looking at the pre-Citizen.

"You think he's on your team?" Rehl whispered back.

"I doubt it. He's way too good looking."

"Pul-leeze," Rehl said as he rolled his eyes. "If you keep talking like that you're never gonna get another date."

The New Citizens department head took his place at the lectern and spoke into the microphone. "Ladies and gentlemen, please take your seats."

The seventy-three men and women in the audience gradually ceased their conversations. Those who were visiting with others or who were standing returned to their seats. Family and friends took to the back rows and quietly sat. The front rows were for inductees.

Now that he had a clearer view, Darreth studied the object of his desire in more detail.

Time and his genes had been good to pre-Citizen Naylon Sente Ress. When the Consortium ordered his family to emigrate to Andakar from Earth fifteen years previous, he barely weighed fifty-four Standard kilos, and was tall and thin. In the intervening years, Naylon had not only grown to a full 1.8 meters in height, but had blossomed to a solid eighty Standard kilos.

Naylon had been talking with a young woman in an adjacent row. Now that his eyes were fixed on the lectern, Darreth observed the sandy-blond haired man. Nice jaw, cute small ears, and nice rounded shoulders, Darreth decided. *I wonder if he's with someone*, he thought. *Hell, I wonder what his name is!* He would shortly find out since everyone's name was called over the loudspeaker as they came up to shake hands and be sworn in by the chief of the New Citizens department. But Darreth had an in. In case he didn't get to meet him, his father could easily get him access to data on any new Citizen.

Naylon was trying to listen to the chief but his attention kept being diverted to his left. He noticed one of the nearby military personnel staring at him. Naylon had to force himself to keep his eyes forward, yet was compelled to glance ever so often at that good looking man in the crisp blue uniform. The man averted his eyes each time Naylon peered at him. Naylon drank in details with each glance. Perhaps four centimeters taller, and beefier than he, the man had rugged good looks and skin darker than his own, based on the little of it he could see in that immaculate uniform. Even more striking was his salt and pepper hair. That was curious. *He certainly doesn't look old enough to have graying hair. It makes him very distinguished looking*, Naylon thought. He couldn't quite read the badge over the man's left breast pocket, but thought he saw the name James-Po when he glanced a third time. *That can't be*, he thought in surprise.

Naylon scanned the men up ahead of him on the low stage. He easily recognized Chief Councilor James-Po. After all, the man had been in that position for several years. As a public figure, his face was very familiar. Plus, virtually everyone knew him from his work in the entertainment field before being elected to his current position. An extremely popular leading man in holovids when he was in his 30s and 40s, his popularity never waned. His surprising entry into Andakar's local politics was seen as a strange but not unprecedented move. The charisma he exhibited on screen had easily transferred to his new position.

In his mind's eye Naylon tried to compare the two men's faces. Their mouths looked similar and they both had a trace of Asian features on their faces. But that was about all Naylon could discern. Naylon had never seen any of the rest of the family on a vid before. No, wait. He distinctly remembered watching a vid on one of the news streams from at least a year ago. The Chief Councilor's son had been promoted to Lieutenant Commander of one of the Andakar Space Navy surveillance patrols. *Wow*, he thought. *That just might be his son after all. Could he be any cuter? And wouldn't it be kick if he were gay!*

The ceremony ended forty minutes later. In succession, individuals were called by name to the slightly raised stage to receive their Certificates of Citizenship, ending with a formal handshake with the presiding official. It was similar to receiving a school diploma. Citizenship ceremonies were never long drawn out affairs, but necessary to establish official Consortium and planetary records.

After the last name was called, Naylon went to his parents' seats in the back of the room and gave them a hug. Naylon was an only child, so no siblings were present. Naylon was also single, so no partner was present either. His parents were all smiles. The rest of the new Citizens, along with their families and friends, were milling about, some exiting the building quickly, but most lingering. Naylon scanned the military contingent, looking for the man who had been giving him the eye earlier. He was nowhere to be seen.

A tap on his shoulder told him exactly where the man was.

"Um, Citizen Ress." Darreth said.

Upon seeing the uniformed man getting Naylon's attention, Naylon's father spoke. "Your mother and I will be in the lobby. We'll meet you out there," he said.

"Sure Dad." Naylon quickly turned to Darreth. "Hi, uh...," He quickly looked at the badge, making sure he read it clearly this time. It was indeed the name he thought it was. "Mr. James-Po," he said aloud.

"Lieutenant Commander." Darreth pointed to the pips on his collar.

"Oh, sorry."

"I saw you in the crowd," Darreth said. "Congratulations." He stuck out his hand.

Naylon shook it. *Nice grip.* "Thanks."

"I, uh...," he glanced at Rehl who was standing nearby. Darreth could clearly make out the furtive motion of Rehl's blonde head. A motion telling Darreth to ask the question already. Darreth smiled, hoping he wasn't visibly blushing. "was wondering if you, uh, were single."

Naylon's head was swimming already. *Thunder! He is gay.* Naylon didn't answer right away. "Since you're being so forward I will be, too. Are you the Chief Councilor's son?"

Darreth pressed an index finger to his lips. He answered with a grin. "Shh. It's supposed to be a secret."

"Are you asking me out?" Naylon asked.

"You have to answer me first. You are gay, aren't you?"

"You can bet your pips on that. And I'm single."

Whew. "I thought I was climbing a prongtop tree." Darreth's reference to the poisonous breeding trees of Andakar's flying hydrogen-filled creatures wasn't lost on Naylon. In fact, the alarm bells were already ringing in Naylon's head. This was just not right. Just two days ago, he had been engaged in a rather disparaging discussion with friends about military people. Yet, his pulse was putting the memory of the conversation on hold. "I've never been asked out by a man in uniform before."

"I didn't ask you out yet," Darreth reminded him.

"But you're going to, huh?" That much had been obvious the moment he met Darreth.

"Well, yeah."

Naylon was rather enjoying the attention. "You're on," he responded.

"Now that that's out of the way, I have to tell you I don't usually ask people I just met out."

"Right," Naylon slowly replied.

"I swear," Darreth said, raising his right hand. "My buddy over there made me do it."

Naylon looked over at Rehl, mock saluted him, then turned his full attention to Darreth. He smiled warmly. "Tell your buddy I'm glad he did."

Chapter 2

Naylon's initial attraction to Darreth was almost immediately replaced with a sense of dread. It was completely unfounded. After all, Darreth exuded nothing that should have invoked such an emotion.

It was all because of the discussion group.

The group consisted of men and women from Naylon's alma mater. Some were still attending the university, but most had already graduated. The object of their discussions, completely outside the realm of academics, was politics. Naylon had been asked to join because he had a keen intelligence, a unique perspective, and a fascination with history. The media was famous for glossing over important current and social events, never explored cultural trends, and talked about tabloid subjects ad nauseam. The group was a way for them to take a news story and trace its origin to specific events on either Andakar or societies on other Inhabs, find out who major players were, and generally do the in-depth analysis they felt was missing from what they felt were topics of import. In a way, it was like solving mysteries, which all of them had a propensity for doing. It was well known that although information freely flowed all over space it was censored when it came to making sure profits were maintained. Since Naylon's occupation consisted of culling the past for clues to the present, it caused him to pay attention to how civilization progressed as well. The past could be a great mystery, ready for solving, just like the present.

As in all organizations and societies, there were formal and informal chains of communication, formal and informal ways of doing business, aboveboard methods of acquisition and those that existed only in the shadows. There were Citizens and non-Citizens. There were Andakar natives and there were nonNates. Formal communication patterns were pretty obvious due to news sources and how the Consortium ran the underlying structure of the economy. There were various corporate alliances that went across solar systems and there were small contracts that went virtually undetected in the grand scheme of things. Naylon's discussion group debated all the connections and interconnections and what real-world effect they had. Recently, a particularly heated discussion centered on the military sub-culture on Andakar.

Human civilization spanned fourteen worlds, with Earth at the corporate center. Andakar and Rylerra were still the newest links in the long chain of supply and demand. Andakar's economy had generated a huge amount of wealth for its citizens as the years had gone by. Their society benefited directly from this wealth due to the many channels of trickle down that were, by law, in place. This windfall had triggered a levy by the Central Planning and Direction Division, the branch of the Deep Sky Mining Consortium that was directly below the top offices on Earth. Although the levy had been in place for decades, recently more and more people were talking openly about the injustice of such a tax.

There had always been a delicate balance between local planetary management and the corporate entities that answered mostly, if not solely, to Earth. The separation of corporate control over business by the Planetary Director, and local planetary control by provincial managers had been in place on all Inhabs since the first one was established. Such separation had been strictly enforced for hundreds of years.

A recent abuse of corporate control over the local affairs in Ocal province on Andakar, where most of the pharma processing took place, had led to an investigation. Once the evidence had been compiled, four CEOs from the off-world corporations who had meddled far too much in infrastructure affairs had been deported. Further investigation uncovered such abuses in several other provinces. When the full council met to discuss the issue, it turned out the abuses had been going on for quite some time. All of those particular CEOs were nonNates. NonNates were, by law, not allowed to have local internal control of provincial issues on any planet.

One of the ongoing discussion threads in Naylon's chat group had been about why Andakar society needed a military of any kind, despite the intense PR that had accompanied its formation. Since his parents were directly involved with the production of pharmas Naylon knew exactly why it was important. In fact, a large proportion of the population was involved in the vertical markets that eventually shipped raw and finished pharmas off-planet.

Nonetheless, Naylon had always been conflicted about this issue. The military was needed to protect their precious products, but in his mind, the personnel who volunteered for the job were thickheaded and not so intelligent. That meant they were dangerous in his estimation. Yet, the military was completely outside the realm of academia, where he kept 99% of his focus. Because of that, he had never even bothered to be acquainted with anyone in the Space Navy. The discussion had always been purely academic for him. Given this aversion to military types, Naylon never thought he'd be dating one. Despite finding Darreth supremely attractive, he declined both times when the man called to ask him out.

Naylon wasn't sure why he so steadfastly refused to even try the guy on for size. But he had to admit one thing. Darreth was easily the most handsome man he'd ever met. In an attempt to make excuses for his decision, he blamed it on the influence of the other people in his group. A terribly irresponsible excuse for sure.

The third time Darreth called, Naylon ran out of excuses. If anything, Darreth was persistent. He liked that in a man.

"Hey," Darreth greeted with a wide smile on the vidscreen.

Naylon could tell that Darreth was calling from orbit. There was a very dark window in the background with the cloudy limb of Andakar further beyond. Darreth could be directly overhead. It was odd knowing that.

"Hey," Naylon returned, trying not to be too enthusiastic. He tried, but failed to suppress a smile. Darreth's handsome face was beguiling.

"You know why I'm calling, I'm sure."

"I think I do," Naylon said, stalling.

"I'm going to be planetside tomorrow. I was hoping you might be free for a few hours. Perhaps for dinner? I've made reservations." A map and the address of the restaurant appeared on Naylon's display.

"You did?" Naylon asked with a nervous voice. It looked like there would be no backing out this time.

"How about I meet you somewhere beforehand."

"That restaurant is nearby." Naylon was at work in the museum. "You could, uh, come here first."

"Great. I can't wait to see you." Darreth smiled to himself. *Yes!*

Naylon's official title was Ph.D. His had earned his advanced degree from Tokaias University in paleo-microbiology. He had worked for the Tokaias Museum of Natural History for the last two years, cataloging fossilized flora and fauna, a job that, to most, would be fabulously boring. Naylon had always had an inquisitive mind and this particular line of work provided him with just enough mystery as well as hardcore science to make a long day interesting.

It was a half hour after sunset in the middle of the week. Naylon was in the museum's lab. The leading edge of the distant Tovar Nebula stretched across the quickly darkening sky. The beautiful silvery-green haze lit up the dark as brightly as would three full moons on Earth. Andakar may have lacked even a single tiny moon, but the nebula's brightness and beauty made up for that loss.

Per Naylon's instructions, the museum guard had been expecting Darreth. The guard escorted him through the lobby, then down the back hallway to the spacious lab. Large picture windows spanned a good length of the hallway, which was one wall of the lab. Naylon saw them approach.

The guard returned to his post as Darreth greeted Naylon.

"Lieutenant Commander," Naylon acknowledged.

"Uh, that's reserved for when I'm on duty," he said, smiling. "You only get to call me by my name."

"Good. I was hoping our date wouldn't be formal."

"I'm only formal when I'm in uniform."

Naylon took note of the implication and drank in the sight of his date. Not being particularly romantic or one to believe in love at first sight, he was nonetheless enamored with Darreth's appearance. Darreth was wearing a light green two-piece tunic typical of Andakar society. Since the climate was almost always hot and humid, virtually all clothing was light and efficiently designed to wick away perspiration. Darreth had obviously gotten a recent haircut, too. His salt and pepper locks were cropped short. A perfect clockwise swirl graced his crown. Product in his hair made it shine under the lights in the lab.

Naylon's clothing was very similar, except for a lab coat, which he was still wearing. He wondered if he should have at least shaved, then promptly forgot about it as he watched Darreth's every move.

Darreth wasn't hunky in a classical sense, but he was filled out where it counted. He sported firm biceps and ample shoulders. Naylon loved a well-developed upper body. But Darreth's face was of particular interest, especially his delicious dark brown eyes, the long dark lashes, and those full pouty lips.

Darreth glanced around the lab. Naylon's desk was a flat white surface with dozens of glass slides sitting in marked trays. Several pieces of equipment sat on the desk as well, the most conspicuous one being a scanning vector microscope. Two small toaster oven-shaped devices, one with its small door ajar, were to each side. One was labeled Quantum Spectrometer, the other Radiometric Dating Analyzer.

"So, what is it you do here?" Darreth was completely unfamiliar with the equipment.

Naylon glanced at his wristcomp to check the time. They had plenty. "I can show you around, if you'd like."

"Maybe a quick tour. The reservation's for 2000 hours."

"Sure. It's not like I can actually show you a lot of stuff. Most of what I do is research and cataloging." Naylon turned to the microscope. "The museum's lab depends on a team of paleontologists working all over the continent. They bring in samples for us to analyze. Our job is to sort, date and catalog them. But I'm working on a special project."

"Which is?"

"To determine why higher life forms never evolved on our planet."

"For what reason?" Darreth asked, intrigued.

"It's part of an ongoing project that started ninety-seven years ago."

"That's, uh, when Andakar was first colonized."

"Exactly. After the first colonists arrived and discovered that the superocean was teeming with life, but the continent wasn't, they were totally puzzled. After all, our sun is half a billion years older than Sol, so why higher forms of life never evolved on land like they had on Earth was the big question."

"Isn't that already known? We have no moons and barely any tides. I thought you needed good-sized tides to evolve higher life forms on land. Plus, Andakar has no record of super-volcanoes. I was sure I learned that a planet has to have a periodic destruction of its ozone layer from huge volcanic eruptions to help solar radiation mutate DNA."

Naylon was completely taken aback. He surely wasn't expecting Darreth to know such esoterica. "Wow. Where did you learn that?"

"I don't remember exactly. Grade school, maybe?" He grinned. In fact, he had done a quick background study of what a paleontologist did, having had only a cursory understanding of the profession.

"Well, those are the prevailing theories. It's still a mystery actually. It's one I hope to help crack," Naylon told him proudly. "That, and maybe add more clues as to why the life forms in our superocean are so bio-available for pharmas."

"I don't get it. How does research about our past help produce any product for export?"

Naylon was the first one to know what Darreth meant by a statement like that. A pure research position was somewhat unusual. "I'm working under the budget of a special grant."

"Really?" he exclaimed. "Who's funding it?"

"AshtaPharma, Ltd, of course. Who else?"

"Of course. The largest pharma corp on the planet. I thought they only cared about profit."

"They have an extraordinarily large budget. The military isn't exactly a profit center either." The words shot out of Naylon's mouth before he could stop himself. *Oops*, Naylon thought. *I can't believe I even said that.*

Darreth's voice took on a defensive tone. "We make sure profits are kept and product is not stolen. We earn our keep."

Naylon quickly sought to make amends with a quick apology and tentatively patted Darreth's muscular shoulder with what he hoped would be a sign of peace.

The seven other employees in Naylon's department had long since gone home for the day, so they had unrestricted access to the lab. Naylon showed him the rest of the equipment and they left for dinner shortly thereafter.

Darreth took Naylon in his hovercar to a four-star restaurant overlooking Pier Five on Koehkelko Bay. Darreth had reserved a table for two at the far wall of windows. From their third floor vantage all they could see was the tip of several piers below them, along with a few cruise ships docked nearby. The wide expanse of dark water beyond was broken by lights reflecting on the surface from the curved shoreline and the glow of the nebula overhead.

The waiter returned to their table moments after he had left. He showed Darreth the label of the bottle he was holding. Darreth nodded, the man uncorked it and poured them both a third of a glass. Darreth had selected a bottle of selkwine, a drink similar to wine on Earth. Native to the Inhab Alkuros, the product's many variants were some of its most sought after exports. He was glad to see they had had a 2809 vintage, considered one of the best years. The waiter took their orders and they were finally alone. Darreth picked up his glass. Naylon did the same. They clinked them together and each took a sip.

"You know, a much less expensive restaurant would have done nicely for our first date," Naylon said.

"No way. I love this place. They serve the best kinerfish in the entire city."

Naylon's mouth watered at that remark. They had both ordered the kinerfish. He had ordered his rare with a spiced overripe quidwe fruit sauce. His favorite style.

"I'll be honest with you. I was a little apprehensive about going on this date with you," Naylon confessed.

"Why?"

"I've never been out with a military man before. Plus, you're the Chief Council's son."

Darreth rolled his eyes for the briefest of instants. "Forget about that 'Chief Council's son' part. It was an accident of birth."

"You're no accident," Naylon remarked, as he took in Darreth's square set jaw, his short hair standing up at his hairline, and the tunic shirt opened at the top. Naylon could just see a few dark hairs peeking out.

"Neither are you," Darreth replied with a grin.

"You're embarrassing me," Naylon stated.

"You started it."

There was a brief moment of quiet while the two men took another sip.

"So, tell me about your job," Naylon said as he set his selkwine glass down.

"Well, my ship's the ASN *Challenger*."

"I'm not all that familiar with the ships," Naylon admitted.

"It's a scout ship."

"Isn't it seriously dangerous on one?" He was only familiar with them being much smaller than passenger ships.

"We have all the latest weaponry. All the latest scanning equipment, too. The nav is a fully bio-neural holo interface. And the *Challenger* has the best shielding for a ship of its size. My squadron's recovered the top number of tons of stolen pharmas with no casualties on our side." Darreth didn't elaborate. Naylon wasn't sure he wanted to know more either.

The two men's salads arrived. Made with tangy shredded nopa leaves, the succulent inner skin of ripe jastacren pods, and drizzled with chilled leron sauce, they dug right in.

"What did you do after the citizenship ceremony?" Darreth asked after his first bite.

"I went back to work."

"Too bad it wasn't quitting time, huh? You could have just ended the day with a big party."

"I didn't mind really. Can you believe my father even mentioned that back on Earth I'd have to go back to work, too?"

"You used to work on Earth?"

"Nope. I was born there."

"Seriously?" he said, giving Naylon his full attention, his salad forgotten for the moment.

Naylon nodded.

Darreth's demeanor shifted slightly at that news. "You're a hollowhe…uh, I mean a nonNate?" Darreth almost said 'hollowhead', which was an extremely derogatory expression used for those not born on Andakar. "Sorry. I didn't mean that. I swear. I didn't know…"

"I'm a naturalized Citizen. I think you were there," Naylon flatly stated. He wasn't sure whether to be insulted or not.

To Darreth this bit of news completely shifted the tone of their date. For the majority of his life he had harbored a secret prejudice against nonNates. Most of the prejudice stemmed from being a third generation Andakari. In addition, he had first hand experience of what off-worlders wanted when they came to his planet. He'd met dozens of them because his father had to entertain many delegates, mostly from Ulult and Ajica Prime, the closest Inhabs other than Rylerra. By far though, the worst people he'd ever met were from Earth. Most of them were arrogant, petulant, and had an offensive sense of entitlement. Yet,

Naylon was clearly not like them. "You seem different," Darreth told him.

Another insult? "Different?"

"I mean your attitude. You don't seem like a typical Earther."

Whew. "I was fourteen Standard when we left. I barely remember Earth."

"Oh." Darreth quickly tried to re-establish their rapport, sorry about his slip of the tongue. "Uh, what country were you born in?"

"New Zealand."

"Let's see if I remember my Earth geography. Canberra's the capital, right?"

"Nope. That's Australia, which is next door. Wellington's the capital. I was born there."

Darreth briefly looked down at his food then back up to Naylon. "I'm sorry about saying that. Really. It just came out."

"Don't agit," Naylon told him. It wasn't the first time he'd been called a hollowhead.

Darreth returned his attention to his salad and took another bite. "Do you miss it? Earth, I mean."

Naylon shook his head emphatically. "Not even for a second. This is my home. My parents are the ones who talk about missing it. They keep talking about going back for a vacation. Personally, I don't see why. It's a long trip."

"What kind of work do they do?"

"They're both pharma techs. That's how we ended up here. The Consort forced them to emigrate because of their specialties…. Hey, enough about me. I'm guessing that since your dad is the head of the Council you've got a pretty high profile."

A corner of Darreth's mouth went up as he stabbed his salad. "I've got a recognizable name, of course. But I'm treated just like everyone else."

No way. "But you must get special privileges," Naylon insisted.

"Seriously. I have to follow the same rules as everyone else."

They finished their salads. Shortly afterwards their steaming plates of kinerfish arrived.

Dinner consisted of more small talk and Naylon trying to figure out where their relationship was going. As the evening progressed, he welcomed the realization that Darreth's hollowhead remark was nothing more than a harmless, unconscious reflex.

"You don't live in Sakirse?" Naylon asked as Darreth's hovercar whizzed past the last entrance gate. Sakirse was the compound just outside Tokaias's city limit where a large number of Andakar's Space Navy personnel lived.

"Nope. I've got my own place nearby."

"Okay, so you get at least one perk by being a James-Po."

"You got me there," Darreth admitted. "It's the only perk I really have."

Darreth continued for another kilometer and turned onto a street to the right, then went two more blocks. He touched down onto an oval landing pad three houses further down. Naylon touched the control on the door after the car came to a stop. The gullwing lifted up. He stepped out, observing a nice bungalow separated by the ones next door on two sides by brick walls. A short fence delineated the front yard from a sidewalk. A ring of chairs around a circular table was near the front door on the front porch, illuminated by an overhead light. It was a nice cozy place.

"I have to work tomorrow," Naylon said in a non-committal tone.

"I'll get you back in time to get ready."

Naylon was pleasantly surprised. His date had gone a lot better than he had anticipated. After the initial gaffe by Darreth during dinner, Naylon noted the man had nearly fallen over himself to make sure he was the perfect gentleman afterward. He was impressed by that alone. He had been sure Darreth was going to fulfill his low expectations of what a person in the military would be like. Darreth should have been full of bravado and machismo, perhaps even be completely stupid. Instead, Naylon found him to be charming and quite intelligent. Plus, he sprang for a really nice dinner.

The bungalow was sparsely but tastefully furnished. The ceiling of the combined living room and den was at least three meters high. The dark translucent wall was obviously a holo interface, while the others were a mustard color. The kitchen off to the left had all the latest appliances and was spotless. After all, Darreth spent most of his time in orbit aboard the *Guardian* space station.

"How often do you get to come planetside?" Naylon asked playfully.

"Hmm. Which definition of come are you referring to?" Darreth asked playfully as he turned on the music center and adjusted its volume with his neural control implant. A light jazzy sound came from the soundfield generator.

A common control and communications device for the majority of the adult population of their civilization, Naylon also had an implant. Connected directly to the language center of one's brain by a thin network of semi-organic tendrils, the implants took the place of remote controls and short-range communications devices.

Naylon chuckled at Darreth's comeback. "Whichever definition you want to choose."

"There. How's that volume?" Darreth asked as he took a seat close to Naylon on the couch.

"That's fine," Naylon told him.

"To answer your question, I travel planetside at least three times a month. I try to come a lot more often though."

"Will you be coming tonight?"

"That depends on you." He shifted a little more closer to Naylon.

"I'm trying to play hard-to-get since this is our first date, but I have a feeling I'm not going to do so well." Naylon already felt a stirring in his loose trousers and placed a hand at his crotch.

Darreth smiled impishly and glanced down at the now obvious bulge. "You hiding a swella?" With that, he leaned over and placed a kiss on Naylon's neck.

Naylon didn't answer as he turned his head to lock lips with Darreth. Naylon was ecstatic. Darreth was bold but without the harsh edge he expected. In addition, this guy was unlike his long and unsuccessful string of dates with academic types. And while he normally didn't have sex on the first date, Darreth's hot breath had already made him relinquish that protocol.

Forty minutes later, wrapped in the sheet Darreth had pulled from a small hall closet, they still lay on the couch, which had been pulled out flat. Both of their clothes were in a pile on the floor next to it. It had been rather quick by Naylon's standards, but very satisfying.

"I really have to get back home soon," Naylon said with a yawn.

"It's not even 2230." He leaned into Naylon and French-kissed him again.

"You taste like my come," Naylon told him.

"I hope I can sample more of it."

"Are you asking me out again?"

Darreth just nodded his head. A huge smile showed his perfectly white teeth.

Naylon had been sure after tonight he'd be history. "Are you serious?"

Darreth rose up on an elbow as he nodded again.

"You *are* serious."

Chapter 3

Dr. Alista Kosovil was tall. Standing a full 1.88 meters, she was four centimeters taller than Naylon and almost a year older. Her hair was straight but soft, cut short and very platinum blonde. It hung like a mop around her head, complete with bangs in front. With her long thin facial features and olive skin, the style looked exotic on her.

She sat in the workstation pod next to Naylon in the museum's lab, wearing the same type of lab coat as did he. Alista and Naylon had worked together since the day Naylon was hired. She was the one who suggested him out of the three candidates they had interviewed. Her specialty was paleoclimatology. Her job at the lab was to place the fossils Naylon identified into their proper climatic periods. She was only the second person on Andakar to work as a paleoclimatologist. Hers was the first full time paid position at the lab. In the last three years she had added two new climatic time periods to the still-developing chart. She had long suspected Andakar had undergone several cooler time periods, but had only identified two such periods so far. It was only a matter of time before she was sure some of Naylon's research would turn up the next one. Naylon's work on the fossil record would provide the vital information she needed.

Naylon was using an ultrasonic pick on a small chunk of rock under a microscope. The work was somewhat routine, so they were able to talk while they processed samples.

Alista had a reference flimsy on the work surface to her right. She touched the forward icon on it. The previous page faded out and was replaced by the next. Her search string was highlighted in red. She moved the data to a field on a spreadsheet she was filling in. "So, how did the date go? You haven't talked about him at all."

The last bit of limestone particles fell off the tiny fossil Naylon was cleaning. He rolled the fossilized object around with the micro tweezers. Another spiral *elagiva novus*. Nothing unusual had turned up so far. "He was one of the military contingent at my Citizenship ceremony the other day."

"And…"

"And he's really good looking."

"And…"

"And yes, we had sex."

"Of course," she said matter-of-factly.

Alista knew Naylon very well. They ate lunch together almost every day and hung out with the rest of the lab crew after work quite a bit. Their group was tight knit and it was almost impossible to keep secrets from each other. It was the camaraderie Naylon liked the most, making them a substitute family of sorts.

"And he wants to see me again," Naylon added. He pulled his eyes away from the magnifier panel and briefly rubbed them with a free hand.

She was quiet for a moment. "I'm jealous," she finally admitted.

"Why? It was you who kept pushing me to find a totally different type guy to date."

"I didn't think it would happen so fast." But she was smiling. She may have felt a brief bit of jealousy but it had already faded. She felt a slight bit of possessiveness about Naylon despite being happily married. In fact, Naylon was the godfather to her two-year old daughter.

"I'm surprised I like him so much," Naylon offered.

"Why's that?"

"Well, he is military," he said.

Alista knew what he was talking about. She knew all about the discussion group Naylon was involved in. She scrunched her eyebrows together, a not so pleasant look for her unusual features, and regarded Naylon's involvement with Darreth. "He's the Chief Council's first born, right?" she prompted.

Naylon nodded. "He seems to be mostly unaffected by that kind of privilege."

"How do you know? You just met him. I bet he's just hiding behind a happy face since you're so cute," she goaded, but smiled as she said it.

Naylon grinned. "Well, I've spent the night with him. He's given me his comm code," he added. His comm code would allow Naylon to talk to him directly through the use of his neural implant.

Alista regarded all of that. "Okay. But we'll see," she said skeptically. "When he's broken your heart who are you going to turn to?"

Naylon scooted his chair over to hers and turned slightly. He made a goofy grin, leaned in to her and laid his head on her slender shoulder.

"What in thunder are you doing, Dr. Ress?" she inquired, trying to sound serious.

Naylon twisted his head and looked up at her with a twinkle in his eyes. "Just proving you're my true confidant. If things don't work out you'll be the first to know."

Alista couldn't help but break into a smile as she pushed Naylon away. She pointed to his desktop. "Turn the magnifier light off, we have lunch to attend to."

The student union building at Tokaias University stood in the center of campus. Seven sidewalks radiated toward the building from the surrounding grounds. The university property looked like campuses had for the last millennium and a half. Tall stately buildings, graced with stone walls, massive Roman columns, and blocks of tree-lined sidewalks. The only difference between this campus and ones on Earth was that the trees were towering fernlike vegetation with fire-red spiked leaves that swayed in the breeze. Instead of verdant grass covered hills, this campus's grounds were blanketed with deep purple and bright red moss-like plants called fumilworts. The tough plants had a velvet feel and were amazingly resilient even when used as impromptu sports fields. Instead of birds nesting in the eaves of the buildings or in the trees, the warbling and whirring vocalizations of a dozen species of hydrogen-filled flyers greeted day students, while nocturnal hydrogen-filled flying insect sounds greeted the night class students' ears.

The escalator brought Naylon up from the underground transit stop to the campus's south entrance. He walked quickly to the student union building, passing dozens of students coming and going to classes. The tall streetlights provided ample illumination down onto the walkway. It was a typical night on campus.

His retina scan remained in the building's database since he kept his alumnus dues up. The door recognized him as he approached and opened to allow him entry. He headed down the corridor to the meeting room. The student union had many such rooms. Some had bare walls, others were adorned with artwork. Many had plush furniture. Some only a few stools. All were used for various activities, such as games, acting classes, storytelling, and in this case, the discussion group. Room 6 was one of the smaller ones. It had three couches, several coffee tables, a small food dispenser machine recessed into a wall, and a small bathroom. As Naylon neared the doorway he heard voices coming from the other side. The door quietly slid open and he entered.

The entire group had already convened. Naylon subvocalized the word 'time' and the universal time clock responded in his auditory cortex. He was sure he had been early. It appeared everyone else was early instead.

Tonight, only one of the seven people in the room was a current student. Naylon was the second academician present. All briefly greeted him as he took a seat next to Caddo, one of the graduates. Droon, the cute blonde graduate who worked at one of the local hydrogen generation stations, was just pulling a tray of baked chocoyams from the food dispenser. The delicious aroma had already filled the room. As soon as the tray hit the coffee table everyone except for Traig immediately snatched them up. Traig didn't care for their bitter aftertaste. A pitcher of light green jelnak tea was on the table next to the tray. Naylon poured some for Traig and himself, then settled back to savor the warm chocoyam confection.

Droon selected a seat next to Naylon and briefly looked at him with a smile on his face. He was the only other gay person in the group. Long ago Naylon had decided his mop of blonde hair, which constantly fell into his eyes, was his most endearing feature. After a brief liaison shortly after they first met, Naylon decided that although Droon was young, cute and terrific in bed, he was a bit too thin for his taste. Droon was also too radical for him. Droon found conspiracies in just about everything, up to and including the algae used at the station to generate hydrogen. Paranoia aside, Droon had a natural intelligence that lent itself well to the group. His pithy remarks and insightful commentaries constantly drove the group to take notice of what he had to say. Even though their partnership hadn't met Naylon's expectations, they had remained friends. Droon had long since given up hope of Naylon becoming his boyfriend.

Naylon realized Droon, as usual, was waiting for him to ask the question. Obliging him, he asked. "Well, is he getting the message?"

Last week Droon had asked Naylon to suggest the best approach for getting a co-worker's attention. Droon was becoming mildly infatuated with a guy who worked in his department. For some reason, he didn't think he'd have a chance with him. Naylon wasn't sure what the problem was. After all, it was Droon who had come on to him when they first met.

"I asked him," Droon announced excitedly.

"And?"

"I have a date."

"It's about time," Naylon said with a sigh of relief.

"Thunder, he's so cute," Droon stated with a grin.

"Like you've said a million times. I hope it works out for you." He nudged Droon in the arm with his elbow.

Their conversation was cut short by Kirin, the self-appointed leader of the group. She was the other academician and had a knack for public speaking. That and she had a preoccupation with keeping everyone on schedule due to her pre-teen children at home alone with her husband. They rarely went over two hours because of her sharp reprimands when someone got long-winded.

Tonight's topic was about a recent new tax issue Siaron province was expected to levy against every Citizen. The directive came from the Planetary Director's office, which in turn got its executive orders from much higher up in the Consort. Taxes weren't unusual. Indeed, taxes were expected. After all, it was one of the ways the wheels of the Consort were greased. This particular tax though, was little discussed in the media. Most people usually didn't notice taxes since they mostly affected company bottom lines. However, this one was an energy tax that affected the general population. It was highly unusual for a tax of this type to be levied against Citizens. Energy was generated locally through the use of hydrogen-producing algae, jet stream-powered wind fan kites which were tethered aloft over the landscape, from geothermal sources, or the microwave power plants in low orbit that beamed their converted solar energy to ground collecting stations. An energy levy was virtually unheard of. But this one passed into existence almost entirely unnoticed, mostly because the news media wasn't reporting the issue.

"I thought that by law all provincial governments were funded from the Development Division of the Consort," Ecca commented. She was one of the most outspoken people in the group.

"You are correct," Traig said, his head inclining toward her.

"Then why are they turning right around and siphoning that money back into their department? In effect, it ends up being a reduction of what they're giving us in the first place."

Naylon spoke up now. "It's because of our planetary resources. They think we'll never notice. Hardly anyone will if they take more away, bit by bit."

"It doesn't make any sense. The Consort makes enough money to do whatever they want. Why do they need to pick on us?" Sopka asked in her nasally whine, which sometimes got on Naylon's nerves if she droned on too long.

Naylon cut in quickly, hoping his comment would sufficiently answer her question, thus heading off the possible ranting tangents she was well known for. "They think we have some sort of privilege they need to get rid of, I guess. You know, tax us and it reduces our ability to purchase some sort of good or service we could enjoy."

Kirin added her own thoughts immediately, with the same goal in mind. She gave Naylon a quick wink, which Sopka couldn't see from her angle. "Yet, energy has never been a privilege. It's a right," she emphasized. "It's entirely possible something's changed that we're simply unaware of. Some policy or procedure or-or perhaps a reshuffling of personnel has occurred. What if someone with a bone to pick with our planet is now in place in some division we don't even know exists!"

The speculation went on for quite a while. It was great fun attempting to tie together the disparate threads of seemingly random events that popped up in their lives from time to time. Yet, fun was only part of the game. This one had the tag of true mystery all over it. Naylon suspected something far more nefarious was brewing at the Planetary Director's office complex, but without any sort of proof he didn't feel comfortable articulating it.

While the discussion went on, Droon confirmed by way of his neural implant that there was no record of any other Inhab having had an energy tax imposed at any time. Proof enough that Andakar was being singled out, just as everyone suspected.

Naylon had no way to confirm his other suspicion. Perhaps since Andakar was becoming increasingly wealthy, and as its pharma interests were becoming more and more lucrative, the Consort was feeling threatened. Earth had always been the wealthiest planet. No Inhab had ever come close to its level of prosperity. Maybe, just maybe, the accounting types in the Consort on Earth had determined Andakar was starting to catch up too fast and wanted to slow down their progress. Catching up would make them not only a rival, but an equal. *That*, Naylon thought, *would never be allowed*.

Eventually, the two hours were over. Despite the continuous speculations and questions, and not an answer to their questions in sight, everyone left the meeting to go their separate ways. Answers would have to wait for another day.

Chapter 4

It was rare nowadays for Darreth and his father Siloy to have dinner together with or without the rest of the family. His mother and two younger siblings were away, visiting their second home on Velcay island north of Tokaias. Darreth's mother Kyana demanded the time away periodically. Their high profile life took its toll on the family and she tried her best to give her children a break from it all.

When the Consort first started developing Inhabs, corporations ran everything. After all, that's the way governance had been structured for centuries leading up to the exploration of deep space. For centuries, the Consortium had owned and operated virtually everything. That included local political administration. Politics, as it had been known up until only fifty years previous, had been run by Local Boards of Directors, management teams, staff and laborers.

But the realization that corporate control at the local level was a growing impossibility had led to a complete overhaul of planetary governance. Slowly but surely, it had become recognized that some of the old ways were actually more efficient and beneficial. Thus, the return to a Provincial Board of Managers to act as governors, a mayoral structure to run cities, and district administrators to provide for infrastructure issues. There was a return to a limited form of politics as it had been known in the ancient past. Everyone involved welcomed a democratically elected slate of candidates. For the first time in centuries, control over the basics such as water, energy, communications, and infrastructure was totally in local hands and not controlled by someone from Earth, who previously would have made decisions for the locals, never having given them much thought.

Despite natives having local control, the Earth-based Consortium still owned and controlled everything else. That was why all fourteen Inhabs had a Planetary Director, appointed by the Earth Central Planning and Direction Division, who lived in the Inhab's administrative center city. This person was always Earth-born and trained. The PD reported directly back to Earth, which in turn reported to the Supreme Board of Directors, all of who resided on Earth.

Siloy's position as Chief Council, the highest elected official on Andakar, required him to wear many hats. First and foremost, the ten other provincial managers reported to him. The managers mostly met holographically. In fact, most council business was conducted in that manner. At least once a month though, planetary by-laws required face-to-face meetings. One of his other hats was to meet directors and division heads on their many visits to Tokaias or when they decided to tour a major facility. Siloy's many other jobs included making sure corporate law was upheld at the local level and to report any unemployment issues. His staff handled most of the day-to-day affairs and funding to various key departments, essentially acting as a traditional city council. Siloy was only the third Chief Council ever elected on the planet. So far, he had turned out to be the best one.

"Not so much ice, Dad," Darreth told him through the opened back door. Siloy poured them drinks, set the glasses on a tray, and brought them out to the back deck.

Darreth turned a succulent stuffed hejbird on a spit in the raised fire pit. Darreth rather enjoyed spending time with Siloy. His father's position had him working long hours most of the week. He was rarely three meters away from at least one local official. It was barely any different for Darreth. As a scout ship pilot, he was in orbit or on patrol and away from the family for long stretches as well.

But tonight was different.

Darreth had never had a problem discussing his personal life or work with his father. Despite Siloy's high-level position, he always had time for his children. But there was one topic Darreth had never broached with him. He had been working up the nerve to discuss it. Why he felt so nervous discussing this concern was a mystery to him, but finally he couldn't contain himself any longer. "Dad, I don't know if I should even discuss this with you, but there's something on my mind I have to talk about," Darreth had said while they watched wisps of smoke rise from the grill.

"You can talk to me about anything, son," Siloy told him warmly.

"It's corporate business."

Siloy took a sip of his drink then put it down on the side table next to the comfortable recliner he was sitting in. "That may be different.

I'm off the clock, as it were," he replied with his famous grin. His body language told Darreth the opposite though.

Darreth took a deep breath. "I'm beginning to think some of the directives issued by the Planetary Director's office are way off base."

"In what way?" he said, settling comfortably into his recliner, his attention immediately piqued.

"Don't you think it's a little odd we're not allowed to pursue pharma pirates if they're in our space," Darreth began somewhat nervously. "I mean, the directive says we're only allowed to fire on them if they've boarded our freighters. In addition, we're not to pursue them if they leave. We've never been able to recover a single nav crystal from any of their ships. We still have no idea where they're basing themselves, who their leaders are, or anything of importance I've been privy to. It's as if we're not allowed to fully do our jobs," he finished, his anger rising. "What good is it to call us a military force if we're not allowed to use that force?"

Space Navy contracts with the pharma division were clearly defined. Only starlanes were to be patrolled. Only events that directly affected the transport of goods and materials in the starlanes were under the jurisdiction of the Space Navy. Consort law controlled the military arm and dictated what was to be enforced. The Space Navy was not a separate entity that could just pursue anyone at any time. They were not under the command and control of separate military leaders. It had taken a full year, but Darreth was only now becoming irritated at the restrictions placed on their readiness.

Siloy was normally a composed man. Used to his position at the pinnacle of local power, he was rarely surprised by anything anymore. But this indeed surprised him. His eldest son, the one who, at an early age was the model of conservative thinking, had apparently been pondering this issue for quite some time. That was a good thing in his mind just now. "Go on," his father coaxed.

"It's been gnawing at me for months now, ever since the request was made to the PD's office for clarification and amendment of the directive. I've been reluctant to say anything to my superiors, but the more I've thought about it, the more I realize she might not have our best interests at heart. It's almost as if she wants the pirates to steal our property," he blurted.

Siloy was paying a great deal of attention to all the details, then cracked the barest of smiles. He had rarely seen his son so worked up and was unprepared for what Darreth was saying. It wasn't just the words. Darreth fairly shook with pent up anger, his head up, eyes blazing. The tone of his voice only added to this look; there was more he needed to say. This was very good indeed. There was something he needed to say to his son, but he wasn't sure how much to divulge just yet. "And," Siloy said for him, "you want someone to find out why."

Darreth nodded. "But I also didn't want to drag you into this. As far as I can tell, I'm the only one who thinks this way. Well, me and a few others who don't want to talk too much about it."

Siloy took another sip of his drink, set it down again, then went to the railing that surrounded the deck. He scanned the yard. The grounds were well secured. No one was within half a kilometer of them.

Darreth pulled the hejbird from the grill and placed it into the large waiting plate. Siloy retrieved both their drinks and they retreated inside. Darreth laid the plate on the counter in the kitchen.

Siloy turned to face Darreth. "You can never tell anyone about this. No one."

This was odd, Darreth noted. It wasn't like his father to take such a serious tone like that with him, especially out of the blue.

"You're not alone with that concern," Siloy told him. "There are others who have been discussing this issue. Lots of others. It goes way beyond just questioning contracts as to when to engage pirate raids." Siloy paused so Darreth would notice and look him in the eye. There was no other way to broach the topic, so Siloy just came right out with it. "Some of us have been talking about independence."

Darreth's first reaction was to laugh merrily. After all, such a thing was impossible. Once his laughter subsided, he noticed his father wasn't even smiling. "You're not… laughing with me," Darreth offered.

"I'm not."

"Why?" he asked slowly.

"Because I'm completely serious."

The residual smile that had remained on Darreth's face faded. He took on the same serious look as did his father. Darreth was suddenly alarmed. He had never heard his father talk like this before. He was sure independence would result in anarchy. Not to mention it was unprecedented. None of the Inhabs were independent. If anything, they were all totally dependent on the Consort to provide everything from raw and finished materials, to the contracts that made business run efficiently, to the technology and fuel which made star travel possible.

"As you know son, the bulk of the wealth our planet generates doesn't stay planetside. Sure, the Consortium provides us with everything we need. The starlanes are open as a direct result of them. But there's an important point Earth's ignoring. Local control to determine when a contract is a good one or not, for instance. Or the purely psychological need to be the masters of our destiny. They dictate much of our policy at the district council level, even though they say they're not allowed to interfere with internal affairs. Sure, I was duly elected, as were all the other provincial managers, but there's something that's been discussed amongst some of us, which we think we should adopt here on Andakar."

"Which is?"

Siloy's face took on a meaner, harder look. "A very old form of government, one that hasn't existed for over eight hundred years. It's called a republic."

"You mean like the ones on ancient Earth?"

"Exactly."

Darreth emitted a harrumph. "I doubt obsolete forms of government could possibly help us."

"Some of us feel otherwise," Siloy told him firmly.

Darreth noted his father distinctly used the word 'us'. He didn't know what to say. He was already anxious. His father's announcement had been like having the rug pulled out from under him.

The hejbird certainly wasn't going to stay warm by itself. His father pulled the arretz root casserole from the oven, raised the lid, and sprinkled some ground yeet on the top. A pungent aroma rose up into his nose. Darreth caught a whiff of it as his stomach rumbled. He started to carve up the meat. Moments later, with plates filled, they sat at the dinner table. Their voices stayed low as Siloy continued to discuss the matter with Darreth.

"Think back to your history. I'm sure you're steeped in it by now," Darreth's father said.

"Of course. History lessons come with the territory. Historical military missions give us perspective on the present."

"Exactly my point. By the same token, we've pulled historical data from the ancient past and have come to an inexorable conclusion. Independence is only a matter of time. The return to a formal governmental structure will follow," he said, with a note of conviction and determination in his voice.

"But-but where's the mandate? Sure, I have a grievance with policies. Who doesn't? Sure, the Consort makes some stupid decisions, which get funneled down to Inhabs. But why not just have contracts amended instead of calling for independence? What you're saying sounds like-like sedition."

Siloy assessed that comment before answering his son. "Sedition is an interesting choice of words; one that I would never consider for a second. What we're quite informally talking about is merely a change from a central corporate authority to a true representative form of government that's purely local. No more interference with our affairs. No more profits siphoned off for the good of who knows what."

Darreth didn't know what to say. It was a lot to absorb.

Siloy continued. "Our Planetary Director doesn't represent any local corporate interests, only those who have the closest ties to the interests of the Central Planning and Direction Committee on Earth. As PD her sole concerns revolve around maximizing profits."

"I've never liked Director Alarr," Darreth stated acidly. It was starting to come out now. Siloy could tell that Darreth had been holding back. "She's a hollowhead," he said with distinct disgust.

"Like the boy you're seeing?"

"He's... different. We're... dating. He's a Citizen, and naturalized. She's not. She's can't be by law." He said it that way more to make it more real for himself than anything else. He was desperately trying to make sure that in his own mind he had a nice neat distinction between Naylon and the Planetary Director.

"Then you agree..."

"Agree? With independence? I don't see how we could ever achieve a complete separation from Earth. After all, the Consort built Andakar. Their researchers discovered the secret hidden in our ocean. They're the ones who started the first pharma development facilities as a result. They built the space stations. They fund the division that employs me. I could add a couple of hundred other things to that list."

Siloy assessed the fervor with which Darreth argued his case. "You're waffling," he finally said, looking Darreth straight in the eye. "You said it yourself. You're not happy about when and where not to engage pharma pirates. Try looking at this on a much larger and grander scale. Independence isn't about who built our infrastructure or who settled our world. It's about having a far greater say in our destiny than we do right now. All of the Inhabs, including us, have very little control over internal affairs despite appearances. The Consortium has tremendous say over local affairs and we have absolutely no say over how they run Earth or the rest of the Consort."

Darreth was dead silent, mulling it over. He knew the history of his planet. The Consort was sort of a benevolent taskmaster. When Andakar had been settled, Deep Sky Mining had been running everything for centuries. Although most of the corporations that did business on Andakar were locally owned now, all had to ultimately answer to a chain of command which lead back to Deep Sky Mining Consortium, and thus to Earth. It had been that way ever since the first Mars mining concern began in the Sol system. Virtually all corporations were in one way or another tied to mining. Andakar was different in that it had a planetwide ocean teeming with life forms that were discovered to have nearly miraculous medicinal benefit to humanity.

"You'd need military help. As soon as Earth finds out about this, all hell will break loose," Darreth offered.

"Trust me. That's being taken care of." He didn't dare tell Darreth what he meant just yet.

Darreth studied his father's face. "I've not heard a word about it from other Citizens."

"You will soon. Very soon. But remember. Not a word about this to anyone."

"What about Director Alarr? How are you going to keep this a secret from her?"

"She's not been invited to some of our, uh, more informal council meetings," his father said.

"Once she finds out about this, and you know she will, then what will you do?"

Siloy grinned then started cutting his slices of hejbird. "She's not going to find out any time soon."

CHAPTER 5

Lieutenant Commander Rehl Takaramyus stood casually in the corridor looking out the window on the *Guardian* space station. The ground shuttle had just arrived. Darreth was onboard. The pod was still docking as Rehl watched.

"*So how was your date?*" Rehl asked through his neural implant. The close proximity of their tiny encrypted transceiver signals made it seem like they were actually vocalizing their discussion.

"*Yummy,*" Darreth answered.

Rehl heard the faint sound of the docking clamp engaging. "*You had sex on your first date?*" he asked with feigned shock.

"*Well... sorta,*" Darreth replied sheepishly. No actual penetration took place that night.

"*You're worse than me. Or maybe your date is,*" Rehl mocked. "*Merrin made me wait until we'd gone out four times before she let me get past third base.*" The outer door opened and Rehl walked to the docking ring door on his side of the airlock. "*What's his name again?*"

"*Naylon Ress. He works at the Tokaias Museum of Natural History on the north end of the bay. And don't forget. Women are different. If you were on my side, you'd have had a lot more sex before you married her.*" The inner docking ring door cycled open. Rehl could see Darreth and the two other men with him on the shuttle.

"*Listen to you. She was just making me wait for the hottest dessert I could imagine. She's still the best dessert I've ever had.*"

"She's very nice," Darreth genuinely noted, now speaking out loud to Rehl as he approached. "And I'm sure she's a great dessert, too."

Rehl elbowed Darreth in the ribs playfully. Their friendship was such that they had never had any issue telling each other anything.

The *Guardian* space station was the main operational center for patrols warping to and from the space lanes on the look out for pharma pirates. Due to the prevailing technology, a starship was only able to make a journey of twenty light years before its energy ran out and the wedge failed. It was entirely due to the power source. The only known power source dense enough to create a warp bubble was cryo-crystalline Helium-3 Tetra Ganide, or Tetra-G for short. Although warp engines had been improved upon over the last half millennium, the fuel source had never changed.

Tetra-G was only available from sources located on Triton in the Sol system. A unique power source, it was carefully controlled by the Consortium, although it was considered a commodity for trade purposes. When it was discovered that the compound had an unusual volatility as well as being a dense source of Helium-3, an impressive array of testing was begun. Within months, an amazing discovery ensued. Under intense pressure in a properly coated reaction chamber, and under bombardment by a highly focused sound wave, a beam of anti-tachyon particles could be emitted from a containment vessel. Under the right conditions, a stable field that 'wrinkled' then 'pushed' spacetime away from a ship could be created by this energy emission. It was an unprecedented discovery. Once the implication of the steady stream of anti-tachyon particles was fully analyzed, the results were clear. Mankind could finally go to the stars!

Within thirty years after its initial discovery, all the remaining interrelated systems needed for a warp ship were put into place. It took such a short time because the theoretical designs for all of them had been established for as long as anyone could remember. The last hurdle had been finding a power source energy-dense enough to create a sustainable and stable spacetime warp field. Field-testing found what was at first considered a severe limitation. The twenty light year limitation. A standard sized container (exactly 314.206 kg) of Tetra-G could cause a wedge of spacetime to be 'wrinkled' only that far before the energy ran out. Once out of the 'wrinkled wedge', as it became known, the ship was only able to use sublight engines while the FTL drive, more commonly called the wedge drive, was recycled and reset. This created a three-hour delay before the next leap could take place due to fatigue on the wedge drive. A ship kept as many containers of Tetra-G onboard as would fit in storage. Thus, allowing for essentially unlimited travel. Unfortunately, trying to restart a wedge drive in a shorter time than the speced three-hours resulted in severe and costly damage.

It could have been different from the very beginning. Two wedge drives could have been installed in the ship, but thermal dissipation considerations and cost overruns had removed it from all blueprints.

Ultimately, more and more starships were built with a single engine simply because demand for FTL ships was so great. There had never been a second engine in any starship due to their extremely high cost anyway. By default, the single wedge drive design became *derigeur* for all starliners, cargo ships, fighters and all other starships. Luckily, one could exit the wedge and reenter it as long as the ship didn't exceed the twenty light year distance. Thus, short wedge runs occurred all the time within star systems and between adjacent ones.

Rehl wasn't assigned aboard the *Challenger* as was Darreth, but rather was co-pilot of the *Wavefront*. Nonetheless, since they had attended flight school together they had been buddies since the day they met.

With Rehl following, Darreth continued down the corridor to his locker. He glanced out the window to his left. The transparent transduranium alloy afforded a completely safe view of the sun at the far edge of his vision to the left, while still allowing him a beautiful view of Andakar's night side.

Night across Andakar was bleak when the continent wasn't in view. Except where thunderstorms illuminated the clouds, the auroras lit up the polar regions, or the Tovar nebula reflected enough light from the ocean surface, the night side was pitch black. Population centers on Andakar were confined mostly to Koehkelko Bay, the cities and towns along the shores of the other provinces, and the scattered islands that mostly lay within a few kilometers of the continent.

Looking down at the landmass during a clear day as the station passed overhead was a sight to behold. The Patoria Mountains took up more than a third of the continent and ran down to the foothills just tens of kilometers beyond the city limits of Tokaias. Only a single peak, ten kilometers west of dead center of the continent was high enough to be snowy, and that was only in some years. Most of the Kattan continent, except for the highlands, was a tropical jungle environment, with patches here and there of what could loosely be called grassy savannah, and a couple of small deserts. The two volcanoes to the west had long been extinct and had never been pyroclastic. Ancient lava fields spread out from both of the low shields they had created millions of years previous. All of the known active volcanoes were either underwater or spilling lava into the ocean from various seamounts that dotted the planet.

Darreth's locker was located in a changing room several dozen meters from the airlock. He quickly shucked his flight suit and donned his work jumper, which was a typical light blue one-piece affair with an array of zippers holding it together at the sleeves and legs. Their removal made for a much more comfortable experience when strenuous work was required.

"Hungry?" Rehl asked.

"Yeah, I didn't have breakfast."

Darreth closed and locked his locker, then they headed down the corridor once again.

The corridors were wide enough for six people to walk abreast. The station looked like a huge cylinder in space. The central core ran along the length of the station and held the graviton generators, which kept one standard g at all times. The mess hall was three decks 'up', and had plenty of windows with which looked out into the cold of space or at transport vehicles as they arrived and departed the station. There was rarely a time when traffic wasn't visible somewhere in their field of view.

After they made their food selections from the buffet line, they took a seat near one of the windows.

"Okay, let's hear more," Rehl prompted, a grin spreading across his handsome face.

"More about what?" Darreth replied, with as innocent a look as he could manage.

"That guy, of course."

"Why are you so interested in him?"

"I'm not interested in *him*, but rather what you think of him."

"Oh, you had me worried for a second."

"Not a chance, pal."

Darreth grinned.

Rehl pointed his fork at Darreth. "You needed a date. I helped you out. So you owe me to let me know how you think things might go with him."

Rehl was right, of course. He had needed a date. He'd been spending way too much time off world. It was beginning to be a pain not having intimate contact with someone. And his persistence had paid off, too. After being blown off twice he wasn't about to give up so easily. After having a nice dinner with Naylon, he was surprised at how easily he found himself enthralled with the guy. It helped that Naylon was his perfect type, if a little younger than he normally was attracted to. But that was okay. He found himself equally surprised at how he so easily dismissed that Naylon was from Earth. Maybe he'd been a little harsh about his usual blanket dismissal of Earthers.

"I asked him out again, if that's what you mean."

"Now that's more like it," Rehl replied with a wide smile. "My boy's growing up."

"Eat me."

"Nope. Just this bite of yast." He poked the forked piece into this mouth and began chewing contentedly.

"Well, it's going quite well. He's nice, actually. Someone I didn't expect either."

"In what way?"

"I guess mainly because he's from Earth and I didn't expect to like him that much."

"Oh. Sorry," Rehl said slowly, with sincere regret in his voice. "If I'd known…"

Darreth dismissed the apology outright. "Don't agit. He's Andakari through and through. And he makes me laugh."

"Huh?"

"You know, the expelling of air and all when you find something humorous."

Rehl rolled his eyes.

"He's got a unique perspective on things. He's in academia. He works in a lab and does some pretty interesting stuff." Darreth elaborated on Naylon's job.

"Really. Well, I'm glad it's working out. It's about time you found someone you could relate to, even if he's light years ahead of you in the brains department."

"Fruck you," Darreth replied with a grin.

Chapter 6

It was Friday. Even on Andakar, the days were named after those on Earth. It was the same on all the Inhabs that had near 24-hour rotations. The main difference was that months were renamed because no other planet except for Earth had a 365-day year.

Darreth had been on spacelane patrols the entire previous week. After that was another week in orbit on the space station. Now he was on a five-day planetside rest and relaxation stretch. He had placed vids to Naylon twice in the last week while still in the sky. He was quite surprised at his continued infatuation with Naylon. It wasn't because Naylon was an easy lay either. He'd had that before, yet more often than not getting laid, especially on the first date, rarely happened. Most of the time a second date didn't materialize at all.

A broad, stiff, white mesh canopy was draped on a dozen three-story tall poles above the downtown plaza. The plaza was a good city block square and was one of many such outdoor spaces scattered around the urban area. The canopy worked well to bring down the heat but did nothing to mask the high humidity, both of which were just this side of tolerable. Naylon sat on one of the many benches near a huge circular fountain; his overnight bag was next to him. This was their agreed-upon meeting spot. It was the nearest bench to the entrance of the underground shuttle station from where Naylon knew Darreth would emerge.

The large fountain to his left was quite noisy and when the wind kicked up, droplets hit his skin even from this far away. With the humidity as high as it was, it wasn't evaporating all that well from him. He decided he'd move if the wind didn't shift.

While he waited, he wondered what he saw in Darreth. Maybe it was because the man was such a smooth talker, unlike what he expected. They still only knew each other but a few days. He was surprised that on his first date they had sex. Sort of. It made sense though. Darreth was hot. He was still the best looking man he'd ever had the good luck to date. But there was more just under the surface of Darreth's beautiful skin. Naylon had been on dates with guys before where the chemistry just hadn't happened despite there being an attraction. Maybe it was the way Darreth kissed. Naylon had already decided that Darreth's lips were genetically designed to produce perfect kisses. Maybe it was simply that Darreth was paying an awful lot of attention to him despite him being gone so often. It intrigued him as he tried to figure it out. Finally, not getting anywhere, he sighed, watched more people go by, and let the thought go.

Darreth appeared through the crowd several meters ahead of him, making a beeline toward the bench. Naylon stood, all smiles, watching Darreth approach as he casually maneuvered his way through the throng of men and women who were milling about taking pictures, eating lunch and socializing. He was dressed in a loose thin planetside jumper with his rank insignia on the epaulets, making it obvious he was a Space Navy officer. It wasn't altogether unusual to see someone wearing a military division jumper on the plaza, but it wasn't an everyday sight either.

"Hey," Darreth greeted.

"Yum," Naylon said before he realized it.

"Yum?" Darreth asked as he scanned Naylon up and down.

"I, uh, meant hi."

Darreth chuckled. "Yum will do. In fact, I should have just said that to you." With that, he licked his lips seductively.

"I'm already embarrassed and now you're making me even more so."

Darreth grinned. "So, where to?" he asked.

Naylon pointed. "The restaurant's that way." They headed diagonally across the plaza, then down a flight of stairs below street level. They pushed their way through the revolving door. The restaurant was cool inside. The dehumidifiers were quite effective. They were seated immediately.

A huge illuminated tank of marine flora and fauna stood in the center of the restaurant. Along one wall, illuminated from above, was another long narrow tank where dozens of multicolored jellyspinners swam. Each was the size of a person's head. They had spiral ridges along five sides and spun on their axis, which propelled them through the water. Darreth noted them briefly as they sat down near the tank.

"I study their ancestors," Naylon stated as he jutted his jaw out toward the tank.

"You really find that kind of work interesting?" he asked with a puzzled look.

"Absolutely," Naylon told him, his face lighting up. "You wouldn't believe how interesting it is. Of the seven Inhabs that have higher life forms, Andakar is the oldest, geologically speaking. Even older than Earth. My research adds to the evolutionary knowledge of not only our planet, but helps develop the parallel evolutionary tree information we're piecing together."

"Parallel evolutionary tree? What's that?" Darreth flipped his menu over and looked at the back. He spied a drink he liked in the refreshments section and decided on it.

"Sorry about that. It means we piece together how life developed here and compare it to other planets. That way we get a broader perspective of the conditions necessary for life to evolve."

"Oh. I can see why that's important," he said as he nodded slightly.

Naylon noted they were serving stuffed julutbe sandwiches, one of his favorites. The waiter came, read off the specials, then they ordered. Darreth studied the slow moving jellyspinners. The ridges of the nearest one were flashing with an iridescent glow in the subdued light of the tank. They were quite beautiful.

"About our last date," Naylon began.

"Yum," Darreth mocked.

"I just wanted to say that just because I was horny that night it doesn't mean I'm a complete slut... anymore."

Darreth ignored the excuse. "I was going to see what you were up to this evening. There's a new vid I've been meaning to see. It's a recent release from Earth. I thought you might like watching it with me. You can, you know, point out the sights to me."

"I guess I have to remind you we left Earth half my life ago. I barely remember anything about it."

"I've never been there. You can still tell me all about it anyway," Darreth told him.

Naylon draped his shirt over the chair at the counter in Darreth's small kitchen. Darreth's was next it on the seat. Many men preferred being shirtless, as their culture was conducive to being scantily dressed in the first place. Darreth was impressed that for an academic type Naylon had a nicely proportioned upper body. He wasn't exactly buffed but he had scant body fat. Naylon on the other hand reveled in Darreth's look. Darreth had a more athletic build than he. Nonetheless, Naylon didn't feel all that self-conscious about the difference in their bodies. He felt he was just fine the way he was.

One of Naylon's favorite Earth foods was fresh popcorn. Corn wasn't something readily found on Andakar, since it wasn't grown on-planet. But Naylon knew the stores that catered mostly to nonNates, and had secured a small container of it the day before. It had been stowed in his kit bag. They were in the kitchen with the popcorn emptied into a large pot with a glass lid on it, shaking it occasionally. No automation for him. He was making it the old fashioned way.

Darreth took a big whiff of the aroma that had filled the small bungalow. "That's coming from a bunch of dried seeds?"

"Kernels," Naylon corrected. "It used to be a staple crop on Earth."

Darreth took another deep breath, savoring it. "That is *kick*."

Shortly, most of the kernels were popped. Naylon dumped them into a bowl and shook some salt over them. They both headed back to the couch.

Darreth sat back and activated the holoscreen across the room. Naylon offered the bowl to Darreth, who took a kernel, then another, then proceeded to devour an entire handful.

"This is great. I can't believe I've never even heard of it before," Darreth told him.

"We'll have it more often if you like, but it's expensive."

The vid started, a story about a love triangle focusing on an astronaut on her way to Mars. It was an historical dramatization of the almost mythical story about the planet's first colony.

Many times while the vid was playing Darreth grunted or chuckled or even outright laughed heartily. Naylon was enamored with Darreth's short outbursts, the way he'd touch Naylon's arm when something particularly funny was said or done, or the time he turned toward him and rubbed Naylon's stomach in a slow and sensual way, giving

Naylon a partial swella in the process. Darreth briefly grasped Naylon's tumescence through the gauzy fabric of his pants at one point. Darreth's action was spurred because of the love scene between two of the main characters, a man and a woman. But he didn't try to do anything else after that to elicit a further response. Naylon was surprised, but didn't pursue it.

After the vid ended Naylon decided to spend the night. The two men lay in bed side-by-side, clad in nothing but their smiles. Naylon felt unbelievably relaxed.

The meter-wide window had been de-energized, making it transparent. The window started at the floor, went up the wall and, following the roofline, angled at forty-five degrees. It stopped halfway to the apex of the ceiling above them. The nebula's illumination had already filled up the sky, brightening the night with an even glow. The yard outside was swarming with nocturnal flying insects looking for a meal. The two men were insulated from them in the quiet of the room, now with low sound of music playing behind their heads.

"You don't mind spending the night with me?" Darreth asked.

"Are you kidding? It's not every day I get to spend the night with a man. At least not recently."

Over the next hour both men told the other about their most recent relationship and how it had ended. That led them to talk about their childhoods.

Darreth told Naylon about his first crush in primary school. Naylon said he must have been a late bloomer. It wasn't until he entered secondary school that he developed a crush on his next-door neighbor. Neither man had ever experienced discrimination of the sort that had plagued gay men and women in centuries past. Both had read stories about when society wasn't as advanced as it was today. It was simply inconceivable that religious and political opposition could have led to the discrimination of an entirely normal part of society. All of that had ceased long ago, longer than space travel had existed.

"So, do you still see him?" Darreth asked.

"Which him?"

"Jento."

"Not since he moved to Kehail province."

"What's he doing there?"

"Teaching at the university that just opened in their provincial admin center."

"See, you have to date outside your specialty."

"What does that mean?" Naylon asked warily.

"You've been dating only academic types. What you need to do is keep dating me instead."

Naylon was silent for a moment, watching a hoverbat dive close to the window with its large maw wide open and scoop a swath through a swarm of insects. Naylon turned onto his side and ran his hand up and down Darreth's chest, felt his nipples grow hard, and watched his penis lengthen. He briefly ran the palm of his hand across the top of his hardening shaft, then cupped his balls before letting go. "Maybe you're right. Maybe I've been going about this completely wrong."

Darreth turned to face him and rested the side of his head on his opened hand. "You know, I really like you. You're good looking, nice, and like I said before, you don't have that Earther attitude I can't stand."

"Stop it. Look what you've done to me."

Darreth did the obvious and grasped Naylon's rock hard swella. "No kidding."

"Really? You like me?"

"I'm letting you spend the night, aren't I?"

"Really," Naylon insisted.

"I'm not kidding. You're different."

"I'm not so sure those differences are ones you might like."

"In what way?" he asked, curious.

"I think our views on a lot of things aren't the same."

"Like what?" Darreth asked.

"I'm not exactly conservative."

Darreth didn't answer. He didn't want to get into a discussion like this right now. Regardless, the conversation he recently had with his father came to mind, making him momentarily feel tense. He was feeling particularly amorous though and instead of letting Naylon continue that thought he started planting kisses on his mouth while he slowly climbed on top of him. Viewpoints could wait until a later time.

CHAPTER 7

The first time a starship left the Sol system under powered flight control was on February 12th, 2316. The 500th anniversary of that date had been anticipated for two years now. The newsgrid had been covering the scheduled festivities, a scale model statue of the first faster than light ship named *Arion* and its three-person crew was to be unveiled later, speeches had been given, and a time capsule was to be buried in Tokaias' main plaza. The exact date of the quincentennial for each Inhab was sort of arbitrary due to time dilation factors, but this was the day when Andakar decided to celebrate. The newsgrid held retrospectives of the first through the fourth centennial celebrations. They covered the expansion of the Inhabs over that time, then the official kickoff of today's event, which started in the late morning. The requisite speech had already been given by Corren Grusics, the Consortium First Executive on Earth, and had been recorded for re-broadcast on Andakar before the fireworks were to begin tonight.

The fireworks display at Provincial Park along the waterfront was to be held in a few hours. The grounds could hold over two hundred thousand people, and they had been streaming in since early morning to stake out a spot. The park was already quite packed despite its ample space. Luckily, it had been nice out all day with no rain in the forecast.

Siloy, the rest of the Council, and the wait staff, along with a contingent of security people, were milling about in the huge administrative building overlooking the park. The building's location provided for a spectacular view of the bay, the foothills in the distance, and the mountains further inland. The city, which spread out along the crescent shape of the bay, completed the view.

Darreth had been with his father since morning. Due to the high level functions associated with such a memorable event, Siloy was obliged to be very visible for the celebration. Darreth not only accompanied him as his son, but also in an official escort capacity as well. Thus, he was in dress blues, which, although they looked heavy and hot, were in fact light and airy, just like a tunic. Official uniforms on Andakar had always been fashioned to be comfortable first, with their functional look being second. Regardless of his official capacity, Darreth told his father he had to leave briefly to meet Naylon at the entrance foyer. That was where he had asked Naylon to wait for him.

He had sent Naylon an official invitation flimsy earlier in the week by courier. Without it, he wouldn't be able to enter the building. Naylon was stunned when it arrived. It meant Darreth had given him access to one of the most high-level parties in town, perhaps the most high-level party of the entire year.

Darreth passed by dozens and dozens of people as he headed toward the foyer. As usual, there were the subtle looks of disgust here and there. His uniform was the reason. He knew that. There were still a significant number of people who opposed having a military space station in orbit. Regardless, Darreth ignored the occasional frowns. He had long ago decided it was unbecoming of anyone to do so.

"Wow, you look really nice," exclaimed Naylon after Darreth found him.

"I was wearing the same uniform when we first met."

"But you look different now." Naylon knew why, too. He was beginning to have familiar feelings of losing control of his emotions when he was around Darreth. It had happened only once before when he was seventeen. His romance with Keldis during his last year of secondary school had taken his breath away whenever they were together. After all, it was his first real relationship. It was nearly three months before he regained control of himself. It was only afterward when he realized that although he and Keldis were great when they were naked together, they had little in common once they were clothed. Keldis complained about the way Naylon dressed, was oddly rough when he should have been gentle, and more than once had said he liked girls. Both eventually moved on. Naylon to another boy and Keldis to a girl. Despite that, they remained friends for the rest of the school year. Their friendship eventually faded altogether when they attended different tertiary schools.

That was a long time ago. Naylon was a completely different person then. Darreth wasn't Keldis, both he and Darreth were adults with their lives well underway, had careers to concern themselves with, and experiences in and out of relationships to temper them. But it was happening to Naylon again. The heart palpitations, the steady thoughts about what Darreth was up to day and night, the fantasizing about Darreth's lean body. All of it.

"You look pretty good yourself," Darreth told him, sizing up his formal tunic.

"Thanks. I wouldn't have missed this for anything." He looked around the foyer. Marble Doric columns supported the high ceiling. Ornate stonework extended along the molding clear to the far end of the room. There the hallway opened up to a huge room with tall windows and a sizeable patio with a wide semi-circular balcony that jutted out over the park. The windows were so large that even from this distance Naylon could easily see a huge expanse of the bay.

"I never knew this building was so elaborate inside," Naylon told him as Darreth pointed the way.

They stopped halfway to the end of the long foyer. There, a corridor ran left and right. "Those two wings have quarters for up to five hundred people," Darreth told him.

"That many," Naylon stated, impressed.

"Most of the building's for conference space."

"So, who's here I should know?"

"Who's here is every member of the Council. And lots of the big shots from every major corporation on the planet. There are even some people from Rylerra. I'm not sure you would know any of them. Most can be quite stuffy, if you ask me." He had grown up enduring functions like this and had become kind of jaded by them now. Darreth led the way down one of the halls.

As they continued toward the end of the long foyer, Naylon studied the busts that lined it in their alcoves. Heavy tapestries provided soundproofing to the otherwise highly sound-reflective stonework. The walls were also ornamented with a series of paintings, most of which depicted people Naylon didn't recognize. The open doorway at the end terminated at a marble balcony that overlooked a large rectangular floor below filled with people. Wide staircases off to the left and the right wound downward to the floor. A wide bar that faced opposite the huge bank of windows was packed with people ordering drinks from eight bartenders. Diffuse sunlight streamed in through the wall of tall windows that faced the park, illuminating the hundreds of formally dressed people who were gathered in the room.

Even amidst the sea of famous and not so famous people, Naylon already identified Darreth's father standing with a small group of people down and to their left. The small group was close to the bottom of the staircase. Darreth and Naylon went left and proceeded down the wide staircase to their level.

Darreth leaned toward him before they got there. "I want you to meet him before it gets too crowded."

"This isn't crowded?" Naylon managed to sputter. There must have been hundreds of people there already.

"You wouldn't believe the number of people they can pack in here."

Siloy saw Darreth and dismissed the two men and woman he was talking to with a broad smile and a slight hand gesture just as Darreth and Naylon got down to the last step of the stair.

Siloy James-Po wasn't exactly an imposing figure, but rather a commanding one. He was several centimeters taller than either Darreth or Naylon. His formal dress, completely white with black sashes, multi-colored patches and the gold inscribed bar over his left pocket that indicated his station, went well with his distinct, angular face. Naylon right away noticed Siloy's genuine smile. The man reached out first with both hands to shake Naylon's, too. Naylon immediately felt comfortable in his presence. This was nothing like the quite impersonal view he had of the man during his Citizenship ceremony.

"So, this is the man my son's dating. It's a pleasure to meet you. Doctor Ress, it is? I hope you won't mind this stuffy formal event."

"Please. Call me Naylon. It's a pleasure to meet you, too, sir. You have a fine son." Naylon couldn't believe he said that. It sounded awkward and trite.

"Fine son, indeed. I'm glad he's dating an academician for a change. He needs a lot more intellectual stimulation than he lets on."

He'll get plenty of another type of stimulation from me too, that's for sure, Naylon thought with a grin.

"Please dad." Darreth shook his head as if to stave off the inevitable stories of his youth or other such embarrassing anecdotes. He glanced at Naylon.

Naylon knew he needed to change the subject before that happened. Before he could do so a woman and two teenagers approached. The woman clasped Siloy's hand in hers and smiled at Darreth.

"Mother," Darreth greeted. "Uh, Naylon, this is my mother Kyana. Mom, Naylon."

She reached out and had Naylon take her hand.

"Nice to meet you Ms. James-Po."

"I've not heard a lot about you Dr. Ness, but what little I've been told I like. Now that I've met you I like you even more." Naylon felt awkward at such an unusual greeting. It sounded almost like a come on. He wondered if his cheeks had gotten red enough to be noticeable.

Darreth spoke up right away. His mother could be forward. He hadn't prepped Naylon about his family and wanted to keep the introductions short and sweet at this point. "This is my sister Kella, and my brother Tann."

Naylon briefly shook their hands and realized they were the same age. "Okay, I'm gonna guess. Fraternal?" he asked Tann.

Tann grinned and nodded. "She's older by three minutes."

"I didn't know you had siblings," Naylon told Darreth.

"Now you do."

"Secondary school?" Naylon asked.

"They have a year left," Darreth told him.

Naylon couldn't help himself. In his head he was already making the age conversion, a habit he'd never gotten out of. That made the twins almost eighteen Standard years old.

In their formal attire, the teens could have easily passed as a prom king and queen. Tann had curly brown shoulder length hair just like his sister. His was parted in the middle while hers was parted on one side, with part of it in a thin braid. There was a length of shiny material woven into the braid. Her formal outfit was a skin-tight silk tunic. It was butter yellow with a bright twisted gold sash around the waist. Tann's light green tunic was also form fitting to his waist. A highly decorated short pleated skirt hung down just enough to cover bulges, front and rear, as was required for formal events. The style had been in vogue for a very long time for such occasions. In centuries past it would look as if they were wearing the other's clothing or had jumped out of a medieval play.

A waitress came by with an empty tray. She noted none of them had drinks in their hands. She spoke to the tiny transducer on the tray, ordering the drinks as each were placed. She whisked away to pick them up from the bar.

"I understand you work at the museum. Is that correct Dr. Ress?" Kyana asked.

"Really, Naylon will do just fine. This may be a formal event but I'm just fine without the formal title."

"Naylon it is then." She nodded and smiled.

"I'm the lead paleo-microbiologist at the lab."

"Fascinating. You'll have to tell me all about it when we have you over for dinner."

Naylon nodded, speechless. They had just met and already he was being invited to dinner?

She turned to Darreth. "Which will be when, son?"

Darreth looked distracted since he had been surveying the room. He turned his attention back to her. "Uh, as soon as I can schedule it. I'll let you know later."

The waitress returned in record time given the crowded room. She clearly was giving the Chief Council's family priority. Each took their drinks, including Tann and Kella.

Siloy spoke up, "To another five hundred years," he said. They all clinked glasses.

Naylon and Darreth were both standing opposite Siloy. Naylon watched Siloy's eyes. He could tell the man saw someone he recognized coming through the crowd. Naylon briefly looked over his shoulder to see a man and woman approach their group. They joined Naylon and his entourage without being invited. He thought he recognized the woman right away but wasn't sure. He knew he had never seen the man before.

"Director Alarr," Siloy acknowledged as he greeted her.

The Planetary Director, Naylon thought. He recognized her now. He'd seen her enough times on newsvids to recognize her.

"Chief, we're having a lovely time. I do hope your family is enjoying this, too," she told everyone.

Naylon knew next to nothing about her except for what he'd seen on the vids. It took only that one sentence for him to instantly dislike her. Her gaze slid right past most of them, too insignificant to rate eye contact.

Everyone nodded and smiled. The brief interaction made Naylon realize they all knew her.

Inandra was thin and pale. As if to call attention to her thinness, she wore a sleeveless tunic that accentuated her bony shoulders. Her thick dark hair was piled up high. Thin wires were sprouting from the coiffure. The entire length of the wires were changing colors; slowly running through the spectrum from red to blue and back again. Her necklace consisted of a dozen strands of the same color-changing material. The necklace drooped down to ample and obviously artificial cleavage. Cleavage, which Naylon was busily trying to ignore, but failed to do.

"Zelin and I are having a wonderful time, too." She turned to her companion and touched his shoulder, then took a final sip from her drink before depositing it on a passing waiter's empty tray.

Darreth leaned into Naylon and whispered as Inandra talked with Siloy. "He's Zelin Raxi, the Chief Operations Manager of the mining interests on Rylerra."

"They're not having their own celebration?"

"I'm sure they're having one, too. He and Alarr have a thing going on. He's from the same continent she's from on Earth. Some place in Eurasia, I think. He shuttles back and forth from Rylerra to see her."

Zelin was a short fat man. Balding, with a red face and a squat ugly nose, Naylon couldn't figure out what she saw in him. He glanced down at Zelin's crotch. *He must be huge,* Naylon thought.

Inandra and Zelin dominated the conversation for several minutes. Naylon took it in stride despite the fact that nothing interesting came out of her mouth or had anything to do with anyone but her or the 'hope for increased future precious gem exports' from Rylerra.

Odd, thought Naylon. He was going to be making a trip to Rylerra soon. Manager Raxi was the perfect person to talk to about it, but he couldn't bring himself to do so. He guessed it was the proximity to Inandra that turned him off to the very thought. Nonetheless, he was sure that even if he discussed his forthcoming expedition to the man's Inhab he'd get nothing more than a blank stare from him.

The Director saw someone else she knew nearby and attempted to flag them down. Instead of having them join their group, she left with Zelin in tow. Their circle immediately grew a lot quieter.

"I thought she'd never leave," Tann said, loud enough for Naylon to hear.

Naylon saw Siloy pat Tann's back and shake his head ever so slightly as he looked Tann in the eye. But Naylon couldn't have agreed more, glad Tann had voiced what the others didn't, or couldn't.

"That's my cue, dad," Darreth announced. "We're going to mingle and take in the view. We'll be back in a while."

Kyana took Naylon's hand. She hadn't spoken much so far, but due to having been immediately enamored with Naylon, wished him well. "Don't make yourself scarce tonight. We're at the head table after the fireworks. You two have a place next to us. Don't let any of these overfed corporate types put you off."

"We'll be right along," Darreth assured her.

Darreth led Naylon to one of the large picture windows adjacent to the wide bar. The view was breathtaking. The park stretched out to the left and right. People had already settled into spaces below them amidst the trees and sculptures that graced the walkways and open areas. Further out, the placid bay shone in the setting sunlight. A barge set up for the fireworks was anchored just offshore.

"Your family is different than I imagined," Naylon said. He took a sip from his glass.

"They're just a family, probably like yours."

"Not as prominent, of course."

"My dad's the only prominent one. But let's not talk about them." Darreth gave him a wide smile then looked out over the park. Naylon stared at Darreth's face, taking in the smile-turned-grin, the strong jaw, the tasteful uniform, and found himself enjoying this time with him.

Darreth turned to Naylon. "Hey, let me show you around."

"It's kind of crowded in here for a tour."

"I mean upstairs."

Naylon looked up at the staircase where they had descended from before they had joined the crowd.

Darreth pointed toward the other staircase at the far end of the room. "Up and around. There are bedrooms."

They eventually made it to the other side of the crowd and ascended the stairs. They took a perimeter walkway along the windows. As they traversed the several dozen meters down the hallway the noise of the throng below became a muted roar, then the hallway became almost completely quiet as the thick plush carpeting helped dampen the sound.

Although most of the doors along the corridor were closed, several were open. They had passed a study, a holographic projection room and several common bathrooms. Darreth stopped in front of a closed door. He pressed his forefinger to his lips, then placed his ear against the door, listening for a moment. Satisfied, he touched the sensor pad next to the doorframe. The door slid open. Inside were a bed, a dresser, an attached bathroom and a small kitchenette. There were no windows. Darreth looked in. There was no sign it was currently being occupied. He was sure all the rooms would have been booked. At Darreth's behest, they entered. Darreth touched the door close sensor and pressed the lock icon.

Naylon whispered. "Whose room is this?"

"It's for guests, but surprisingly this one isn't being used."

"How do you happen to know that?" Naylon asked.

"I didn't know this one was empty, but I've been in this building several times for various functions, all due to my father. I've even been in this bedroom before."

"With someone else?" Naylon responded jealously.

"No, just snooping around." With that, he took Naylon's hands in his own and faced him. Darreth slowly took him in a long passionate kiss. It was so sensual that Naylon nearly lost his breath. Naylon pulled back after several moments feeling lightheaded. "Whoo…"

Darreth reached down and grasped Naylon's swella through his pants.

"You're in dress blues. How in the hell are we going to…" Before Naylon could finish the sentence Darreth was maneuvering Naylon to the bed. Naylon sat on the edge and watched while Darreth removed his coat and gloves. He went down on his knees, spread Naylon's legs apart, then fished out Naylon's penis through the buttoned slit in front. Darreth went down on him immediately. Naylon leaned back on his elbows trying to stifle the involuntary noises he was emitting. He wasn't doing a very good job of being quiet.

The moment was so exciting Naylon came within minutes. Darreth was careful. He made sure not a single drop of semen ended up anywhere else except in his mouth. When he was done he continued to lick Naylon's softening penis until Naylon pulled him off. There was a mischievous look on Darreth's face.

Naylon couldn't believe how intense the moment had been. Not only was Darreth handsome, he was bold. The guy was a lot more exciting than Naylon expected.

Darreth placed his hands on both of Naylon's thighs. The full length of Naylon's softening penis along with his scrotum was still poking out of his pants. Darreth continued to stay on his knees and stared at Naylon's face. Naylon sat upright and stared back. Nothing was spoken for several seconds.

It was as if some sort of energy passed between them at that moment. Simple desire was transmuting. A bit of play was becoming serious. Darreth's grin turned into a smile. The part of Naylon that he had been holding back because of Darreth's station in life disappeared. He reached out to Darreth's face and caressed his chin, then his cheek. Naylon leaned forward then dropped to the floor. Both were on their knees on the thick immaculate carpeting. Darreth had no intention of getting even semi-naked. He had only wanted to bring Naylon to orgasm. They embraced carefully so that Naylon's still-dangling genitals wouldn't touch Darreth's uniform. It wasn't just the orgasm that had brought Naylon a little closer to Darreth right then. It was something more. Something impossible to place just yet.

Darreth pulled back then reached up and unbuttoned his collar. He pulled up a chain from around his neck. He lifted the necklace up over his head and dangled the objects at the end in front of Naylon's eyes. "I want you to have this," Darreth told him. On the chain were two items. One was a thin green disc with a hole in the middle. A polished torus of jade. The other object was a coin. A very old one. It too had a hole in the center, a square one. Darreth pointed. "Jade, from China."

"On Earth," Naylon stated.

Darreth nodded. "Where the Po side of my family originated."

"This coin must be worth a lot. I-I can't. You can't give me this."

"It's about fifteen centuries old but it's not worth much. They just represent our family's past." He chuckled. "From a place I've never been and will probably never visit either. I want you to have it. Think of it as a symbol of us together."

"Us? Together?"

Darreth just nodded.

"Wait a minute," Naylon told him. They both stood up. Naylon went to the adjoining bathroom to clean up and straighten his clothing.

Darreth glanced in the mirror above the dresser and checked his uniform. He re-buttoned his collar then re-donned his gloves.

Naylon emerged from the bathroom and sat on the bed. Darreth stood over him. "But why?" Naylon asked. He opened up his hand to reveal the items.

"It means I like you an awful lot. Please?"

Naylon didn't know what else to say. Darreth was driving the relationship. That was a switch for Naylon. He usually led. At that moment though, Naylon realized maybe it wouldn't hurt to be subordinate. At least for now. Darreth was certainly serious about the relationship already. That alone provided new possibilities for him. Possibilities Naylon hadn't even considered yet.

Indeed, Darreth was slowly but surely stealing his heart.

The semi-precious stone and the coin jingled as Naylon placed the necklace around his neck, then dropped them down his collar. For a brief instant the objects were cold against his chest. He stood and Darreth kissed his cheek, then headed for the door. He pressed the open button and stuck his head out to see if anyone was looking their way. There were three people at the far end of the hallway but they were intent on something against the wall, perhaps one of the many sculptures in the various alcoves along the way. The two men exited without being seen.

Naylon wondered what just happened in that room. Okay, so Darreth got a little frisky. It's not like he'd ever experienced that before. What he was most concerned with was that Darreth had some sort of grip on him he'd not experienced before. It was just a little so far. He knew if he didn't contain himself any better he'd lose complete control of the situation. That wasn't right. After all, Darreth was a military man. It was still extraordinary he was even dating someone in the military. Darreth's family was completely non-corporate. Another unprecedented situation.

And Naylon was enjoying every second of it.

Moments later they rejoined the crowd. Forty-five minutes later, they both watched the fireworks begin over the park with the rest of the James-Po family.

Chapter 8

It was shortly after eight a.m. and Naylon just arrived at work.

"There's a vidmail you have to open," Alista told him as he sat down at his desk.

"Who says?"

"I do."

"How did you know I have a vidmail I *have* to open? Have you been *snooping?*"

"My, aren't we the defensive one today. I heard the tone your workstation made after it was received. Plus, I overheard some certain board members talking in the hallway late yesterday."

"The grant!"

Alista just smiled.

He quickly sat at his console. After activating the workstation screen, he quickly watched the vidmail from Director Jerty.

> *"Funding for Museum Expedition B/654 has been approved. Request to take samples from Rylerra for possible matches to existing Andakar fossil record is hereby granted. Please meet with the Director's Grant Board to receive grant stipulations and funds transfer information."*

"Kick!" Naylon exclaimed. Months previous he had written up a grant proposal for this very expedition. He had requested the funds because of a drawer of fossils that had lain forgotten and unmissed in one of the sub-basement vaults from decades ago. While he and Alista were cataloging them, they had come across some ambiguously tagged ones. The scant information on the samples indicated they had come from an amateur who had found them in what appeared to be ancient rock strata on Rylerra. The holovid in the drawer's viewer database didn't have any data on the exact latitude and longitude of the samples, much to the disappointment of them both.

Naylon had performed a microscopic examination of one of the samples. It had revealed something completely unexpected. As far as Naylon was able to determine, the structure of the microscopic *hartneria codomanum* was almost identical to a similar species of the long extinct, mud-burrowing mollusk-like carnivores on Andakar. That would mean only one thing. They were related. Upon further analysis it had became evident that the only way to prove the two worlds had parallel evolutionary life histories was to go to Rylerra, try to determine where the fossils originated, and retrieve more. If he found what he expected,it would certainly put Naylon's name in the history books. Proving that their two planets had had even some cross-pollination would be monumental. The accolade was something he desperately wanted to have in his academic record. He had talked up the right people at the museum, had gotten their opinions, then was asked to write up a full grant proposal.

Alista was waiting for Naylon in the lab after lunchtime.

"Well, what did the grant board say?"

Naylon had made a holocopy of the meeting. He placed the crystal on Alista's workstation counter and pointed to it. "It's all there. The proposal, the grant and the approval. Merek was even approved to be my partner." Merek Soliciellio was a graduate student who worked in the museum's children's science wing. He was eager to work his way up the academic ladder. Merek had heard about Naylon's request months ago and had asked to join Naylon's team. So far, they were the sole members of the team. Naylon was happy to have a partner, too. Merek's work was quite important at the museum, he was well-liked, and Naylon needed the extra hands. Participation in the dig would put Merek in good standing. The paper he'd write up about it would put him in a perfect position for placement in the Ph.D. program at Tokaias University. Alista had no interest in accompanying him off world. "Only one thing's missing," he told her.

"What's that?"

"A pilot."

"Huh? Why would they approve a grant and not give you a pilot?" She gave him a bewildered look.

"I have no idea. They said available ships are scarce right now and it'll be a few months before they can get someone who's willing to take us there. Our window of opportunity will either be in the next two months or we have to wait for over a year and a half. I have no intention of going there in the midst of a northern hemisphere winter."

"I don't get it. We get mining shipments from Rylerra all the time. What's wrong with one of *those* ships?"

"I asked the same question. Corporate law doesn't allow non-mining personnel to travel on mining ships."

"Well, what are you going to do?"

"What do you think? I'm gonna wait," he said, exasperated.

They were quiet for a moment while both of them thought about the silliness of approving a grant while not providing all the requisite components.

"At least the dig next week doesn't rely on a pilot," Naylon stated, breaking the silence.

Alista crossed her arms, feeling as dejected as did Naylon did about the 'partial-grant' he'd been offered. "At least," she echoed.

"That's everything," Merek said. He added his backpack to the items in the back of the vehicle and pressed the button on the hatch. It closed slowly, then snapped shut.

Naylon was in the driver's seat already and pressed the on-switch. The vehicle rose up several feet moments after Merek took his place on the passenger side.

Darreth studied the map on the back of Naylon's seat. He had insisted on taking this trip with Naylon and his entourage. He wanted to see what it was they did on a dig. This was the perfect opportunity for him to see what it was all about. He adjusted the screen's brightness, then zoomed the image out slightly. "Balmoral Keep. It's hot out that way."

"It'll be thirty degrees, if not more," Naylon told him. He set the coordinates and the navigation system laid out the course. The estimated arrival time was in three hours and eight minutes.

"Thunder, it's thirty-five degrees out there," Darreth said as he glanced at the display on the dash. The side door popped up. He stepped out onto the sidewalk and shaded his eyes. It felt like he was inside an oven. They were all on the main street at Balmoral Keep. He looked down the road. Heat waves shimmered at the end of it.

The town had been built at the edge of the Gartenda desert region. It was small as towns went in the interior of the continent. The main street was slightly over one kilometer long. Several more streets, perpendicular to the main one had shops, labs, a small administrative office, restaurants and the homes of the permanent residents of the town. Naylon knew several of the shop owners. He had been at this dig site six times previously.

The dig site was eight kilometers west of town. Before they could leave, they had to check in with local authorities to let them know where they were going, and re-supply their vehicle with water and food.

The dig site was as primitive as they had been for well over a millennium. Tarps on poles shielded the paleontologists and students from the blazing heat over large open pits. The pits were marked in a grid comprised of short metal poles and string. Several different layers of strata were exposed and half a dozen students were busy brushing dirt away with whiskbrooms, tiny picks and even screwdrivers. Everything was done manually. None of the normal automated tools were ever used when it came to students. Nonetheless, a couple of them were using a shovel bot to move overburden, which had to be removed to reach the level of strata they were interested in analyzing.

Naylon was expected, so it took scant minutes to check in with the head of the dig, a professor from Tokaias University. His old major professor, to be exact. Normally, digs of this nature would be off-limits to anyone not specifically involved with the university. But this one was different. Teams of people had been working the site for years now on a constantly rotating basis, mostly for class projects. In fact, the current team would be finished by this evening. Then it would be just Merek, Naylon and Darreth. Darreth welcomed the chance to be in the outdoors under a real sky for a change. As much as he loved his job he still felt the need to be planetside and *outside* as often as possible.

Naylon's objective was to gather some samples from a fossilized streambed he had discovered a while back. He needed them for a special project he'd been researching on some early single-celled microorganisms that had cleverly used salicic acid to construct their shells, thus uniquely fossilizing them. This dig and the project associated with it were completely unrelated to the project and the fossils he needed from Rylerra.

Before anything was unloaded from the transport vehicle, they decided lunch was in order. They found a location to put up the tents shortly thereafter.

Naylon was quite impressed Darreth would bother to follow them into a hot dusty desert. The space station and crafts that shuttled through their system were pristine environments. He figured Darreth would hate being in this one.

"Are you kidding?" Darreth told him upon hearing that. "I love being out in wide open spaces. Fresh air is ten times better than any of the scented bottled air on any ship in the fleet."

"Oh I just figured…"

"You just don't know me all that well yet. I hope I can change that as rapidly as possible." He drew Naylon close and kissed him sensuously. None of the nearby students who saw that take place so much as blinked an eye at their open display of affection.

That evening, after a short dinner, Merek talked a lot about the amount of money he thought was being spent guarding pharmas. Darreth tried to be polite, but as the barrage of criticism continued, he felt he needed to set the record straight.

"Look, our world has ample resources for very long term profits. I'm not a manager, a profiteer or a capital investor but I can tell you what we do is extremely important."

"Important enough to kill for?" Merek retorted, almost as if baiting Darreth.

"Whoa," Darreth shot back, becoming more irritated. "What's that supposed to mean?"

"There are a lot of people who think the Space Navy represents something Andakar shouldn't stand for."

"Like what?" Darreth coaxed. He'd heard it all already but wanted to know what Merek thought, too.

"Hegemony. Murder. War. That's for starters."

To Darreth it sounded like Merek were deliberately trying to antagonize him with those accusations. "What? We don't murder people. We're protecting Andakar from pirates. That has to be something everyone can agree on." He looked back and forth between Merek and Naylon.

Naylon had found the exchange amusing for a moment, then realized he'd better settle it right now before Merek got himself into real trouble. "Uh, Merek. You do remember that Darreth follows the trade routes. He does the patrols that keep pirates from stealing our stuff. The stuff that makes our planet as wealthy as it is. You might want to reconsider all of that."

Merek was suddenly alarmed. "Sorry." He looked genuinely embarrassed. "I don't know what I was thinking."

The next morning at breakfast Darreth and Naylon were up before Merek. Darreth was still miffed at Merek's assessment of the Space Navy. "There must be an awful PR firm running offense for us planetside," he told Naylon.

"About what?" Naylon asked after he licked the spoon from coring a purple noga fruit.

Darreth lowered his voice. "Merek used the word murder to describe my job. Where do people come up with those ideas? We protect planetary assets. How many times do I have to tell people that? That has to be worth a lot more than false accusations. I'm glad you don't think that way."

"I know you don't murder anyone. But there are some people who think the Space Navy invites people who want to slaughter and oppress." He instantly knew he shouldn't have said that. There were only two people he knew who thought that way and they were in his discussion group.

"Oh, now it's *slaughter* and *oppression*, too," Darreth said slapping his thighs. "When has the Space Navy ever been about that?"

"Well… not yet anyway."

Darreth was completely taken aback by the tone the discussion had already taken. He wanted clarification now. "Care to elaborate?"

"Some people think differently about the Space Navy."

That much he knew for sure. "Do those someones include you?"

Naylon only stared back, not sure what to say.

"Look, if you don't want me here just say so and I'll leave," Darreth offered, suddenly wondering what had brought this up from Naylon. He had known Darreth was in the Space Navy since they first met. Why now, when things were going so well between them, did this come up?

Naylon dropped the spoon with a loud clatter onto the tabletop. He stood, walked around the table then sat down next to Darreth. "I'm sorry. The answer is no," he said, vigorously shaking his head. "I've, uh, been listening to too many of my friends, that's all. And I guess Merek's heard me talking about it."

"What friends?"

Naylon gave him a very short explanation of the discussion group he'd been attending. He left out most of the details.

"They don't sound like friends to me. What I do is protect planetary assets," he said as he tapped the tabletop with the last three words. "And I'm damn good at what I do, too," he added, now feeling genuinely offended and hurt.

"I know. I know," Naylon looked into the distance. Clouds were coming in from the west near the mountain range further on. "My parents would be proud."

"I don't need your parents' approval."

"No, no. It's because they're pharma techs," he explained. "They'd be proud of what you do because you're helping to make sure that what they do makes a profit." The wind kicked up a dustdevil not more than five meters off to their right. It swirled around briefly before vanishing as abruptly as it started. "I'm sorry," Naylon told him. He leaned over and kissed Darreth. "Really. You've opened my eyes to the need for your job."

Darreth smiled and smoothed back Naylon's hair. He was quickly forgetting all about his and Merek's collective academic misunderstandings.

Eventually Merek woke up, got ready and ate breakfast with the two men. After everything was cleaned up, Darreth accompanied them both to the dig site several hundred meters away from their encampment.

"See these long flat rocks here?" Naylon indicated to Darreth. He pointed to an exposed area that looked like it had recently faulted, geologically speaking. One side was half a meter lower than the other. There was a distinct one meter thick layer of long round rocks embedded within the exposed face.

"Yeah, they're pretty obvious."

"This is where we're going to dig. First, we pull out some of the longer flatter rocks. Then find the cracks along the sides. Like this one." He dug one out of the fault and pointed to a hairline crack along its side. He set it down on the ground on its edge and rapped it along the crack with his rock hammer. It required three such hits before it split in two, like a pre-scored English muffin. Inside were some squiggles and a long line that looked like a burrow of some sort. It was quite a bit darker than the rock material.

"Thunder! How did you know it would split like that?"

"That's what I do. Merek, this one's a go." He handed the two halves to Merek, who placed them in an a-grav cart.

Naylon used a laser cutter on a section of the exposed hillside. He didn't need to be exceptionally careful about using it since the laser wasn't designed to burn into rock, but rather to loosen the much less dense fossilized mud that surrounded them. After a good section of it had been removed, Merek used the radioisotope analyzer to determine the age of the strata, which was within ten thousand years of what they expected. This was precisely what they were looking for. Next Naylon aimed a rock tomograph at some of the flat rocks to determine if any of them were suitable for retrieval. He decided on fourteen, which were all placed in the a-grav cart. They worked for three more hours retrieving the samples they wanted.

The evening brought temperatures cooler than they anticipated. The three men were sitting under the tall open gazebo tent they had erected against a vertical rock formation. Their trek to the exposed hillside was long behind them now. The rocks they had collected for the day were packed in containers and already loaded into the transport.

Balmoral Keep had access to a brewery, which was located twenty-five kilometers away in the savanna-like area that marked the transition of the desert to the mountain highlands further on. The beer was much favored in this province. Just after the students packed up their gear the day before, Naylon's former professor had offered them a nine-pack. The three men had enthusiastically accepted the offer. Now with three open bottles, all of which were half gone, they were watching the stars appear.

Merek was reading through some of his vidmails on the handheld comm unit he had. He was enveloped in the device's soundfield. It was designed in such a way that no one else could hear any of the communications with the speakers facing his way.

"Naylon!" Merek suddenly blurted out from the silence. He sounded very excited.

Merek's outburst startled them both. "What?" Naylon responded.

"The grant was approved. You didn't say anything!"

"Did you watch the entire vidmail? We have no way to get there."

Merek was quiet for a moment as he watched the rest of the vid. He slammed his nearly empty bottle onto the arm of the chair he was sitting on. "They only partially approved the grant? Why would they do that?"

"It's the usual corporate misunderstanding. You'll get use to it."

Merek looked agitated now. "That's ridiculous. It's going to delay my paper even longer."

Darreth spoke up now. "What grant?"

Naylon told him all about it.

When the explanation was completed, Darreth shook his head.

"What's that all about?" Naylon asked.

"For an academic type you sure don't know how to network."

"What's that supposed to mean?"

"Who are you going out with?"

Naylon looked over to Merek.

"Don't look at me," Merek told him. He took the last swig from his beer.

Naylon looked back at Darreth. "You."

"What is it I do for a living?"

"Uh, you run pirates out of the starlanes."

"More specifically?" he urged.

"You're a pilot?"

"Exactly."

"But you're in the military."

"The spaceport at the Nona Ice Station on Rylerra is ninety-one kilometers from your dig site. I've been to that station three times. I know it pretty well, too. I also have clearance to take anyone there. Military or not."

Naylon sat upright, feeling the strained muscle in his back that he'd gotten earlier in the day. "Why didn't you say so?"

Darreth held his hands out and grinned. "I just did."

Chapter 9

"Just act normally. You've already met everyone. It's not like you're going into this cold."

Naylon stood on the broad front porch of the elegant James-Po home in the foothills of the Patoria Mountains with Darreth. From this height, they could see the lights of the city below that followed the crescent of the bay. The sun was just beginning to descend toward its placid surface. In another hour, the sky would start turning purple as it reached the horizon.

Darreth's presence triggered the front door to open. He ushered Naylon inside a spacious entryway. To his left was a sunken living room. Two halves of a tall sliding glass door along the far wall facing the pool had been slid back into the wall. The huge gaping opening brought the outdoors directly into the living room. The setting sun was streaming into the room turning everything golden.

Outside Kella and Tann's tanned bodies glistened as they finished some very noisy laps and were standing in the shallow end of the pool.

"Kids, they're here," Naylon heard from somewhere to his right. It was Siloy's voice. Naylon was already nervous. He didn't like being paraded in front of the Chief Council and his family. Both Kella and Tann climbed out of the pool and went for their towels.

Kyana appeared from down one of the hallways. She was dressed quite a bit more informally than the first time Naylon met her. She had on a thin button-up top and shorts with sandals. She greeted Naylon with a big smile and led both he and Darreth to the kitchen. Two servants were busy preparing snacks.

Siloy joined them directly. "Dr. Ress, uh, I mean Naylon, nice to have you over."

"The pleasure is mine, sir," Naylon told him as they shook hands again. *Nice strong grip*, he thought. *Just like Darreth's.*

Siloy held up his finger. "If I can't call you 'Dr. Ress' there will be no sir allowed in this house either," he said, smiling pleasantly.

"Uh..."

"Siloy will do."

"Siloy," Naylon responded. He breathed deeply and exhaled quickly, letting go of even more nervousness. *Thunder*, he thought. *I'm more wound up than I realized.*

Kella and Tann, now dried off and changed, joined them. They both dove into the snacks as soon as they were presented. Everyone moved to the sunken living room and sat down on the plush furniture, where drinks were served, too. Naylon's nose was teased with the aromas from several courses being prepared in the kitchen as they chatted. Shortly, the call to dinner was announced and everyone found seats around a comfortably round, but not overlarge, dinner table.

Finally, after talk about a recent water main leak that had flooded a part of the downtown district, the topic came around to Naylon's research. Naylon gave a brief overview of his work, including the recent approval of his grant.

"Naylon," Kella asked, "why would you need to go to another planet to study life on ours?"

"Good question. It's not asked often enough either. In fact, I had to put plenty of detail about that in my grant request. You see, long ago it was determined that if there's life on one planet in a solar system, there's most likely a signature of life all over the entire system."

"A signature?" Kella asked.

Naylon almost felt uncomfortable bringing it up but he had to. Because it was about Earth. He didn't want to even say that word, mostly because of Darreth. "I'll explain. The theory was brought to the fore about eight hundred years ago, back on Earth." He looked around. Good. No one so much as flinched when he mentioned Earth. Not even Darreth. "In the late 20th century a meteorite was found on one of the icy continents in the southern hemisphere."

"Antarctica," Tann stated glibly.

"Right," he said, impressed. It came as a surprise to Naylon that Tann might know Earth's continents. "Once it was examined, they determined it had been ejected from Mars, the fourth planet in the system; most likely jettisoned from a large meteorite impact. Further examination led to the tentative conclusion that it contained fossilized remains of Martian life forms. The claims were never proven with that particular meteorite, but another one found elsewhere on Earth about a century later provided ample proof. Once regular expeditions started going to Mars they discovered that fossils had been carried back and forth between Earth and Mars. They even learned that DNA from live microbes had survived the fiery re-entry into each of the planets' atmospheres. Later, once the Jovian moons were explored, scientists discovered microbial life forms in the subsurface Europan and Ganymedean oceans with the same DNA coding as those in the inner planets. The theory that life in a solar system mixes between planets had been proven beyond any doubt."

"Serious?" Tann asked.

"Serious as star travel. In my humble opinion it's one of the most important discoveries in human history."

Siloy spoke up now. "So, you think the same thing has happened here in our two systems."

"That fact has been established for quite some time now. The DNA evidence is all there. It's just that the environments on Andakar and Rylerra created completely different evolutionary paths just like in the Sol system. Our task is to find out where the Rylerran samples came from and determine if there are more. We'd like to determine when the mixing occurred and when the two evolutionary paths diverged. It's quite unfortunate the samples we found in the museum weren't properly labeled. That would have narrowed down the search considerably. As it is, we've had to use Rylerran satellite survey information to isolate probable sites to start our digs. As you know our solar systems are unique in that we have two planets in two life zones. None of the other Inhabs have two planets that harbor life on temperate worlds."

Siloy nodded, aware of that fact, but never giving it much thought until now. "This grant that the museum provided. It's fully funded?"

"Nearly. They didn't provide for a ship or a pilot. But that's been taken care of."

"How so?" Siloy asked.

"Darreth offered to pilot a ship for us. Our primary site's in the northern hemisphere and it's summertime there right now. At least for the next four months. It's almost shirtsleeve weather."

Tann looked at his brother. "How are you getting there?"

"An H-180."

"Who's going?"

"Me, Naylon and his colleague Merek. I have the time off so I'm staying with them, then flying them back."

"Those shuttles have room for eight," Tann announced in a suddenly hopeful manner.

Kella looked up at him, her eyes wide, knowing what was coming next.

Darreth pointed his fork at Tann. "No," he said with a decided dismissal.

"Darreth," Tann said in a decidedly pleading tone. "You promised."

Naylon looked at the two of them staring at each other. "Promised what?" he asked Darreth.

Darreth ignored the question. "There's no way," he firmly retorted, still looking squarely at his little brother.

Naylon leaned back in his chair, watching their interaction take place. "What did you promise him?" he asked softly. Naylon glanced over at Siloy who looked like he was enjoying the interaction.

"That I'd take him to Rylerra the next time I went. Just to look around. You know, to visit another planet."

Naylon looked first at Darreth's father, then to Kella, then into Tann's pleading eyes. Finally, he took in Darreth's steadfast gaze at his brother. "I can authorize clearance, Darreth. Insurance covers everyone. It's only for fifteen days anyway. That's with transit time. He'll have to stay with us the entire time, but I can assure everyone it will be an adventure he'll never forget."

Darreth shook his head then waved the idea off with his hand. "It's too dangerous."

"Darreth!" Tann interjected. "He just said I could go!"

"I said you can't."

"He'll just need warm clothing," Naylon told him.

Siloy intervened, heading off an obvious argument. "I think Darreth's being overly cautious, as usual. I say he can go," he said with a ring of finality in his voice. He looked at Naylon. "When are you leaving?"

"Darreth said he can have the ship ready in three weeks."

"Perfect. Tann's out of school by then."

Tann was so excited he stood up, almost knocking his chair over in the process. He shot his fist into the air with almost childlike enthusiasm. "Light speed!"

"I can't believe you said that," Darreth told Naylon. "He has no business on Rylerra."

"It's not dangerous unless he gets frostbite. What's the big deal?"

Chapter 10

Inandra Alarr's quarters were plush. Not that other Earthers on Andakar didn't have nice quarters. It's just that hers had to be the very best. In fact, it was one of her first demands when she had arrived several years ago. The walls of her living room all had the latest holo-tech in them so she could surround herself with familiar images of her hometown near Vienna back on Earth. That included full sound quality of tourists on the walkways along the lake, the din of the small shops that faced the water, and the traffic further beyond.

Virtual reality aside, her backdoor opened out to a huge swimming pool on a raised deck overlooking a fair-sized portion of the midrises of Tokaias' western district. She had two servants, both of whom were born on Andakar, but were soon to be Citizens. She reminded herself she'd need new ones soon. It was rare when a Citizen would continue working for an off-worlder, regardless of the pay, after obtaining that status. It came with the territory and she knew it. She was well aware of the tacit tension which frequently accompanied interactions with the natives of this Inhab. It was particularly intense on Andakar.

Taking charge was burned into Inandra's genes. From the time she was a little girl, when she was first allowed to accompany her father to a business meeting, or more accurately, to the dinners afterwards with some of his clients, she knew she would eventually be someone of rare importance. At first, it was because of the radiant smile that won the favor of her father's most important clients. Then it was her precocious realization at puberty that it wasn't just her smile. Smiles alone didn't win her father important contracts.

After sleeping with the Nattor Designs division headquarters chief the day after her fourteenth birthday, and her father won the contract with them the day after, she realized her gifts weren't necessarily rare, but were important. Important enough to give herself freely every chance she got.

She was sure her father knew the dinner dates with 'friends' were really with division heads, upper level managers, and with the corporate lawyers ready to approve richly rewarding contracts. But daddy never spoke about it. Since those contracts were always lucrative when 'little Inandra' was along, she discovered that daddy was also important. Daddy provided her with ways to hear things little girls didn't often get to hear. Like who was really in power. Who really had direct lines of communication to even more important people. Small things like that.

Inandra's older brother Lerut was directly in line to take over when the time came. Family run businesses demanded that. Inandra knew that although Lerut was large and sounded important, he had a very limited capacity for obtaining major contracts her father had so deftly solidified. After all, Lerut was male. Nor was he good-looking. Later, when he married, his wife was no match for her own prowess. Indeed, Inandra's sister-in-law had no intention of sleeping around to obtain contracts. She was well-aware of corporate law.

Inandra knew once her father retired it would be impossible to sustain the level of profit the family had enjoyed since she had reached the age of consent. So, although family members suspected Inandra was the direct cause of the most lucrative contracts in recent years, no one had ever proven how. After all, none of the businessmen, most of whom were married, had any intention of divulging their liaisons. They also knew corporate law. She kept her trail cold and her emotions in check.

A defect in the airlock of the transport ship had caused an explosive decompression coming back to Geosynchronous Station One from Mars when she was 23 years old. It was a once in a lifetime event, which resulted in a lawsuit that went on for years. The accident not only killed her father, but Lerut, his wife, and two of the lawyers assigned to negotiate the contract with Gusev Dome Builders. Lerut didn't get his chance to succeed his father after all. Inandra immediately became president of Alarr Offworld, Ltd. Her mother had no interest or inclination to do so as long as money kept coming in and kept her in the luxurious lifestyle to which she herself had succumbed.

That unfortunate circumstance immediately positioned Inandra with the means to follow her true aspirations. She didn't intend to stop with just being president of a corporation. She wanted more. She craved more. She had even had that dream twice. The impossible dream. Each time it had woken her from a dead sleep. Her ruling an entire planet. It was something no female in the history of the Consortium had ever managed to do. Earth Central Planning and Direction Committee appointed the planetary director to each of the Inhabs. There were only 13 such directorships, since Earth was excluded from such appointments. In the history of Deep Sky Mining, only four women had been appointed to be Planetary Directors.

Zelin Raxi was born and raised in Bonn. Zelin was single for the second time, and 38 years old, when he met the radiant Inandra long after she had become her father's successor. Right away, he knew he was dealing with someone formidable, yet with desperate needs. He intended right away to fulfill at least one of those needs, and get one of his satisfied along the way.

Zelin had an almost supernatural knack for extracting information from people, even when they were least aware of it. It was one of his natural talents, which he had exploited for years. He was a catalyst of sorts. Socially, he had an uncanny ability to bring disparate people together. In his business dealings, he played the role of master negotiator. In his personal life, he was smooth enough to melt even the most jaded women. Fortunately, for him that included Inandra. She had actually met her match.

It was after their second night of passionate lovemaking that Zelin discovered Inandra's innermost desire. Zelin was absolutely surprised to hear it, thinking it was just prattle at first. But he noted her tone. He could nearly feel her desire for such an office. Here was his chance, he realized. He figured he would be able to use her as she was using him. After all, she was sleeping with him to obtain a very lucrative contract with Kekliv Waveguide Systems where he had been working for over a decade. Zelin was tired of the non-stop work with Kekliv and longed to run a mining operation instead. After all, it was his innermost desire. Something out of the way. Something quiet. Something as lucrative but without the frenetic schedule of sales meetings he had to attend. When he discovered they both had unfulfilled goals, it was a simple matter of waiting for the right moment. He knew a few things Inandra had no idea about. He had contacts Inandra knew nothing about.

Forty-six days later, an opportunity presented itself to him.

Nels Hodofar was already in his early sixties when he had been appointed by Central Planning and Direction to be Andakar's Planetary Director. He had held that post for almost eighteen years. He had been generally liked by most of the population. He was fair most of the time, although he always had Earth's interests at heart. That's why he was in the position. His death was met with great consternation with the Committee. Through a series of extremely lucky contacts in the Committee and a small payoff, Zelin was able to bring Inandra's name to the top of the list of possible replacements. Her reputation was well known. Lucrative ventures always got news. The Committee had its pulse on who was who and who was not. In addition, he lobbied each voting member of the nominating committee that they wouldn't find a better candidate than her. It was less difficult than Zelin thought to convince the right people.

Within a month, Inandra was offered the position. She had to decide between continued ownership of her corporation or choose a lifetime appointment on Andakar. She already knew which choice to make. One of the first people she told was Zelin. He could barely contain himself when he saw the look of sheer joy on her face during the brief vidcall. She was unaware of the amount of time he had put in to make this happen.

A message arrived a week later in Zelin's vidbox. The mining operations manager named Bov Ghendeed on Rylerra was expected to retire in the next year. Now it was his turn to be overjoyed. Zelin's quiet little spot might be opening up far sooner than he thought. And the favor he needed from Inandra would be due far sooner than he ever believed possible. Zelin had visited Rylerra twice several years previously on business trips. He had made a special side trip each time to visit Bov. Both times, he had wined and dined the man. Never quite knowing when his effort would pay off, he nonetheless realized that several things had finally converged in a manner he couldn't possibly have predicted. By the time Bov retired, Inandra would have been on Andakar for quite some time. She would have ample power and significant influence with the Central Planning and Direction Committee. Recommendation by a Planetary Director for him to fill Bov's position had immeasurable weight. In Zelin's estimation, there was nothing better than this merger of events.

Well, perhaps there was something better. How about the wonderful bedtime favors Inandra was so talented at? Her talents seemed to have ruined it for him. There wasn't another woman alive he was remotely interested in anymore. How that was possible, he wasn't sure since he had long ago lost count of the number of encounters he'd had with women. But ventures with other women, romantic or otherwise, paled in comparison to the haughty attitude she exuded, her lithe thin body, her long flowing hair, the impossible angles she could be taken in. Perhaps it was her wonderfully smooth skin, the deep green eyes that haunted him at times, and now she would soon be Andakar's next Planetary Director, all due to his skillful maneuvering.

And the last item alone was to be to his supreme advantage. Zelin knew what he wanted and now he could force Inandra to get it for him.

Two weeks before Inandra was on her way to Andakar, he had her over to his private Montreux suite overlooking Lake Geneva, the very same Montreux that was Inandra's hometown. It was a night of celebration. A night where they had both gotten very drunk. Zelin covertly activated a holorecorder. The questions he asked her were how she obtained those very first contracts for her father when she was so very young. He had his suspicions already, but he wanted to hear it from her lips. She confessed it was because she had slept with key people. It didn't matter that she had whispered it. The holorecorder's audio system was very sensitive and very good. Zelin told her that it turned him on to hear about the men she had slept with, so she told him more. At first he thought everything she had said was nothing more than boastful lies. But the voice stress analysis he later performed told him that everything she had said was completely true. Unfortunately for her, it was highly illegal.

The Consortium was indeed the overseer for all other corporations on all the Inhabs. The Consortium was also the largest single legal entity humans had ever created. Its efficiency was enforced by a very rigid set of laws. Laws that were strictly enforced, since it was the only way business could be run on an interplanetary scale and still work for the good of everyone. It was the Consortium's business to make sure the population was clothed, fed, created or had jobs, and paid taxes. That required rigidly fixed standards of business. Under normal circumstances, Inandra's private life would have prevented her from obtaining any position other than the one she currently enjoyed, which in itself was only due to nothing more than an unfortunate accident. But she had been very careful. Until she met Zelin.

Zelin had a way of making sure that everything he did had a legitimate purpose and was well documented. Bribes were always donations. Private meetings always had a record of legitimate business containing a well-traced trail to legitimate dealings, even when they weren't necessarily so. He wasn't quite criminal since he was very meticulous about what he did and with whom he dealt. Thus, the holorecording. Which she suspected the next morning.

She spied him at his vidstation watching some sort of vid. She was sure that was her in the vid, although she couldn't be absolutely sure from where she stood. She had peeked at him through the partially opened door of his study after she was finished dressing. Zelin's lair was supposed to be perfectly private. This was one time he slipped up.

She had arrived at his lake house again two days after the recording had been made. She stood in his front doorway.

"Well, are you coming in?" he had asked. "The door is going to close on you if you don't."

She looked around at all the corners, floor and ceiling that she could see from the front entrance. He noticed that right away.

"Something wrong, dear?"

"I'm not your 'dear', Zelin." With that, she ushered herself in and strode past him.

The house was quiet. None of his housekeepers were there. The large windows were filled with a view of the mountains to the south. She wasn't sure how to tell him, so decided on the direct approach. "Your little celebration wasn't exactly what I thought it was."

"Come again, dear?"

"Stop it with the 'dear'. You know I hate that."

Zelin had already gone to the nearby table that contained crystal containers of various liquors and had poured her a brandy. He pointed to the couch. She looked at the drink and decided she needed it. She tossed half of it back in two gulps. French. Her favorite.

"You were just getting information from me that night, weren't you?" she stated, her voice hard.

"Information?"

She tightened her mouth to pencil thinness, not sure why she had bothered to even explain it. She sat the glass down on the coffee table. "Don't play games with me, Zelin. You recorded everything I said that night. And now you're going to use it against me. Why?"

Of course Zelin was going to deny all of it. "You're kidding, of course. I recorded you? Why on Earth would I do such a thing?"

"Because you want to ruin me, that's why. Now that I'm going to be a Planetary Director, you want to take me down. Why?"

He tried his best to suppress a look of surprise. Somehow, she knew about the recording! So there was no use lying about it. He didn't know how she had discovered his ruse. Perhaps he wasn't as careful as he should have been. He shouldn't have started reviewing the recording so quickly. At least not until she had actually left his suite. "I recorded our little… liaison so I could make sure you help me out."

"Zelin, dear. Whatever are you saying?"

"Well, let's just say I've just taken out an insurance policy. You see, if you help me with a little, er, problem I have, well, then you can have the recording."

"If that means we're having sex right now, the answer's no."

Zelin shook his head and issued a barely perceptible grin. "No, my dear. That's not what I had in mind." Actually, he wouldn't have minded at all, but he had a different purpose already set in stone. He excused himself and went to the study. After he returned, he aimed the scanner at her. Satisfied that he wasn't being recorded he decided to let her in on everything.

"I have higher aspirations than just being a well-paid manager at Kekliv," he began. "I'd like to make sure I get something very important in the near future. Besides, you owe me. After all, it was me, my dear, that got you the Directorship."

Inandra wasn't sure she heard him right. Zelin had some sort of hand in her getting the Directorship? How was that possible?

He told her how he had spoken with key committee members. Gave her exact quotes from people she was sure to know by now. Then told her about Bov. About the nice quiet manager's job that was soon to open on Rylerra. It was just a coincidence that Rylerra and Andakar were in the same double star system. A happy coincidence, he had decided.

During the next hour, while Zelin explained everything, her thoughts strayed as far from the conversation as they could. The situation wasn't as bad as she thought. She'd get the holovid though. There was no way anyone could ever get their hands on it or she'd be ruined. He could have his little manager's position, too. She was positive that could be arranged. In fact, her thoughts strayed even farther. Since she wasn't a native of Andakar, she would never be able to actually run the entire planet, per se. There were local provincial managers who would be reporting to her. But that was a minor legal issue to be resolved in the years, perhaps the decades, to come. She would eventually figure out how to remove native local managers and become the sole legal overseer. She knew enough lawyers. Consortium law might be rigid but it wasn't fixed. Somehow, she'd be able to do it.

Somehow.

Amazing what sleeping around had accomplished for her.

Chapter 11

The shuttle that Darreth had signed out was part of an interplanetary fleet. There were twenty of them. All were the same model. Darreth had flown on several missions to Rylerra in one. The H-180 shuttle was unlike cozy passenger ships though. Designed to move military personnel from ground bases to orbiting stations, or as a station-to-station transport vehicle, it could easily traverse planetary distances in a reasonable amount of time. It could hold eight people comfortably and could store up to two weeks of frozen or freeze-dried rations, along with plenty of water. It had short and long-range sensors, several comm buoys, and an advanced holofield navigation system. Although not designed to be a fighter by any stretch of the imagination, it had defensive shielding and offensive weaponry just in case. After all, it was a military shuttle.

Naylon stood in a long corridor on the space station awaiting the surface pod's arrival. This one had fifteen passengers. One was Tann. Naylon's face brightened as he saw Tann come in through the airlock door. "Hey. Good to see you," Naylon told him.

"I can't believe I'm finally here. I thought this day would never arrive," he said with boyish enthusiasm.

"Have you been on the station before?"

"No."

"Neither have I. It's not as bad as I thought it would be."

"Whadda ya mean," Tann asked curiously as he looked up and down the corridor. Several people passed them by and two more were crossing an intersecting corridor several dozen meters up ahead.

"I thought it would be a lot more… stark."

It was far from that. The shirtsleeve environment was a steady 22 degrees. A breeze could be felt in all the carpeted corridors. Evenly spaced windows gave the impression of an open loft space.

"Where's Darreth?" Tann asked.

"Prepping our ride in Shuttle Bay 2. He asked me to meet you." Naylon pointed to the bag riding on Tann's shoulder. "You must have more than that."

"The steward said my stuff would be routed to the right place. I hope he was right," he said anxiously.

Apparently, baggage was being offloaded through another pressure door, Naylon guessed. "Hungry?" he asked as they proceeded through the corridor.

"I'm too excited to eat."

"We're going to pass the visitor's mess up ahead. I thought you might want something for the 'road'."

Tann shook his head. "I've got some snacks in here," he said as he patted his bag.

Naylon noticed Tann was all smiles as they took off toward the shuttle bay. He was taking in all the sights.

The station was huge. In fact, it was larger in volume than the largest cruise ship on Andakar. Dozens of people were going about their business in the wider corridors. About half of the personnel they saw were in uniform. Now that Tann had finally gotten to see the station his brother spent a lot of time occupying, he had a newfound respect for the facility and for his brother. This is what profit could provide: a station with all the latest amenities, the latest shuttle pods, and the best anti-pirate weaponry and detection systems in the entire Consortium.

Two-thirds of a kilometer further they finally came upon a row of windows that overlooked a huge gaping room. Eight H-180 interplanetary shuttles were lined up next to each other. Naylon and Tann descended an elevator to the main floor. The elevator opened to an airlock, which opened to the shuttle bay.

Tann and Naylon immediately saw Darreth with a vidPAD in hand standing outside the open shuttle door talking to a maintenance technician. Darreth handed the man the vidPAD and the maintenance man left just as Naylon and Tann approached. The shuttle's designation was in large bold black letters.

"*Siaron Viper*," Tann said aloud as he touched it briefly.

Darreth smiled upon seeing his brother. "Hey, kid. How was the ride up," he asked as he gave Naylon a quick affectionate peck on the cheek.

"Took all of twenty-five minutes." He quickly passed right by Darreth and took a look inside the shuttle's open door. He stepped in and looked around. Less than three seconds later he exited the craft. "This is it?" he exclaimed.

Both Naylon and Darreth turned to look at him. The shuttle bay airlock door opened at that moment, too. In walked Merek. He had a bag slung over his shoulder. He was pulling another one behind him on rollers. He had just checked out of his visitor's room. Naylon and Darreth looked back to the still stunned-looking Tann.

"It's a military shuttle, not a yacht," Darreth told him.

"Where are we going to sleep?"

"The acceleration chairs slide all the way flat. They make for a very comfortable bed. Plus, they have noise cancellation fields. You knew it's going to take a few days to get there, so don't complain."

Naylon grinned at Darreth.

Merek approached the two men with his baggage. "Everything's stowed already?" he asked Naylon.

"All the equipment's in the storage lockers. Your stuff can go in back. Need help?"

"Nah."

An a-grav sled came out of an open door to their far right, led by a porter. On it were Tann's two bags. The porter had Tann put his thumbprint on a vidPAD to sign for them, then deposited them at the shuttle's door. The man guided the sled back out of the shuttle bay and was gone a moment later.

Merek was busy strapping his things down in the storage lockers at the rear of the vehicle while Tann brought his things in.

"Tann, is it?"

"Yeah," he replied.

"Merek. I work with Naylon." He extended his hand. Tann shook it. "I hear you're the pilot's brother."

"Yeah," Tann replied, sounding dejected.

"You don't sound so happy," Merek observed.

"I thought we'd get a better shuttle."

"Better? They're all like this one," Merek pointed out as he looked around.

"So I hear," he said, with a note of disappointment in his voice.

Clearance for departure was granted two hours later. Darreth was in the pilot's chair. Naylon had taken the co-pilot seat to Darreth's right, although he had no idea how to work any of the controls. Merek was directly behind Naylon, and Tann was behind his brother on the left. Tann's view was through a large window on the port side. In front of him was a large display screen, but Tann was much more interested in the real view.

Darreth's view wouldn't be real at all. In fact, a real view would have been fatal. All interplanetary shuttles and other FTL ships had a standard holofield nav interface, which enveloped the pilot in his own bubble of sensory data. The interface gave the pilot the unique experience of sitting in an imaginary point in space surrounded with all the sensor array information the ship possessed. With voice commands and a few hand controls, the pilot could view, call up, display or otherwise interface with every computer aboard the ship and have instant access to whatever important data was needed at the moment. All of it would be projected into space in front, to the side or even to the rear of his holo-universe. Even if the pilot forgot to access specific data when required, that information would be displayed anyway.

Distances were projected using logarithmic scales in thousands of kilometers, local system AUs, or light years. Navigational stars could be labeled in the pilot's holographic universe with their name, distance, spectral type and an array of other information that might be relevant. Course plotting was projected in front of the pilot. Weapons array levels were displayed in real time. Environmental controls, landing points: everything was viewable when necessary. It was not only a very efficient interface, it was one that gave Darreth a thrill every time he strapped in and activated it. He was in total command of the ship the moment the field was turned on. It was one of the many reasons he enjoyed what he did.

Ships were not allowed to activate their FTL drives within six million kilometers of a planet's orbit. The reason was that wrinkling spacetime created a huge graviton distortion wave. That wave was disruptive to communications, navigational beacons and any other nearby photronic device. The waves spread out in a spherical shape from the insertion point, so it was standard to wrinkle a wedge at a considerable distance from any Inhab. Thus, they would be traveling sub-light at .46c to a point designated by the glowing red X in Darreth's nav field. Once they were the proper distance away, Darreth would activate the FTL engine.

With all systems checked out and clearance authorized, they left the station's shuttle bay and were out into open space. Instantly, Tann felt a thrill like he'd never felt before. His first trip away from Andakar! He intently stared out the window hoping to get a glance at anything that might pass as they cleared the docking ring. Maybe he'd see a bit of the station as they left it behind. Perhaps he'd see one of the numerous satellites in orbit around their world. Anything. But he was disappointed when the station and his world quickly receded and were only specks in moments.

Thus, Tann had to resort to sensor arrays after all. He knew how to run the display in front of him since it had a standard interface. Extreme magnification allowed him to watch Andakar recede. Within an hour, their velocity had increased enough for the planet to be too small to discern any viewable detail from the rear vid cam, even at maximum magnification.

"Okay Tann, ready to assist me?" Merek asked. Unknown to Tann, Naylon had sent a message to the heads up display in front of Merek asking him to divert Tann's attention.

Tann looked over at Merek. "Assist you? How?"

"I need to run some diagnostics on the equipment we brought. I'll need your help."

"I don't know any of your equipment."

Merek shrugged. "I'll show you what to do and you can tell the computer to run them."

"Oh. Okay."

They both un-strapped and went to the rear of the shuttle. The equipment bay was through a small door just past the entrance hatch and the head, which also doubled as an ultrasonic shower. Merek winked at Naylon just before he shut the door behind himself.

Naylon activated his internal comm. *"Darreth?"*

Naylon wasn't sure he should interrupt Darreth while he was enveloped in the nav field. But it didn't hurt to try.

Without looking at him, Darreth's reply came appearing in his head as a fairly loud voice. *"What, cutie?"*

"Okay if I talk to you?"

"Sure."

"What's it like?"

"The nav field?"

"Yeah."

"It's spectacular. These shuttles are great to pilot since they're so nimble."

"Any bumps in the road?"

"Not a one. According to the chronometer we're on schedule to wrinkle a wedge in two hours."

Just short of two hours later Merek and Tann finished the diagnostics checks on all their underground sensor equipment that would be used in the field operation once they arrived. The equipment would be used to map fault lines, determine where and how sedimentary layers were deposited, perform short and long distance t-mode scans of objects beneath the ground, and do chemical as well as radiological analyses of samples. Merek ran the diagnostic on the t-mode unit himself. The t-mode or terrestrial mode unit was simply named but would perform the most important tasks. That of taking 3D underground pictures using a wide swath of the electromagnetic spectrum. It had the uncanny ability to help them determine ahead of time whether a spot was worth digging or not.

The storage room door slid open. Merek and Tann returned to the main shuttle cabin.

"Hey, just in time. We're only a couple of thousand kilometers from the insertion spot," Naylon told them.

Standard procedure was for all personnel to be strapped into their acceleration chairs before going FTL. Although an FTL procedure hadn't gone wrong in hundreds of years, protocol was protocol. They both sat down and strapped in.

A few minutes later Darreth counted down for them. "Insertion in 5-4-3-2-1."

There was a slight shudder throughout the cabin, a noise from the rear of the shuttle, that of the FTL engine sound chamber engaging, and instantly the view outside the ship turned gray. Tann knew they were no longer in normal space. Even so, it was disheartening to not have a bit of a view. For the next eighty-four hours he'd have to rely on the music chips he'd brought with him, the vids he had downloaded into his vidPAD and the ships broad entertainment database to keep him company. Short-term boredom was the small price he would have to pay for the awaiting big adventure.

Darreth immediately disengaged the nav field from around him. There was no use for it as long as they were FTL.

"Whew," he exclaimed. "I'm hungry. Break out the sandwiches."

Chapter 12

At first, Naylon thought he'd made a mistake in insisting Tann come along. In this environment, he seemed a bit whiney. Naylon thought the James-Po family's position would have made him a better sport. In a way, he had insisted because the boy had expressed a profound interest in visiting another planet. Well, the opportunity was right there, so why not have him come along? Yet, despite Naylon's initial regretful observation of Tann's demeanor aboard the shuttle, he was pleasantly surprised to see that Tann adjusted rather quickly. Yes, the shuttle was Spartan and cramped, but he ceased sounding bratty within hours. Naylon hadn't been on a trip like this before either, but he'd been on plenty of multi-day overland road trips to various dig sites. As a seasoned adult, he never minded the dust, the rain or the long hours where he could barely stretch his legs in the transport vehicle. Luckily, though, Naylon could just barely touch the cabin's ceiling with his middle finger when he stood upright on his toes. The cabin might have been small, but it wasn't nearly as bad as an overland trip.

Sleeping was better than Naylon anticipated, too. When adjusted to the sleeping position, the acceleration chairs immediately conformed to their body position. After they turned in Naylon was surprised to find he had fallen asleep within minutes.

There were advantages and disadvantages to the method of FTL travel the Consortium had control over. One of the advantages was that as long as one was inside a wrinkled wedge they were perfectly protected from normal space. Thus, the entire night passed without so much as an alarm. The main disadvantage was that it wasn't an instantaneous process. 'Normal' time passed on board the ship while traversing the distance. It's just that the amount of time was considerably less than if spacetime wrinkling hadn't been discovered.

At 0500, Darreth hit the head then checked the control station readouts. It wasn't at all necessary since the shuttle's computer would have instantly transmitted warnings of any kind audibly. Nonetheless, it was habit. Darreth went back to sleep shortly thereafter.

An hour later, the interior lights slowly brightened, mimicking a sunrise. Naylon rose and made his way to the facilities, too. Tann was asleep on his back. Right away Naylon noticed the boy's morning swella under the light blanket. He looked away with a slight grin on his face. Darreth's was the only one he had any interest in. Tann was far too young for his taste and straight as far as he knew. He immediately set himself to making a pot of coffee. By the time it finished brewing, everyone else had woken up.

The entire day was spent talking, eating, periodically doing some light isometric exercises, which Darreth led, watching a couple of vids, then it was free time for everyone. Naylon went over his copious notes with Merek. Darreth explained every one of the shuttle systems to his brother, who patiently listened to every word. Naylon glanced up every once in a while to note Tann's reactions. He was completely different now than when he first came on board.

Breakout from FTL in the Kaskalon system was only moments away. Everyone was wearing a heads up display so they could watch the transition back to normal space. No satellites, buoys or other ships were allowed in the sector where breakouts occurred because they were hazards. A ship that hit one would be instantly destroyed. Thus, when a ship appeared inside the nav field not more than 100,000 kilometers off the port bow Darreth was duly concerned. He saw the visual warning a split second before the nav's voice expressed its displeasure at the object.

"What the...?" Darreth said with noticeable unease.

Tann's gaze shifted left as he saw the speck in the display. All other eyes went there as well. The data on the display associated with the object was only understandable to Darreth.

"What is it?" Naylon asked.

"A frucking ship. They're not supposed to be in this part of space. It's off-limits," Darreth told him.

Darreth immediately told the nav computer to identify it. A half-second passed, then a full second. *"No transponder code present,"* the computer responded, after it completed a sensor sweep. The sweep was only able to log the vessel's type and class but nothing more.

The hair on the back of Darreth's neck went up. This couldn't be happening. Only pirates didn't transmit identification codes. But in Kaskalon space? If it had happened before, he was unaware of it.

"Everyone strapped in?" Darreth asked.

Everyone responded in the affirmative.

"Good. Because I have to make an emergency maneuver."

Although the inertial dampeners were good, they couldn't keep up with the emergency turn to starboard. That put them on a heading directly in line with Rylerra.

Naylon whispered it. "Pirates?"

Darreth knew his nod would be seen, although he couldn't see Naylon.

"Why are we running?" Tann asked.

Darreth took a moment to answer. He wanted to make sure what he was reading was accurate: the pirate ship was vectoring toward them. "They're in pursuit," he announced.

"But we're a shuttle!" Tann said with noticeable apprehension. "We don't have any pharmas, do we?"

"No," Darreth quickly replied.

The other ship was making an extremely high velocity trajectory straight for them. Darreth accelerated the shuttle. A call for help would have been fruitless. He knew it wasn't going to be possible for defensive support to reach them in time. What was a pirate ship doing going after a transport shuttle anyway? It wasn't like they had anything of value a pirate might want.

Or maybe this particular shuttle did. Him.

Darreth had participated in five sorties which had resulted in a total of nine pirate deaths. No, it wasn't murder, just like he had stated back at the dig weeks ago. They were purely because of the defensive actions he had undertaken. The deaths were something he'd carefully kept from everyone except his superiors. It was all logged and part of the job. No one outside the Space Navy needed to know about it.

Darreth knew that him being the pilot of this shuttle was known to only a small group of people on a need-to-know basis. Records could be culled from flight plan databases, but not that easily. Perhaps someone had gotten hold of that bit of information and was waiting for them to go sublight from the FTL wedge. That was the only satisfactory answer he could come up with right now. The thought that this might happen one day had been in the back of his mind for months. Now it looked like a terrible reality.

Darreth spoke to the computer. "Track incoming ship continuously. Audible readout."

The computer started reading off data in a pleasant voice, quite unlike the tension building in the cabin. Both Tann and Merek were squeezing the armrests, watching the red blip and the distance counter showing the ship closing in. Darreth told the computer to tell him when they were within the two-second delay communications range of the nearest Rylerran comm buoy. But he already knew that at their current velocity, and the subsequent slowdown they needed to achieve once they were close enough, would gain them nothing. Even with a mayday, they would still be on their own.

Darreth told them his plan. "Okay everyone, listen up. I'm going to make an emergency landing. Unfortunately, because of our velocity we're going to end up somewhere other than the Nona Ice Station spaceport."

"Then… where?" Merek asked.

"It doesn't matter. I've just got to elude that pirate ship long enough to get into the atmosphere. There are lots of clouds in the higher climes. We can easily lose them once we're at fifteen kilometers altitude. Don't agit. All systems are working. Once we land, we'll call for help or just lay low for a while. We have maneuvering thrusters for low atmosphere travel, so we're okay."

"Shit," Tann said just loud enough to be heard.

"Hold on little brother. This is what I do best."

As soon as Darreth got the last syllable out the shuttle was rattled by a strong shutter. The nav field sensors told Darreth the outer envelope of a particle beam weapon had grazed the side of the shuttle. The pirates weren't playing around. The *Siaron Viper* was still several tens of millions of kilometers from Rylerra. They had to make it to the atmosphere. It was their only real chance to elude the pursuing ship.

"Raise shields," Darreth told the computer. Immediately several console lights lit, indicating that the energy deflection shield had been activated. "Hold on. This isn't going to be fun." Darreth had made a show of raising shields for his passengers. He was well aware the ship pursuing them was heavily armed. The sensor sweep had told him that. He had deliberately not let his passengers know that. A direct hit to his shuttle's shield generator would leave them nearly defenseless. This was no fighter craft. It was a standard interstellar shuttle lacking the advanced weaponry he was used to controlling. He was sure though that they'd be able to hold out for quite a while. If only he could get them into the atmosphere. Otherwise, they risked being blasted to smithereens in the cold of space and never found.

Darreth initiated an emergency procedure that was not in the best interest of power savings. He altered course slightly. The maneuver would put them on a trajectory where they would eventually skim the atmosphere at Rylerra's North Pole. The magnetic field lines, which stronger at the pole and closer together, were a perfect shield for most targeting sensors. Once Darreth guided them in, they'd be less vulnerable and perhaps force the pirates to use manual targeting for their weapons. They would be significantly less accurate if he could manage to pull it off. At least, that was the theory.

The computer indicated a nav satellite was close enough to relay a message to the Nona Ice Station's landing authority. The delay at this distance would be fifty-six seconds. Not enough time to scramble any sort of defense. Yet, he had to try.

"Nona Station Authority," he began. "This is Lieutenant Commander Darreth James-Po piloting the military shuttle *Siaron Viper*. We are under attack. I say again, we are under attack by an unknown ship. Attacking ship is Helios class. We've been fired upon. Request track... ing."

The blue flash was all the evidence he needed to know his comm would most likely never be replied to. The pirates had targeted the satellite. They were more than serious now. The nav sat, which also served telemetry and comm, was the main one used for nearly all traffic making the run between Rylerra and Andakar.

"Okay everyone," he told his passengers. "They blasted the nav sat. We're on our own until we reach surface communications range." Darreth knew he would have to shed velocity and shed it fast. At the rate he needed to slow down it would take twenty-five minutes before they would be close enough for direct communications with the surface. Darreth nudged another two-hundredths out of the engines for several seconds. That might shed another eight or nine minutes before he definitely had to slow down.

"Why haven't you fired back?" Naylon asked, quite confused that they were just fleeing and making no attempt to defend themselves.

That statement tore at Darreth. Standing orders were that no one had the authority to fire on anyone in Eratil-Kaskalon space. Corporate mandate had made that very clear.

But no one expected this to happen.

It was absurd to think he couldn't or wouldn't fire back. After all, he had his partner, his brother and another researcher with him. Yet he had no real authority to make a command decision like firing back, an action that might ultimately get them injured or killed. The dilemma was staring him in the face, yet he couldn't just do nothing. "Orders," was all Darreth said back.

"Orders?" Naylon replied, quite distressed. "You mean you can't fire back?"

Darreth nodded.

Naylon's mouth gaped open. "*Fruck* your orders! They're trying to kill us! You *have* to shoot back." He bit his lip. Without Darreth at the helm they would have been dead already. Naylon suddenly realized the absolute necessity of having a Space Navy and highly skilled pilots. He certainly hoped Merek realized it as well, he thought with chagrin. Real world issues were nothing like theoretical ones his discussion group usually dealt with.

Darreth was rapidly concluding that the standing order was ridiculous. Indeed, to his knowledge no one had ever had to confront this situation. He had to fire back. But he still had a couple of ideas up his sleeve before he ignored the directive. Besides, he already knew he was outgunned. Luckily, only a few seconds had passed. He was already planning his course of action.

Naylon yanked off his virtual display glasses and glanced back at Tann. The boy's face had gone white. The back of Naylon's acceleration chair was too wide. He couldn't see Merek directly behind him. Naylon's stomach was tied in knots. He quickly put the glasses back over his eyes. He could do nothing more than watch the drama play out and wonder when Darreth was going to start using their weapons.

Rylerra was coming up impossibly fast. It was a ball of mostly white, reflecting light off the huge amount of ice permanently locked in glaciers and the profusion of clouds at the higher latitudes. A wide band of dark ice-free land was rapidly becoming visible along the equator, which was turning at a wild angle as they made their approach.

"Nona Ice Station, this is Lieutenant Commander James-Po of the *Siaron Viper*. We're under attack by an unidentified pirate ship. I say again. We're under attack. Attempting to ditch them. Lock on to our transponder signal."

To Naylon's unskilled eyes, their approach was far too fast to be manageable. He found himself gripping his armrests even tighter, sure that at any second they would end up diving right into the surface and be smashed to dust.

"Calculate fastest safe approach to landmass below and execute," Darreth told the computer. Immediately, their pitch changed. They went into a steep downward dive. The computer was pushing the shuttle's engines and attitude controls to their limit. They weren't designed to try to fly at this speed in the atmosphere, but the pursuing ship was closing in fast. The sky outside the front shield was rapidly changing from black, to blue, then to white. Atmosphere and clouds. Wisps of plasma were starting to lick the edges of their visual field through the transparent front shield. Tann could see its pinkish glow outside the window to his left.

Naylon was having a very difficult time assuring himself that the ship's computer and Darreth's expert piloting skills would bring them down safely. And his main concern was that all around them was white. Was that atmosphere or was it snow? He felt so scared it was if every molecule of moisture in his mouth had evaporated. While in another situation their descent might have been thrilling, even beautiful, Naylon could only wonder where they could possibly touch down. Everywhere below were huge mountain ranges covered with snow. Rivers of ice kilometers wide and dozens of kilometers long, with long dirty channels of dark earth flowing along with them told him that a forbidding landscape awaited them everywhere he looked.

Tann was sure his brother would get them down alive. But the oddest thought arose in his mind. He didn't want to die a virgin. If he got out of this unscathed the first thing he was going to do was have sex with Havest. He'd been pining for her from afar for way too long. But more important than that was trying to hold down the intense sensation of needing to vomit. He had thought he had better nerves, but the situation was totally out of control.

Merek had been quiet this whole time. He didn't want to distract Darreth. His life was somewhat passing before his eyes. He suddenly realized he'd been sequestering himself way too much lately. His desire to get ahead academically, to get the recognition he knew he deserved, suddenly seemed ridiculous. Indeed, recently he'd been living like a recluse. His routine had been going to work and coming home only. He couldn't die. All of it was for the sake of making a name for himself. Strange how it all mattered greatly just this morning and now none of it did.

The lurch to starboard caught everyone by surprise. Not Darreth. He saw the beam reach out from within the nav field. It targeted their port sublight engine. It failed almost instantly, slicing through the deflection shield like it wasn't even there. The computer compensated for the missing thrust almost as fast, but not before everyone had been yanked around quite a bit. Something shifted in one of the overhead bins above Merek. It slammed against the interior latch and popped it open. The container fell edge on directly down on top of Merek's head. The container clattered to the floor.

"Shit!" he yelped. Blood immediately began oozing from a scalp wound.

Something else must have failed, too, since almost as fast, the stench of a shorted photronic component started filling the cabin.

That did it for Tann. As much as he enjoyed speed, the fear of the situation was overwhelming. The stench pushed him over the edge. He had little slack in his harness, which was holding him firmly in place. He puked what little he had in his stomach all over the front of his shirt and lap. The smell instantly pervaded the cabin, combining with the stench of the burned out circuit. The environmental controls immediately attempted to compensate.

"Still pursuing us," Darreth announced. "Naylon."

"What?"

"See that red icon on the display?"

Naylon quickly scanned the panel in front of him. "The square one marked 'Buoy'?"

"Press it!"

Naylon reached out and pressed. Hard, although it was totally unnecessary to do so.

"What did I do?"

"Released a record buoy of everything that's taken place for the last twelve hours. It should contain enough information for someone to find out what happened to us once it gets picked up."

"But it'll be destroyed."

"They're pursuing *us*. You may have just saved us all, buddy."

Right. Me. I think it's more like you're saving all of our butts, Naylon thought.

Darreth spoke to the nav computer. "Calculate safe pull up velocity, engage weapons control, standby for my mark."

"Weapons engaged. Standing by for pull up," the nav computer responded.

"Mark," Darreth said.

The shuttle pulled upward. Their downward descent immediately halted. At the same time three beams of light emitted from the shuttle's stern. The shuttle turned to port slightly. Another beam, then another. They were going too fast for them to hear the result of the weapons discharge. But the sensors told Darreth what he needed to know. Their pursuers had been hit at least once and were already pulling away to a safe distance. Darreth figured that might only buy them a few minutes. They would simply recalculate a safer pursuit vector if they hadn't sustained too much damage. He was sure that without a direct hit to one of their nacelles they would be back on the hunt.

"Continue descent," Darreth told the computer.

The shuttle turned nose down again. That maneuver brought them underneath two layers of thick clouds, then another thinner layer of scattered ones. Darreth had long since switched to LADAR imaging to get them through the clouds without slamming into a hidden peak. The nav computer was winding them through a sinewy course along a deep glacial valley. The glacier, which fed the valley was tapering off and started to disappear into a river. They flew high over a cirque, another one, then came to a wide ice-free valley filled with the unique greenish-yellow of Rylerra's vegetation. For many minutes now there had been no sign of the pirate ship. Darreth took note of their longitude and latitude as they continued along the length of the valley.

Everyone's gaze was fixed on the visual image below. The sun was just starting to crest the high peaks several kilometers to the east. It was only a few hours after local sunrise. The starboard engine sputtered and shut off. Several alarms and warning lights lit up the navigation console.

"*Overload*," the calm voice of the computer announced as it immediately went through a power down sequence. Darreth glanced down at the control panel as systems were powered off.

"The nav computer shut the engines down," Darreth told them. They were gliding for a moment before the chemically fired attitude controls came on. That was another hazard Darreth was hoping wouldn't occur. Chemical engine trails were simple to track. Darreth attempted to find a clear spot for them to land. It wasn't looking good. The entire length of the valley was covered with mohlert trees. Their thin trunks with long thin needles were everywhere. They were typical of this type of wide valley and wouldn't provide a heck of a lot of cover.

The computer warned of an approaching craft. All eyes followed the red blip when the sensor array switched to a camera on the upper rear of the shuttle. The faint dark spot against the clouds was closing in, according to the display. It was too far behind to get a targeting lock. He decided on outfoxing them. He dived even lower. His objective wasn't the present valley they were in, but rather he was going to follow the dry riverbed to the left. Just before they descended too far down, he had noticed that the valley spread into a wide alluvial fan further beyond. It too was covered with mohlert trees, but if he were lucky and quick enough he'd be able to make the sharp turn and temporarily disappear from their pursuers' visual systems.

"Hold on. Inertial dampeners aren't going to help much at these low velocities," Darreth warned them.

Another warning light lit up on the control console in front of Darreth. "Fruck!" Darreth exclaimed.

Naylon tried to discern what happened but was unable to. "What now?"

"Attitude controls are faltering. It's going to be rough."

Naylon had both hands tightly gripping the X-shaped straps across his chest. He was tense, nervous, scared even. Yet while experiencing all that he still noticed Darreth was alert; tense too, and doing an incredibly efficient job of eluding the pursuing craft.

Darreth banked the shuttle hard to the left. They were just skimming the tops of the tall trees. He banked it slightly to the right now. The tops of the trees were above them. They were only meters from the bottom of an ancient dry river valley. The canyon was getting steeper and narrower; and turning to port. Darreth deftly followed the contour of the terrain trying to nurse as much altitude as he could. He hoped the topography wouldn't force him to go up much higher since he had almost no z-axis control left.

Seconds later they emerged into a wide dry valley with a large grove of mohlert trees to port. Out the starboard side was a steep wall of dark sedimentary rock. The trees were less dense in that direction.

So far, there was no sign of their pursuers. Darreth quickly found a flat area at the edge of the trees over a dry riverbed, managed to shed their forward momentum, and set the craft down. Sand and dust billowed up all around them as the landing jets fired.

It took several seconds for Darreth to declare all was clear. He read the outside temperature sensor. It stabilized almost immediately at 15 degrees.

"Grab your jackets. It's going to be chilly. We have to get out of here as quickly as possible. They'll be looking for us."

The cabin was awash in noise as they un-strapped their harnesses. They scrambled toward the back, quickly opened their cold weather storage containers and pulled out coats, gloves and other items. Within minutes everyone was dressed, although Naylon noticed Merek was having a more difficult time than the others because of the trickle of blood still coming down his forehead and covering one of his eyes.

Darreth had no time to equalize their cabin pressure to local atmospheric pressure. He lifted a protective panel and stabbed the emergency release button on his control console. Everyone's ears popped as the airlock door at the back end of the shuttle released with a loud clank. It immediately swung open halfway. Fresh cool air rushed to fill in what was a warm cabin.

It wasn't looking good for Merek. He was swearing up a storm while getting blood all over his clothing. Naylon pulled a med kit from one of the compartments in the main cabin and told him he'd work on stemming the bleeding once they were away from the shuttle.

Behind one of the side panels were several meter-long tubes. In them were containers of rations and water. Darreth unlatched the panel, pulled out four of them and handed each of them one. They had straps attached to each end. They immediately slung them over their heads and rested the tubes across their backs as Darreth urgently directed each past him out of the shuttle and onto the surface.

They were now very vulnerable. They had no hand weapons. It was supposed to have been a simple research trip to collect samples. Not one where they would have to run for their lives!

Chapter 13

Fortunately, Darreth was prepared. It was just part of his nature. He had always carried a small utility pack in a compartment at his pilot's position. In it was an electronic compass, binoculars, an all purpose communications device and several other small items that would be useful in any situation like this one. He had long since had the one of the pack's straps over a shoulder. Only the binoculars were out right now.

He scanned the area. Tall stands of the thin mohlert trees were all he could see. There was little underbrush in the groves. Most of the vegetation was up as high as it could get to take advantage of minimal sunlight. "Over there. Behind that rock," he commanded.

A huge boulder, most likely an erratic from an ancient glacier, stood not more than ten meters away, surrounded by the forest. At least they wouldn't be out in the open on this sandy riverbed.

Everyone raced toward the boulder, then crouched down behind it. Darreth hadn't gone so quickly. He stopped every couple of steps and scanned the sky between the tall branches. Everyone's ears were piqued for any sound. There was very little wind. Lucky for them. The chill was quite evident. It was incredibly quiet, too. Indeed, there wasn't another human nearby for probably a thousand kilometers.

Except for the pursuing craft's occupants.

Now that there was a semblance of safety Naylon broke open the med kit, opened a bandage and attempted to clean up the blood on Merek's head and from his hands. Most of the blood had coagulated, but some continued to ooze out.

"Thunder, this hurts. Is there anything for the pain?" Merek asked.

"I don't know. I've never used one of these kits before."

Tann spoke up now. "Activate the e-doc. She'll tell you what to do. Hit that blue icon on the upper part of the case."

Naylon saw the icon, which said 'Activate Doctor Here'. "Oh," was all he said. He asked the e-doc what to do in this situation and started working through the instructions.

Finally, despite having his bleeding stemmed and his headache manageable, Merek started getting dizzy and had to lean his head between his legs. Naylon told him he would deal with that in a minute or so.

Darreth had returned to the shuttle where it was easier to see most of the sky. There was no sign of the pirate ship. The sky was absolutely silent. Apparently, his emergency maneuver into this valley had succeeded in eluding them after all. Or perhaps he had damaged their ship more than he thought. But, he was still concerned they could be found. The shuttle remained totally out in the open and there was no way to hide it. Finding shelter away from it was essential to their survival for at least the next several hours.

Satisfied they were alone for the moment, Darreth dashed to join the others by the boulder. As he rounded it, he found Merek lying on the ground. His head was propped up by a piece of what passed as wood on this planet. His eyes were closed.

"Is he okay?" Darreth asked.

"Head wounds always bleed a lot, you know, making it look worse than it really is sometimes." Darreth nodded his acknowledgement of that. Naylon continued. "He's complaining about dizziness though. I think he's got a concussion. He's going to need a real doctor to be sure. This med kit isn't going to be much help."

Darreth knelt down to Merek. "You still with us?"

"I really can't stand up," he said.

"Don't then." Darreth looked up at Tann. "Stomach?"

"I'm okay," Tann told him as he pressed a palm against it. He had already unzipped his coat and wiped himself clean. There was a moment of awkward silence. "What are we gonna do?"

"You're going to use this to keep watch." He handed Tann the binoculars. "Up you go." He pointed at the boulder.

Tann put the binocular strap around his neck, then he and Naylon boosted him up the side of the boulder where he could gain a foothold. Moments later, he was standing at the very top of it, almost at treetop level, with the binoculars at the ready.

"We're lucky it's morning," Darreth told Naylon. It could be a lot worse."

Tann heard that. "Yeah, like it could be wintertime. Or-or we could have crashed on a glacier, or...," he announced in response.

"Cut it," Darreth warned as he looked up. He briefly scouted the sky again from his ground level vantage point. Finding nothing coming toward them, he went several meters out onto the dry riverbed. There, away from the forest the open area afforded him a somewhat unobstructed view of the side of the mountain dozens of meters away. He came back to the boulder a moment later.

He pointed to where he had been surveying. "There might be some overhangs along the far bank where we could take shelter. Look after Merek. I'll go look and report back. Naylon, our internal comm should be good for up to a kilometer. You'll hear me if I find anything. He pointed upward. "It looks like it might get a lot warmer. Lucky us."

"Yeah, lucky us," Naylon said.

Darreth took Naylon's hands. He looked him right in the eye and subvocalized so that only Naylon would hear it through their implants. "*Don't agit. You launched the buoy. We'll get out of this.*" He pressed closer and kissed Naylon. Naylon welcomed it and hugged him, thankful Darreth was there to take charge of the situation. He was sure he could have handled himself just fine. But Darreth had such control over the situation it was nothing less than amazing to him.

"Don't be long," Naylon told him out loud.

Darreth kissed him again, turned and jogged through the trees toward the mountainside. Naylon turned his attention to making sure Merek stayed comfortable.

"Anything?" Naylon called up to Tann.

"The sky's clear. Not even a cloud."

"Keep watching," Naylon told him.

Fifteen minutes later Darreth contacted Naylon. "*I found a cave. It's fairly large and there's a pile of rocks in front of the entrance. I very nearly didn't see it. We'll need some lanterns. Any sign of the pirate ship?*"

"– Tann! Anything?"

"Still nothing."

"Good. Darreth's found a cave. He's coming back right now. – *Darreth. No sign of our pursuers. We'll be waiting for you.*"

Darreth, his outer jacket unzipped, was out of breath when he returned. "It's not too far away," he told them. "You okay?" he asked as he looked down at Merek.

"I really don't want to stand up just yet," Merek told him.

Tann was working his way down the side of the boulder. His last jump down to ground level was almost two meters. He ended on his side after rolling a little. "What's the gravity here? I was sure that was going to hurt," he asked as he picked himself up and dusted himself off.

Darreth quickly answered his brother, then turned his attention back to Merek. "Two-tenths of a G less. Merek, you're gonna have to stand up. We have to get out of here."

Merek sat up. "Help, please." Naylon assisted him to a standing position.

"Tann, you know where the lanterns are in the shuttle, right?" Darreth asked.

Tann nodded.

"Go. But just get them. Nothing else. We'll get more supplies later." *Hopefully*, he added to himself. He was aware the pirates could show up at any time. But he kept his own counsel, not wanting to further alarm the others.

Tann returned only minutes later with three lanterns. They moved along the edge of the sparse mohlert tree forest, following the riverbed. Darreth had one of Merek's arms over his shoulders while Naylon had the other. There was virtually no underbrush and few larger rocks, which made it relatively easy to help Merek make the trip. Merek could walk but he seemed to have developed an extreme sensitivity to sunlight along with being dizzy while upright. He had to squint most of the way.

The cavern's entrance had a large boulder in front of it along with several tons of scree around it that had fallen from the slope overhead. The opening wouldn't have been noticeable except that a wide vertical gap was left where the boulder hadn't covered it over.

There were no large predators of any kind on Rylerra. That kind of higher life had never developed on this planet. Thus, they didn't have to be concerned with accidentally disturbing an animal that might have made the cavern its home. On the other hand, the highly active slime molds and insect-like ice mites that were indigenous to the planet could be a real problem. That was the first thing Darreth and Naylon checked for after they and Tann activated the high intensity lanterns. After declaring that no mud or fiber nests, which were indicative of the mite habitats, and none of the purple web-like molds were adhered to the interior of the cave, they pulled Merek inside. Tann climbed atop the large rock at the cave's entrance and scanned the sky with Darreth's binoculars again. Still nothing.

Naylon surveyed his new surroundings. Two branching tunnels radiated into darkness opposite the entrance. Darreth touched Naylon's shoulder to get his attention. "I'll need some help getting the rest of the supplies. Merek, do you think you'll be okay if we all take off?"

"I think so. Just don't make me stand up again for a while, okay?"

Darreth wadded up his jacket and made Merek lay his head back on it. The floor of the cavern was dry and cool.

Darreth and Naylon exited the cavern into what seemed like blazing sunlight. In short order, their eyes readjusted.

Tann picked his way down the large rock and joined them. "Still nothing. I think you did it. You gave them the slip," he told Darreth.

"Let's hope so. It might be really quiet here but it can be deceptive. They could swoop down on us before we hear them if they're fast enough. Stay alert."

The crunching of their footsteps on the pebbles was all they heard as they headed back to the shuttle. All three of them quickly identified the items they figured they needed for at least a few night's stay in the cavern. They quickly transferred personal effects into three containers. The containers were of a standard dimension with grooves along the sides. Darreth pulled out the anti-grav struts and attached them to the awaiting grooves. With handles on the front and back of the struts, they could be adjusted in length by telescoping them out or in. He pressed the activator on the side and a tiny indicator light turned on. The containers, all strung together, lifted slowly into the air and hovered a meter above the ground. Another second later the struts adjusted to local gravity conditions and were ready to be used. Now it was simply a matter of holding on to the strut handles and guiding the equipment along to their destination.

Tann insisted on taking the lead. Naylon took the rear handles as they started back to the cavern. Darreth followed behind and watched the sky every once in a while. Still nothing.

The sun disappeared behind the tallest peak, stretching a wide shadow over the valley. The temperature had dropped considerably, which wasn't a real problem since they already had two radiant heaters on in the cavern. Merek was doing better now. He still couldn't stand for any considerable length of time, so sat cross-legged or just continued to lay down.

They heard footsteps at the entranceway. Darreth was returning from his most recent foray outside the cave.

"Bad news, boys."

"How bad?" Naylon asked.

"Several of the key shuttle systems are shot."

"Key, as in how?"

"Like we can't take off. And short range communications aren't working. Not that they would do us any good down here anyway."

"What?!" Tann exclaimed.

"I ran a diagnostic on all the subsystems and it indicated the primary and secondary thrusters are inactive. That's what took me so long. I was trying to get them back online."

"But we landed," Tann indicated.

"Manually."

"How are we going to get rescued then?"

Darreth didn't want to sugarcoat the situation, but he wasn't going to call it a disaster just yet. He pulled out a small device from his utility belt and held it up.

"What's that," Naylon asked.

Darreth told the device to change screens. He turned it so the screen faced Naylon and Tann. "A list of transmission codes normally used on Rylerra. It'll alert me to whether a ship's comm is friendly." His voice trailed off. "Until then we just get comfortable."

"But no one at the space port knows where we are," Naylon said.

"I don't know if our call for help was received by anyone since they blew up the comm buoy. But since it's been destroyed that'll be a clue something bad happened. We were scheduled to land and we didn't. Everyone will be on high alert because the nav sat is out of commission. Someone will eventually look for us. Unless they assume we blew up, too." He realized he shouldn't have said that last part out loud.

"Fruck!" Tann said as he stamped his foot.

Darreth placed a hand on Tann's shoulder. "The recorder buoy will make its way back home. Once the vids and telemetry are downloaded, they'll determine what happened. At the very least they'll contact the authorities here and they'll come looking for us."

"But it has to get back to Andakar. It'll be nearly a week at best before Rylerra has any data," Merek said.

"Someone will be looking for us long before that." He placed the comm channel device down, making sure its volume was all the way up and the display was facing everyone. "We'll know immediately if any comm traffic is coming from a rescue vehicle."

Tann's stomach rumbled loudly. "It's been hours since I ate," he said.

"Me, too. Break out the rations," Darreth replied.

Chapter 14

The maintenance database on the shuttle was far more detailed than Naylon realized at first. He spent over two hours that evening talking to the shuttle's computer, trying to coax it to find anything which might be helpful in getting the shuttle operational again. He found nothing that helped. It wasn't as if he even knew the first thing about shuttle maintenance. But he knew enough about diagnostic systems to know that he didn't have to be an expert to get information from a computer.

Several diagnostics showed some key systems were simply inoperable. Backup circuits might be active, but the circuit crystals used to bring up the subsystems had simply overloaded in the last blast. Two dozen of them were blackened, their internal circuitry fried beyond repair. He was sure Darreth had already done all he could, but he felt he needed to do something even if it meant following right behind him. Unknown to all but Darreth, the life support subsystem had also been affected. Naylon had discovered that during his maintenance sweep. It was a good thing they hadn't been informed about that, he realized. It would have added unnecessary stress to an already seemingly impossible situation.

Having exhausted the shuttle's maintenance system and realizing that without a viable life support subsystem it was moot anyway, Naylon gave up, exited the craft, then pressed the button to close the back hatch. He zipped up his coat and looked up into the perfectly clear quiet sky. It was eerie and beautiful at the same time. Here they were over 1600 AU from home, thousands of kilometers from the nearest rescue team, and in the bottom of a huge river valley. Actually, he thought they were very, very lucky indeed. At least they hadn't crashed. They would be very dead if they had.

Something else was creeping up on Naylon's thoughts. Why would a pirate crew, whose sole task so far had been to steal pharmas, suddenly change their tack and decide to try to shoot them from space? How could they have known when they would arrive in the Kaskalon system or where they were going to be exiting the FTL wedge? Had they known who was piloting their shuttle? Was there some sort of conspiracy going on?

Now I'm thinking like Ecca, Naylon thought. But maybe thinking like that had merit right now. After all, he'd just come up with some very good unanswered questions. Someone appeared to be after Darreth and they didn't seem to care that innocent lives might be part of the price just to get him.

Naylon stuffed his hands into his coat pockets as his feet crunched on the cold dry pebbly riverbed. He came into the cavern briefly and motioned for Darreth to come outside. Tann was already asleep underneath two blankets. Merek was listening to something on the music crystal he had had packed in his bag. He was sitting up with his eyes closed.

Darreth zipped up his coat and followed Naylon outside into the crisp evening air. They found a rock to sit on.

"I've been thinking," Naylon told him.

"About us?" He reached over to kiss Naylon's cheek. Naylon kissed back.

"In a manner of speaking, yes."

"I'm sorry," Darreth told him.

"About what?"

"The mess we're in."

"Excuse me. You got us down in one piece. But that's not what's bothering me. I think someone wants you dead. Very dead. And they don't care who they take out along with you."

"So, you figured it out," Darreth said casually.

"You think so, too?" Naylon responded, quite surprised Darreth wasn't more rattled at this conclusion.

"It only makes sense. Someone had our flight plan. Otherwise, how would they know when or where we would exit the wedge?"

Naylon was silent for a moment. Darreth had already come to that conclusion. It made him wonder what else Darreth knew that he wasn't saying. "And?" he prompted.

"And… it's apparent there's some sort of clandestine communication going on between Andakar and Rylerra. After all, flight plans aren't just broadcast out into open space. We have to consider that someone, maybe even at the museum, leaked our flight plan data to the pirates, or to someone who then leaked it to the pirates. Pirates who are clearly and obviously stationed here on Rylerra."

"What? You think some of my co-workers would want to see you dead? How can you think that?" he said, startled.

"Everyone's suspect until we have more data. There were a limited number of people who knew I was piloting the shuttle. Their ship was small. It was only about four times the size of our shuttle. Still, Helios class ships aren't designed for extended interstellar flight. It had to be based on a planet with a substantial atmosphere. Since there are no moons in the system with a substantial atmosphere, that points back to Andakar, which is out of the question, or right here on Rylerra, which is the only reasonable answer."

Naylon looked up to the treetops, trying to follow Darreth's logic. He concluded it was impeccable.

Darreth continued. "They haven't returned either. Either I winged them good and they headed back to their base, wherever that is, or we're so far from any inhabited area they simply took off. They probably intend to let us freeze or die of starvation. They know they took out a good number of our systems."

"Well, someone's going to rescue us!"

Let's hope so. "Of course they are."

Naylon stuffed his hands further into his pockets purely out of habit. It was completely unnecessary. The jacket had dozens of sensors all throughout it. It was continuously monitoring his body and ambient temperature, adjusting various zones to keep him warm. "Or maybe we'll die of thirst," Naylon offered forlornly.

"Not while I'm running this show. It's only a matter of time before we're traced down here. We'll wait another full day, then activate the mayday beacon in the shuttle. At least it still functions. The rescue ships would have to be very nearly above us or they won't detect it. Regardless, we'll be rescued one way or another." Darreth stuffed his hands into his pockets, too. "How's Merek doing?" Darreth asked, changing the topic.

"He seems to be getting better. No blurred vision and his dizziness is fading," Naylon said. "I love you," he added. It was the first time he'd said that directly to Darreth.

Darreth smiled broadly. It felt good to hear that. "I love you," he said in return. They stood and molded their bodies together as they embraced and kissed. Both sported isotitanium-hard swellas when they finally peeled themselves apart.

Chapter 15

Inandra knew local provincial issues were none of her business. Strict Consortium law regulated just how meddlesome a planetary director could be in local affairs. Inandra was finding that set of laws much to confining to suit her needs. After all, she was overseeing the second richest planet of all the Inhabs. Therefore, it followed that she was well within her rights to know everything going on below her position. At least, that was how she saw it, she thought with an amused smile, as she slowly paced her spacious office.

Thus, little of the provincial manager discussions that Inandra hadn't been directly involved in had escaped her attention. The program her communications computer used to sift through routine vidmails had picked out incredibly salient ones. Ones that at first alarmed her, then made her very angry. Despite being so far from Earth and despite the autonomy granted by the largest businesses, grumbling was still to be found among those who thought their autonomy wasn't enough. For quite some time the grumbling had extended to the provincial managers. It was perfectly within Citizens' rights to discuss anything they thought important, which they did on a regular basis. But provincial managers were supposed to be immune to chatter such as what she was clandestinely listening to.

At first, the vidmails sounded like nattering, but within two months talk of full autonomy was being opening discussed by the highest levels of the Council. Only two of the vidmails involved Siloy James-Po, she noticed. And they were completely dismissive of the idea. But she was sure he was discussing this issue with them in person. She was sure he was directly involved, despite what the vidmails seemed to indicate.

She was absolutely going to put a stop to this. There was no way they would be able to gain independence, but it was important no one took this issue and ran with it. She had been in office long enough to know that this planet's Space Navy might have a little too much power and control so far from Earth despite the safeguards to prevent such a thing from happening. Although she held the purse strings for their division, she didn't have enough of a background in Space Navy operations to be fully cognizant of how much power they might exert when the time came. So, she knew she had to plan accordingly.

It had been during one of their monthly meetings after having watched the most important of the vidmails that she made her first move.

Gartenda province encompassed a large stretch of desert to the east of the mountains. Shifting sands was slowly encroaching upon two of the settlements. Kals Sanadan, the Gartenda Provincial Manager, and she were discussing upping an allotment of moneys to purchase materials for the erection of barriers, which would help stave off the sand. The existing ones weren't high enough and hadn't been placed in the right locations. They were over forty years old anyway. Inandra had carefully steered the discussion.

"You know Kals, if it weren't for the inept way the Development Division allocates funds, those barriers would have been built right in the first place."

"Say again, ma'am?"

"I mean, don't you think they should have paid a lot more attention to what was required at that time? They clearly didn't have your interests in mind when they first funded that project."

Kals guffawed. "I'm not that old, Director. I wasn't a Provincial Manager then. I'm hardly the one to complain about that."

"But if you had been manager at that time, wouldn't you have said something about it?"

"I'm sure I would," Kals had replied.

"Sometimes I wonder what they were thinking when they were projecting budgets back then." Inandra had slowly but surely projected an aura of concern. And since they were one-on-one, she had the perfect opportunity to sound genuine.

"I, too, have often wondered the same thing," he told her.

"I meant Earth." She glanced up from the vidscreen they were both viewing, and looked directly at him. "The committee that appointed me to this wonderful planet sometimes makes the worst blunders when it comes to projections." Inandra already knew exactly what Kals thought about Earth.

"And you don't have any say as to those figures?" he asked guardedly.

"I have limited say. I rely on those I oversee to report to me with accurate information I can then relay back to my higher ups. In addition, I rely very heavily on provincial managers and them being as honest as they can with our offices to make sure they get full funding. In fact, the more honest the provincial managers are with me, the better I am at dealing with the red tape that inevitably comes from such distances." She licked her lips after that statement.

Kals was married, but was as red-blooded as any man. Inandra had been clearly prompting him for information. And she had been doing it in a way that suggested she was interested in him. He was vaguely aware of her being in a relationship, but didn't know with whom. Nonetheless, although she could be as formal and businesslike as any person could be, right now her charm was clearly in the lead and her business manners non-existent. Another thing Kals was fully aware of was that all meetings were recorded. Holographic storage allowed any disputes to be put to rest once the record was pulled and reviewed. This one-on-one meeting was no different than a group meeting. Kals briefly looked around the room, trying to discern where the cameras might be located. They could be so tiny he had no idea where they might be.

"If you're looking for the recorders you can be assured I've had them shut off the entire time we've been together in here."

"I'm sure I don't know what you mean, Director Alarr." Something about her suggested a cleverness he had never suspected before, despite his libido being front and center now. He had always been attracted to her but never in his wildest dreams would he have thought she would be attracted to him.

"I didn't want our meeting to be... how should I put it... on the official record." She leaned back in her chair, crossed her long slender legs and looked him up and down. "Sometimes I just don't have time to deal with the stuffiness that virtually all the Committee members seem to think is their birthright. Sometimes I wish I wasn't from Earth." She said that last line in her most pouty voice.

"I'm sorry?" Was she actually telling him something so personal?

"I mean it. I-I love Andakar. I wish Consortium law didn't prevent me from becoming a Citizen." She finished in a rush, as if holding on to an emotional dam that might burst at any moment.

Kals didn't know what to say to this intimate confession. Consortium law was very clear and had been so for a very long time. Planetary

Directors simply couldn't become Citizens of the worlds they ran. They already had enough control without being born on the planets they controlled. That's simply the way it was.

"I imagine a day in the future, the near future, mind you, where I can become a Citizen and cut my ties to Earth altogether." She was trolling.

"Cut your ties? To Earth? That-that would be unprecedented." A perplexed frown appeared on Kals' face as he tried to battle what he now suddenly so desperately wanted.

"Perhaps so. But that's my dream. To become a Citizen of Andakar." With that, she sighed heavily. "But enough of that. Let's continue with this budget request. I'm sure you're already bored with my musings anyway."

"No… no, Director. In fact, I'm surprised you would be so bold as to even state such a thing."

Desperate hope was evident on his face. She knew she had won. "I did so because I like you, Kals. You're the council member I feel the most comfortable speaking my real mind with. I don't know what it is about you, but I guess it's because you're… so easy on the eyes." She smiled coyly. With that, she lightly touched his hand with her index finger.

Kals slowly pulled his hand away. It was impossible not to think about her naked now and it was beginning to make him feel a bit uncomfortable. After all, just outside the office were at least a dozen members of her staff.

As if reading his mind her hand moved swiftly to the console on the table. She lightly touched an icon on its smooth surface. The door to her office locked. "I wasn't kidding." She stood with the languid movement of a cat rising from a nap. She looked at him expectantly. He stood as well. Kals instantly felt as if he were magnetically drawn to her. She perfectly molded to his embrace. He kissed her while she brought her hand slowly down the middle of his torso until she rested it at his crotch. As quickly as she had done that she drew her hand away. It was a tease. A taste only. Maybe a promise.

She pulled herself away from him and turned around. "I'm… sorry Kals. I didn't mean to do that. I shouldn't have even considered such a thing. Please forgive me." She turned back to face him, feigning embarrassment.

Kals felt as if he were in a fog. He had some explaining to do to himself about what just happened. It wasn't like him to do such a thing, at least recently. His last such indiscretion had occurred almost eight years ago in Tokaias. The woman had meant nothing to him, but she had been equally seductive. It had led to all night lovemaking. Regardless, he never saw the woman again. What was confusing about this situation was Inandra's confession that she no longer wanted to be a Citizen of Earth. Like that was even possible.

"Director. I'm…"

"Inandra. It's Inandra."

"Inandra… I-I have to leave."

"Whatever I said is between you and me."

"We didn't talk about anything… personal," he told her, confused.

She smiled secretly at his confusion. "Again… I'm sorry."

Kals took the vidPAD, collected the rest of his things and left the room.

Two days later Kals had a vid conversation with Orl Ustiby, the Provincial Manager of West Litok province. He made sure he was on his personal vidmail channel and not on any provincial one.

"Orl, you're not going to believe this. I think we have an unexpected ally in our quest."

"To what are you referring?"

"Independence."

Orl instantly looked at the icon flashing on his screen to make sure the encryption was in place. Satisfied it was on and working he answered. "Who?"

"Director Alarr."

Orl laughed heartily. "That's a good one, Kals. Tell me another."

Kals didn't so much as emit a grin. "She practically insinuated that she's on our side."

"How did such a conversation even come up?"

"It wasn't so much a conversation as it was an attempt to seduce me."

"Another good one, Kals. I know she's a 'gifted' woman, but I hardly suspected her gifts extended to the seduction of a provincial manager."

"Hear me out." He told Orl everything that had transpired during their meeting.

Orl didn't say anything for several seconds after Kals finished.

"She's from Earth, Kals," he said with a scowl. "I don't trust her." Orl and Kals were both second generation Citizens.

"I have to find out what she was driving at."

"You're not," Orl warned.

"I am."

"When your wife finds out you're going to not only lose your marriage you're going to lose your position as provincial manager."

"No one is going to find out," Kals assured him.

"There's something not quite right about this."

"It's worth a try to discover what she's really up to," he said gamely, falling into a trap he had no idea was even there.

Chapter 16

Naylon flipped the blanket back from over his head. Low morning sunlight was breaking through wispy cirrus clouds. A thin shaft of light was creeping into the cavern entrance. He had spent a restless night in a chilly cave, tossing and turning for hours before he had finally fallen sleep. Now it was morning and, in his estimation, just above freezing outside. The cavern seemed to have maintained a semblance of a few degrees above that. Even though he had plenty of experience in the way of short field expeditions, even weeklong ones, Naylon still hated sleeping in his clothing. The last time he had done so was when he was studying for his Ph.D. Oddly enough, these rough conditions were exactly what they were expecting, although not after having been shot out of the sky.

Darreth had stayed up for hours after everyone else had gone to sleep, scanning the comm frequencies and the clear night sky for any sign of a craft.

Shortly after Naylon stirred, the rest of the group awoke, too. Tann opened one of the ration cylinders and pulled out a container of water. An hour later, after everyone, including Merek, who was feeling much better now, had shaved and used a makeshift latrine several dozen meters from the cavern's entrance, all were focused on making breakfast.

"Nothing at all last night on the comm," Darreth told them.

"I can't believe they haven't sent a rescue craft after us yet. We're hours overdue," Merek said. He gingerly touched his scalp where the gash was still tender. In this cold he wasn't able to properly wash his hair and it looked a mess.

"They'll come," Darreth told him confidently. "We have plenty of food and enough water to last at least two weeks. Maybe more if we stretch it out. How's this for a laugh. There's no nearby ice here on icy Rylerra to make water."

"Yeah, real funny, Dare," Tann said acidly. He wasn't looking too happy about their situation at all now. It wasn't like his well-oiled world where everything went just about exactly as he expected. Plus, the idea of staying in this cavern for up to two weeks didn't sit well with him at all. He had hoped for adventure, but a far more comfortable one.

"Don't get all angry about it just yet, Tann. At least you didn't lose any blood like our friend Merek."

Tann looked first to Merek, then to his brother but quieted down.

Naylon realized it was time to divert Tann's attention. "Hey, after we're done with breakfast let's find out what's at the end of that passageway." He pointed to the right. Naylon was getting antsy to do something other than sit still.

Tann went toward the dark passageway and stopped in front of the dark maw. He held both arms up. "I feel a draft. If there's an opening further on maybe we can get to the other side of this mountain."

Naylon looked at him quizzically. "Why would we want to do that?"

"You might have something there, Tann," Darreth told him.

Naylon looked at Darreth. "He does?"

"If our pursuers come back and they happen to find the shuttle, and also happen to find the cave, then we might have an exit route, if it's big enough to get through, of course."

"Oh, that makes sense," Naylon said sheepishly. He turned to Tann after they downed their breakfast. "Let's pack some stuff and head out."

Naylon and Tann unzipped their packs, tossed in their canteens and added a few food bars. Naylon added to his a pack of forty marble-sized glow globes and other miscellaneous items they'd need for a couple of hours of exploration.

"No rope climbing, no slogging through water and no falling down dark shafts," Darreth told them. "If it looks at all dangerous come back."

"We have no intention of getting into trouble," Naylon assured him.

They both stood at the opening while Naylon played his lantern straight ahead. About twenty meters along Naylon noticed that the walls, ceiling and floor of the tunnel had become perfectly planar as far as the light beam could reach. It seemed equally odd that the corridor's corners were perfect right angles and the ceiling was slightly taller than a man. Naylon placed a gloved hand against the wall and picked off some loose rock. It crumbled at his touch.

"This is certainly strange," Naylon commented after they had proceeded forty meters down the corridor, inspecting the walls and ceiling ever so often. He had already switched on and dropped a glow globe every three meters or so. Their intense white light simply acted as a breadcrumb for their return journey in case the passageway turned out to twist and turn in all directions. So far, that had not been the case.

"What is?" Tann asked.

"I could swear this tunnel is manmade."

"I doubt that. We're easily the only people to have ever come here."

"But we've gone quite a ways and we've not seen the usual features of a natural cavern."

"Like what?"

"How about an uneven floor. Or rough walls and ceiling. This corridor has been square since just about the time we started out."

Tann played his flashlight along the wall nearest him. He stopped to inspect the loose material, too.

Naylon spoke up again. "We've not seen a corridor branching left or right or any other way at all." He stopped and pulled off his pack.

"What are you doing?"

"I'm pulling out a terahertz scanner. It might give us an idea of how much further this tunnel goes."

"Oh." Tann was quite familiar with the scanner. It was routinely used to see through solid objects.

Naylon pressed a few icons on the display pad. He pointed it ahead of them and they both observed the graphic. "It just keeps going," Naylon said. He switched off the sensor.

They continued to walk in silence, with only the crunching of their feet echoing all around them. Every three meters or so Naylon dropped another glow globe. After nearly fifty meters, the corridor abruptly shifted forty-five degrees to the left. They stopped and played their lanterns all around them.

"All right, this is a mining shaft. A natural cavern wouldn't switch at a sharp angle like this," Naylon said. The hair on the back of his neck was beginning to prickle. There were mines all over Rylerra. Naylon already knew that. But they were all near habitations and thus, people. If not, there was equipment near or in them or other signs of humans being there or having been there. This shaft was far from the nearest inhabited region and it looked well over three generations old. The oldest city on the planet was barely that age. Plus, they saw not the vaguest sign of equipment anywhere. The implication was simply not possible.

"I see what you mean," Tann replied as he played his light beam all around. Despite never having explored a cavern before, he had seen plenty of pictures of them. The odd part was that the cavern they had all entered yesterday was clearly natural. This passageway was the anomaly.

They continued for another thirty meters. Bare walls, exactly the same height the entire way continued to span out in front of them. Abruptly the long monotonous corridor opened to a huge open cavern much larger than the one they had taken shelter in.

"I'm positive what we just went through was built as a tunnel." Naylon told Tann. "It connects the entrance cavern to this inner chamber."

"Is that sunlight?" Tann asked. Across the dark expanse, slightly higher than where they were standing, was a narrow vertical opening. A shaft of sunlight was beaming across the darkness.

"Looks like a crack in the wall," Naylon replied. "That explains the airflow. Let's see if it's big enough to fit through." He aimed his lantern ahead of him, observing normal uneven ground, which was completely unlike the nearly flat surface they had just traveled down. "Be careful. The floor here isn't like what we were just walking on," he told Tann.

He led the way, aiming his light ahead of him, upward, then to the sides. Tann did the same. The ceiling was at least a dozen meters above them, proving that this chamber was quite large and spacious. From Naylon's estimation, this chamber was at least six times larger in volume than the entrance area they were camped in. All around were the proper elements of a natural cavern system: some evidence of flowstone, a few stalactites, a couple of stalagmites, and lots of large and small boulders strewn about.

As they headed across the open cavern, they both noted something obscuring their view of the opening where the shaft of light was streaming in. They discovered a rectangular section of rock in the exact center of the chamber. Naylon stopped and played his light over it. Its surface was perfectly smooth, looked like highly polished reddish-black granite and had a two-meter diameter cylindrical hole drilled completely through it. Naylon was immediately intrigued.

Tann was instantly curious about the tunnel, too. He approached it from the other end and felt the interior as he played his light inside it. Naylon was at the other end, still inspecting the shiny outer surface. Tann continued on through the tunnel and reached the middle. His light beam reflected and scattered off some sort of barrier that seemed to be draped across the entire diameter of the tunnel. Tann reached his hand out but felt nothing. He decided it was merely an optical illusion caused by the highly polished interior surface. He continued on and reached Naylon seconds later.

Naylon seemed startled. "How did you do that?"

"Do what?"

"I didn't see you coming through there."

"The middle of the tunnel is weird," Tann told him, shaking his head.

"What do you mean weird?" Naylon shone his lantern into it. The beam seemed to scatter and reflect from the dead center. "That *is* odd," he murmured. "This is certainly not natural. Someone went to a lot of trouble to make this thing."

Tann heard him but had his light aimed several meters away. He had seen something glinting a few meters away and went to investigate. Moments later he emitted an ear piercing shriek.

Naylon whirled around. Tann's light beam was moving all around and he was rolling over on the dirt floor. It appeared he had tripped and fallen over something. He stood back up and dusted himself off as quickly as he could. His breath was ragged and he sounded terrified as he kept saying 'Uh! Uh!'. He continued to dust his pant legs off as if he were covered with stinging burynits, which were common on Andakar's southern beaches.

"What happened?" Naylon asked in alarm as he made his way toward the boy.

"Th-there! That-that thing!" Tann replied. He aimed his lantern onto the eye sockets of a skull staring at him.

Startled, Naylon played his light beam on the body, too. His first reaction was one of complete and utter denial. The skull staring out into the blackness of the cavern was slumped against a rock. It was attached to a body, a body that didn't look at all human. It was clearly clothed, albeit the clothing was terribly faded and obviously very old. But what was worse was the implication of what he was looking at. It was completely impossible. Nothing like this had ever been discovered in the entire history of humanity. His mind and his eyes continued to war with an undeniable truth. He was looking at what was clearly a dead alien creature.

Tann's initial fright had given way to intense curiosity as he calmed down. He got closer to the alien body and widened the light beam.

Naylon had already dropped his pack and was pulling out another light source. He wanted a lot more light now that he realized what they were observing. "Th-this is incredible!" was all he could say. He activated his neural implant in an attempt to contact Darreth. He tried three times before giving up. There was just too much solid rock between them. All over Andakar there were transmission towers and repeaters everywhere for just that reason. The internal power source was simply too weak to penetrate solid rock. All he had to rely on here was the energy generated by the nanowires implanted into his right arm. Here, the weak impulse simply wasn't capable of generating enough power to penetrate a hundred meters of solid rock.

"Aliens? On Rylerra?" Tann said in disbelief. "But we've never seen any of their cities."

"I wouldn't believe it myself unless I was standing right here," Naylon told him.

Both of them took detailed mental notes of the dead being. Tann's fright had been because of the tightened skin sunken inside its eye sockets. It made the oversized orbits look ghastly. One was completely closed. The other was slightly opened, which seemed due to the thick eyelid having shrunk more than the other one. The alien appeared to be taller than most humans. It was clearly clothed. A one-piece uniform covered most of the body. Here and there, parts of it had torn to reveal clear white bone and taut grayish skin or hide underneath. It was difficult to tell much of the being's features since so much of it was covered. But one thing was evident. It had two sets of legs. One set was clearly the ones it used the most. That was because it had boots covering the long thin feet. The other set was higher on the hips and shorter. They were terribly shriveled but it was easy to tell they were appendages. It didn't look to Naylon like the being could have easily used them if it stood upright. He wondered if it had crawled instead. But then he wasn't sure since the being's clothing and its position, slumped backward against the cavern wall, indicated that it walked upright. It clearly had hands at the ends of arms, which were as long as a man's, complete with six fingers in a radial pattern. There was no obvious thumb. The head was the most interesting since it was uncovered. There was no hair. It had a high protruding brow line, which ran in a circle around its entire head. The alien looked reptilian, but not. It looked human in a way too, but perhaps only because it was clothed. The long thin feet made it seem as though it couldn't possibly stand erect too easily.

Naylon touched the material of the alien's clothing, wondering what it was made of. That's when he found the hole. He discovered the hide had been penetrated, too.

"Look at this, Tann. He was shot."

Tann looked closely. "Wow! Do you think he was in a battle? Maybe there are others!" He stood up and shone his flashlight all around as he walked the expanse of the cavern. His effort was rewarded a moment later. "Over here!" came Tann's excited voice.

Five meters away, slumped on its side, was another of the alien creatures. He was dressed the same way. The cavern had also preserved this one, too. Naylon looked for signs of a bullet hole. He quickly found one. From the look of the neat circular hole in the alien's clothing, Naylon concluded it had also been shot with some sort of projectile weapon.

"Definitely some sort of shootout took place in here. But what's more important is who they were. There have never been any reports of a civilization on any planet in all of explored space. It's been assumed that we're totally alone. And now this," Naylon said in both a perplexed yet thrilled tone.

"Hey, here's another one!" Tann found the third body laying some distance from the other two. The alien was clutching a bag. Tann carefully tried to lift it from the alien's hand. It disintegrated as he did so. A metallic clinking sound greeted his ears. Out spilled a fist-sized disc-shaped object. He picked it up and inspected it. The object looked as if it had been fashioned yesterday. It had the oddest red and orange iridescence to it that made it seem to glow. "Wow, look at this," Tann told Naylon as he approached.

Naylon took the object, inspecting it closely.

"Think it's money?" Tann asked.

"Maybe. I could have been worth dying for. Who knows?"

"If they died for money," Tann mused, "I don't see why he still has it. You'd think their pursuers would have taken off with the loot. There might be more bags of this stuff around. Let's look."

"Good idea." Naylon placed the disc in his thigh pocket and snapped it shut.

They scanned the rest of the area, finding no more sacks of the objects. Finally though, Tann found another one lying under the mummified hand of one of the other aliens. He carefully pulled it from the dusty cavern floor, taking care not to touch the body. They both examined it, looking for possible clues. It too looked like it had just recently been fashioned.

"Looks like these *were* important enough to die for. Maybe they were money after all. Put it in your pack," Naylon told Tann.

Tann retrieved his pack, placed it into one of the zipper compartments, then swung the pack over his shoulder.

They went to the hollowed out cylinder in the center of the chamber again and inspected it in more detail. It was as if a laser had bored a perfect cylinder out of the stone and polished the inside surface. *Maybe the aliens made this,* Naylon thought. What was most mysterious about it was that no matter what angle they aimed their lanterns the light beams seemed to hit a wall of what Naylon could only describe as static in the dead center of the cylinder.

He decided to walk through the tunnel this time. Tann followed closely behind him. As soon as they reached the center, they both felt as if they had just been spun in an extremely fast loop-de-loop. The length of the cylinder was two and a half meters long. They swiftly made their way to the other side in less than a second.

Tann almost stepped on Naylon's heels as he tried to get past him. He went to the ground onto his knees, breathing heavily. He felt he might vomit again. Naylon was having a hell of a time keeping upright as well. In the same moment that Tann went to his knees, Naylon shot his hand out to the side of the smooth rock surface to hold himself up. Within seconds though, they were both past the sensation, looking at each other with their lanterns pointed at each other's faces.

"What the hell just happened?" Tann exclaimed.

"I have no idea," Naylon replied.

The next second told them something was oddly different. Now that they had passed beyond the odd opaque barrier they could both see that the crack in the cavern to the outside was much larger than they had observed previously. In fact, the hole had somehow doubled in width. Naylon was sure he would have heard something if a tremor had caused it to open up. The only sound was wind coming from the direction of the opening. And something else was noticeable, too. The cavern had become at least ten degrees warmer.

Had they somehow inhaled some dust along the way that had hallucinogenic properties? Had they simply become disoriented due to the inky darkness of the cavern? Whatever had happened to them, something was terribly odd, Naylon decided.

Tann observed the crack in the cavern wall, too. "I don't remember that being so wide."

"It wasn't." Naylon started heading toward it. Tann followed close behind.

Whereas before, the opening was just a crack, it was now wide enough for them to easily pass through. They stood outside the cavern after picking through the large boulders and other debris in their way. They both shielded their eyes, waiting for them to adjust to the light as they looked out over a wide green valley. The mountains in the distance had snow only on their peaks. That didn't make any sense since they had clearly crashed in the far north. Naylon distinctly remembered the higher nearby peaks with snow and ice well below the peaks. It wasn't possible that this vantage was giving him a view of a region that looked like it would be much closer to the equator.

Twenty meters below them was a swiftly flowing river. The riverbed they had landed on must be part of this river, but it was dry as a bone just a half hour ago. Plus, Naylon was vaguely aware that at this latitude there were no flowing rivers.

Naylon looked out over the sharp decline to get a better view. Immediately he lost his footing on the loose talus. Before he knew it, he was sliding down the rocky slope toward the racing water. "Shit!" he yelped as he slid. His pack was securely around his shoulders and was helping to break his slide down the slope. But it didn't help him at all when, seconds later, he reached a point of no return and splashed heavily into the water. The swift current immediately carried him away.

"Naylon! Naylon!" Tann cried out in terror.

Chapter 17

Tann dropped his lantern, threw off his backpack and ran to his right. He ran at an oblique angle almost to the river's edge far below. Breathing like mad from adrenaline and from his burst of exertion, he stopped. He could no longer see Naylon. The water had already carried him out of sight.

He started running downriver, dodging boulders, scree and spongy earth underfoot. He had traveled several dozen meters before he realized he needed to get Darreth to help him. He stopped and tried to catch his breath, but upon looking around, he realized he was totally alone. Frightened at that realization, tears welled up in his eyes. He wiped his face with his sleeves and headed back.

It wasn't easy getting back up. There was hardly a place to gain a foothold that didn't threaten to make him slide back down. Several times he ended up meters below his intended path. Over and over, this repeated until finally, after great exertion, he was rewarded by finding his dropped pack. He quickly picked up his lantern and scrambled through the crack in the face of the mountain.

Mustering as much courage as he could, he faced the darkness and switched on the light. He scanned the far end of the cavern to discern where the corridor was. He had mentally noted where the bodies of the dead aliens were. But each time he pointed his light in those areas he saw nothing except rocks and boulders. Had he completely forgotten where any of them were? But that didn't matter right now. He had to get help and get it fast.

He continued to play the beam along the wall. There. The dark entrance to the corridor was just to his left and ahead about ten meters away. This time he raced as fast as he could in the gloomy darkness. Where were the glow globes? He didn't see a single one, yet they had dropped at least a dozen and a half along the way! Their power supplies were supposed to last a least a week, yet not a single one was lit. Plus, there were what appeared to be wires attached to the center of the ceiling. In some places they had fallen to the floor of the passageway and he had to avoid tangling his feet in them. Where had they come from? He was sure he hadn't seen them when they came this way earlier.

Once the corridor opened up to the cavern where they were camped, Tann was already shouting.

"Darreth! Darreth! Help. Naylon's in trou…ble!"

But no one answered. In fact, there was no light emanating from the cavern except from the entrance. That didn't make any sense. He had personally positioned one of the three light tripods against the wall to the left just yesterday.

Tann stopped to catch his breath. He played his light all over the area where he had bedded down just last night. There were what appeared to be footprints, but they were barely discernable. Immediately he started to panic. This wasn't possible. They had to be here. This was the exact same cavern they'd holed up in to avoid the pirates. He was sure of it. There was only a single way back. There was no way he had taken a wrong turn.

Tann dashed to the cavern entrance. The dry riverbed they had walked across to get here was filled with water. It was running swiftly but not as swiftly as the one Naylon had just fallen into. Was this the same river, just on the other side of the mountain? Or did something much more mysterious happen? Whatever it was, the shuttle was gone, too. For all he knew it had been swept away by the water. Darreth was missing. Merek was missing. All of the gear they had stowed in the cavern was gone. Worse though, was that it looked like he'd never been in this cavern before. It looked like no one at all had been in the cavern for centuries. In fact, his were the only footprints he could clearly identify.

This is not possible, his mind screamed.

No time to figure it out. He had to get back to save Naylon. That is, if he could, he thought to himself, completely confused. He quickly played his light into the other corridor, the one they hadn't explored. He mustered up enough courage to go down it a way. Within twenty meters it was impossible to go any further. The ceiling was way too low. There was no way he had accidentally gone the wrong way.

Quickly he backtracked, returned to the entrance cavern, and immediately went back down the correct passageway. His mind was racing. Was there someone else here? Perhaps a *live* alien? Was something or someone playing tricks with his mind? He fought for composure by trying to control his breathing. This wasn't supposed to happen. They were supposed to have landed at the Nona Ice Station. Now everything had turned upside down. Everything!

He sprinted down the dark corridor, carefully avoiding the wires, and headed back to where he knew the dead alien bodies were supposed to be. He knew he shouldn't do it since the situation was starting to freak him out completely. But try as he might, as he played his light everywhere, he found not a shred of evidence that the aliens had ever been here. Yet, in the very center of the cavern was the exact same perfect cylindrical hole in the rectangular dark stone. He avoided it this time, opting to go completely around it.

Moments later he emerged back into sunlight after going through the crack in the cavern wall. He felt exhausted. All the running and the stress of realizing he was totally alone was taking its toll. He went to his knees, breathing deeply of the warm air as he tried to gather his wits.

His backpack. He dragged himself up from his knees and took it. He stuffed the lantern into one of the compartments before he donned it and started toward the riverbank once again.

Darreth looked at his chronometer. Naylon and Tann had been gone for far too long. The first thing he did was try his internal comm. Nothing. He wasn't surprised it might not work given the expanse of rocks that surrounded them.

"Merek, I can't contact Naylon. I'm going to see if anything's wrong."

"I'd go with you but..."

"Don't agit. I won't be long."

Darreth took one of the more powerful lanterns and headed down the tunnel. He, too, noted that within a few meters the tunnel seemed to have been honed. A passageway this square couldn't possibly be natural. He saw the trail of glow globes and followed them. Minutes later, after having walked briskly the entire way, he entered the cavern Naylon and Tann had entered hours before.

"Naylon! Tann!" Darreth yelled out. He saw at the far end of the cavern, across a considerable dark distance, that a glow seemed to be coming from the wall. No, it was sunlight. He could tell that now. That meant a small opening was along the wall further on. Perhaps they had gone out that way?

He made his way toward the center of the cavern, following the footsteps he saw in the dirt. They were distinct enough. Some of them led to the left and to the right but he was more interested in the structure he saw in the very center of the cavern. As he continued toward it he saw that the footprints had converged back in the same direction he was headed. He continued on.

He passed his light beam along the interior of the cylindrical tunnel, now that he got closer to it. He felt the smooth surface. The huge slab of stone couldn't have been brought into the cavern since it was clearly larger than the size of the tunnel he'd just come down. That was odd. It seemed as though the rectangular slab was cut right inside this cavern. But the rock looked like polished granite. Where could it have come from? There was no granite nearby.

Darreth played his flashlight inside the short, cylindrical hole once again. The shiny interior walls appeared to deflect his light beam in an odd distorted way. Nonetheless, he went through it and was across to the other side in seconds. Darreth tried his comm again.

"*Naylon?*"

Nothing.

"*Naylon!*"

Still nothing.

He yelled out loud again. "Naylon! Tann!" Not a whisper in return.

This was more than strange.

He proceeded toward the crack at the far end of the cavern. The opening appeared to have been weathered from a much smaller crack that had long ago developed along the wall. The hole wasn't exactly facing the outside. In fact, the hole was barely twenty centimeters wide at its widest and barely half a man's height tall. It faced an exterior flank of stones that was so close no one could have squeezed through and made their way into the open air. They certainly couldn't have gone that way. He turned back around.

Darreth was startled when he saw the first dead alien and took in a loud gulp of air in surprise. His second reaction was of total bewilderment. This was impossible. There was no such thing as aliens. But as he knelt to examine the dead body he realized that his assumption, and everyone else's for that matter, about that was false.

And it might explain why the tunnel to this cavern looked more like a mineshaft than anything natural.

He quickly searched around to see if there were more bodies. There. Another one! As creepy as it was in the dark, he nonetheless knelt to examine what looked like a uniform, which covered the long-dead alien's body. It looked similar to his flight suit. He lifted the material with an index finger in an effort to discern what it was made of. What was that object? His light reflected off something obviously metallic after he had moved the alien's clothing. It was disc-shaped and had an orange-gold iridescence to it. He moved aside the clumped fibers and picked the object up out of the dirt where it was half hidden. It looked brand new and neatly fit in his palm.

He pointed his light directly at it in an attempt to figure out if it was some sort of weapon or if it was a communications device. He found no buttons, displays, openings, catches or levers. On the other hand, it appeared to have some sort of writing etched into it. Or was it just designs? It was impossible to tell because of the poor lighting. Perhaps it was a keepsake or a reminder of the alien's family. It looked valuable no matter what it was. But he had more pressing concerns right now—concerns which far outweighed these absolutely amazing discoveries. Where were Naylon and Tann? He lay his pack down next to the alien's body, placing the shiny object on top of it. Aiming his light in all directions, and now unencumbered by his pack, he looked all around the chamber. It was spooky. Dead alien bodies. Not a trace of Naylon or Tann. He yelled out several more times. No responses. In his exploration of the cavern, he found no large cracks in the floor or hidden pits, but did find the third body. So, they hadn't been swallowed up by the darkness. There was simply no trace of them.

He went back to the cylindrical tunnel and knelt down to inspect the jumbled footprints at one end. Not being a tracker of any merit, he knew obtaining valuable information from them would be useless. He played his light along the interior surface of the smooth opening and searched with his hands for any hidden trap doors along its interior.

Slowly, he made his way down its entire length, crossed what appeared to be the optical illusion in the dead center, then continued looking for anything that might indicate an opening. The interior of the tunnel was devoid of so much as a blemish.

Now he was beginning to panic, or more accurately, he felt like he was going to hyperventilate. He had done his best to find his brother and his boyfriend. But he'd turned up absolutely nothing except what clearly were alien bodies. Bodies that his boyfriend and brother had to have seen because of the footprints near them. The situation was more than creeping him out now. He figured he might have better luck if he got Merek to help him out. First though, he'd get some more lighting out of the shuttle.

Half an hour later, and with Merek in tow, they had set up several lights in the chamber. With every corner as illuminated as possible with their scant lighting, they both searched every shadow and behind every boulder. Neither Naylon nor Tann showed up anywhere. There was no way they could have crawled through that little crack even if they had tried. Darreth felt nothing but anguish now.

Hours after they had returned to the entrance chamber Darreth received a hail on an emergency frequency. A team of rescuers from Nona Ice Station Command Response had been searching for them for two days. His message had been received just before the pirates had blown the nav sat from space.

Part II

Chapter 18

The first thing Naylon realized when he splashed into the river was that he wasn't going to sink. His sealed backpack was buoyant enough to help keep his head above water. Realizing that didn't stop him from becoming besieged with panic. His tumble down the slope had happened so fast he hadn't had time to grab on to anything. Besides, there wasn't much to grab on to anyway. Most of the flat stones he had been gliding on top of on his way down into the water ended up in the river with him. Luckily, only some small ones had actually pelted him. Now he realized he was headed downstream at a blinding pace. He saw Tann only out of the corner of his eye before he was quickly swept out of visual range.

Up ahead, a rooster tail of water was rising above the surface. He was vaguely aware that it meant a large boulder was up ahead. Seconds before he would have hit it the water gently glided him around to the right. He found himself momentarily in an eddy, slowly swirling around, before he was again pushed along downstream. Just after that his head went underwater for several seconds. He swallowed a mouthful of water, which he sputtered out when he surfaced. His right wrist smacked against a slick rock. That hurt.

He felt lucky about at least one thing. The water was cold but he was fully clothed. That would help at least a little against the inevitable hypothermia he knew would set in. He hoped the slope would level off soon so the water would slow down. It had to.

Unless, that is, he ended up going over a waterfall first.

But nothing like that appeared to be coming up. The water's slope wasn't that great and the river was narrow here. He was moving in such a random pattern he couldn't get any sort of purchase onto anything.

There. Just up ahead, he was traveling toward what appeared to be a branch wedged between two boulders. If he could just maneuver himself to catch it, he thought, reaching. The water quickly diverted and he went well to the side. Shit!

Further down and to the left. There. A huge mass of spindly branches, partially submerged in the water. It looked dangerous since he might end up being impaled on one of the sharp-looking ends. Naylon reached his hand out and managed to catch his sleeve on the end of one. It stopped his forward movement long enough for him to grab onto it. Just as he did so, it snapped. It wasn't waterlogged enough to be pliable. The water continued to push him along, backwards this time, with the end of the branch still in his hand. But maybe that was a good thing. He had about a meter's length of it still in his possession. Perhaps he could use the extension to help him as the water carried him further and further downstream.

A bend in the river rapidly neared. Naylon was starting to feel quite chilled at this point and was having trouble holding on to the stick. The water was deeper at the bend and, because it was narrower here, he was pushed into the dead center of the channel. The channel suddenly opened out to a broad flat area where he was able to finally touch bottom. But the water was still moving quickly enough for him to be unable to make any headway toward either shore. Slowly but surely, touching bottom wasn't just once in a few meters, but rather all the time. Using the stick as a third leg, he was able to finally maneuver himself to a sandbar to his right. Just in time, too, since the chill of the water was beginning to sap the remainder of his strength. Finally, the water was only waist high. With the help of the stick he was able to make his way to the sand. Immediately, his legs gave way and he ended up on his knees.

Naylon looked all around. Soaking wet, he was alone in the wilds of Rylerra. And he was a considerable distance from his original location. Perhaps even a full kilometer away. The sandbar was on a wide curve with a few boulders scattered here and there. The other bank was quite distant. At least ten if not fifteen meters away. He was having a difficult time focusing his thoughts and realized he might be in real trouble if he didn't get warmed up soon. Just beyond the sandbar, where the bank was steep, creeping vines hung downward, seemingly trying to make their way to the water. Vines? He was unaware of vine-like plants on Rylerra. All of them were only two or three meters in length at their longest. Beyond that were short trees, or were they bushes? He simply didn't know. He had been planning to familiarize himself more with the flora and scant fauna once they had set up their legitimate camp for the dig.

There would be no dig on this venture.

A narrow diameter log of bright orange wood had mired itself in the sand closer to shore. Orange? What a strange color for wood to be. He didn't recall anything like orange wood on Rylerra. He crawled to the log and rested his back against it, facing the river. There, he caught his breath while holding his arms around his chest. His teeth were beginning to chatter. He had to figure out a way to get warmer and quickly.

The sun had warmed this patch of sand quite considerably he realized. There was no wind of any kind here. Naylon shed the backpack then his jacket and shirt. Bare-chested, he was able to at least able to take advantage of the warmth of the sunlight. He squeezed out his shirt and laid it on the log. He did the same for his jacket. Lastly, he shed his trousers and underwear. The humidity was quite low. He figured the items might dry out quite quickly.

Next was his backpack. In it he had a container of water, a few energy bars, the sensor gear, a small toilet kit bag, a change of socks (he totally forgot he'd put them in that compartment), and some other miscellaneous items. Everything was wet.

He returned to his trousers and started to wring them out. That's when he remembered the disc-shaped object they'd picked up in the cavern. He reached in and pulled it out of his thigh pocket. He peered at it to discern what he could of it. That's when he discovered tiny symbols written in a spiral pattern over its entire surface. He was sure he was staring at alien writing. The thought of such a discovery was incredibly exciting, even considering the circumstances.

At least the scientist part of him was excited. The rest of him was becoming quite fearful. He was weaponless, alone and still cold. He was far from where he needed to be to get back to the rest of the group, and there was no way he could reach them before nightfall. It was surely going to be very chilly tonight despite the reasonable temperature right now. Immediately, he tried the neural implant. *'Darreth! Darreth! Can you hear me?'* Nothing. He tried again and again. Still nothing. If it didn't work when they were in the cavern, it certainly wouldn't have worked this far away. It was worth the try anyway and it boosted his morale for a while. But it faded quickly.

He was exhausted from having thrashed around in the water. He could barely hold his eyes open. He finished wringing his trousers and underwear out, then slowly put them both back on. It was difficult due to their being wet and him being exhausted. Maybe after a short nap he'd be able to figure out how to get across the river, if that's indeed what he needed to do. Perhaps by that time his clothing would be dried out. His wet pants were just this side of tolerable. They would eventually dry out from the warmth of his body.

Naylon curled up in as much of a ball as he could. He rested his head on the backpack and shut his eyes. The warm sunlight felt comforting. Soon he fell asleep.

Tasker Ebit's large yellow eyes had been following every move of the mysterious stranger on the sand below him. He had been just about to walk down to the river, hose in hand. His task was to place an end into the water then return to the ship and start the pump. He had gone not more than thirty meters when he saw something dragging itself up out of the river and onto the narrow beach. Immediately, he squatted down onto his belly, looking like a four-legged spider in such a position. He raised his head on his thin neck and peered out through the short vegetation.

Being an alien on this planet, as were his masters, he thought at first he was observing an aquatic native. Within a second, he was sure he saw nothing more mysterious than a Terran. But this Terran wasn't part of his party. Although Tasker Ebit was unable to count as such, he knew everyone was accounted for, including the other Taskers.

This Terran was alone, too. Tasker Ebit was sure of that. He saw no others nearby. Carefully, he sniffed the air when a slight breeze made it his way. The Terran's scent wasn't on that one. He shifted his position slightly, crawling sideways very slowly, to align himself more with the shifting breezes. The wet Terran below him wouldn't be aware of him unless he presented himself visually. But who was this one? How did he get here without his master's ship? Was he a Telkan in disguise? No, all the Telkans he had ever seen were much larger and had thick grayish-black skin. This one was surely Terran. There. The breeze definitely told him this was a Terran. But the stranger smelled noticeably different from the ones on the ship.

It was time to report back to his masters about this mysterious arrival. This man might be a danger. The water he was supposed to filter could wait. He was sure this was more important.

Captain Rodigue Pacudas, leader of the band of nine handpicked men from his infiltration patrol, sat behind a wide table in his cabin. The cabin was inside the specially upgraded troop ship named *Cortés Libre*. They had landed on this planet a day and a half ago. The captain had already named it Déstica. It was an exhausting and stressful journey which had taken several weeks.

Their journey couldn't be made through the use of the normal space routes. Telkan warships monitored the spacetime conduits that merged into Telkan space. In fact, there wasn't a single known conduit that connected Terran and Telkan space that didn't have a dense network of mines surrounding it. But the Telkans didn't have a complete map of Terran space. Nor did they consider that Terrans might actually use a conduit connecting neutron stars.

Although spacetime conduits existed all over space, there were many of them that were far too hazardous to use. Those that terminated in systems with supergiant stars, giant stars, triple star systems, neutron stars and stars that had gone nova were always avoided due to the gravimetric shearing at the mouths of the conduits, the instability of the openings, and the severe radiation hazards inherent in such systems. Indeed all systems with a giant or supergiant star had conduits that opened within their coronospheres.

Several years previous, a recon team determined a neutron star in a triple star system in Terran-held space opened into a single neutron star system with a dense asteroid field in what was thought to be Telkan space. The end of the conduit on the other side was dangerously close to the star's solid crust. Five probes had been sent through and only two retrieved. Both had provided telemetry proving the opening was indeed in Telkan space, that no comm traffic had been detected, and the conduit didn't open too close to the neutron star's radiation axes. If a way through could be found for a much larger vessel, the conduit might provide a strategic advantage.

Pacudas had volunteered for the mission. The *Cortés Libre*, normally a standard interstellar troop transport ship, was outfitted with eight radiation deflection systems instead of the normal two, along with specialized ablative and reflective shielding, and the latest armament. They were to provide a detailed map of the conduit at the far end, determine where the other conduits were in the system, then find out if any of them were being monitored. If they could traverse the system, they would be able to assess troop strengths in the systems they passed through, and discover if there were another way around the dangerous route. Few knew he and his team were on this mission. Everything in any database on the ship that could point to where they had come from and how they had arrived here had been carefully encrypted into a single holocube, which was hidden in Pacudas' storage locker. Determining its significance would be essentially impossible if they were caught. A good deal of the technology being used on their ship was brand new. If successful, the shielding and the holocube technology would become standard on all interstellar ships.

The odds of their returning, or even having made it successfully through the asteroid field at the far end, had been calculated several times. None of the calculations predicted a success rate of greater than forty-three percent. But each one of them was up to the task. They knew if they succeeded, not only would they be heroes, the Empire would be in their debt. Indeed, a significant promotion would be in Pacudas's future if they returned with enough data to change the course of the war. After all, the mission would put them deep behind enemy lines. It would be extremely hazardous, but any data they could provide would be intel that would be impossible to come by otherwise.

With engines at nearly full after exiting the conduit they sheared away with only two point three seconds to spare before gravimetric forces would have taken them to the star's surface. They had sustained only minor damage to the outer hull, all of it because of the asteroid field they had ended up in. Getting clear of the field took three days. Once in relatively empty space and a full ninety degrees from the neutron star's magnetic field, they were able to use the onboard conduit detection system to find another one thirty-nine hours away. Getting into it was cause for great concern. A tremendous amount of interference from the neutron star's intense radiation field prevented opening the mouth of the conduit until the fourth try. Finally through, they continued on their journey to the second, third, then the fourth jumps. Not a hint of Telkan occupation had been detected until they reached this system.

Telkans used a very narrow band of comm frequencies, which the Terran fleet constantly monitored. When they reached this system, it was obvious there was a significant presence due to the amount of comm traffic. Discovering the least amount of comm traffic on this planet, and determining it was habitable, they landed. The captain dubbed the planet Déstica and decided it was time to not only perform some repairs, but also to access how heavily the rest of the system was occupied. Preliminary scans had told them this was a binary star system with at least two occupied planets, one orbiting each star in the system. And, he considered his men, who had been cooped up for far too long inside the small craft. He had morale to keep up. Once it had been determined no Telkans were in the immediate vicinity, he had given permission for the crewman to leave the ship in small groups but only for an hour at a time. His crew was grateful for any time at all because they understood the risk the Captain was taking on their behalf. At least the planet had a Terran-like atmosphere.

The war with the Telkan Ascendency had been waged for three decades. Long ago Pacudas had lost his brother and mother in a Telkan bombing raid. That raid had been in retribution for their own earlier raid on a Telkan colony world deemed dangerously close to Empire territory. It was well-known that Telkan technology was superior to their own, yet they lacked spirit, and thus had to be thoroughly provoked before they fought back.

It mattered not a bit to Captain Pacudas that diplomacy had not entered into the equation even after three decades of war. Against an enemy that refused to be conquered. But he wasn't a diplomat. He was a soldier. Besides, it was unheard of for Terrans to hold diplomatic talks with a sworn enemy.

Captain Pacudas could trace his ancestry back well over fifteen hundred years. In fact, he could trace his lineage directly to the family of King Philip of Old España. It was a long and extremely proud history, filled with large families. In every generation since then, at least one able-bodied man had joined a military unit and fought for their country or planet.

Pacudas felt honored to be part of that family tree, one that had eventually helped take over most of Terra, expanded into space to colonize the Sol system, then eventually fifty-six exosolar worlds. He had relatives on seven of them, some holding important political positions, too.

But the easy pickings of inhabitable planets came to an abrupt end when it was discovered that the Telkan Ascendency lay at the edge of explored space. Since conquest had been in Terran blood for as long as recorded history, it was only natural Terrans would conquer what they considered interlopers in their expanding empire. An alien race simply couldn't bring their expansion to an end, especially ones that existed so close to Terran-occupied worlds.

But the Telkans refused to be conquered. In fact, they seemed to be masters at hiding their strength and numbers, all of which seemed far greater than Terrans. It was even possible there were trillions of Telkans still not accounted for.

Much was known about Telkan physiology. They had six appendages, two of which were removed through a surgical procedure at birth. It was said they were vestigial legs, but no Terran had ever seen the limbs because no one had ever seen a live Telkan birth, much less analyzed a young one. They were very easily poisoned; tiny doses of fairly common compounds, which might cause a Terran minor irritation, could make a Telkan writhe in agony and bring on a painful death. That is, if one could pierce their incredibly tough hide. Although such compounds aided in interrogation, it had long since been discovered they never got any accurate intelligence that way.

Captain Pacudas had several display devices in front of him. One had a topographical map of their immediate area taken from imagery they shot before their descent from orbit. Another contained an inventory of the ship's store, which proved they were running low on water. Another contained a complete personnel roster, including the Taskers assigned to them. Tasker Pas was an excellent cook. Tasker Ebit was incredibly strong and could work all day, if directed. Tasker Vak was used to keep the interior of the craft clean. It didn't seem possible they had as much energy as they had, given how they were all thin as rails. But it was so.

A hologram of Captain Pacudas' wife and his two sons were in the holocylinder to the right of the display devices on his desk. As he reached for another of the report flimsies, he scanned the holocylinder ever so briefly. It held a thirty-second loop of the three of them smiled out at him. The fighting and now this extremely dangerous reconnaissance were for them. One of these days he'd be with them permanently. They'd settle on a planet at the other end of Terran space. He already had his sights on Galea. It was far from any front line. But that was a thought for another day, he knew, as he continued to go over the displays.

The door chime sounded. It was Commander Jao Selaye. The commander wasn't supposed to report for another hour. He pressed a button at the table and the door slid open.

"Captain," the commander said as he came in and stood at attention in front of the captain's desk.

"At ease."

Selaye put himself at ease. "Sir, Tasker Ebit has reported something unusual. Something about a Terran on the river."

"A what?"

"A Terran, sir. He's quite adamant about it. I've checked and everyone's accounted for."

"Then he's wrong."

"Tasker Ebit is not given to excitement, sir."

"Then see what it is. It's probably an animal he's mistaken for a Terran."

"I'll check into it myself, sir."

The commander stepped backward one step, then turned around and exited the cabin. The door slid closed. He looked at Tasker Ebit, then turned to Lieutenant Navar, the leader of the soldat team, who had been waiting in the corridor. The lieutenant was in charge this shift, and thus in charge of whichever Taskers were awake.

Taskers were unable to speak. They had no speech center with which to do so. But they served their purpose. Nearly eight hundred years previous, when Terrans first went into space, slavery was the norm on Terra. Shortly thereafter, a social movement had been growing to do away with that trade. It was simple luck that one of the first earthlike planets Terrans settled had a large population of a semi-sentient species of simian-like creatures. They couldn't be classified as mammals, although people had a tendency to view them as such. In fact, they were oddly insect-like, more like spiders, what with their unusual stance on four legs. They mostly moved like that, but all could stand and walk erect. Their rubbery necks and large yellow eyes made them extremely odd-looking. But it was their docile nature, amazing dexterity, their near unlimited energy, and abundant numbers which instantly intrigued Terrans. By a happy coincidence, they became the replacement for human slaves. After all, that institution had existed since the beginning of time and it surely wasn't going to end just because Terrans had conquered space travel.

At the same time the human slave trade on Earth was being dismantled, the Taskers on Ebórica 4 were being rounded up, implanted with cybernetics, and taught to understand human speech by way of RNA learning injections. Within four years, the techniques used to create a Tasker had been standardized. The serum used to teach them to understand Empire Spanish was patented with the name Pelinex. Taskers had been part of human culture just as human slaves had been in previous centuries. Kept in their place because of limited brainpower and the use of Pelinex, no Tasker had ever turned on its master. And none needed to either. They had become an invaluable part of life, were as common as cats and dogs, and were kept well-fed and healthy. The only drawback was that their planet's natural rotation was much faster than Earth's. Their days were only eighteen hours long, which made Tasker circadian rhythms totally different from a Terran's. Nonetheless, Terrans had long ago gotten used to the fact that at regular intervals a Tasker would simply shut down in what appeared to be a narcoleptic state, which lasted up to five hours. Special sleeping chambers for Taskers were a common part of any household, business or military unit.

The holographic commbar attached to the Taskers' forearms contained word symbols. They were able to position the symbols in such a way to create rudimentary sentences, much like what apes used over a millennia ago to communicate with their captors. All of the higher primates had long ago disappeared from Earth's biosphere, but the methods used for Terran-ape communication still came in handy, even though the subject of that communication method was a totally alien species.

The Terran encounter with Taskers became the foundation for how to deal with Telkans. Telkan physiology was much more sophisticated. Their brains were as developed as Terran brains. After all, they had space travel, speech and held many worlds of their own. Although not much was known about the worlds the Telkans inhabited, recon had determined there were colonies on at least eighteen planets. Pelinex provided two-way communications between Telkans and Terrans. It's just that Telkans learned Empire Spanish, not the other way around.

"Tasker Ebit, you're sure what you saw is a Terran?" Lieutenant Navar asked.

Tasker Ebit bobbed his head left to right, which was his best attempt to mimic a human nod.

"And you say he may be damaged, uh, hurt?"

Again the bobbing.

"I'll get the doctor just in case," Commander Selaye told Lieutenant Navar.

Dr. Doratzo Ranarde, captain by rank, was the chief medical officer aboard the *Cortés Libre*. The team he tended to was small, but they had had their share of mishaps already. Mostly accidents, he admitted, yet at least he was able to use some of his skills. He volunteered for this mission because of his knowledge of the three T's: Terran, Tasker and Telkan. He was looking forward to interrogating any Telkan they might manage to capture. He hoped the soldats would show restraint and not kill each and every one of them first. He was well aware of the blood sport which seemed to accompany most raids nowadays.

Commander Selaye entered the infirmary and spoke to the doctor at length about what Tasker Ebit had 'told' him, since the entire conversation had been through the symbol board. The doctor was eager to get out of the ship and breathe in some much-needed fresh air anyway.

Less than twenty minutes after Tasker Ebit's discovery of Naylon on the sandbar, he was leading the three Terrans with him back to that location. When they arrived, Naylon was still fast asleep. He was sure the men standing over him when he was woken up were pirates. What the other thing was he had no idea, but it scared the crap out of him.

"Uh! W-what in thunder?" He quickly reached for his shirt, which was still lying stretched across the fallen log. It served its purpose of being a psychological barrier to the gun-wielding humans in front of him. It served as no barrier to the fact that an alien was with them. At least the shirt was dry now.

This person was indeed a Terran, Selaye noted. "Qen ere, i com llegast'qui," he asked. He was quite informal with his speech. Whoever this person was, the commander didn't need to address him in the honorific.

Naylon was puzzled beyond anything he'd ever experienced before. Here were humans, one speaking a language he had never heard, while standing behind them was a thoroughly bizarre-looking alien creature. The humans appeared to not know the alien was accompanying them.

Naylon's eyes told them everything. He pointed at the Tasker and tried to crawl away. The one who had spoken, who was also the taller of the three, pointed a weapon at him as he moved. Naylon stopped and pointed at Tasker Ebit. "Th-there's an alien behind you!"

The doctor and commander looked at each other. What did this stranger say? "Comtést-me!" demanded Selaye.

Navar stood a meter behind the doctor and the commander on purpose, with his weapon at the ready.

Again with the strange language, thought Naylon. *Are they dense? There's an alien standing behind them!* That's when Naylon realized something odd was going on here. More odd than everything that had transpired since he woke up this morning. The alien was with them! In fact, it looked like the alien had some sort of photronic display attached to its forearm. But the creature wasn't like any of the alien bodies he'd briefly examined in the cavern. Okay, it had been a few hours back, and he had been thoroughly traumatized by having slid off the side of the mountain and unceremoniously dumped into the river, but he was sure that the shape of the alien's body he'd examined, even in the pitch-blackness of the cave, wasn't anything like the one standing in front of him.

"W-would you guys tell me what in thunder is going on here?" Naylon implored them.

The doctor and the commander again looked at each other. This time the commander realized their captive Terran wasn't speaking Empire Spanish. In fact, he'd never heard the language this person was speaking, and he spoke three languages himself.

"Ve con sotro," Selaye told Naylon. He pointed to Naylon's things and motioned for him to don his shirt. While he did so, Renarde spoke with Selaye. "I'm not familiar with that language."

"He's trying to pull a fast one," Selaye replied. With that, he eyed Naylon. He was waiting for a reaction that didn't come. Perhaps the man hadn't understood him after all.

Naylon donned the shirt and took his jacket in hand. Lieutenant Navar had already taken Naylon's backpack and looked through it. He had determined there were no weapons in it but handed it to Tasker Ebit anyway. They led Naylon back toward the ship with Navar in the rear with his weapon drawn on him. Tasker Ebit stayed behind them all, as was protocol. Naylon looked back every once in a while, wondering if the alien was a guard or something.

"Naylon," he said to Navar, pointing to himself. "Naylon," he said again to the two men in front. These people didn't speak Lingua, he realized. How that was possible was beyond him. To his knowledge, there wasn't a soul on any of Inhab that didn't speak at least some Lingua. But there was more. No world in known space harbored an alien species. None had ever been discovered. As far as humanity knew, they were entirely alone in the Orion Arm of the galaxy. Yet, within a day he'd personally seen at least two species unknown to humans. Unbelievable.

The two men ahead of him didn't say a word to Naylon but rather talked between themselves. "I guess his name is Naylon," the commander offered.

"What kind of name is that?" the doctor asked.

"It's not one I've ever heard before."

Naylon listened to the conversation, unable to follow it at all. He heard his name mentioned so he was sure he had gotten through to them. So, why weren't they responding to him?

Soon enough they arrived at a clearing. The taller man, the one who was obviously in charge, spoke something to a communications device on his wrist. Immediately, it was as if the very air opened up to reveal the interior of a ship as a door opened at ground level.

Thunder! Naylon thought. *A cloaked ship. No such thing exists, but-but I'm sure I'm looking at one right in front of me.* Such technology had been science fiction for hundreds of years. Small objects could be hidden using portable cloaking technology, including people. But as far as he knew, nothing as massive as an entire ship could be cloaked.

Naylon was taken inside through an obvious airlock, then led to the end of a corridor, which opened to a larger room. It appeared to be a mess hall of some sort. He was pointed to a bench where he sat down. Even the mess hall made this the most sophisticated looking spacecraft interior he'd ever seen. The shuttle they'd flown in to Rylerra was nothing compared to this.

The man in charge finally decided to tell him his name. "Comdant Selaye," was all he would say as he pointed to himself. Well, that was a start.

Naylon watched as gesticulating and a long discussion took place in front of him. Finally, the man who seemed to Naylon to be a physician was ordered to leave. He returned with a young female in full military uniform. She introduced herself to him as soldat Daníl Ocio.

Soldat, Naylon thought. *Somehow, I've stumbled onto a secret military organization. Since when did the pirates become a full-fledged military organization? And why doesn't anyone speak Lingua?*

Commander Selaye asked Daníl to ask Naylon something. She cleared her throat.

"English speak?" she asked with a thick accent.

"English?" Naylon asked back. He wasn't prepared for the unusual way the question was asked.

"Yes, English?" she asked.

English was the old word used centuries ago. All languages changed and morphed over time. English had been no different. No one had used the word English for almost half a millennium. "No, Lingua. Ever heard of it? Lingua," Naylon told her.

There was much conversation between the female soldier named Ocio and the older man after that, none of which Naylon was able to follow. Finally, he was taken to a room off the mess hall, ushered into it, and the door was locked. He looked around. It was a storage room. There was nothing to sit on except the floor. There were food containers all around him. At least he wouldn't go hungry.

"I have no idea where he came from, Captain. It was the doctor who suspected the man spoke something similar to English. Possibly a dialect of it," Selaye said as he took a seat in front of the captain's desk.

The captain frowned. "How did he know that?"

"He activated some sort of computing device the man had and looked through some of the documents. Ocio was able to identify a few word of the language on the documents or we wouldn't have been able to confirm that."

The Captain mulled over their surprise visitor. His effects had been thoroughly examined. Whoever this man was, he was of little or no threat since he had no weapons on him. In fact, the man seemed completely surprised to see them. Perhaps he was no spy as his commander had suspected. As far as they could tell the man had either swam the river or had fallen in to it and crawled onto the sandbar to dry off. Everything the man had was damp.

"He says his name is Naylon but that's all we could get out of him," the commander said. "His effects don't explain a thing. Sir, I don't think he speaks any Empire Spanish." He slid Naylon's vidPAD toward the captain.

"That's impossible." The captain had never met anyone who didn't speak at least some Empire Spanish. He activated his desktop screen and looked through a few maps. "According to this there are barely three million people who speak English. There have never been enough speakers for it to develop a dialect. In fact, this says it's a dying language." He leaned back. "It's entirely possible an English speaker has never been in space."

The commander shook his head. "It's all moot, sir. The doctor has a solution to our mystery."

"How so?"

"How do we interrogate the Telkans?"

"Of course," the Captain said as he nodded his head. "Of course."

Chapter 19

Tann was completely terrified. This was literally the first time in his life he'd ever been completely alone in every sense of the word. It didn't seem possible everyone could just have disappeared, including the dead aliens. But it had happened. And now, with not a shred of evidence that they had taken shelter in the cavern, his only alternative was to attempt to pursue Naylon. But how to do that was proving to be nearly impossible. There were no neat paths near the river for him to follow. Rocks and boulders, rises and vegetation prevented him from simply following the riverbank. Very quickly, despite the slightly lower gravity, he was becoming winded. Twice, he had to stop and catch his breath when he felt himself hyperventilating from a combination of fright and exertion.

Finally, breathing heavily, he stopped. He leaned forward, resting his palms on his knees. "There are no wild animals here. The pirates haven't returned. You're going to be okay," he said out loud only to reassure himself. Even as he did so, tears again sprang from his eyes. Still leaning forward, he wiped them away then looked over to his left where the river was rushing. A tall rise of rocks was directly in front of him. He repositioned his pack straps and heard his canteen sloshing inside. He should have filled it completely up before they went exploring, he realized. Too late now.

He'd have to skirt the rocks by going to the right and around to get back to the water's edge. That took several minutes. He couldn't hear anything the entire time he was attempting to get around the rocky rise. No sound from the rushing river. Only the wind in his ears as he ran. Otherwise, it was eerily quiet.

Slowly but surely, the intensity of the situation started to lessen. He felt himself becoming much more focused on the task at hand and found himself thinking, 'What would my brother do?' 'How would Darreth handle himself?' Somehow, it made him feel a lot more courageous.

Completely around the rise now, he was finally able to follow the river, although from a much higher level than right at the water's edge.

That gave him an advantage he didn't have before: he could see much further. He stopped and scanned both banks as far as he could see. He yelled out Naylon's name over and over. Nothing. He'd have to go much further downstream, he realized. At least the vegetation was thinner right here, and much lower. The bushes very nearly hugged the ground and were much more circular in shape. That made for many open spaces where he could see the ground more easily. The rise started sloping downward. Tann trotted through the low bushes, finding himself back near the river bank. Ten minutes later, after having run the entire way, the river took a bend and widened considerably. He stopped again to catch his breath and pulled out his canteen. After taking several gulps, he slowly scanned both banks. There, on the right, hundreds of meters further on was a wide sandy bank. It appeared to be the only open area on either side. He took a course through the underbrush, which had become taller this close to the bank, and made his way toward it.

"Lieutenant," Captain Pacudas said to Navar.

"Sir."

"Send a team to see if there are other Terrans out there."

"Sir, our scans didn't show even one Terran biosign before we landed."

"The scans were wrong, weren't they?"

The captain treated his crew with respect, but he was still a hard taskmaster. The lieutenant knew this and said simply, "Yes sir."

Soldats Marco Zapante, Daníl Ocio and Tiso Urret quietly left the safety of their cloaked ship and headed toward the bank. They used the cover of the low brush to stay out of sight as much as possible. Soldat Zapante had a handheld scanner in front of him and activated a diagnostic just to be sure it was functioning properly. It would take another three minutes for it to complete the diagnostic test before it was ready to use. Zapante knew the ship's survey of the area before they landed had determined they were completely alone. Apparently, their survey was flawed. That was highly unusual since their sensors were the best the Empire could provide, and were specifically tuned to not only Terran but to Telkan life signs. How this Naylon person was missed was a complete mystery. Thus, he paid particular attention to the diagnostic.

Soldat Urret went a dozen meters downstream, used the binoculars to scan the far bank, then lowered them so he could simply watch the water as it rushed downstream several meters away.

Ocio was several meters upstream, almost at the water's edge. She knelt down to check her weapon. Her finger was next to the trigger instead of over the trigger guard, as trained, while she examined the power pack. Moving at a pretty fast clip, Tann came out of nowhere. He very nearly stumbled over her. His sudden appearance startled her. In her haste to pull her weapon up, she accidentally pressed the trigger. Ocio instantly rose to a standing position and pressed her comm badge. "Urret, Zapante, get over here. I just shot a Terran."

Tann had landed on the ground face down. Daníl had already pulled him over onto his back and checked his pulse. *Whew,* she thought. He was alive. Both of her comrades were with her in seconds.

"It's a teenager!" Urret said in surprise. "What is a Terran teen doing on this world?"

"Why did you shoot him?" Zapante asked.

"It was an accident," Ocio told him angrily. "Luckily, my weapon was on a low stun setting. The blast didn't hit him head on either." She called the ship. "Captain Renarde, we've got an emergency. We just found another Terran. A teen. I accidentally stunned him."

"Stunned him?"

The frustration was obvious in her voice. "Accidentally!"

"Get him to the infirmary."

Zapante checked for any obvious weapons in Tann's jacket pockets and pants, then unzipped the main compartment of Tann's pack. He discovered nothing that could be construed as weaponry. He unzipped the smaller compartments and found nothing threatening there either.

Ocio was supremely angry with herself for not paying better attention, especially while in the field. It went against all of her training, but she certainly didn't expect someone to burst through the underbrush seconds after she had gotten into position. In fact, she wondered if she needed a hearing test.

Another two minutes went by before they were able to get him in the ship and onto the bed. The doctor removed Tann's jacket, his shirt, then his t-shirt, and set them aside. He placed the scanner that was attached to the ceiling over his bare chest and checked for any obvious injuries. Finding none other than the shock to his body from the low level stun, he felt satisfied the boy was going to be all right in an hour or so.

While the doctor examined Tann, Urret took that time to look at the tags on Tann's clothing. None of what he read was recognizable.

"Hey, Ocio, know what this means?"

None of it was in Empire Spanish, but she guessed it was the same language as Naylon spoke. "I don't read the language. I just recognized a few words."

"Well, look anyway."

She tried to make out the fifteen words on the inner lining of the jacket but was unable to make out a single one. Shaking her head, she sounded quite exasperated. "Doesn't this ship have a language database?"

He spoke into his comm badge. "Shipcomp, this is Urret."

"*Service*," the shipcomp replied.

"Access language database for English. Translate the following word." He spelled out one of them.

"*The language database is limited to the four primary languages of the Empire and Homeworld Telkan. That word matches nothing in any of those databases.*"

"Shit," Urret said.

The captain interrupted them. Ocio listened to her comm. "*Soldat Ocio. I will see you in my ready room now.*"

Urret looked at her. "He better go easy on you about this."

Ocio whispered back, "I can take a reprimand. It's more than you can say," she taunted him playfully.

Soldat Urret gave her a face and a rude hand gesture just before she swiftly left the infirmary.

The captain, the doctor and the commander stood next to the med table where Tann lay still unconscious. "The boy was only stunned. He'll wake up shortly. He'll have a headache, but that's about all," the doctor told the captain.

"Think we should tell our captive we've found one of his cohorts?" the commander asked the captain.

Pacudas nodded in the affirmative. "I want to find out what's going on here as soon as possible. Have our 'guest' taken out of the storage locker and feed him. Water, too. When he's finished bring him in here. I'm sure the man can identify this boy. Notify me if you discover anything of importance. I need to go over the sensor data."

"Yes, sir," Selaye said.

The captain returned to his ready room while Selaye went through the corridors to the mess hall. Soldat Barcega was on guard duty outside the locked storage room door.

Selaye raised his chin. "Open it."

Barcega nodded and unlocked the door. Naylon stood up. He had opened one of the myriad lockers that lined the walls of the small room, had pulled out a large can and had been sitting on it. It was more comfortable than the floor. Barcega had a weapon and waved it at Naylon, trying to usher him out. Naylon immediately raised his hands.

Selaye pushed the weapon down and nodded to Barcega, indicating that he could stand down. Naylon got it and issued a tight smile while he lowered his hands.

Knowing his captors wouldn't understand him, he pointed to a smaller empty can. He had taken out what he thought were food bars and had put them back into the locker. "Since you didn't let me out I had to pee in that can." Barcega briefly looked in it after Naylon left the storage room. He grinned. No language was needed to see what Naylon was trying to say.

Selaye led Naylon to the same table he had been seated at before. He spoke, although he knew Naylon wouldn't understand a word he said. "I'm going to heat you something to eat. I'm sure you like chicken. I've added some vegetables, too." He pulled out a container from a refrigerated compartment and placed it in what looked like a small rice cooker. It hummed briefly. A tiny bright green light illuminated on the lid a few seconds later. It smelled delicious. Selaye pulled out a cup from behind a small cabinet door and filled it with water. He set both items in front of Naylon, along with a napkin and some cutlery.

Naylon immediately started devouring the food and thirstily emptied the cup of water. He offered the cup to Selaye, indicating he wanted more. Selaye filled it up again and handed it back. Naylon downed half of it then set it down. He finished the rest of the food in record time.

"English?" Selaye asked.

Naylon responded by vigorously shaking his head. *Enough with this misunderstanding.* It was not English. "Lingua," he said with emphasis.

The commander had only understood the word Naylon had spoken to mean 'language'. He shook his head. He still couldn't understand how this man could possible have arrived on this planet.

A klaxon sounded throughout the ship. Instantly, Selaye stood up. Naylon felt his heart hammering. *What now,* he wondered.

"All personnel: stations. That Telkan ship has been spotted again," came the warning over the ship's intercom. A long-range scan had indicated a craft in flight only fifteen minutes previous. It had almost immediately gone out of range, but was back now. This time it was a lot closer and headed their way.

Selaye held his wrist up and spoke into his communicator. "Lieutenant Navar, are your soldats ready?" They had been waiting for this turn of events.

"Lazcún and Agrida will be in position in two minutes."

"Excellent."

Selaye grabbed Naylon's plate and cup and tossed them into a waste chute. He pointed out the mess hall doorway and motioned him to follow him. Selaye didn't want Naylon out of his sight and there was no time to put him back in the storage room. Naylon went with him. The captain had already decided, with Selaye agreeing, that Naylon posed little threat. He didn't look tough enough to know any type of hand-to-hand defense, so was basically harmless. The commander took him to a cabin several meters down a central corridor. Naylon finally got to see another part of the ship as he swiftly accompanied the officer.

At this point Naylon wasn't sure whether he'd been rescued or captured and was slightly panicked and bewildered. Who these people were, he had no idea. Indeed, although he hadn't been following every make and model of shuttles, this one appeared to be much more sophisticated than anything he'd ever seen before. He had already considered these people to be from a colony far outside the reaches of the Consort. If that were so, what were they doing on Rylerra and why had no one ever heard of them before? Had Rylerra been invaded? Was Andakar next? His mind raced at all the possibilities, each more outlandish than the last. He consoled himself with the thought that at least they hadn't shown any sign of wanting to hurt him. And they had fed him. That was a good sign, right?

Selaye motioned for Naylon to take a seat in an acceleration chair behind a console that had monitors and displays all over it. Selaye picked up the ends of the straps and pantomimed to Naylon how to secure himself in the chair. Naylon quickly picked up on what was going on. Selaye also made a motion across his throat, then pointed to the console arrays. Naylon knew exactly what that meant: don't touch.

Selaye strapped himself in next to Naylon then pressed several icons displayed on his console. Monitors showed fore and aft views of the surrounding area. Naylon realized what was happening. They'd been discovered by someone or someones. Or maybe it was the other way around. He couldn't tell just yet. Were these people the pirates after all? Maybe the pirates were after these people! It was impossible to discern. Maybe Darreth was wrong. Maybe the pirates were pursuing these guys and not Darreth after all! Whatever was going on it had the entire ship on alert. Naylon could do nothing but watch.

Selaye spoke to the captain over his comm. "Looks like a scout ship. It's six kilometers off port. Coming in rapidly."

The captain responded quickly. *"Wait until they pass us, then proceed south to the clearing we scanned earlier. Cloak is still activated?"*

"Aye," Selaye responded after glancing at one of his screens.

Naylon watched the vidscreen in front of him. Coming directly at them was a blip making a beeline toward them. It started to slow as it reached the edge of the short forest that surrounded their cloaked ship. By the time it was in visual range, cameras were on it, tracking. The display started showing lines of text now on both sides of the screen, along with the image. Naylon had no idea what the ship's designation was. Before it reached them though, it abruptly turned west and followed the course of the river, upstream. Moments later it was gone.

Selaye grinned at Naylon. "They didn't detect us."

Naylon shrugged his shoulders. He had no idea what the commander had told him, but he was quite smug about it. That much he could tell. He could also tell they were trying not to be found by that ship. But why? Wasn't their ship cloaked? Perhaps it was only cloaked to the visual spectrum.

Selaye tucked that shrug into his mind. Was it possible that this Naylon person was completely oblivious to the Telkan threat? The display clearly indicated it was one of their ships.

The captain spoke again. "*Commander. Move the ship. Bearing one zero six degrees.*"

Selaye spoke through the ship's comm this time. "*All hands. Prepare for departure.*" He touched a few of the icons on the console in front of him. Naylon looked on. He realized the ship was preparing to take off. To where? The thought nearly terrified him. Who knew how far they were taking him? More importantly, how would he get back here if he had no clear way to communicate with them?

Selaye spoke a couple of commands to the navigational computer and it started the take-off sequence. Seconds later they were airborne.

Naylon continued to watch the display in front of him. It was a forward view. As they ascended, he was able to get a much better lay of the land. He saw a swath cut through the low forest where the river's course traversed. He calmed some as he saw the bend of the river, which had brought him to the sandbar where he'd been found. At least he was able to recognize some landmark. Now they were headed downriver, roughly following its course. Within minutes, after traveling at an almost supersonic speed, they touched down, again near the river, next to a rock outcrop, hidden in the midst of towering greenery. *Fern-like trees*, Naylon thought. That would imply they were in some sort of temperate clime, perhaps even tropical. That wasn't possible. Tropical regions didn't exist on Rylerra, or so he thought. The mystery of where he was deepened.

After they touched down, Selaye un-strapped himself and motioned for Naylon to stay put. Naylon did so. Whatever had happened, it had been an emergency and now Selaye seemed to be checking something out. He was more than surprised to be left alone.

Selaye exited the nav cabin and went to see the doctor. "How's your patient?" he asked.

"He'll come around in a few minutes. I think it's time to ask Naylon some questions."

"Agreed. That's why I came back here. We're thirty-eight kilometers from the Telkan ship. Lazcún and Agrida are in position and have activated the sensor probe. We're receiving data. It indicates the ship's crisscrossing the area. I'm pretty sure they came across our approach ion trail and are scanning for us. Of course, we won't be there." A wide grin appeared on his face.

"Then it's safe to proceed?"

Selaye nodded.

"The hypo will cause them to appear as if they're in a coma for at least two hours."

"Interesting. Same as with the Telkans." Selaye raised his arm and called for Ocio. "Bring Naylon to the infirmary. He's strapped in at my nav station."

Tann, strapped to the med bed, had woken up ten minutes ago. At first, he wasn't sure if he was back on the shuttle or not, then realized that the voices he heard weren't Lingua. He had glanced around the room, then shut his eyes again. His quick glance told him he might be in a pirate ship's hospital cabin. A hospital cabin on a pirate ship? Were their ships big enough to have room for one? Maybe they were. He wished he knew more about the different types of ships the Consortium's starship division manufactured to determine that for sure. He wasn't entirely sure if pirates used Consortium-built ships. His brother might know what was going on here. His brother! Where was everyone?

Moments later Naylon was led into the hospital cabin. "Tann!" he cried out immediately.

Tann's heart ramped up to hypersonic speed in an instant. He quickly opened his eyes and looked in the direction of what he was sure was Naylon's voice. Selaye assessed the situation. Clearly, they knew each other.

Tann raised his head up. "Naylon, tell them to let me go!"

Selaye was clear about the interaction, too. These two were either collaborators or friends. He wasn't sure. But that point was moot. As soon as both of them received the Pelinex, the crew would be absolutely sure about how the two had arrived here and who they were.

Naylon quickly went to the med table, with Ocio right behind him. She grabbed his shoulder and attempted to pull him away from it. He angrily pulled himself from her grip. She raised her weapon and aimed it right at his face without a trace of emotion showing on hers. That wasn't good at all, Naylon quickly realized. He raised his hands into the air and emitted a nervous laugh. "Don't move, Tann." Tann didn't. In fact, he barely breathed now, terrified that Naylon was going to be shot any instant.

Ocio motioned for Naylon to take a seat on the table next to Tann. Tann felt especially vulnerable because he was still shirtless and unable to use his arms due to the straps.

Naylon was still only wearing his t-shirt, his now-dry trousers and his boots. The doctor casually took his upper arm and very calmly placed one end of a five-centimeter long metal cylinder against his tricep. An almost inaudible hiss emitted from the device. Naylon wasn't prepared for the sensation. At first, he felt exactly like when they were in the cavern and the intense vertigo had overcome him. The vertigo! Maybe that had something to do with what had happened to them. But the thought quickly faded, as did his consciousness. The doctor and Soldat Ocio took hold of Naylon as he slumped over, then laid him out on the adjoining table.

"What did you do to him? Let me go! Let me go!" Tann screamed as he struggled against the straps, getting red in the face while doing so.

The doctor took another one of the cylinders from a case in a cabinet, held it up against a scanner, and decided the dosage was appropriate. He took a few steps toward the still struggling Tann. Tann saw it coming. He tried to pull himself out of the straps with all of his might, making fists and grimacing as he exerted himself. The doctor touched Tann's upper arm with the device. Instantly, a wave of vertigo overcame him and he stopped struggling. His eyelids fluttered as his conscious slipped away.

"Assist me, please," he told Ocio. He then proceeded to un-strap Tann from the restraints and put his t-shirt back on.

"How are our 'patients'?" the captain asked Selaye when he returned to the main bridge.

"Sleeping it off." He looked at his wristcomp. "The doc said he would contact us when they're awake."

The captain looked up briefly from the display he was scanning and nodded.

Their interlopers would soon divulge who they were and what they knew about the Telkans. He had a nagging suspicion they were spies. If they were, it would be the first time he'd ever heard of a Terran helping Telkans in any way.

Chapter 20

Despite the oddity of the situation, Dr. Doratzo was certain he had done the right thing. The language RNA injection he'd just given the two Terran's had precedent, but not in his own experience. He had only injected Telkans for interrogation purposes. He had never met a single person who didn't speak at least some Empire Spanish or any of the other languages spoken in the Empire. Thus, the reason for the scans of his patients while they slept. Something just didn't add up about these two.

The RNA-encoding was extremely fast acting, so much so that the injection had a sedative in it. It kept the person from realizing the changes that were taking place. It was true no matter what type of RNA injection was being administered. It had long ago been recognized that encoded learning caused intense sensory disorientation. In this case, an entire language database was literally being inserted into the fabric of his two patients' brain cells. The changes were so intense that it was much easier for a patient to simply sleep it off while their language centers were being modified.

The doctor pulled the flat plane of the full body scanner from the arm on the ceiling and positioned it above Tann first. The youth looked familiar. In fact, he looked very much like his nephew who lived on the DeSoto peninsula back on Earth. The peninsula stretched many hundreds of kilometers south into the warm waters of the Arawak Sea. A nice place, if one liked heat, humidity, endless pine tree forests and flat sandy land.

As the doctor mused about the familiarity of the boy, he noted the scan read negative for any hidden nanotech weaponry. That was something he was only somewhat familiar with, but nonetheless made sure none had been placed subcutaneously. His scan completed, he switched off the device and logged the report.

Next, he switched on the scanner over Naylon. Naylon was taller and required two sweeps of the short scanner. It was during Naylon's upper body sweep that the resonance scan took the doctor completely by surprise. *What are those tendrils*, he wondered, shocked. *They're in his brain!* Had the man been taken over by some sort of metallic organism? If so, the doctor had never heard of such a thing before. His mind was racing now. He immediately changed the scanner's resolution. A closer examination revealed dozens of tiny strands of something snaking all over the communication and speech center in his brain. They trailed down Naylon's neck to his shoulder. As the doctor traced the fine lines he noted that they converged on a tiny flat device implanted underneath his right shoulder blade. This was no invasive organism. Only a surgical procedure could have done this. This was tech! Who was this Naylon? The doctor was completely taken aback at the implication. The only living being he'd ever seen with tech inside its brain was a Tasker. It was illegal to interfere with the higher functions of a Terran with Tasker tech. Doing so would result in the revocation of one's medical license, a jail sentence, and probably even the death penalty. Who in his right mind would dare to have done this to the man?! Was that the reason for him not speaking Empire Spanish? Perhaps this was a botched operation. If so, did he completely miss seeing the tendrils in the boy, he wondered, more mystified by the moment.

The doctor switched off the scanner and turned back to the still-sleeping Tann. He lowered the scanner again and adjusted it over the teen's head. He energized the panel, then turned up the resolution. He looked and looked, but found not a single tendril. *There must be a rogue doctor someplace who experimented on the older one*, he reasoned. That was the only explanation he could come up with.

"Commander," he spoke to his comm, "you better come in here. I've found something inside the one who calls himself Naylon that you must see. I believe it's a matter of utmost security."

"*Did you say inside him?*"

"You'll have to see it for yourself, but I think someone tried to turn the man into a Tasker."

Selaye was at his nav station. "*What?*"

"Just come here, please."

The commander was in the infirmary in seconds. "What's this about?" he demanded.

"Look for yourself." He adjusted the display so that the commander could see.

The doctor pointed to the tendrils and to the disc under Naylon's scapula. Selaye wasn't at all sure what he was looking at. "You'll have to explain it to me," he told the doctor.

"There's tech implanted inside this man. Only Taskers can legally have that kind of operation performed on them. He has a lot of explaining to do when he wakes up."

Selaye was quite aware it was illegal to implant a human with tech not associated with limbs or minor implants. Years of analysis had provided enough evidence to conclude that the same technology used to keep Taskers docile could also be used inside a Terran. That's why even a simple cochlear or retinal implant required a lengthy legal process and a detailed medical follow-up.

Selaye shook his head. "I'll have to tell the Captain."

"By all means!" the doctor agreed.

"But not now. The Telkan scout ship is still scanning the area we left. He's keeping track of the sensor data to make sure they don't come this way. If they land, Urret and Agrida will get them. I hope you have plenty of Pelinex left for survivors."

"Plenty. And there better be survivors, commander," he said more calmly, cracking a slight smile. He had no trouble dealing with Telkans.

"If there are survivors, at least one will be returned to you. Of that you can be sure," Selaye told him with mock gravity.

Naylon woke up feeling oddly refreshed. He felt like he had been sleeping for days. He noted the chronometer on the wall opposite him. Only a few hours had passed. Or was it twelve hours plus? He wasn't sure.

The doctor was turned away from him, facing Tann. Naylon opened his mouth to speak. Something odd came out. Something he didn't say, but rather did say anyway. The sensation was impossible to explain. It was as if someone else had spoken his words. "Where am I?" he had said, now puzzled at what he thought he heard himself say.

The doctor turned around and observed his patient.

"Just a moment, please. Your companion is finally coming around."

"So, you do speak Lingua," Naylon replied accusingly.

The doctor grinned.

Naylon shook his head. It seemed as though he were observing his thoughts from some distant location. He looked over at Tann, then scanned as much of the small room as he could. There were only two beds. He was on one and Tann on the other. Drawers and cabinets were labeled as in any hospital room. Medical devices and instruments were obvious behind a clear panel to his left. But it was the labeling that grabbed Naylon's attention. He read one to himself. The word he pronounced in his head had a familiar, yet unfamiliar ring to it. But the spelling! He was sure he'd never seen the word before, but at the same time he knew exactly what it said. His curiosity about the situation was cut short as Tann groaned, sat up, then swung his legs over the side of the table.

"Let me go right this minute," Tann immediately demanded. His eyes grew wide as he realized the same thing as did Naylon. He wasn't speaking his native language anymore.

The doctor stood back so he could observe the two of them. "As you heard, you speak Empire Spanish now."

"What's 'Empire Spanish'?" Naylon asked.

The doctor grunted. *What kind of statement is that? If Naylon thinks that's going to curtail an interrogation, he has another thing coming,* he thought.

Selaye sat across from Naylon and Tann in the mess hall once again. Tann was wolfing down the same meal Naylon had eaten earlier. Two of the soldats stood at the doorway with weapons drawn, observing their every move.

"I'll ask you again. What are you doing with tech inside your head?" Selaye asked.

"I already told you. Any adult can have a CU-900. It's a standard one, in fact. It doesn't even have all the extended features."

Selaye looked at Tann. "And you? Why don't you have one?"

"I'm not old enough," Tann replied between bites. He was ravenous.

The commander looked back at Naylon. "Who installed this device?"

"I don't recall the exact name of the woman," he said in exasperation, "but it was at the comm clinic on Addison Street in Tokaias."

"Tokaias," Selaye repeated flatly, wondering what kind of game the man was trying to play.

"Yeah, Tokaias. On Andakar?" he replied sarcastically. He could play the man's ridiculous game, too. "Surely you know Andakar. After all, you guys regularly steal pharmas from our ships."

Selaye was sure that statement was a ruse. He declined playing Naylon's hand.

"Andakar," Selaye said. "Where is this Andakar?"

Naylon leaned back as much as he could on the backless bench and crossed his arms. "Where is Andakar. Let's see. It's just down the road a little way. You know, the nearby water-covered planet?" It was still quite odd speaking this strange language he had no recollection of learning.

Selaye laughed heartily. "Good try. But your lie will do you no good."

"He's not lying," Tann insisted.

"I didn't ask you," Selaye shot back. "Yet."

"Well, I'm telling you. I was born on Andakar."

Selaye let the statement go. He could have made some comment about insolence, but decided against it. It could be far better to let the kid stay angry. Anger, Selaye knew, had a way of making people blurt out all sorts of things they might otherwise hide.

"Where were you born, Naylon?" Selaye asked, in the friendliest tone he could muster.

"I emigrated from Earth a long time ago."

"Earth. From where exactly?"

"New Zealand."

Selaye had never heard of that country. He energized the vidPAD he had in front of him. He spoke to it and the screen displayed a Mercator projection of the earth on it. He said the name twice. Each time it beeped. "Point to the place."

"It's irrelevant. I'm a Citizen of Andakar. What does that have to do with anything anyway? If you're holding us for ransom I want to know what your demands are," Naylon said boldly.

Selaye slid the vidPAD closer to Naylon. Naylon looked into Selaye's eyes briefly and, realizing he wasn't going to get an answer from the commander, touched New Zealand on the screen. The two islands instantly filled the display.

"Maoriland," Selaye said.

"They died out centuries ago."

"What did you call it again?"

"It's got only one name I'm aware of. New Zealand," he said pronouncing each word separately and with emphasis, as if explaining something that should have been painfully obvious.

"New Zealand. Where's the old Zealand?"

"I have no idea. Why do you care anyway? I demand to know what you're going to do with us."

"I know," Tann said suddenly. He pulled the vidPAD closer to himself.

"Know what?" Naylon asked.

"Where the old Zealand is."

"How could you possibly know that?"

"Earth history class. Someone did a report on it. I remember it because it was funny that there was a new and an old Zealand on opposite sides of the planet."

"Okay, where is it?" Naylon asked him.

"It's an island in the European Confederation."

Selaye studied Tann's face. "What European Confederation?"

"On Earth," Tann said. He realized he could move the map around by simply using his fingers pressed against the screen. He slid the image over until Europe was centered. He looked all around, but most of the country boundaries were wrong. He used two fingers to zoom in, then slid the map all over, looking for anything labeled Zealand. He was sure it was south of Scandia. At least he thought it was. But only a couple of the borders were where he thought he remembered them. The look on his face grew from concerned to alarmed. The map was all wrong!

Naylon looked at the two of them going back and forth about what he considered a non-issue. "Look, we're a long way from there. It doesn't make any difference. What in thunder do you want with us?"

Selaye stood. "Where is your ship?"

"It was shot down. You should know. After all, *you* shot it down!"

Selaye dismissed Naylon's assertion. "What's its designation? When did you arrive here?"

"It's an Andakar Space Navy shuttle. They make runs to the Nona Ice Station all the time. I'm sure you know all about that."

"Nona Ice Station," Selaye repeated solemnly.

"What are your demands?" Naylon stated again, now tired of what he perceived to be the man's pretended ignorance.

"Demands? That you answer my questions," the commander shot back with a hard look.

Tann was still poring over the map. Something was very peculiar about all of this. First, he couldn't find his brother. Then the cavern seemed to have been completely deserted when he returned. Where their disabled shuttle had been in a dry riverbed, there was a running river instead, and no shuttle. Now he was speaking a language he couldn't possibly know! To top it off, the map of the Earth he was sure he knew with some familiarity was totally wrong. Country borders and most of the names were different except for some on the African continent and some in Asia. He looked around the room now, scanning everything. Definitions to unknown words appeared in his consciousness when he read a label or the various screens on the walls. Something had happened to them. Something very strange. And Naylon was so busy trying to get the commander to answer him he wasn't aware of all the clues.

"We've got a dilemma here, Naylon. You show up on Déstica, yet say you don't have a ship…"

In frustration, Naylon nearly shouted. "Déstica?" He had never heard that name used for Rylerra before. "You shot our ship down!"

"Our scans showed nothing but a Telkan ship here."

Naylon shook his head. "Telkan ship?"

Selaye chuckled. A Terran who's not heard the word Telkan before? Naylon was playing his part quite entertainingly, if not all that well. He had to commend the man's performance though, because he sounded quite convincing. "Come now, Mr. Naylon," he said, shaking his head and mocking Naylon with his tone.

"It's Doctor Ress to you."

"Oh, medical doctor?" Selaye asked, sure it was a lie.

"I have a Ph.D."

"In what?"

"Paleo-microbiology." He was surprised to know even that word in this new language.

"You come to this planet and claim to be a microbiologist?"

"Paleo. Look, we're not carrying pharmas. Check the shuttle. That's all the proof you need."

"Naylon," Tann interjected. He knew the shuttle wasn't there and needed to tell Naylon. But there was far more he needed to say.

"What?"

"They're not the pirates."

"Like hell."

Selaye was sure Tann was goading him. "Pirates! What kind of notion is that? We're a legitimate fighting force." Yet, Selaye realized that whoever these two were, they seemed to be at a loss as to what was going on. Both of them were working from different angles on their supposed 'confusion' over their situation.

"They're not the pirates," Tann insisted. "Look." He slid the vidPAD toward Naylon. "This is not a map of Earth."

"Of course it is."

"Not the Earth you're from."

Tann was insistent, which made Naylon stop dismissing him. "What do you mean?"

"Look at those countries. Which ones are you familiar with?" he prompted.

Naylon scanned the Asian continent. He recognized the Chinese border and the Mongolian Republic, but none of the other nearby countries were recognizable. Tann placed a finger on the image and slid the graphic to North America. The continent look like it had been split up into odd-shaped quadrants. There was a smaller country along the southeast coast that didn't belong there. That was not the North America he was familiar with.

"Does any of that look familiar?" Tann asked.

Naylon's head swam as he searched his memory. It had been a long time since he'd even looked at a map of Earth. But this map was decidedly not familiar. Something was very wrong with everything. And it seemed to have begun when they found the aliens in the cavern.

Chapter 21

The quarters both Naylon and Tann had been led to was the only unoccupied one on the ship. It was at the end of the corridor away from where the rest of the soldats were quartered. In the room were two bunks, two small closets, a small open area with two chairs to sit in, a sink, and a separate shower and toilet closet. There was a panel built into the bulkhead, which served as the communications center, but the screen was dark. The two guards who had been standing watch over them in the mess hall were currently outside the door, keeping guard on them.

"When you were talking with that commander guy I remembered something," Tann told Naylon.

"Remembered what?"

"I couldn't find the shuttle."

"What do you mean?"

Tann whispered as fast as he could. "After you fell into the water I ran back to get Darreth. When I got back there was nothing there. Everything was gone. Darreth wasn't there, Merek was missing and the shuttle wasn't there either. Everything was just… gone. I couldn't get them so I had to go back by myself to try and find you. The last thing I remember was seeing that woman soldier. I think she shot me or something. What do you think is going on?"

"I don't know, but it's as if we're not on Rylerra," Naylon told him.

"That makes sense. I've not seen any ice anywhere. But when did we get transported off-planet?"

Naylon shook his head. "I'm just about positive now that those dead aliens had something to do with it."

Tann opened his backpack. Both packs had been thoroughly searched, then given back. At this point, they were merely being held against their will, due to the captain not understanding where they had come from. All of their effects were still in the packs. Tann pulled out the disc-shaped object he'd taken from the cave. "Think this has something to do with it? Maybe it's some sort of transportation device." He held it up to the light and watched as the surface seemed to ripple as if it were a liquid. "It's not hot or glowing. At least I don't think it's glowing. And it doesn't appear to have any sort of energy source or even any buttons."

Naylon took it and felt along its smooth surface as carefully as he could. He found no hidden grooves or pits that might be controls. "I don't feel any biometric pads, but who knows how this thing works. After all, it's alien." He placed the device on top of Tann's pack.

"Speaking of aliens, what about those aliens they have on board? What did they call them? Taskers?" Tann asked.

"There are no aliens. They're just aren't any. But I've counted three of those creatures on this ship; and everyone seems to be hiding from some entirely different ones. It's almost as if we're in some sort of alternate reality or something. Hell, I know I don't speak Empire Spanish! I've never even heard this language spoken before. How the hell can we both be speaking it?" Naylon sputtered in frustration.

"They somehow made us learn it," Tann realized.

Naylon snapped his fingers. "The injection. I bet it was RNA."

"You mean genetic RNA?" asked Tann.

Naylon nodded. "Did you ever learn or hear about that war that happened hundreds of years ago? On Earth. Some military general named Mala...Maladito. No, Malán Zas. He used cloning, then RNA injections to create a whole army of soldiers to do his bidding. After that, cloning tech, RNA encoding, and all genetic alterations were banned from being used or developed."

"I remember a vid about it. I don't know any of the details," Tann told him. "I'm pretty sure I fell asleep watching it."

"Well, those guys have RNA technology. They're using it. And they've somehow perfected it. They've used some sort of RNA injection to teach us their 'Empire Spanish'."

Tann threw up his hands. "But why?"

Naylon shrugged and shook his head. "Okay, let's try to put this together. We know these guys can't be the pirates. They have technology that's far superior to ours *and* they have technology that was banned centuries ago."

"That's not much to go on."

"And," Naylon continued, "as you pointed out, they don't have the right map of Earth. So, they're either not from Earth or don't have a clue to what our Earth is really like."

"That was definitely a *map* of Earth. At least the continents look the same. It's just that the country boundaries were mostly wrong," Tann offered.

Naylon nodded in agreement. "Which means we have to ask them a bunch more questions to figure out what's going on here."

Tann picked up the disc-shaped device. "This thing *has* to be a clue." He was sure of it.

Naylon brought his thumb to his mouth and bit the nail. "Think, Naylon. Think," he mumbled to himself.

"The cave," Tann blurted out.

"With aliens," Naylon returned.

"Another glaring clue which totally eludes me right now," Tann said. "That cylindrical opening we went through. It couldn't have been natural. You said so yourself. You already figured out that the corridor that led us to the dead aliens must have been manmade or alien made. That much is true, right?"

Naylon nodded then took the disc from Tann. "You had one and I had one of these when we went through that opening. This thing *has* to be some sort of transportation device. Hey, wait a minute. Remember when we shone the light through the tunnel? Some sort of weird interference made the light scatter."

Naylon handed the disc to Tann. "Yeah," Tann agreed eagerly. "Like a screen or barrier was in the way," Tann said as he eyed the device. "Hey! I went through it once without this thing on me and nothing happened. When both of us went through it we were carrying one apiece and *that's* when we felt that weird sensation." Tann carefully placed the object on the desk next to the bunk. "I'm not touching it again. Look what happened to us! It's like we're in the past or the future or something."

"No. It's weirder than that," Naylon continued, thinking hard. "Whoever carved out that perfectly smooth tunnel knew they had to use the thing to get through it. Right?"

"How do you know?"

"Well, we're here, aren't we? It's someplace other than the Rylerra we're familiar with. When we had that device on our person we crossed over to here. Without it, we didn't. I think you're *right*."

"About what?"

"I don't think we're in our *universe* anymore."

Tann's whole face reflected what Naylon felt: complete shock mixed with terror.

Chapter 22

"Olton Avela, Nona Ice Station Rescue," the large man said to Darreth as he offered his outstretched hand.

Darreth shook it. "Lieutenant Commander James-Po," Darreth said in return.

Merek was standing next to Darreth and also shook the man's hand. They both had just watched the small ship land not far from the mouth of the cave.

Darreth was supremely worried. It had been a full day and he had found not a trace of Naylon or his brother. He and Merek had scoured the cavern multiple times looking for anything which might provide any clue to explain their disappearance. They had come up empty. They had deliberately not touched the alien bodies, but had disturbed nearly every square centimeter of the dirt floor in their search. There were footprints everywhere. Naylon and Tann's footprints had been completely obliterated. It was the most disconcerting situation Darreth had ever been confronted with. By now, they were entirely used to viewing the aliens, but it didn't provide any comfort to the fact that two of his party had simply disappeared.

Darreth was suspicious that the mysteriously smooth cylindrical tunnel, for lack of a better description for the cutout, had something to do with it, but couldn't prove it. He had aimed his communications PAD at the device and tuned for every frequency it was capable of receiving, but his effort was futile. The cylindrical area, seemingly cut from the solid rock, emitted no electromagnetic radiation he could detect. There were no wires, antennas, switches, biometrics or anything along the surface of the large stone slab it had been cut from to indicate it was made by human or other hands. In other words, it appeared to be solid rock. All except for the mysterious translucent barrier, like a highly localized atmospheric distortion, in the dead center of the tunnel.

"Where are the other two?" Olton asked. The other three men from his rescue team stood at the ready behind him.

"They've, uh, disappeared," Darreth said. "But there's more. We've, uh, discovered aliens in the cave."

Olton wasn't sure he heard Darreth right. "What?"

"Dead ones."

Protocol was such that incoming ships that didn't touch down when and where they should caused Olton's team to go on alert. The mysterious disappearance of the *Siaron Viper* shortly after the nav sat went offline had given Olton's manager, Yason Birovich, just enough pause to put Olton's group on standby alert. Their orders could change in a minute. He had been made aware that the pilot of this particular missing shuttle was a provincial manager's son. Despite being a good pilot, the son of a provincial manager was considered important enough to keep tabs on. Weather was frequently unpredictable on Rylerra despite the latest weather sensor technology. Thus, Yason made it absolutely clear to Olton that he was to find the passengers or the wreckage ASAP. Olton and his team had earned their pay.

Darreth and Merek were assigned temporary quarters at the ice station, then briefed the rescue team about the details of what happened to them. As far as they knew, pirates had pursued them, fired on them, taken out the orbiting sat, and forced them to make their hasty landing.

Yason was quite concerned about the loss of the sat. There were dozens of ships and FTL comm buoys constantly making runs between Rylerra and Andakar. Commerce had been disrupted but wouldn't entirely cease. Nonetheless, its loss was bad for business and bad for the one hundred twenty-six thousand inhabitants of the eight domed cities and un-domed outposts on Rylerra, including their station. It would take at least two months to replace the damn thing.

Yason's big concern now was that their lives would be intruded on by Space Navy vessels, as well as personnel from Andakar, a lot more frequently. They might even demand a permanent berth. He didn't like that idea at all. Rylerra wasn't theirs. The two planets were merely trading partners. Granted, they were relatively close as Inhabs went, but it didn't mean his authority should be bypassed. He would personally speak with Rish Illigan, their Planetary Director, about it later. He figured Rish would be angrier than he. He was counting his blessings that his planet had only raw materials, a few precious mineral resources, and refined ores, which no one would consider worth stealing. After all, the majority of it was bulky, heavy and not much more than a commodity. The logistics of stealing them would be beyond what he could imagine anyway. If Rylerra had to have their own Space Navy even half the size of Andakar's, they'd all be bankrupt within a year. The very thought of having to maintain a military made Yason sick.

The mysterious part of this whole episode was the missing persons. They weren't considered dead and they hadn't been obviously killed. They weren't even injured as far as he knew. They had somehow vanished. But what made this report impossible to believe was the description and brief vid of dead aliens in a cavern. He was well aware aliens didn't exist.

Yet they did. He saw the vid himself.

Zelin Raxi was his next call. Zelin needed to be kept in the loop on anything that might affect mining operations.

"They're alive?" Zelin tried his best to not sound disappointed. After all, Inandra was not going to like this one bit, he thought with some trepidation. He had experienced her temper more than once.

"We have the pilot and one of the passengers," Yason reported. "Two of his party have gone missing. But there's more than just that. I have vid of three dead aliens in the cavern where they took shelter."

Zelin issued a short laugh.

"Look for yourself," Yason countered. "He sent the vid along his communication line.

"Impossible. There-there's no such thing as aliens," Zelin stammered as he watched. Not only was his little operation a failure, but aliens?

"Apparently, we've been wrong."

The news had already circled both globes before Darreth and Merek had returned to Andakar four days later. Their return didn't ease Darreth's mind at all. He was wracked with guilt about not having even a clue about what had happened to his boyfriend. Plus, how could he explain his failure to protect his little brother to his parents?

Rescue team personnel cordoned off the cavern to keep anyone on Rylerra from 'just happening by'. A thorough survey of the cavern by investigative personnel might reveal some new clues to the mysterious origin of the dead aliens, which, it was speculated, were hundreds, if not thousands of years old. Not a sign of Naylon or Tann was found. No one had a clue what to do next.

Darreth and Merek's return was greeted with a curious mixture of amazement, relief and suspicion. Clearly, the vids showed that aliens existed. As far as everyone on both planets was concerned, they had discovered what everyone since before the advent of space travel said didn't exist. Rumors had somehow started that Darreth had made his two companions disappear. Speculation was rampant about why he might want to off his brother and partner. First, it was suggested an accident was being covered up. Then this 'accident' was because Darreth had let his partner handle the ship and that was why it had crashed, killing an unknown number of innocent bystanders. Many conveniently forgot his report of an unknown assailant pursuing them to the surface of Rylerra. Maybe, the speculation ran, they mentioned this supposed "discovery of aliens" to shift the attention away from the real cause. An unnamed junior officer was even quoted as saying he had seen Lieutenant Commander Darreth James-Po drinking during patrols.

Unfortunately, Darreth heard all of it. Until this incident, not more than a handful of people even knew he and Naylon existed. Now he was practically the talk of the entire planet. And nearly everything he heard was a fabrication.

Squadron Master Yoon Wakanabe, who was both Darreth's and Rehl's immediate superior wasn't all that happy with the speculations either. But he had to take action for the sake of the Navy's reputation. He grounded Darreth.

"Sir, I had nothing to do with their disappearance," he argued. "Why are we letting rumors dictate military policy?" Darreth asked.

"Rumors are not part of this issue," Wakanabe responded. "It's politics, plain and simple. If I let you continue to pilot patrols, the repercussions will be far wider than just missing people."

"Sir, I did not murder my own brother!"

"No one said you murdered anyone."

"No one?" He nearly spit out the words. "How about this article." Darreth handed the commander a news flimsy with the article's title in bold letters.

The Squadron Master briefly scanned the heading. "No one at this command says or believes anything of the kind. Those are baseless and false accusations. There's no evidence of foul play. Naylon's assistant, Mr., uh, Soliciellio corroborated your story."

"Then you can't reasonably ground me."

"I have to reasonably ground you for the sake of appearances," he tried to explain patiently, even though he backed Darreth completely. "In fact, you're not to leave Andakar for any reason until the investigation into this matter is concluded."

"Which will be when?"

"Four weeks."

"Four weeks!" he raged. "I'm supposed to sit here when I could be helping find Naylon and my brother!" Darreth said bitterly.

"That's an order Lieutenant Commander."

"What about the ship that shot us down?" Darreth demanded.

"An investigation is being held on Rylerra. Don't expect anything to come of it any time soon though. I'm getting some very peculiar resistance," Yoon said with an edge to his voice.

Darreth was just about to say something about that.

Yoon held up his hand. "Don't agit. We'll get to the bottom of this."

"Disobedience of a lawful Consortium order, failure to adhere to Space Navy protocols, unauthorized passage into Rylerra's atmosphere without official entry authorization, and dereliction of duty. There are several other charges as well," Darreth's father continued, running his eyes down the list as the two of them sat comfortably in his study.

Darreth rose from his chair. "Who could possibly have produced these trumped up charges!" he said in exasperation. He began pacing, his anger near the boiling point.

"I'll give you three guesses."

Darreth shook his head. He had no idea.

"Alarr," Siloy said flatly.

"She's in no position to charge me with anything!"

"Quiet down. She's merely bringing to everyone's attention how she sees things."

"She's blind then. My brother disappeared. She honestly believes I deliberately lost my own brother!"

"I'm sure that's not what she means. But she's sent this communication to your commander. I suspect you'll hear about it later today."

"Maybe I should send my own communication to her. Better yet, have her clear her schedule today so I can have a nice tête-à-tête with her," Darreth said acidly.

Siloy eased back in his chair. "Son, don't give her anything else to put on this list."

Darreth had no real intention of talking with her. He already didn't like the woman, now she gave him more reasons to dislike her. But his main concerns remained unanswered. What had happened to Tann and Naylon?

Chapter 23

Darreth entered the hearing room and stood at attention. Behind a long curved table against the left wall sat Darreth's immediate superior Squadron Master Wakanabe, his adjutant Sefana Veoc, and a staff lawyer from the planetary director's office. Ahead of him, behind a raised bench, was a judge who had been brought up from the surface. He was from the main Space Navy office in Tokaias. To Darreth's right was a long desk, behind which was a Space Navy secretary.

On the wall behind the judge was the seal of the Andakar Space Navy. Its gleaming gold and blue were prominently lit from behind. The room was carpeted and extremely quiet. Darreth was surprised Director Alarr herself wasn't present. But he knew she was either watching live or would watch the salient points after the hearing had been edited later for her consumption.

"This hearing will come to order," the Space Navy secretary said to everyone present. "Please be seated."

The judge made a brief statement that this would not be an informal hearing but rather a formal establishment of charges. He would be determining the merits of the arguments and make his judgment immediately. Darreth had been led to believe this would be strictly an informal fact-finding hearing. He was greatly concerned now that this was going to be a formal hearing instead. It seemed they were cutting straight to the political chase, as it were.

Darreth sat with as much military bearing as he could on the slightly raised chair. It was hard and uncomfortable. Most likely on purpose, he figured.

Yoon's adjutant Sefana was Darreth's defender in this case. He had met with her briefly before the hearing and had been assured that the procedure was standard, would take forty-five minutes at most and was simply to establish a permanent recording of the charges being brought against him. But the rules had obviously changed. The judge had already said so. Darreth was still fuming about the charges that had been levied against him and had decided it was a political ploy of some kind. In the days preceding this hearing, he had done some research of his own and had come to the not-so-surprising conclusion that he had broken no real laws. No, this hearing was for something other than to charge him with trumped up 'crimes'. As to what that purpose was, he hadn't figured out so far. Nonetheless, the feel of politics hung heavily in the air.

The planetary director's staff lawyer was a small man to Sefana's left. A nameplate on the desktop identified him as Orin Atimlet. Immediately, Orin stood and pulled down the hem of his crisp gray tunic shirt. It was embroidered with dark piping to indicate his office. It seemed to Darreth that the man was not just a corporate lawyer but was going to try to be his judge as well.

"You've been advised of the charges against you?" Orin asked Darreth.

"Yes."

"You are aware that these charges are per corporate and planetary law?"

"Yes." Darreth told him, only to be on record although he didn't believe it.

"What do you have to say in your defense?"

"I have already submitted my defense. I have nothing else to add." Darreth was not required to answer directly to the charges. His defender, Sefana Veoc was going to do the speaking for him. In fact, he was beginning to find this formal tribunal humorous. It was simply for show and had little to do with whether he was 'guilty' or 'innocent' of the charges. Orin sat down.

Sefana stood next. "I motion that all charges be dropped as submitted in our written copy."

Orin had also already read their submission. He answered simply. "Denied."

Sefana calmly expected that response. She continued. "Lieutenant Commander Darreth James-Po was acting in accordance to page 85, section 7d of the Uniform Pilot Code. Section 7d is quite specific with regard to the safety of passengers and crew of an interplanetary shuttle. I will submit said passage for the record." With that, she pressed an icon on the flimsy she was reading from. The passage was immediately transmitted to the flimsy Orin was holding.

Orin read the passage's mere two sentences, then added his comments. "This statute covers Space Navy personnel only. It does not in any way cover the transport of Citizens."

Sefana countered. "We submit that the safety of any crew or passengers in a Space Navy vessel takes precedence over and overrides any other law or statute that may otherwise neglect the safety or the lives of any Citizen or pre-Citizen."

Orin knew that he was on thin ice going into this hearing. He had logged four hearings regarding Space Navy issues in the past. He had lost three of them due to superior arguments from the adjutant's office and the weakness of the charges. In fact, he was quite surprised he would have to even attempt to defend the law over the protection of Citizens who had been clearly in danger. In his own personal opinion, the Lieutenant Commander deserved a medal, a commendation, and an award for his outstanding handling of the bizarre circumstances he had found himself in. Regardless, he had had no choice in this matter. Director Alarr had been very clear. It wasn't his place to question her authority. He was merely a corporate staff lawyer assigned to this Inhab. With all due respect to Director Alarr, he would have rather stayed in bed, saving himself from this farce of a 'hearing'.

Darreth watched in amusement. It was less than five minutes into the hearing and Darreth could already tell that Orin was way over his head. Clearly, this was nothing more than an attempt to either humiliate him or at the very least, embarrass him. It wasn't working. Darreth tried his best to suppress a very satisfied grin.

Four minutes later Orin ended his argument.

Darreth was instructed to remain seated as the principals left the room. Sefana and Orin went through one door and Darreth's superior officer and the judge went through another. The room was completely silent except for an occasional beep from the flimsy the court secretary was reading as she scrolled through it. Darreth amused himself by taking apart one of the nav consoles in his head. It was an interesting exercise in that he had to slow down quite considerably as he visualized what he was doing. It was modular and had to be disassembled in a particular order. It was a simple diversion that served its purpose. He had removed three of the components when, not more than five minutes later, the side door slid open. Sefana and Orin took their seats. Moments later Yoon came in and seated himself.

The judge took another minute before he returned. He read through the flimsy he was holding and pressed several icons on it before he spoke. "It is officially judged that all charges are dropped," he announced.

It was as simple as that. His direct declaration of acquittal was all Darreth needed to hear. But there was more.

"It is also officially judged that Lieutenant Commander James-Po is on probation and will stay grounded until an official recommendation can be made as to his fitness to command a ship."

Definitely political, Darreth thought. *And petty.* The question he harbored now was who was this political statement aimed at? Himself? His father? *Most likely Dad*, Darreth realized. *But why?*

It suddenly occurred to him that maybe, just maybe, the subtle talk about independence had a far larger audience than he was aware of.

The judge tapped on a tiny silver bell with a small gavel and let the gavel drop to the tabletop with a decided thump.

Chapter 24

Authorization to remove the alien bodies from the cavern took place the day Darreth and Merek had returned to Andakar. Olton Avela assigned three of his best men to set up lighting inside the large interior cavern, and to provide stasis chambers to put the bodies into. Plenty of equipment to perform live rescues existed on Rylerra. After all, two to three men and women a month had to be removed from cave-ins, ice crevasses, or from storm-covered outposts. The hazards of living on this Inhab were continuous, numerous, and would only get worse. The loss of Rylerra's planetary magnetic field wasn't new information. Rylerra's nickel-iron core was cooling faster than normal for a planet of its composition. That had been known for decades. The complete loss of the planet's magnetic field wouldn't happen for centuries. Only then would the entire surface become downright deadly. In the meantime, Olton foresaw a long and lucrative career in this industry, that is, if he himself weren't killed in some accident or frozen solid in an ice storm.

The bodies of the dead aliens had been carefully removed from the cavern and sent to the same facility Darreth and Merek had been processed through in the Ready Response Department. They had several large domes and plenty of ready cold storage. The stasis chambers had transparent tops, which provided the local news access to take plenty of vid and still photos. Those vids and stills were being sent to the entire human population. Within two months, the news would have been received on every Inhab. It would have been impossible to keep something like this a secret.

There were no archeologists or anthropologists on Rylerra. There were none on Andakar either. With no previous civilizations ever having been discovered on any of the Inhabs, someone with the appropriate background who would be willing to trek to Rylerra was going to be difficult to find, at least in the short run.

Olton stood on a gangway above the throng of news people in the building that housed the aliens. He was particularly curious because the aliens had been killed. The pathologist at the clinic had established that even before a basic forensics examination. But who had shot them? And why had evidence of whoever had done it never been discovered on the planet? Was it possible that glaciers had completely obliterated all trace of a previous Rylerran civilization? The area where they were found had been ice-free for at least fifteen hundred years, so they thought. Olton speculated the bodies had to be at least that old. That would predate the colonization of Rylerra by nearly a millennium and a half. Ultimately, someone would figure it out.

The detailed result of the forensics scans took another day. They debated the results for hours. It wasn't a matter of how to interpret the results, but rather how to explain what they conclusively discovered. The forensics experts determined their morphology didn't resemble any of the body type patterns found on Rylerra. Indeed, no sign of any sentient creatures had ever been found on the planet. Their conclusion was that the bodies had to have originated off-world. Speculation as to what world could possibly have produced the creatures abounded.

Luckily, Olton's office was in close proximity to where the bodies were being studied. As a result of the pathologists being so close by, he managed to have several discussions with them about their conclusions. It wasn't difficult to cull from them what they had discovered. Apparently, they had decided that the aliens could only have originated from somewhere beyond the Tovar Nebula. An astro-cartographer had even come up with a theory that they had come from one of the stars that lit up the nebula. But what was potentially more challenging was trying to determine who had killed them since no weapons had been found. They certainly didn't shoot each other. One of the aliens had an object lodged behind a rib bone. It was a fragment made of a simple titanium-lead alloy. It was quickly determined that the object was a projectile from some sort of weapon. No other projectiles had been found in the cavern or in the other bodies. Olton was enough of an armaments buff to know that projectile weapons hadn't been made for hundreds of years. In addition, humans had only occupied this part of space for not even one hundred years. Thus, he reasonably concluded that no humans had caused their death. Ultimately, he had to speculate that the dead creatures were the ones who had made the projectile weapons. It was a curious and delicious mystery.

The oddest conclusion made by the pathologists was their time of death, more accurately, the century of death. They had determined that the aliens had been dead for more than two thousand years. The unique nature of the cavern's constant climate, until very recently, when a crack had appeared in the wall, had preserved the bodies in a near perfect state of mummification. Enough desiccated tissues were available to determine that.

It was a stunning discovery, to say the least. After all, if aliens had been sitting dead in that cavern for over two thousand years, why had not even a *trace* of their civilization ever shown up on the planet or anywhere in the general vicinity of the Kaskalon-Eratil star system. Surely, Andakar, with its much more accessible climate would have been the perfect place for their race to have colonized. Olton wasn't sure what to conclude about that. It was just an amusing speculation for him.

Olton managed to obtain a report that had him even more mystified. It had to do with the odd block of stone that was in the center of the cavern. The perfectly smooth cylindrical tunnel in it was giving everyone a headache. An academic headache, that is. It defied attempts to discern how it had been made. The entire block refused to show up on scans as to its chemical composition. All attempts to determine if a power source was causing the strange static that appeared halfway through the cutout, failed. Vid, holos and photos of the static showed only an opaque blur. It was impossible to photronically record a proper image of the odd static. The mystery was deepening. But Olton knew that mysteries had a way of being explained.

The energy sources that fed Tokaias, as well as all of the municipalities in the rest of the provinces, were many and varied. The Andakar GeoWorks Energy Division had employed Caddo Nebbi for over eight years. Caddo's specific job there was to oversee a team of technicians. They made sure the software that ran the sensor photronics for the pipes sunk into Andakar's crust to access hot spots worked as efficiently as possible. The continental crust underneath the Kattan continent was particularly thin 18 kilometers south of Tokaias. Finding hot spots was mostly a matter of drilling a hole deep enough, inserting the pipeline, cracking the nearby rocks, flooding the cracks with water, then drawing off the steam for power generation. Many Inhabs used this method of inexpensive energy generation. Caddo was one of the day shift supervisors. He normally didn't bother to follow what the Planetary Director's office did. But for the last several years he had been noticing that high-level Consortium rulings were intruding more and more into what should be purely local affairs. By the time the new energy generation tax was announced, he had sufficient access to his division's databases to determine that a significant amount of money was being siphoned off world from his company. He was a software designer by training and a supervisor now. It wasn't his place to decide how the funds were to be used. Regardless, it irritated him. It was just in his nature to be irritated by seemingly arbitrary corporate rulings. Thus, his discovery of the discussion group on Tokaias University's campus. It gave him a forum to discuss topics he felt needed airing. The mainstream media wasn't going to contradict anything a corporation said. After all, they were the mouthpieces of corporations. That much was a given. But he could at least vent with like-minded people.

He had no idea he was about to get past the seemingly impenetrable shield that was Inandra's office. Her private network codes were supposed to be unbreakable. Even the attempt to crack them would have landed him in front of the GeoWorks Division head if he'd been caught. But someone had left a gap in her security system. One that Caddo knew how to exploit.

Caddo presented his findings to the discussion group the same night the news was broken about the aliens on Rylerra. He felt comfortable enough divulging such a clandestine effort due to the sentiments the group members all held. The Planetary Director's office had been the subject of much discussion over the last several months. And he was not alone in his disdain for Director Alarr.

The timing couldn't have been worse. What Caddo had discovered rivaled, if not superseded, the announcement of what had been discovered about the alien bodies.

During their meeting at the university, Julun activated the holoscreen on the wall. "Shh," she told the group. "Here's the announcement."

The reporter was wearing a parka, mostly for effect. It wasn't all that cold today at the Ice Station. Plus, she was inside the huge storage facility, which was only just below shirtsleeve temperature anyway. In the background were several vehicles coming and going inside the building behind where the bodies were being housed.

"Shani Kuhenvik reporting from the Nona Ice Station Search and Rescue headquarters fifteen kilometers from the Rylerran corporate capital. The alien bodies discovered here have been studied and analyzed in great detail for the last week. Evidence shows they're approximately two thousand years old and don't appear to have originated on Rylerra. Since there has never been any evidence to suggest an ancient civilization existed on either Rylerra or Andakar, the tentative conclusion is that they come from outside our star systems. No clues were discovered in the cavern to suggest their exact origin. Their clothing was ragged and torn and had mostly disintegrated due to their extreme age. A few items roughly similar to our photronic technology discovered next to one of the bodies suggest they had a highly developed civilization. They may have taken shelter in the cavern or they may have been dropped off there to die. Regardless, the possibility is that the cavern may have been the site of an ancient triple murder."

The reporter went on to discuss how the bodies had been mummified due to their long interment in the dry cavern and that holes from projectile weapons of an unknown design had been found on each of them.

There was no talk or speculation by the reporter about the mysterious stone block, which Caddo was sure he'd heard about earlier. That made him even more suspicious about what the news decided to tell the public. As usual, corporate interests took precedence over public divulgence.

After the report was over, vid of interviews of the pathologists, as well as a couple of the people who had pulled the bodies from the cavern, was aired. The five women and six men in the discussion group sat in stunned silence. The idea that the bodies were thousands of years old led to lots of speculation about why no one had ever come across this obviously spacefaring civilization. Had their species died out at the same time?

After a half-hour of repetitive and circular discussions, Caddo decided to change the topic. He had brought a flimsy with him that contained a huge number of intercepted comms from the Planetary Director's office.

"You have what?" asked Grevi, somewhat loudly.

Caddo held up the flimsy. "You heard me."

"You brought that here?" Ecca gasped, incredulous.

"Where else would I bring it?" Caddo told him, somewhat impatiently.

"You could have left it in your office," Julun retorted. "It's totally illegal to have that kind of data!"

"No, it's totally illegal for the Director's office to tax our energy production. Don't you get it? Something's going on here that needs to be dissected. And we're going to do the dissection."

Grevi had stated her concern because they were in a public part of the university. This was the student union building. The door wasn't exactly sealed shut.

"I'm going to divide up the comms for each of you. Just run the program I wrote and see what it catches," Caddo told them.

Caddo was becoming a lot bolder as the weeks went by, Omley noted, as Caddo copied a chunk of the comms to his flimsy via the wireless link. Caddo then cut and pasted eight more chunks of data to each of the flimsies the rest of the group had with them. They started the program and watched while specific comms were flagged on the left sides of their screens. The algorithm took fifteen minutes to complete for most of them and another five for Naram and Sked since they had larger chunks.

Grevi scanned the flagged files as they were being listed on her screen. While they were waiting for Sked's files to finish being analyzed, Grevi noticed a peculiar pattern emerging in some of the comms. They weren't from the Planetary Director's office. They were intercepted comms from local provincial manager offices. "Hey, look at this," she stated, now quite interested.

The comms were all sorted by date and time in one column. Images of the sender and receiver were part of the vidcomm headers and were all sorted next to the file names. Maps indicating the origination and termination points were displayed as well. But none of this particular batch was to or from Alarr's office. That immediately raised a red flag with Caddo.

"Pay dirt!" he announced triumphantly.

Sopka had never heard that phrase before. "What does that mean?" she asked.

"It means we caught her ass," replied a thrilled Caddo. A huge grin covered his face. "Alarr has these vidcomms, which means her personal files contain intercepted ones from the Council. This is evidence of her not only meddling in our affairs, but doing it illegally."

Everyone was terribly excited about the find. Even Grevi forgot her prior cautiousness and began to search with renewed intensity. Now it was a matter of going through the files to discern what it was Alarr was after.

Caddo took Grevi's flimsy and adjusted some of the parameters of the audio output. He encrypted the data so everyone in the room would only be able to hear the audio portion of the vidcomms through their neural implants. Encryption would prevent anyone from eavesdropping on them. He started the first file and they all watched. By the time they had finished with the nineteenth file, most everyone was upset at what they had discovered. Grevi took the flimsy and shut it off. She took a deep breath.

Everyone was looking at each other. Caddo had hoped to find some sort of incriminating evidence, but nothing as big as this. Secretly, some of them hadn't really cared if anything was found. To them, this was just a mental exercise. But reality had rudely awakened them. It didn't seem possible all these events could have converged as they had, but they had direct evidence for one of the most egregious breaches of planetary trust they had ever even heard of.

Caddo was the first to speak. "Not a word of this to anyone. Hear me? No one." He looked at everyone in turn. "Grevi, you and Traig have got to get to Darreth as soon as possible. Like tonight."

"Why me?" Traig asked.

"Because I didn't sleep too well last night, it's late and I have to get up early for work tomorrow."

Chapter 25

Darreth had been in contact with Naylon's parents several times over the last couple of days. Both Jaron and Temorrah Ress alternated between being concerned with Darreth's state of mind and their own sense of loss over the mystery of their missing son. Darreth did his best to assure them that there was every reason to believe Naylon was still alive.

Darreth's mother insisted everyone come to their home and have dinner. She and Naylon's mother were just about in tears throughout most of the evening. As far as Darreth was concerned, it was a very awkward evening since he was there as well. It was a nice gesture on his mother's part. She had insisted. But it only served to deepen his own sense of despair. Scenarios of what could have happened to his brother and Naylon played over and over in his mind. He hated to admit it, even to himself, but bad ones outweighed the good ones by a fair margin.

Naylon's parents had left three hours ago. Darreth lay awake in his parent's spare bedroom. This was the second time he'd awakened in the last hour. Under normal circumstances, he wouldn't even be considering sleeping at their house. He had his own quarters and could have just simply gone home. But he was feeling lost and somehow felt more comfortable in the house he grew up in.

It was the first time in his entire life he remembered feeling this way. Dread. Sorrow. Confusion. Anxiety. Unable to sleep. A terribly complex swirl of emotions was beginning to eat into his normally calm demeanor. Two people very close to him had simply vanished and he had no idea what to do.

The chime on his comm next to the bed stirred him from his reverie. He reached over and looked at the display. He didn't recognize the name or the number and almost decided not to bother answering it. Something told him to bother.

He sat up and pressed the on icon. "Lieutenant Commander James-Po," he said quietly.

"Darreth?"

Darreth didn't recognize the voice. "Who is this?"

Darreth heard a muffled voice say something to the caller then the caller answering in equally muffled tones.

"Who is this?" Darreth asked again, becoming frustrated. If he didn't get an answer this time, he would simply press the 'end' button.

"Name's Traig. I'm a friend of Naylon's. I've got some information you want. But you have to meet me."

Instantly, Darreth was wide awake. "You know where Naylon is? What about my brother?"

"I don't know any of that."

"Then why are you bothering me?" he demanded.

"I need to meet with you about the smear campaign."

"What smear campaign?"

"The one directed against your father, you and the rest of the Council. Can you meet me?"

What? "Where."

"There's a building named The Triangle on…"

"I know that building."

"There are two back doors. One has a blue light above it. I'll be in there."

"How do I know this isn't a trick?" he growled suspiciously.

"You don't. But I can tell you this. If you don't get the info I have you're going to be in worse trouble than you already are."

Darreth smoothed back his hair. *This is crazy*, he thought. "When?"

"An hour. We know you're at your parent's place. That's why we chose a building close by."

"You have the code to a door in The Triangle?"

"Of course I do. It's the back door to my father's office," Traig told him flatly.

Darreth entered the proper code on the entry pad next to the back door forty minutes later. The door silently slid open. Expecting a dark interior, he was surprised to find the entryway well lit instead. This was the back end of an office all right. To the left was a bathroom. To the right was a glass door revealing some computer equipment. The rest of the hallway wasn't lit. He saw a man who appeared to be somewhat younger than him at the far end. Traig beckoned Darreth into a room off the corridor.

Darreth may have been grounded but he still had his stunner. It was holstered but he had deliberately left the safety off in case he needed to pull it out quickly. He started down the hallway. As he approached Traig, he noted right away that the man didn't look threatening in any way. Darreth instantly relaxed, then yawned. After all, it was one o'clock in the morning.

"In here," Traig told him as he entered the room.

Darreth entered a large conference room behind Traig. Inside, two other people were already seated around a circular table that could easily seat eight. They were Alista Kosovil and Traig's girlfriend Grevi.

Traig extended his hand. "I'm Traig Maverol." He pointed. Alista. And Grevi." They both introduced themselves.

Grevi started doing the talking right away. "We're sorry this sounds so mysterious and all, but we have some very important information. Believe me, we're all sleepy, but we felt it was far more important than waiting to tell you in the morning."

"Tell me what," Darreth asked a bit impatiently.

"Your life is in danger."

"Is that all?"

"You don't care about that?" Grevi asked, quite surprised at his reaction.

"My life is in danger every time I go into space. How is this day any different?"

Traig shook his head and immediately upped the ante. "It's because of the plan to secede."

Darreth felt as if the heat were rising in the room. How could they possibly know about that? It was supposed to be a Council secret, and at that, only a few people on the Council were even discussing it. He had barely heard about it from his own father.

"What do you know about any plan to secede?" Darreth demanded.

"Look, we have a lot of information you need. Will you listen?" Grevi pleaded.

Darreth's body language told them everything. He was prepared to listen.

"Look, we know about the plan to secede. We also know that Director Alarr knows, too despite the Council thinking it's a secret. She's communicating with someone on Rylerra and telling them about scheduled shipouts to the starlanes."

"She *is* involved!" Darreth exclaimed.

"So, you do know about this," Traig said. "We figured you had to be privy to something as important as seceding from the Consort."

"Yes. I do know about it. And I've had my suspicions for quite some time about her involvement in something nefarious. Who's she communicating with?" Darreth asked.

"We don't know. The message headers are scrambled."

"What message headers?"

"We, uh, intercepted some of her vidcomms."

"What kind of organization are you?"

Traig answered for them. "We're just a discussion group. Naylon was one of the members. He contributed his thoughts just like the rest of us. One of our guys, uh, tapped into one of the Director's comm archives. We sorted through some of them and uncovered what looks like a well-concealed plan to thwart everything the Council wants to do. What's more is that some of the vidcomms went to Rylerra. I personally think she's got a lover there or is in communication with a spy or something. We just don't know exactly because she couches even those comms with damn odd phrasing. Your shuttle was shot down after she sent one of her comms to Rylerra. She had something to do with it, we're sure of it."

Darreth was duly impressed. "You figured all that out from a few comms?"

"Caddo's pretty good at mysteries. He's got a naturally suspicious nature. Long ago we learned not to underestimate him."

"Caddo?"

"He's the guy in our group who dug all this up."

"I want to meet him."

"He's asleep. He needs it," Traig told him. "He's not so good when he gets woken up before he's had his eight hours."

Grevi nodded at that assessment.

"About my life being in... danger. What else do you know?" Darreth asked.

"Just that. Look, we've all been friends with Naylon for a lot longer than you've been seeing each other. We want him back like you do. But you have to understand we could be in serious trouble if you let anyone know how you found out what Caddo did."

"No doubt. Spying is punishable by some seriously upheld laws. Did Naylon know anything about this?"

"Caddo dug this up after Naylon disappeared."

Alista interrupted Traig. "Naylon and I have worked together for quite a while now," she told Darreth. "He was terribly excited about going to Rylerra. He's pretty good at what he does and had pressed quite hard to get the funding to go off-world. To tell you the truth he was thrilled you were going to be the pilot, too. He's got a thing for you, by the way. He's even used the 'L' word."

"Huh?" *He told someone else?*

"His exact words were, 'I think I love Darreth'."

Darreth leaned back ever so slightly. His eyes started to smart. This wasn't supposed to happen. He wasn't supposed to get all emotional about this. His sole purpose for being here was to discover what they knew and put the rest of the pieces together. But this added an extra emotional dimension and impact to the situation that he wasn't expecting. He swallowed in an attempt to clear the ball rising in his throat.

Grevi spoke up now. "Look, I might as well tell you that as soon as we heard Naylon had gone missing we immediately suspected you."

"What? Why?"

"Because you knew Naylon was involved with us. Not a single one of us is exactly sympathetic to Consort interests. Your job is to make sure those interests are maintained. See the link?"

"No, I don't. I've known about this discussion group for months. He and I talked about it."

The group glanced at each other briefly.

"Maybe you don't realize my brother is one of the missing people. I had nothing – *nothing* – to do with their disappearance," Darreth added angrily.

Grevi waved her hands. "Don't agit. We know that. Boy, do we. There's lots more."

Good, at least I'm not on their suspect list anymore, he thought. "Go on."

"Alarr knows that the Council has discussed pulling out of the Consort. She's using her usual underhanded ways to put a stop to it. It wasn't a pirate ship that blasted you. It was someone operating under her authority."

"How can you be sure about that?"

"Didn't you scan the ship?" Traig asked.

Darreth issued a slightly audible sigh. *Boy, do they have a lot to learn.* "Of course I did. It's standard procedure. The scan only determined what type of ship it was and that they weren't using a transponder code."

"And no positive ID on them being pirates, right?" Alista added.

"Right."

"That's because they weren't pirates. She was using someone else to get rid of you as a bargaining chip to keep your father from agreeing with the others on the Council."

Uh, oh. Just as I suspected! "I'm being used to get to my father?"

All heads nodded.

"You think my death will influence what the Council wants?"

Traig answered. "We don't think anything like that. Alarr does. Look, she successfully had several trumped up charges leveled against you, had you grounded, and that alone has prevented the Council from discussing independence any more. She's getting her way. Even though you didn't die. You have more weight than you give yourself credit for. You're the Chief Council's son. That's the only bargaining chip she needs."

"You said there's more," he said.

Grevi sighed. "A lot more."

"Such as?"

"We've discovered she's involved with the 'real' pirates."

"I thought there weren't any pirates," Darreth replied, confused.

"The real pirates that you go after. Not the pilot of the ship that shot you down. Apparently, she has some sort of deal worked out with someone named Anoon Tilshar. Ever heard of him?"

"No, should I?"

"We did a search on that name. He was killed in an accident on Agica Prime five years ago."

"If that's so he seems to have made a remarkable recovery."

"He never died. He went undercover. He's either a leader or working for one of their leaders."

"If that's even remotely true I have to bring it to my superior's attention," Darreth told them.

Traig was immediate with his response. "You can't."

Darreth snorted. "I can't, huh. And, why would that be?"

"I told you he wouldn't understand," Traig told Grevi.

"Traig," Grevi warned.

Alista intervened. "You can't because you don't know who to trust."

It was as if the room suddenly reached its flashpoint. In fact, Darreth started sweating now. Where had he heard that before? From himself. It was all beginning to make sense, too. For too long he hadn't wanted to be wrong about his work. He kept having to tell himself he was performing a duty that was greater than himself. Now he wasn't certain who he was really working for. His interest, training and full-time employment was routing out pirates, which was supposed to be for the greater good of Andakar. But it was beginning to become quite clear that someone in his division, obviously someone high up, might be working for Inandra and not have Andakar's best interests at heart after all. Who could it be? Someone directly above him? Or was it much further out of sight? It was impossible to tell who he could trust. Just as Grevi said, he realized. Was it possible someone might actually be paid to look the other way while he was out risking his life to keep pharmas out of the wrong hands? As far as he could tell he was doing legitimate work, but clearly someone else was seriously trying to keep him or others from discovering the truth about the pirates.

Grevi spoke next. "We need proof of *your* true loyalty."

"You want to be a little more clear than that?" Darreth shot back.

"Specifically we need to know if your loyalty is to Andakar or not."

Darreth stood up. His chair slid back and bumped the wall behind him, startling the three people. "My loyalty to Andakar has never been questioned until this very minute. You better have a good explanation for even asking me that."

There was a moment of silence in the little room.

Traig's voice broke that silence. "We think the so-called pirates are on our side."

Darreth slowly sat back down.

Traig let the silence drag out a moment longer before he decided to explain himself. "We've sifted through enough of the information garnered from her comms to determine that the Planetary Director's office has been involved in a massive cover up. Years ago, before the Space Navy was beefed up to become a full-fledged military division, there were huge debates on Earth about how much to fund you guys. As you know, a corporation whose purpose is to make money isn't necessarily interested in planetary security."

"You're dead wrong. Planetary security is achieved by guarding profits. It's not hard to understand."

"I figured you might not connect the dots," Traig said acidly.

"Traig. Stop it," Grevi said sternly. She stared at him until he looked down at the table.

"What Traig was going to say," she said, "is we suspect the pirates are trying to fund a breakaway from the Consort, too. They're just going about it all wrong. They're stealing pharmas and reselling them for profit to finance their own narrow interests."

"There is no way that can be true. I would have heard about it," Darreth countered.

"But you haven't," Traig retorted. "Which means that the propaganda machine is working."

From what Darreth had heard so far, they had to be accurate on that point, too.

Traig continued. "Caddo figured it all out. The pirates are operating on an unknown world by stealing pharmas from us then reselling them to the highest bidder on the black market. That much everyone knows. But what he figured out was that those credits are being used to purchase ships and pay off officials to maintain their secrecy. What those officials don't realize though is that they're being duped. The pirates are attempting to withdraw completely from the Consort or have already done so."

Darreth was already shaking his head. "How could there be 'some unknown world'?"

Grevi decided to fill him in. "The Consort has developed only 14 worlds. That leaves about 18,400 planets…"

Traig interjected the exact number. "18,435 surveyed planets."

Darreth knew the exact number, too. It was part of his pilot training. Stellar cartography was imperative to use the nav system aboard the vessels he piloted, although there was no way anyone had ever been to or named all 18,435 of them.

"…and umpteen moons," Grevi continued, "they simply have never bothered to Inhab due to atmosphere, gravity, orbital period, radiation issues…"

"Yes, yes," Darreth interjected this time. He was well aware of the number of undeveloped planets due to their less than perfect conditions and lack of material resources to exploit.

"Let me finish," Grevi responded. "So, it's a simple fact that the pirates could easily be on one of those other planets, far outside the normal travel and shipping lanes the Consort has established."

Darreth had been in many meetings about this issue already. There were a little over four thousand possible planets and moons large enough to inhab humans, and reasonably close to star lanes, where the pirates could be making a stand. There were so many potential locations and they were scattered so randomly it would take decades to find them at the rate the Space Navy had been proceeding, even by using remote probes.

"They couldn't possible make enough money to break away," Darreth told them.

"And they don't know that Andakar is attempting to do exactly what they're doing, but at a much slower pace," Grevi said.

"So they're making themselves into criminals in the meantime. That doesn't make it right. They have no right to steal our assets," Darreth said.

"No, it doesn't make it right. So, be aware that one of the paid off officials is Inandra," Alista added very quickly.

"Why would Alarr give them the time of day?" Darreth asked.

"Caddo suspects she's buying time to discover where their hideout is. She'll eventually find it. That way she can be the 'hero'. Everyone will rally around her and make her something she's not. As a result, someone's bound to offer her even more power than she has right now and that could seal the fate of our entire planet."

Darreth took that assessment in, considering it for a moment. "I've never heard anyone say or even elude to these pirates being organized. If anything, they appear to be semi-organized, at best. I'm not privy to any of the information extracted from those we've captured, and none have talked in my presence. It would make sense that she's been hobbling our division's attempt to find out where their base is so she can do it herself."

"Hobbling or paying off," Traig told him.

"So, you're speculating that she has some very highly placed people working for her and against us," Darreth mused.

"We're sure of it. Unfortunately, no names have turned up yet," Grevi offered. "We didn't sort through every comm."

"What about those Council vidcomms."

"She's had an extraordinary amount of access to their private conversations. Caddo found two between provincial managers that were significant. That's how he discovered the aim to leave the Consort. The third was between a provincial manager and your father. Your father was very good at couching his phrasing in such a way to not implicate himself in any direct way regarding withdrawal. But Caddo figured it all out. She wants to stop all talk about independence before it gets too far."

Darreth bit his thumbnail. This was potentially disastrous. At best, it was a complete breach of privacy. He had to have a conversation with his father as soon as possible to warn him about not saying anything else, even over what he considered secure comm channels. Certainly, no standard photronic means of communication would be appropriate to contact his father at this point now that he knew what she knew. What if she even had access to his neural implant conversations?

"She's clever, but not foolproof," Grevi said with a smirk. "She's getting help on Rylerra. Any idea who that might be?"

Darreth's head was spinning. She was guilty of attempted murder as far as he was concerned. And for the first time he was asking himself the right questions. How was it possible that not a single person in the Space Navy had come up with any good leads on the pirates, but this totally amateur group had? Was it because no one suspected her or her office in all of this? Were there really no tentacles reaching out from his division to discover things like this? Were there higher ups or others who were keeping the lines of communication closed between divisions?

Who in his chain of command was blocking all of this? How was it possible that the Planetary Director had as much power as she did over his life? It appeared as if she personally had the power to make sure his life came to an end! It was like suddenly having a veil lifted from his eyes. It was becoming extremely obvious to him that Inandra had blocked a thorough investigation into this incident by planting the idea that it was pirates who had shot down his shuttle. That way no one would suspect the ship had originated from Rylerra.

"I have a damn good idea," he told them angrily. "His name is Zelin Raxi. He's a mining operations manager. It's rumored they have a thing going on. Long distance, of course, but a thing nonetheless."

"A lover. I knew it," Traig said as he wrote down the name in his vidPAD. "I'll have Caddo do the research on him."

"Why haven't you brought this to anyone else's attention. Someone in authority," Darreth asked.

Traig answered. "As you've already pointed out, breaking into the Planetary Director's communications grid is highly illegal. Then there's the issue of who to really trust with this information. We don't know who Alarr has on her informal payroll. We don't know who else might mysteriously disappear. After all, you and your passengers were supposed to have been the first."

Alista indicated she wanted to speak. "I'm not a part of their group. That's why I came here with them. They contacted me because I've known Naylon so long. They knew you might not trust them, so I tagged along. If you ask me, these guys are doing work that should have been done long ago. There are a lot more problems on this planet than meet the eye."

No kidding, Darreth thought. "I want to see the data Caddo dug up."

"If you do and we're caught you'll be implicated, too. Are you sure you want to do that?" Grevi told him.

Alista chimed in. "They've shown me some of it already. I think they're right. The pirates are just a radical faction of regular people like us who're fed up with the status quo. The pattern of corporate corruption that's been finding its way to our planet goes all the way back to Earth. I don't dare say I understand all the legal and financial machinations taking place to allow it to happen, but one thing's obvious: the Planetary Director's office has been sticking their noses into our local affairs more often than ever before in our history. It's getting worse as the weeks go by. Your shuttle being shot down was just the latest indicator of that."

Darreth was still reeling at how these ordinary people had been able to sidestep all the data security to be able to dig this up. Was it really possible he was an unwitting pawn in a game the Planetary Director was playing? If what these people had uncovered was in fact not a ruse by them for some as yet unknown purpose, then he had been duped far more than he could possibly have imagined.

"This is as much about getting Naylon back as it is about exposing the Planetary Director's offices. Will you help us?" Alista asked.

"You want my help," Darreth stated.

"It makes sense you'd help us. Look, she targeted you. Instead of you disappearing, your brother and your boyfriend disappeared instead. Your position in the Space Navy gives you access to people and data we don't have."

"Such as?"

"I'm sure I don't have to spell it out."

"Spell it out anyway."

Traig sighed heavily. "Your father, her offices, official business, etc. Need I go on?"

"I still can't believe you've not gone to the authorities with this information."

"You're all the authority we dare tell. We do not want to be on her list of people who disappear!"

Alista, Grevi and Traig left the Triangle through the main hallway entrance. Darreth exited through the back door where he had entered. He stopped as the door shut and looked everywhere to make sure no one was spying on him before he took off. His head was swimming with the information he'd been given about Inandra, but mostly about how his father was clearly in danger now. It was surprising to him that the Planetary Director's office hadn't had his father arrested already. The fact that nothing had happened meant she had little direct evidence of his involvement in the discussions by other provincial managers, didn't have enough authority yet, hadn't found a law that had been broken yet, or was simply waiting for the right time. Yet, he couldn't think of a single charge she would be able to levy against anyone on the Council for simply discussing the matter. Of course, that hadn't stopped her from having false charges hung on him for everyone to see.

The meeting had lasted only a little over an hour and a half. It was still dark out when he returned to the house. The side entrance door slid open and let him in. The door quietly slid closed and he headed back to the guest bedroom. The house was completely quiet. His mother and father were still asleep. Although Darreth felt tired, especially after not gotten any decent REM sleep, his adrenaline was still pumping. His father would be awake in another hour.

Chapter 26

Darreth was in the adjacent bathroom when he heard the water running in the kitchen. His father was making a pot of coffee.

"You're up early," his father said upon seeing him fully clothed.

Darreth sat on a stool across from his father at the peninsula in the kitchen. "We need to talk," he said.

"Coffee first," Siloy replied, empty cup in hand.

They had retreated to a small basement tool room. Siloy had been listening intently the entire time. What Darreth had presented to him was a huge cause for concern. He searched his memory several times to determine how many vidcomms he'd accepted from other provincial managers that contained any discussion of independence. He determined there were only two. Both of them had been brief and neither he nor the other party had ever openly discussed the issue. He was well aware of prying ears and eyes no matter how well encrypted comms were. Regardless, he never suspected he was being outright spied upon. His private conversations were not supposed to be in the common domain, nor were they supposed to be viewed by anyone, much less a Planetary Director.

But the vidmail from Kals on his personal account deeply disturbed him. Kals had implied that Inandra might be closer to their sentiment for independence than they suspected. He had responded that nothing could be further from the truth despite what she had alluded to. Siloy's assessment of the meeting was that she had been on a fishing expedition. Now that he knew what she knew, it was clear she was attempting to get Kals to warm up to her so he would tell her what she wanted to know. Siloy was going to put a stop to any further discussions with that woman immediately.

"You realize no one can go public about any of this due to the highly illegal nature of what that group did," Siloy told him.

"You don't think it's highly illegal what she's been doing with private vidcomms?" Darreth asked incredulous. Wasn't his father appalled by this egregious breach of privacy, not to mention a couple dozen Provincial laws?

"Of course I do, son. It's just that until I can work my way through some channels this can't be discussed by anyone."

Darreth's wide shoulders sagged, a mixed look of chagrin and relief flooded his face.

"It's all right, son," he said, looking into Darreth's eyes with a smile. He reached out and grasped Darreth's arm now. "Don't agit. This will all be worked out. Trust your old man to act when it's appropriate." He looked at the time. "Look, I'm going to be late for my morning meetings. I'm going to cancel my afternoon ones though and head right out to West Litok to discuss what you've learned directly with Manager Ustbe. I can't risk saying anything else to him via a vidcomm."

Darreth nodded.

"You look a wreck," Siloy said with fatherly concern. "How much sleep did you get?"

Darreth emitted a sigh. "Not much."

"I'm sorry you're involved in any of this," Siloy said with serious regret. "I guess, though, that it's a good thing I had mentioned this 'issue' to you so you wouldn't have been broadsided by it."

Darreth noticed he was biting his thumbnail a lot lately and pulled his hand from his mouth. He straightened up, too. Shoulders back, his face set. "About this 'issue'. I want you to know I fully support it. One hundred percent. Say the word and I'm there."

Siloy looked surprise.

"Wouldn't you after what Alarr's done?"

A slight grin found its way across his father's face. "When the time is right I'll let you know who you can trust in orbit."

"Huh?"

"A very high level officer on the *Guardian* space station has backed us from the very beginning."

Both men went back upstairs. Siloy emptied his coffee cup in the sink, then went back to his bedroom to finish dressing for his full day. Darreth went back to the guestroom in a failed attempt to get some rest. His thoughts continued to stray to Naylon and his brother. In his semi-fatigued consciousness, his thoughts were drawn to the backpack he had had while on Rylerra. It was sitting on the floor of the closet back in his bungalow. Despite his profound sleepiness, he bolted upright in the bed as a forgotten memory surfaced. In one of the zippered pockets was the strange disc-shaped device he'd found in the cavern. He only just now realized it was still there.

He arrived at his own place a half hour later. He pressed the button on the frame of his closet to open the door. The overhead light illuminated the closet's contents. He knelt down and unzipped the compartment. Underneath several miscellaneous items was what he was looking for. He pulled the alien object out, then inspected its curious shape and the unusual designs etched on the surface. The device had to have some connection to their disappearance.

He had already given a complete statement about what had transpired on Rylerra, with Merek corroborating everything, yet leaving out the existence of this 'souvenir'. Even Merek didn't know anything about it. If he presented the device at this point, he knew he could easily lose his commission for having withheld information during an official investigation. Due to the political masquerade which had surrounded him since his return, he knew there was no way he could add to what he had already stated.

Darreth sat with his back against the wall, breathing hard as he thought. Rehl. He needed to talk with Rehl as soon as possible.

Chapter 27

Soldat Epo Agrida looked at his wristcomp. It had been only fifteen minutes since their ship had left them alone. Soldat Jarien Lazcún was hidden next to Agrida in the brush. Both were crouched inside the stealth field by way of portable shield generators they had set up before their ship had taken off. Two of them had been placed three meters apart. The invisible field draped over them like an umbrella, masking their biosigns or the energy signatures of the weapons they had fully charged and at the ready. The portable stealth field generator was stronger than their personal stealth fields, thus providing them with a larger area of protection.

The small Telkan scout ship crossed their position twice before returning. It began a slow circle around their hidden location. As expected, the ship was steadily scanning the clearing their ship had occupied. Agrida's sensors had detected the particular frequency used by them doing so. The scan had crossed near them twice, but never actually over them. He was sure the stealth shield was doing its job. If it hadn't, they would have been burn spots in the vegetation.

"It doesn't get any better than this," Lazcún whispered to Agrida, jazzed that everything was going according to plan. The ambush they had set up was making his adrenaline surge like mad.

Agrida grinned as he nodded. He glanced at his pulse cannon's power indicator. It showed a full charge. He would first disable the Telkan energy shield, then they'd pierce holes into the side of their ship. He knew exactly where to fire. He'd been through sixteen simulations and had already shot a ship in the same manner eight months previous. Eight months between shooting a Telkan ship was too long as far as he was concerned.

The ship clearly hadn't detected them. It began landing procedures not more than ten meters at their twelve. Agrida took aim. Lazcún did the same with his cannon. Agrida pressed the trigger as soon as the landing thrusters shut off. Although he could have easily let the targeting computer do the work for him he preferred doing it the old fashioned way. Lazcún wasn't as confident and let his targeting computer determine the optimal firing pattern.

The first blast from Agrida's weapon severed a tiny junction at the primary power coupling on the starboard engine nacelle. His second shot completed the job. Lazcún fired at three points. He knew what he was aiming at. During a landing procedure the ship wouldn't be shielded like it would be for interplanetary flight. Agrida's disruption of their primary energy grid helped. His first shot pierced the hull at a strategic location. His next shots burned out the three backup and redundant energy nexuses. Within two point eight seconds of landing, the Telkan ship was totally disabled.

The two soldats held their position for only a moment longer before deactivating the stealth generators. Now with personal stealth shields operational, Agrida assumed the nine o'clock and Lazcún the three o'clock positions. They knew that once the Telkans manually opened their outer airlock their first course of action would be to fire on the positions from where the strikes had taken place. The stealth shield only masked energy signatures, it wasn't a true defensive shield. They would have been smoke if they had been fired upon.

Agrida raised his wrist and spoke to the comm. "Agrida here, sir. Mission accomplished."

Dozens of kilometers away, Commander Selaye grinned. *"Good work, men. Standby. Out."*

The commander raised the captain on the internal comm. *"Sir, the fire team has taken out the Telkan scout ship."*

"Excellent. Plot return course for insertion."

"Yes, sir."

Naylon discovered that the comm screen on the wall had no particular security codes with regard to its activation. Thus, after he ordered the screen to energize he inquired about outside cameras. There were twenty.

"Tell it to give us a forward view," Tann told Naylon.

"Why not," Naylon offered.

A forward view activated on the right half of the screen. Both were surprised to discover they were in flight. The inertial dampeners had completely masked any sensation of movement. Tann had suspected something was up though because they both heard a high-pitched whine start only moments before.

Tann tried his luck with voice commands, "Full screen mode," he said.

The image immediately filled the screen. Moments later they noted their ship was hovering at a distance from the same clearing they had earlier left. Both of them saw a ship in the clearing. It was obvious right away that the ship was different, even from the craft they now found themselves in. Both looked at each other, wondering what was next.

As they slowly descended, Tann told the display panel to center the closest camera on any activity outside the ship. The panel responded while they landed not more than ten meters from the alien vessel. They both recognized two of the soldats from the crew, who were already there, apparently left behind. They both had handheld weapons trained on something or someone inside an open airlock door.

Tann spoke to the panel. "Magnify view fifty percent." The monitor instantly complied with that request.

Two soldats waved their weapons and were obviously yelling. There wasn't an outside microphone pickup, so they were reduced to just watching the vid. Moments later, an obviously alien creature slowly moved down the ramp. Naylon and Tann both sucked in startled breaths at what they saw.

"That-that's one of the aliens we found in the cavern!" exclaimed Tann.

"It certainly is," Naylon returned, mightily intrigued. He also noticed that instead of the creature having six appendages, it had only four. Perhaps it was a different species? He was intensely fascinated at what was going on and wished there was an audio feed. Clearly, these creatures were the Terran's enemies. It looked like this one was going to be in for some big trouble, too. It appeared to be two against one so far, as well. "So that's what they look like when they're alive," Naylon added.

"What are they doing?" Tann asked.

"Looks like they intend to capture or kill him, uh, it."

Tann tried another camera to get another view of the drama unfolding outside the ship. "There's another one. It looks dead."

The other Telkan lay face down in the sand near the nose of its craft. There was a dark stain on his clothing and it didn't move. Naylon was sure it was dead.

They continued to watch the action on the forward screen. The Telkan had descended the ramp and was forced down to its knees. One of the soldats approached the creature and forced it to place its hands on top of its head. Then he yanked a weapon from its holster. The soldat then removed the belt that went around the creature's waist and flung it far into the underbrush. On the belt hung various apparatuses besides just the previously holstered weapon. Naylon could only guess what the other items were, but apparently were determined to be dangerous.

The gesturing and evident yelling continued. The soldat covering the Telkan with his weapon motioned for it to stand now. With its hands still on top of its head, it was lead away from its craft and toward their own. They were bringing the creature inside the ship! Seconds later the view was just of the Telkan ship and nothing more. Nothing Tann asked the monitor to do could produce an image of the interior of the ship.

Soldat Ocio had been in the corridor covering Tann and Naylon's quarters. She opened their door once she got word that the prisoner had been secured in the infirmary. Tann had just turned off the monitor with a voice command. She was unaware they had been watching what had transpired outside the ship.

"Come with me," she told them. Her weapon was at the ready.

"Why do you need that? You already know we're unarmed," Naylon asked her.

"Orders," was all she would say.

Naylon shook his head ever so slightly. She motioned for them to head toward the infirmary, then pointed for them to enter a small adjacent observation room just before they reached it. They could see the Telkan through the wide window that separated them from the infirmary. It was strapped down on the same exam table Tann had been on. Naylon could barely believe there was yet another alien species in the ship. It was as if these people were used to them!

The two soldats who had been in the clearing were in the infirmary with weapons drawn and trained on the Telkan, who was obviously completely under restraint. Captain Pacudas was standing at the foot of the table while, to the side, the ship's doctor was preparing a cylinder of Pelinex. Naylon thought the Telkan was dead at first, but then saw it breathing. Moments later the doctor stuck the cylinder against the Telkan's neck and withdrew it. He nodded to Pacudas, who turned and exited the room. He joined Ocio, Naylon and Tann in the observation room.

"Wha-what is that thing?" Tann exclaimed.

Ocio exchanged glances with the captain. "What kind of question is that?" she asked.

Tann shook his head. "We saw some dead ones."

"Where?" Pacudas demanded, greatly interested in what Tann had to say.

"In a cavern upriver."

Naylon watched the brief exchange from a different perspective. It was beginning to dawn on him that they probably shouldn't tell their captors too much. The very idea that they knew something might implicate them in the bizarre alien war these soldiers seemed to be embroiled in.

"It was a cave we took shelter in before we ended up here. There were three of them there. I guess you guys took them out," Naylon said for Tann. He knew they had been dead for far longer than just recently. In addition, they weren't in the cavern on 'this' side, as he had recently concluded, especially after Tann had told him they had seemed to be missing when he had tried to find Darreth.

Ocio shook her head. "It couldn't have been us, sir."

The captain was the one who had ordered Ocio to bring Naylon and Tann to the small observation room. He had wanted his 'guests' to see what they were doing to the Telkan, wanting to observe their reactions and body language. Tann's statement was completely unexpected. "Answer her, Tann. What kind of question is that?" the captain demanded.

"What are you talking about?"

"What do you mean you have no idea what he is?" He pointed his chin in the direction of the Telkan.

Tann stood his ground. "You just don't get it, do you," he said defiantly.

"Tann," Naylon warned.

The captain's ready room was small but could fit four people comfortably. Right now, it had only three people in it. The captain sat behind his small desk. The commander stood next to the desk. Tann sat in front of the captain. The captain had a stylus in his hand, tapping it on the table.

"How is it possible you don't know what a Telkan is?"

"Telkan," Tann repeated. That was the first time he'd heard a name used for their species. He was feeling considerable anxiety. When they had led Naylon away, back to their quarters, and he was directed to follow the captain, he was sure it wasn't going to be pleasant. But he got the hint from Naylon just before they were separated. Don't say too much, seemed to be what Naylon wanted to tell him. "If I never saw one before, how could I know what they are?"

"You saw dead ones in a cave."

"Yeah, *dead* ones."

"Was their clothing homeworld, colony or military?"

"I have no idea what that means."

"Sir, he's not lying." Selaye lowered the sensor device he had in his hand and set it on the captain's desktop.

The captain leaned back in his chair, trying to absorb all that had transpired over the last several hours. First, these two Terrans who had never spoken Empire Spanish just 'happened' to be on the very same planet where they were doing recon. There certainly were not supposed to be any Terrans within two-dozen light years of here. Then they both insisted they resided on a Telkan Held World. It had to be a completely fabricated story. None of it made any sense. The captain called for Ocio who came and led Tann away. The door shut behind them.

"He's lying," the captain told his commander.

"Sir, the sensor is accurate to point zero zero one."

"Have it re-calibrated. There is not a single Terran in the Empire who's not heard of a Telkan. Bring in the other one," he ordered, an edge to his normally calm voice.

Selaye pressed a button on his wristcomp and spoke to Ocio. Shortly, she brought Naylon into the ready room.

Naylon was motioned to take a seat in front of the captain.

"We'll start again. How is it possible you don't know what a Telkan is?"

"So, that's what you call them."

The captain glanced at the commander, then reached into a drawer and pulled out the necklace Darreth had given Naylon. He dropped it on his desktop. Naylon thought it was lost in the river.

"That's mine," Naylon said angrily.

"Where did you get it?"

"A… uh… a friend gave it to me." It was obvious he needed to be very careful. Although Naylon wasn't used to having to guard his sexual orientation, he was beginning to realize this military unit wasn't his culture. It was completely different than anything he'd ever encountered before and something nagged at him to be very cautious indeed. He was sure anything he said or did could be construed incorrectly if it went too contrary to what was expected. After all, he was in the minority on his own planet. Gays were in the minority on all Inhabs. That's just the way it was. Who knew what harm might befall him if such a minority status was against the law with these people.

"This coin. It's Chinese, no?" The captain poked at it with the stylus.

"I was told it was."

"Known contraband. And you admit it's yours."

"I don't know what you're talking about," Naylon said. That was one of the most bizarre statements he'd heard so far. Apparently, Chinese coins were forbidden! How such a ban could be in place he had no idea. Chinese culture was just about ubiquitous on every Inhab. Granted, not all that many of them actually lived on the Inhabs. Darreth was only one-eighth Chinese. But their goods were certainly everywhere. And had been for centuries. But apparently, that culture was not welcome in this alternate universe! This whole experience was becoming more and more bizarre by the minute. It's a good thing after all he didn't reveal that his boyfriend had given it to him!

Pacudas was beginning to be supremely frustrated at what he felt was total insubordination. Regardless, he decided to play into Naylon's hand to see what he might divulge. "Tell me more about your… society." He opened the drawer and pulled the necklace back until it dropped in. He shut it firmly. The captain was beginning to entertain a new hypothesis about Naylon and Tann and needed some more input to confirm his suspicions.

Damn it, Naylon thought. *That's mine!* "It's certainly not like yours." The possibility that he and Tann had somehow entered some sort of dimensionally parallel world was at the top of Naylon's list. Given everything that had transpired so far, it was the only explanation that fit the facts. Clearly, it mattered little, if at all, about what he might tell the captain as long as he didn't divulge too much about his personal life. "For starters there's no military running the show. There are no aliens of any sort and there's certainly no war between our species."

"Go on," the captain said. An amused smile started across his face. Naylon's story sounded impossibly naïve. *If he thinks I won't catch his lies, he's sadly mistaken*, the captain mused.

Naylon continued, trying to sound convincing, but realizing the man probably wouldn't believe him anyway, no matter what he said or how he tried to convey it. "I can't imagine who funds your little operation here, but it's certainly not the Consort. They had enough trouble deciding to fund an upgrade to our Planetary Transport Security Division."

"On Ozol," the captain responded.

"Ozol?"

"You called it Anda-something."

"Andakar."

"And this Andakar is where you live and work?"

"Maybe you'd like to scan for it. We've both established it's not too far away. Last I checked it was .26 light years from here."

"Of that, we're quite certain. Indeed, I'm betting your Telkan friend in the infirmary is from there. Since you're both from there I will assume you know him."

Naylon chuckled briefly. "You can assume no such thing."

The captain ignored Naylon's denial. "What is this-this Consort of which you speak?"

"Large and powerful companies that run everything."

"Where is its base of operation?"

"Earth."

"Earth," the captain repeated.

"That's where their central business operations are located, but they're on all the Inhabs."

"Inhab. That is not a word."

"Occupied planets, then. Ones with businesses."

"All sixty-seven of them," the captain stated.

Naylon's mouth fell open, taken by surprise. They had inhabbed sixty-seven worlds? Things were far different here than he suspected. "All *fourteen* of them," he replied.

"And one of them just happens to be Ozol?" The captain's face was openly scornful.

"No, one of them happens to be Andakar," Naylon insisted.

"Troop strengths on their bases. Tell me about that," the captain countered.

Naylon decided it wouldn't matter if he played along now. Pacudas indeed didn't believe him at all. "If you mean the Space Navy, I'd say somewhere around, oh, ten thousand." It was a total exaggeration, but at this point Naylon didn't care.

"He's lying, sir," Selaye said from behind him. It was the first time he'd said anything since the questioning had begun.

Naylon looked back at the man. Selaye issued a grin and held up the sensor to Naylon. He hadn't had time to recalibrate it. Besides, he knew it was functioning perfectly. Naylon eyed the device, trying to determine if it really could determine whether he was lying or not.

"Again, Dr. Ress. What is the troop strength?" Captain Pacudas asked quietly.

"Three hundred, give or take." Naylon really had no idea. Nonetheless, there was no response from the commander.

"And what are their armaments and weapons?"

"Look. I'm a paleo-microbiologist. I don't keep track of that kind of stuff."

"Tell me more about this Consort." The captain was digging. He figured it was nothing more than a command center or a cover name for their operations.

"Like I said, it runs all the corporations and divisions that span the Inhabs. Tell me more about your Consort. Who funds your army?"

The captain wasn't in the mood for games but he decided to help Naylon give him more information. The more friendly he sounded the more Naylon might reveal.

"Funding is an odd word to use, but perhaps it's because of the Pelinex. The Empire has always been built around the engine of expansion. Expansion is paved by the military. The military oversees the building of the infrastructure and the people occupy the conquered territory. It's a simple equation. You know it. Everyone knows it. And everyone supports it. That's why it works so well."

Conquer. Territory, Naylon said to himself. "You're going to invade them, aren't you?"

The captain leaned forward and looked Naylon squarely in the eyes. "You're working with or for the Telkans, aren't you?"

"What?" *Uh, oh*, Naylon thought. The man was accusing him of collaborating with their enemy.

Commander Selaye kept the sensor trained on Naylon.

Naylon was fed up with this. He wasn't going to divulge that he and Tann had come through some sort of dimensional tunnel. Their way back might be lost forever if he did so. These people even had some sort of scanner that could determine whether he was lying or not! Knowing that, he wasn't going to divulge anything that might prevent their return. "Look, you know as well as I do that I know nothing about this little war you have with those aliens." He looked back at the commander after saying that. "We don't know any of them and we've never heard the word 'Telkan' until you people said it."

"Little war. Another interesting choice of words, Dr. Ress. What is the name of the Telkan we just captured?"

Naylon stayed silent.

"We'll just have to ask him. You and your young friend will be present when the questioning begins."

Naylon was escorted from the ready room and brought back into the quarters with Tann. For the moment, they were left alone. Both of them stood in the middle of the room trying to make sense of what they had gotten themselves into.

"The captain asked me all sorts of stupid questions. At least we know what those aliens are called," Tann told Naylon.

"And from what I've been able to piece together so far, they think we're collaborators," Naylon replied.

Tann shook his head. "But we're not!"

The door slid open a few minutes later. Ocio motioned for them to accompany her. She stood aside and they went ahead of her. "To the right," she said. They walked down the corridor to the air lock. She pressed a sequence of buttons on the bulkhead and the inner door opened. Naylon watched. The panel had two rows of three buttons. Top left, twice. Bottom right, once. Middle left, then middle right. The three of them entered the small compartment. Naylon repeated the sequence in his head several times until he'd imprinted a visual memory of it. She pressed the reverse sequence in the inner chamber and the door closed. Once it was sealed the outer one opened with a press of a large green button next to the keypad after a safety cover was lifted. Naylon noted that, too.

Outside the entire crew was assembled in front of the Telkan, who had been brought outside. It was restrained and it had obviously gained consciousness after the injection, since it was standing up. It had been stripped of its clothing except for a ripped piece of cloth that dangled from its waist. It barely covered what were obvious genitals. The alien creature was at least a third of a meter taller than anyone there. Its arms had been lashed to a metal pole. The pole was across the Telkan's shoulders and attached to a metal ring around a collar that had been fastened around the alien's neck. There was no way it would be able to defend itself in that position. There were manacles around the creature's lower limbs. It had no boots or shoes on. Its feet were long and narrow with long toes that resembled a frog's. The creature was breathing heavily.

Both Tann and Naylon noted the being's thick, dark brown, shiny skin. It reminded Naylon of hippo or elephant hide. He had never seen either animal in real life, but had been through a holo zoo plenty of times. Wading in a river right next to them had been one of the most fascinating things he'd ever done when he was a teen. Since the Telkan was nearly naked, Naylon could see distinct marks above its waist. Vertical scars. Long ones. But they looked old, not fresh. Maybe this wasn't a different species after all. Maybe this one had had its smaller limbs removed for some reason. There was no way Naylon could be sure.

"Speak, snake!" Lazcún bellowed.

There was no utterance from the Telkan prisoner.

"I said speak!" With that, he punched the Telkan in the stomach with the butt of the staff he was carrying. The alien didn't do much more than grunt. Based on the amount of force Lazcún had to use, in Naylon's estimation the Telkan easily weighed 125 kilos, if not a lot more.

Finally, it spoke. "I am Second Tier Ranger An'Arka J'selnof. You are trespassing on a Telkan Held World. You will leave."

Naylon and Tann were astonished. The alien spoke perfect Empire Spanish! It was more than bizarre to hear the odd toothy sound coming from the creature's mouth.

Tann whispered to Naylon his surprise. "They can talk."

"Quiet," Ocio told him.

The captain stepped up to An'Arka, dismissing what it had said. "What do you know about these two Terrans?" Ocio turned her rifle horizontally and used it to push both Naylon and Tann forward from behind.

An'Arka gazed at them. "I do not recognize their markings."

"You lie," the captain said flatly.

The manacles around An'Arka legs rattled slightly as it stood taller. "You accuse me of collaboration with my enemy. It is not so. You dare to set foot onto our Held World. You imply those Se'leth collaborate with the Telkan Ascendency. If it is so then you have lost control of your people. Your time is at an end."

The captain took the staff Lazcún was holding and pressed it against the Telkan's bare chest with one hand. He pointed at Naylon and Tann with the other. "What do you know about those two Terrans!" he demanded angrily.

An'Arka closed its eyes, seemingly waiting for what was next. The captain pressed a button on the staff. Although it emitted no sound, An'Arka instantly went stiff, then fell to the ground nearly flat on its face.

Tann was sure they would be next. "Stop it!" he yelled. He was almost in tears. He was totally unprepared for the cruelty he was witnessing. It was like watching an animal being tortured.

The captain turned to Tann, his eyes fierce and intense. "If you want him to live you will tell me everything I want to know."

Naylon wasn't sure whether the captain was going to kill the Telkan prisoner or not. Nonetheless, given that the other Telkan was still face down in the sand near its ship made it clear they didn't care much for these creatures. Whether they were really going to witness a cold-blooded murder right here was another matter though. Naylon attempted to scrutinize more of the captain's intentions. Was it possible he could be so cruel? They were completely alone, with no other authority anywhere nearby. Anything could happen and no one higher up would be the wiser. That thought alone brought great concern to him. They were both in serious danger now.

An'Arka stirred then tried but failed to stand upright. It took twice before he could right himself. Despite what appeared to be excruciating pain, he stood tall once again. Sand covered the side of his face. He shook his head to remove some of it, which rattled the manacles again.

Tears had welled up in Tann's eyes. There was nothing he could say to appease the captain because he simply didn't know anything.

"You can save him, Tann," the captain goaded.

Tann felt momentarily bewildered, then supremely angry at the accusation. "You know I can't!" he spat.

Naylon realized Pacudas was baiting Tann. "Stop it!" he yelled. "Just stop it!" The anger in his voice was evident to everyone.

Soldat Zapante was standing directly behind Naylon. He leaned forward. "You would choose a snake's life over your own?" he hissed.

That was the second time Naylon has heard the word 'snake' used to describe the Telkans. It was obviously derogatory. "No, I wouldn't. I wouldn't because I don't know this creature. Neither of us do." He looked directly at the captain this time. "We've never seen this-this Telkan before. We don't know him and he doesn't know us. And you *know* that." Naylon realized he was pleading with the captain.

Pacudas heard everything he needed in Naylon's tone. His show of force worked. He was sure now that neither Naylon nor Tann knew their Telkan captive. In fact, both of their emotions were genuine. The little one was actually sniffling. The sniffling wasn't because he knew An'Arka either and feared for a friend. It was because he was actually concerned about its plight. Pacudas found that both remarkable and disgusting. It was cause for genuine concern for him, too. Clearly, he was facing something he didn't expect. Terrans that truly had never heard of the Telkan Ascendency and thus had compassion for these creatures? How these two didn't know about the war, he wasn't sure. But tonight he was going to find out.

The captain stared at An'Arka briefly, then turned to Lazcún. "Stake him."

Lazcún turned to a long narrow bag that lay in the sand next to his feet. He unzipped it and pulled out a two-meter long grey metal cylinder. He placed the pointed end of it against the ground and pressed a button near a vertical seam. Lazcún held his ears, as did a couple of the other crewmen. An audible hiss emitted from the top, a puff of smoke came out, then a very loud pop sounded. A stake inside the cylinder rammed itself into the ground. Secured by barbs that pointed upward, only a half-meter remained above the surface. There was no way An'Arka would be able to pull up the securely anchored post. He pulled upward on the cylinder and tossed it aside. He attached a short chain to the manacles at the feet of the Telkan. The other end he attached to a metal loop at the top of the stake. He clamped two links together, which appeared to fuse solid at his touch. The Telkan wasn't going anywhere.

Tann and Naylon were ushered back into the ship. The Taskers, which were not outside during the interrogation, were standing idly by in the corridors as the crew filed back in. It was an eerie sight to Naylon, what with all the different aliens around them. The remaining crew turned and followed except for the captain and soldats Barcega and Zapante. Naylon figured the captain was probably going to do a real interrogation on their prisoner. That made sense. After all, that little show was only to mess with Tann's emotions.

Barcega and Zapante entered the Telkan ship to remove the data modules from the command console. They stowed everything into containers they had brought with them. The ship had standard data modules, of which they were familiar. In their own ship were adapters that would be necessary to extract tactical information from them later on. Once the items they deemed valuable had been removed, they placed thermal scramblers at points in the Telkan shuttle's interior. Once activated, they would destroy the shuttles command components and spread a toxic cloud throughout the interior, rendering it totally unusable. They sealed the outer airlock and waited until they heard muffled thumps. The two men both had satisfied grins on their faces.

The captain continued to hold the stick at the ready as he asked the Telkan over and over again about troop strengths, weapons, and ships that might be nearby. An'Arka said nothing.

Barcega looked at An'Arka, trying to discern if it realized they had effectively disabled his only ability to leave the planet. The Telkan didn't have the same muscle structure of a human face and thus, there was no way to tell what emotion it felt. He grinned as he watched the captain circle the prisoner with the stick. He didn't know how long the interrogation would last and wondered if it would make any difference anyway.

Soldat Efren Llarena, the Chief Engine Technician by training, had been the last to enter the shuttle after the rest of the soldats. He had looked back at the Telkan, still standing proudly in his chains, then back toward the airlock door. Discovering Terrans on this planet was indeed a mystery, but one that provided a glimmer of hope for him. Whoever they were, they had actually never heard the word Telkan! Was it possible there was a Terran planet untouched by this endless war? A planet that didn't speak the word Telkan with a vehement desire for blood?

Naylon and Tann had been led back to their quarters. The door was shut on them unceremoniously. Tann sat on one of the bunks, his eyes red, tears still welling up but not quite enough to run down his cheeks.

Naylon sat next to him in an attempt to calm the boy down. "The captain did all of that because of us."

"How do you know?" Tann sniffled a couple of times, then wiped his eyes, already regaining his composure.

"We weren't staked out there like that alien. We weren't mistreated, just verbally abused. The captain needs us. He thinks we know something. I'm sure he's going to take a completely different view of us when he decides to talk with us again."

"Which will be when?"

"I can't be sure, actually."

Tann sighed, then took a deep breath; stood, then activated the view screen. An'Arka was standing tall, his arms still lashed and totally vulnerable. They both watched as the captain circled his prisoner, stop, gesticulate, point the stick at him, then wait. Naylon desperately wished there was a microphone pickup that accompanied the vid. Both of them watched this go on for several minutes, sure that at any moment the captain would jab the stick at the alien and kill him, apparently by electrocuting him. But that didn't happen. He ceased his questions as his soldats re-emerged in the camera's view with a container of something taken from the Telkan's ship. All of them left the scene and headed back in.

"How long do you think they'll leave him out there?" Tann asked Naylon as he told the display to de-energize.

Naylon shook his head. "I don't think they take prisoners." That much was evident since they weren't in any sort of brig or formal lockup either.

Tann fell silent. He knew what that meant.

"Don't try to feel sorry for it… er, him. This is their war. We can't take sides," Naylon tried to point out.

Naylon's argument wasn't having its intended effect. Tann felt panicked. "We have to escape," he whispered. "We have to get back to that cavern. We still have those things that got us here." His desire to never touch one again was gone.

"I know," Naylon replied. "That option might take days though. We'd have to steal food and water. They might take off again, too. We have no idea where we might end up next. We'll never be able to find our way back if we get too far from that river. Then there's another problem. They clearly have biosensors. They could easily find us if we're on foot. And who knows how many other Telkan patrols are nearby. We wouldn't last long if we're caught. After all, we're 'Terrans' now. We're the enemy."

Tann put his head in his hands and rubbed his eyes, then his forehead. The fear and frustration in his quivering voice told Naylon Tann's exact emotional state. "This wasn't supposed to happen. I just wanna go home."

Naylon hugged him. Hard. "I know," he said. "I know."

The captain was taking his time Naylon noted, in questioning them again. He knew it was inevitable though. At 1800 hours, according to the clock on the view screen in their quarters, he heard talking outside the door. Tann pressed his ear against it briefly to hear the exchange.

He stepped away and whispered to Naylon. "I think they're changing our guard." No sooner did he say that when the door slid open. Llarena stepped in and the door slid shut.

"What now?" Naylon asked. He hadn't had any opportunity to focus his attention on this soldat until now. The man was two meters in height, had short dark hair and brown eyes. This close up, Naylon decided he was extremely good looking. That alone reminded him of Darreth.

"I'm Soldat Llarena, the Chief Engine Tech. I need to know something. Truthfully, do you really come from a planet where we're not at war with the Telkans?"

Instantly, Naylon could tell that this soldat wasn't asking in the name of the captain. He was asking for himself. That meant they had a bargaining chip!

Llarena noted Naylon hesitating, sizing him up. He sweetened his request for information. "Look, my weapon is shut off." He clicked a switch and holstered it. "It's unheard of to keep Terrans under arrest unless they've committed a crime. You've committed no crimes. But we've been ordered by the captain to hold you here until you talk. Where are you really from?"

"Both of us are from Andakar." Naylon briefly looked at Tann. Tann quickly nodded.

Llarena shook his head. "There is no such planet."

Tann spoke up. "I was frucking born there. Let us go and we'll take you."

Llarena laughed. "Good one. But you know I can't. Regardless, you have to know there are many of us, and many more every day, who are not happy about this situation. The war is going on its thirty-first year."

Thirty-one years! Naylon thought. If that was true, then he and Tann had a lot more going for them than he originally figured. But he had to prove their hypothesis. "Llarena, what's your first name?"

"Efren."

"Are you from Earth?"

"I am," he said as he nodded.

"What do you know about your Empire's history?"

Tann looked at Naylon. *What does that have to do with anything*, he wondered.

"I know everything about it."

"When did the Empire first go into space?" Naylon needed to know if their suspicion of where they were was correct.

"January 24th, 1902. It is an indelible date."

Naylon wasn't exactly sure, but he thought humans hadn't gone into space until the mid-20th century.

"What do you know about General Malán Zas?" As far as Naylon knew, a soldier from Earth had to have at least heard of the man.

Efren thought for a moment before he answered. "I have heard of no such general."

"He was a dictator in South America."

"Where is South America?"

Naylon shook his head in frustration. "On Earth."

"I know of no such country."

"It's the name of a continent."

"You are thinking of another planet. No such continent has that name on Earth."

"Tann, help me out here."

Tann threw up his hands. "With what?"

"How far back did your Earth history studies go?"

"Uh, to the Roman era."

"I trace some of my ancestors almost that far," Efren stated.

"Seriously?" Naylon asked, quite astonished.

"Of course. A lineage trace is required for active service. Some of the soldats on this vessel who were born on Earth can track their families back over twenty-seven hundred years."

"Whoa! Well, uh, what do you know about a country named England?"

Efren snorted. "You mean Angla."

"Angla?"

"Angla province. The name 'England' hasn't been used for centuries."

"Province?" Tann asked.

"It's a province in Europa," Efren said.

"Europa," Tann repeated, not sure he had heard the word correctly. Part of what Naylon was getting at was beginning to sink in now.

"The collective provinces are called Europa. That includes the province once called England. Old Spain is Europa's First Land," Efren told him.

"Provinces? You mean countries." Naylon said. He was confused now. What Efren was telling him was quite a bit different from what he knew about Earth.

"That word is very old and not used anymore," Efren told him.

"What happened to England... er, Angla? How did it become a province?" Naylon asked, trying to pick up another piece to the puzzle he was trying desperately to put together.

"King Philip conquered it long ago. It is the defining moment in our Empire's history. It began everything. How could you not know that? It's required knowledge on every world." Efren was becoming quite suspicious of Naylon's questions now.

"We come from a backward planet," Tann replied sarcastically.

But Naylon had enough pieces of the puzzle now. It wasn't his area of expertise by any means, but he'd read enough articles on the subject to make some bold assumptions. He was firmly convinced now they were indeed in an alternate universe. Amazingly, this one wasn't really too far off from their own. He had figured some detail of history was different and had caused a divergence from his and Tann's timeline. Surprisingly, his questions may have already led him near or to the divergent point. He wasn't at all sure why this particular version had so many alien species in it or why this Rylerra wasn't a ball of ice. Naylon knew that England was still a country, even to this day. Granted, it had been part of the European Confederation for nearly a millennium, but as far as he knew, it had never been 'defeated' by anyone named King Philip.

"Tann, what do you know about Spain?"

He shrugged. "Only that it's in the Confederation. We had to study the history of three Inhabs this year. Look, I didn't remember everything."

Efren looked back and forth between the two of them. He was quite confused with this conversation. "You mean Europa," he emphasized.

"Never mind that," Naylon said. "Didn't Angla ever claim land in the southern hemisphere on Earth?" Naylon was well aware the English had settled Australia and New Zealand more than a millennia ago. After all, he was born on North Island and knew where his family had originated.

"Why do you keep asking about Angla? They have never had any land except for their islands off the North Sea."

"Who claimed the Western Hemisphere?"

"The Spanish, the French and the Holandés, of course. Enough of this-this history lesson," Efren told them, irritation evident in his voice. "What planet *are* you from?"

Naylon needed no more convincing. He turned to Tann. "We are definitely not in our universe."

Tann pursed his lips. "No shit."

Efren's suspicions were added to by frustration since his questions weren't being answered. "What universe?" He didn't get his answer because the comm strapped to his wrist buzzed. He looked down at it then pointed to them both. "Not a word," he told them sternly. He spoke to the comm unit next. "Llarena here."

"*Zapante here. I'm in the engine room. The regulator is showing that anomalous reading again. Can you come back here and look at it?*"

"Uh, I'm guarding our 'guests' quarters."

Zapante grunted. "*Our 'guests' are harmless, as you well know. Just come back here and take a look.*"

"I'll be there in a minute." He pressed the door control. He pointed a finger at Naylon. "We never had this conversation." He exited the room quickly and the door slid shut.

Naylon immediately noted the indicator light on the doorframe. It didn't show red after he left, but rather green. Every time previous it had been red after their guard had left. Whether by design or sheer forgetfulness, Efren hadn't locked the door.

Chapter 28

"*You've got to be kidding me!*" Rehl sub-vocalized it as loudly as he could. "*You've got an alien device and you've not told anyone?*"

"*I told you, didn't I?*" Darreth sub-vocalized back.

"Yeah. Way after the debriefing! I am not about to get involved in this," Rehl said out loud this time.

"I just need someone who's willing to analyze it and figure out what it is. Someone who'll keep quiet about it. I-I just want to see if it can give me a clue, anything really, to explain their disappearance," Darreth told him with a hint of desperation in his voice. After all, it had been over a week since Tann and Naylon had gone missing. Plus, he felt guilty for letting Tann join them in the first place. *Frostbite*, Darreth thought, remembering Naylon's warning. *This was far worse than frostbite.*

Rehl looked away from the table and out the window to the street. His lunch was getting cold in the little diner where they were seated. Darreth had gotten lucky. Rehl was going to be planetside for only another day before he was supposed to go back into orbit. Darreth had caught a little over an hour of sleep, then was able to see him shortly after calling him. They were silent for quite a few minutes before Rehl spoke. "Maybe Kestin will do it," he offered.

"Who?"

"Kestin Dryter. He's a friend of my wife's boss. I met him at an office party at their house a couple of months ago," he explained. "He's a physicist. We got to talking. We must have talked for over an hour. He's one of the most unusual people I've ever met. Smart as can be. He's quite the brain but he wasn't pretentious at all. I can give you his comm code." Rehl told the comm link on his wrist to add the contact information to Darreth's. "Ready?"

Darreth activated the transfer link. The data included a holographic photo of Kestin as well as his address and two of his comm lines.

"I have no knowledge of this little 'omission' on your part," Rehl told him.

"Rehl, lay off. I was way too freaked out about the whole situation to remember I had it on me."

"I wonder where your training went. It's not like you to be forgetful."

Darreth wondered, too.

Darreth's call to Kestin was brief and cryptic. Mentioning Rehl's name though brought an instant response. Yes, he remembered Rehl from the party some months back. Yes, he'd be happy to take a look at this object Darreth insisted on presenting to him. And yes, he would do so under strict secrecy. It was a very unusual request, but Kestin was interested because of the intrigue. He didn't mention it but he was quite familiar with Darreth. After all, he watched news vids like everyone else. Darreth's father wasn't exactly an unknown figure either.

Kestin told Darreth to meet him at his office. It took all of twenty minutes to get there after Darreth entered the address into his hovercar's nav. The vehicle pulled off the lane and descended toward the parking lot. He met Darreth at a side entryway. The holo-pic Darreth had of Kestin helped to identify him right away as the man let him into the building.

Kestin was a short, thin man of forty-nine. His hair was just beginning to gray on the sides. He stuck his hand out to shake Darreth's. "Nice to meet you," he said. His bright eyes and rapid speech immediately told Darreth the man was intelligent.

"Likewise. Thanks for taking the time to see me."

"No problem. I'm always interested in examining something that might be new. Let's go up to my lab. It's private."

The elevator took them up seven floors and opened to a wide corridor. There were plenty of windows letting in the late morning sunlight. Kestin's lab was marked with the number ten on the door. His presence made the door slide open. He ushered Darreth in and the door slid shut.

It was a typical laboratory, not unlike Naylon's, Darreth noted, except this one had far more sophisticated equipment and was easily twice as large. Clearly, none of it was used to dig into the past, Darreth thought, as he nervously looked around the expansive lab.

Kestin noted right away that Darreth seemed to be hiding something. He reached for a flimsy on a countertop and pressed a few icons, making a show of it so Darreth would notice. "No one will question why I've turned off the security recording. We can talk freely."

Regardless of the assurance Kestin just gave him, all of a sudden Darreth wasn't so sure this was such a good idea after all. But the thought of never seeing Naylon or his brother again made up his mind for him. It was try this, or nothing. He unclipped the small pack he had around his waist, then unzipped the front and pulled out the device, which he had carefully wrapped in a cloth. He set it down on a countertop. "Before you examine this, you have to swear to me that whatever you discover about it doesn't get to the media," Darreth told him.

Kestin noted the tone with which Darreth spoke his very clear warning "Why? Is it stolen?" He glanced down at the cloth-covered object, dying to see what it was.

"No, just… not accounted for. And can't be at this point."

"What does that mean?"

Darreth told him how he had acquired the object and the debriefing, which followed. He sat on a stool at the counter. Kestin sat on one next to him. "If you say anything about this, it won't take long before you go down with me," Darreth added in a dark tone.

Kestin didn't speak for several seconds as he thought about the implication. He didn't want to be involved in any criminal matter. He looked at the object, still wrapped up, then back up at Darreth. Curiosity won out. "Agreed. Now let's see what it is."

Darreth unfolded the cloth. The unusual way the disc reflected light gave Kestin pause. "It's not radioactive, it is?"

"I think I would have exhibited some symptoms of radiation poisoning by this time if it were," Darreth responded.

"That's the first test I'm performing on it."

Kestin placed the object into a glass container. Darreth followed him to another part of the lab where it was placed into a small compartment in the wall at the back of the lab, furthest from the windows that lined the hallway. Kestin closed the compartment door and sealed it with a vacuum. Darreth sat next to him as Kestin started the tests.

"Good. Radiation is nominal," Kestin read out loud. "I'm only getting the usual background amount." He retrieved the container and withdrew the object from it. He placed it on a tray and then into a different analyzer. As each test completed, Kestin noted the results out loud.

"This analyzer indicates the object is made of bismuth, silicon alloys and some type of polymer. That's odd. The polymer has a very unusual molecular structure."

Next, the display they were both watching ramped up to the X-ray range. Kestin noted its internal structure. "Nothing unusual here. No, wait a second." He changed the resolution for a closer look. "That coil looks familiar."

"In what way?"

"I'll have to check the historical database. I swear I've seen that structure before." He slid a flimsy toward himself and pressed a few icons on the display. A few seconds later he found what he was looking for. "Yes. That's it. The similarity is impossible to ignore. The coil looks like an antenna used in an old style pass card."

"What's a pass card?" Darreth asked.

"It was one of the original electronic security devices, before the days of photronic and biometric technology. They were originally used for things like entry through a door or to identify a person. It's basically just a coil of wire attached to a simple memory device that contains not much more than a code. When one passed the card in front of a sensor, the coil or antenna caused a remote database to respond. It allowed an authorized person access or entry if there was a proper match. Hey, what the heck?" he interrupted himself, baffled.

"What? What?" Darreth said eagerly.

As Kestin had been talking, the analyzer was ramping up through the electromagnetic spectrum, producing a log of what it had recorded. He had also been watching a flimsy as the results were being displayed. "That low terahertz result can't be right."

"Well…?"

"Just a moment while I check the calibration." Kestin pressed a couple icons on the display flimsy. Instantly it changed to a different mode. He went through several of the diagnostic screens. All calibration parameters showed normal. He pressed the 'return' icon and the display showed the device inside the test chamber in visible light. He pressed the spectrographic display icon again and pushed the flimsy closer to Darreth. "This graph simply can't be right, but the test chamber is properly calibrated."

Darreth wasn't sure how to read the graph but he saw that a portion of the spectrum had dropped off. It was as if, when a particular frequency range bombarded the device, the energy disappeared or was swallowed up instead of reflecting back readings. Darreth shook his head. "What does that indicate?"

Kestin scratched his head, thinking furiously. "It's not possible, but it can only mean one thing. This object isn't here."

Darreth eyed Kestin. "That's ridiculous. We're looking right at it," he told the man, pointing.

"I know. So there's only one other explanation," he said excitedly. "It means this object doesn't belong to our quantum universe."

Darreth's head jerked backward a couple of inches. "What the hell does that mean?" he said, more than a little confused now.

"Everything in the universe has a quantum signature. Think of it as say… a resonance that an object gives off because it 'belongs' to our universe." He pointed to the area of the spectrum that had dropped off. "This area here always displays a particular value. All objects that belong to our universe resonate at a particular frequency that shows up in that spot. This observation has been known for centuries. But there is absolutely no reflected energy there. It can only mean the object isn't here. Since we both know it's here the only other answer to this anomaly is that the object isn't a part of our quantum universe." Even as he was explaining it, Kestin was having a difficult time comprehending it himself.

Darreth stood, took a step backward and nearly knocked the stool over he had been sitting in. Unbelievably, he had all the clues he needed now. The impossible but neat disappearance of Tann and Naylon made complete sense. The object was the only one he had found in the cavern, and only a single alien had one. There were no others anywhere to be found. That much he was sure of, since he and Merek had spent hours searching everywhere for clues to their disappearance. They would have stumbled over another one if it had been in that cavern. Even if he and Merek had missed something, he would have heard about more of the objects having been found once the bodies and anything else that might have been found had been brought to the recovery facility on Rylerra. He had heard nothing. It was true no aliens had ever been encountered anywhere in known space, which also added to the clues. It was making even more sense now. There were three aliens. There was only one of these objects. That could easily mean two others were missing! Those two missing devices might be in Naylon and Tann's possession. Now that Kestin had discovered that the device didn't belong in their quantum universe at all, it further added light to the mystery. It seemed evident that Naylon and Tann had somehow slipped into some alternate universe by using them. Most likely by accident! He had to conclude they were in the universe where the aliens most likely originated. The only way that could have happened was if they had gone through the perfectly smooth tunnel. After all, the tunnel had some sort of odd shimmering in its middle that neither he nor Merek could see through. What if one needed the disc device to 'see' through it. Or in the case of Naylon and Tann, go through it.

"You said the object is just a pass card," Darreth said.

"There's nothing to indicate anything more complicated than that. The only unusual thing about it is that it's not from our universe."

"Then it's just a simple piece of technology when it comes down to it."

"Basically. It just looks complicated due to the intricate design on the casing."

"Can it be duplicated?"

Kestin emitted a short laugh. "Are you kidding?"

"No, I mean it," he insisted. "I need another one. And I need it as soon as you can make it." Darreth was already working up an idea and needed Rehl to help him get Naylon and Tann back.

Chapter 29

Tann had also noticed the door was left unlocked. Was it a trick of some sort to see if they would act on that discovery?

If Naylon thought the same, he didn't care. "Get the packs," he ordered.

Tann looked at the door again, hesitating.

"Didn't you just say we need to get out of here? We're going," Naylon told him. He pressed his thumb against the sensor and the door slid open. He briefly stuck his head out and looked down the corridor. So far, so good. No one was in view, not even one of the Taskers. Tann was already zipping up their packs. He handed Naylon his jacket.

Naylon stepped out and slid down the corridor with his back against the wall. He reached the junction of the next one and looked both ways. It was clear, too. He waved his hand for Tann to follow. Tann stepped out of their quarters and pressed the smooth pad on the doorframe. The door slid shut. He pressed a tiny red indentation next to the doorframe. Its pad glowed red, indicating the door was locked. They quickly made their way to the airlock. Naylon looked at the control panel. The ship was small, but apparently everyone had something to do right now because no one was in sight. Naylon pressed the sequence he had memorized earlier. The panel's buttons were totally silent but they lit up as he pressed them. The inner door quietly slid open. Tann was too busy being terrified they'd be caught at any moment, and didn't ask Naylon how he could possibly have known the code. They both stepped into the airlock. Naylon enter the reverse sequence to shut the door. He whispered to Tann to keep to the far wall away from the port in case someone happened to come by. Naylon then lifted the safety cover next to the control at the outer airlock door and pressed the green button. He could only hope an alarm wouldn't sound when he did that. Nothing noticeable happened. The outer airlock door slid opened. The panel on the outside of the shuttle had the same set of buttons as did the inner door. He had never seen the door being shut from the outside but it had to be the same sequence as shutting the inner door. He pressed the button in the reverse order and the door smoothly shut. *Whew*, he thought. As far as he could tell, their trek outside was completely unobserved. Now he had to hope someone monitoring a vidscreen wouldn't see their hasty retreat away from the shuttle. He pointed to the nearby bushes and they both rushed to take cover behind a low boulder further on. From there they waited a few moments, observing their surroundings and listening intently for any sign of pursuit from the ship. It was odd being just outside the ship's cloaking field. They both knew it was there but they couldn't see any of it now that they were several meters away.

Yes, there was an energy fluxuation again in the regulator that supplied the entire ship with power, Llarena noted. It had started acting up after they were first struck by debris in the asteroid field in that neutron star system where they first emerged into Telkan space. In a way, it was expected. The extra shielding added to their ship drew much more power than normal, adding a strain to the regulator. But this was Llarena's main strength in the ship. He knew the details of all the command circuitry, how to run all the key diagnostics and what to do with the results.

"Ocio, this is Llarena," he said to his comm.

Ocio was in the galley and had just finished making a sandwich. Across the glass partition that separated the mess from the Tasker cubicles, she watched two of them as they slept. They were docile while they were awake, and looked particularly vulnerable when they were asleep. She realized she probably did, too and shook her head so as not to think about it.

"*Ocio here.*"

"I'm in the engine room."

"*Uh, why are you there? You're supposed to be on guard duty right now.*"

"The regulator is showing that fluxuation again. I need to run my corrective diagnostic. Can you cover my post until it's done?"

"*How long,*" she answered. "*I'm making a sandwich. It's dinnertime, you know.*"

"It'll take fifteen minutes. Seriously. I'll bring you a dessert when I come back," he promised.

Ocio acknowledged the request and strode down the corridor to the quarters Naylon and Tann had just exited. She briefly noted that the door lock light glowed red. This was becoming tedious, she decided. There was no reason to hold these mysterious men. They had shown no aggression and they certainly weren't going anywhere. She had no idea what the captain had in mind about them, but it wasn't her place to question orders or to try to discern his motives.

No sooner had she arrived, when the ship's comm barked. It was Selaye this time. *"All hands. Long-range scans have detected a Telkan ship patrolling the area. Prepare for liftoff."*

The captain had decided not to tangle with any ship. Despite being fully cloaked, he wasn't itching for a fight just now. He was well aware it was probably looking for their missing ship anyway. Less than two minutes later, the ship lifted off and fled to the south.

Naylon had just decided all was clear and that they should get as far away from the Terran ship as possible when they heard a whine. It had to be their engines. Both knew right away it meant the ship was preparing to take off. Their timing couldn't have been better, he decided.

"They're leaving!" Tann whispered loudly, totally astonished.

"Which means they have no idea we're not in the ship."

"Why do you suppose they're taking off?"

"I have no idea, but it's our good fortune." It meant they could at least attempt to make it back to the cavern by following the river, which Naylon was sure was down the slope nearby. They waited as the ship apparently lifted off. They had to rely on sound and the fact that air rushed all around them to determine that. When they could no longer hear it, they both stood.

"That way?" Tann asked as he pointed up river.

"Hang on. We can't leave that Telkan chained up. Who knows what might happen to him before he's rescued. If at all," Naylon told him.

"What? Didn't you tell me back there that this is not our war? We have to get out of here," Tann urged, pulling Naylon's arm.

"We have to at least try to release him."

Naylon's response to the situation was unexpected as far as Tann was concerned. He thought he had been the only one who felt disgust at what they had seen the captain do to the Telkan.

Naylon hesitated though. He knew they had to leave as soon as possible. But Tann's reaction earlier had made him stop and think about it. He seemed compelled to at least attempt to rescue the helpless being. The Telkan was on the other side of the small clearing from them. Its disabled shuttle was between them and the chained alien, preventing them from seeing it. They both moved out into the open and rounded the ship. The alien was staring at the sky, apparently attempting to discern the direction the cloaked vessel was taking. Upon seeing Naylon and Tann, he turned his head and studied them intently.

They approached at the same time. Naylon held up his hands to show the creature he had no weapons. "An'Arka," Naylon said.

The Telkan said nothing but the chains at his feet rattled slightly.

"We mean you no harm." It was terribly trite, but it was the truth. "We're, uh, we're not with them."

"Release me," An'Arka said defiantly.

"We intend to."

An'Arka wasn't sure what to make of that statement. He was sure these two Terrans had been left behind to torment him. His demand to be released was simply his way to let them know he had no intention of being made the victim any more than he already was. But their instant compliant tone was surprising. "You intend to remove these bonds?" he asked suspiciously.

"Yes. We're not with those other people." Naylon inspected the manacles tightly bound around the Telkan's ankles. They looked solid. He wasn't sure he'd be able to do anything after all.

An'Arka intently watched Naylon's every move. He looked toward the bushes to their left. "There," he said with a quick jerk of his head. "You will find my utility belt. Your companions threw it that way. Find it and bring it here," he instructed.

"Why?" Naylon asked.

"It contains equipment that can remove those restraints."

After a twenty-second frantic search, Tann came across the belt. Dangling from it were six items in various holsters. "Found it," he yelled to Naylon. They quickly returned to An'Arka. Tann lay the belt at An'Arka's feet.

The unexpected need to find the belt weighed heavily on Naylon. He was starting to feel pressured to leave. He had intended really only to figure out if there was an easy way to release the Telkan, but it had instead turned out to be a bit more complicated.

"There is a knife in the black sheath," An'Arka said in a toothy, yet stern tone. "Cut the ropes."

Tann pulled the knife out and handed it to Naylon. An'Arka bowed at the waist to allow Naylon to cut the ropes that held An'Arka's arms around the pole and around his neck. The tight bonds had already drawn some blood around the alien's wrists. It was a bright yellow liquid with flecks of green. Naylon quickly discovered the blade was extremely sharp. He easily sliced through the rope around the Telkan's neck and then his wrists. An'Arka's arms flopped uselessly down by his sides. Naylon threw the metal pole aside. He realized the creature's circulation had most likely been cut off. He wondered briefly if the sensation of it returning was as painful for it as it was for humans.

"Are you okay?" Tann asked.

"Why do you care?" An'Arka asked.

"We had nothing to do with you being tied up."

An'Arka didn't response.

Naylon looked up and scanned the sky. With no sensor equipment of any kind to discern approaching crafts, it was up to a visual inspection only. And that was useless if a ship were cloaked. "Tann, let's go."

"Tann." An'Arka stated.

"Yes. Tann. That's Naylon," Tann told him as he pointed.

"This restraint around my ankles can be removed by a tool in one of the pouches of the belt."

None of the objects in the semi-transparent pouches looked even remotely like a weapon. He slid the belt closer. With great effort and two fumbled attempts An'Arka was finally able to open a pouch and withdraw what looked like nothing more than a rectangular piece of obsidian. With it, he touched the metal collar around his neck with it, then the manacle around his ankles. Within seconds, the metal crumbled. Naylon watched with awe. The tiny device had effectively broken what appeared to be the molecular bonds of hardened metal!

Again, with difficulty An'Arka reached in to another pouch and withdrew a small flat round object. It had a red oval in the center. He placed a slender finger on it and pressed. He dropped the object into the dirt, unable to put it back in the pouch.

Naylon saw him do it and wondered what that was all about. It was alien technology and made the action was next to meaningless to him. He addressed the alien. "Can you get back to your people?" Naylon asked.

"They will be here shortly," An'Arka assured him. He looked up into the sky.

What does that mean, Naylon wondered, uneasy at the alien's tone. But he could discern confidence even though the voice saying it wasn't human. In fact, the Telkan seemed as if he was expecting something. The hairs on the back of Naylon's neck prickled. He looked upward in the same direction as did An'Arka. Sure enough, just as he suspected, he saw a vapor trail coming from what he assumed was the east. Was it the Terran ship? Probably not. It should still be much closer to the ground despite it having left earlier. No, this was a different ship. Most likely it was the one An'Arka was referring to. *Uh oh*, Naylon thought. *Our captors took off because they knew that ship was nearby!*

Tann also saw what Naylon was looking at. Immediately he realized they had clearly done the wrong thing. They shouldn't have stopped to help the Telkan. It wasn't at all clear if they could avoid being captured a second time, but they weren't about to find out. With Tann right on his heels, Naylon scrambled away from the Telkan as fast as possible down slope. As they made their way through low brush, they reached the river's edge a few minutes later. But there was no place to go. There was no neat trail at the bank.

Naylon was breathing heavily as they stopped to get their bearings. His heart was pounding mercilessly and he felt terrified. "I'm sorry, Tann. I didn't know he had a homing beacon. Maybe we can outsmart them. We have to find shelter. Look for some rocks or anything where we can hide."

"I only see bushes."

"Then we'll have to dig."

"Dig! Are you crazy?"

"I mean under a boulder or something."

"But-but there's nothing like that anywhere. What would we dig with anyway?" he told Naylon as he looked all around.

"Then we have to get away from here as fast as we can." Naylon pointed upriver. Several springs along the way had made the ground soggy, then downright muddy as they made their way through the brush. He quickly realized this was going to do them no good. No one needed sensors to track their obvious footprints. Regardless, he figured the further away they got from the Telkan, the better.

Naylon had been sure the Terrans would re-capture them within minutes after they had escaped. When that didn't happen he figured they had at most a few hours before it was discovered they had gotten away. Now though, Telkans would most likely capture them instead. All because he felt sorry for An'Arka.

Ten terrifying minutes later, after getting their clothing snagged countless times on branches and twigs, and after having their boots thoroughly covered in mud, they came to a highly tilted rock outcropping. Naylon rested his hand against it as they stopped to catch their breath. He realized there was no way they could get far enough to elude them at this rate. His foot slipped on several of the large pieces of thin rock. *This is shale*, he thought. All around them were large and small pieces of it. Some of the sheets were massive. Perhaps too massive to move, even with both of them trying. But that's all they had. Maybe they could use thinner layers of them to make a lean-to! Maybe if they stacked enough of it they could hide in the triangular-shaped tunnel they'd end up 'building'. Maybe the rocks would be thick enough to mask their bio-signs. It was a whole lot of maybes, but what else could they do? After all, he was sure they'd be tracked on foot or the Telkan ship would simply scan for them.

Naylon quickly described his idea to Tann.

"You think it'll work?" he asked anxiously.

"What other choice do we have right now?"

They quickly shed their packs and started stacking what they could. Tann huffed and puffed with Naylon as they placed the gray stones in layers against the side of the tilted strata. Soon they had enough of them erected to hide the lengths of both their bodies, and then some; and crawled through the narrow tunnel. Naylon went in head first from one end and Tann entered head first through the other. They pushed their packs ahead of themselves. Seconds later they were only a few inches from each other's faces. With their packs under their heads, they could at least rest there.

"How did you know the airlock code?" Tann finally asked.

"I watched Ocio use the button panel when we were taken outside the first time."

"Oh," Tann said. "My canteen is low," he then told Naylon in a whisper, as he sloshed it. Both of them had greatly exerted themselves and had drunk most of their store.

"Mine's not exactly full either. We can refill them from a spring once we determine if the coast is clear."

Fifteen minutes later, with nothing to disturb them and having been worn out from their exertion, Naylon fell into a restful reverie while Tann fell completely asleep. Their respite was short lived. A few minutes later both became wide-awake when they heard a whine from somewhere downriver. As it grew louder, both of them realized it was coming from above them. It was impossible to tell which ship they heard. Was it the Telkan one or had the Terrans returned? It sounded as though the ship was crisscrossing the area, but never came near their hiding place. The whining sound ceased several minutes later.

"Should we head out?" Tann asked.

Naylon shook his head. "Not yet. We don't know whether it's really gone or if it landed nearby. They could easily be searching for us on foot."

Tann took another sip of water. He shook the canteen, concerned once again that it wasn't full.

"Fruck," Naylon said under his breath as he watched. He knew they couldn't lay under the rocks all day.

Leader Sa'Par, commander of the patrol ship *Mu'Anelko*, was alerted to Ranger An'Arka's signal only moments after they had started their orbital descent. The fact that a Se'leth ship had recently been detected on M'jas'la led him to believe his planetside scout team might have encountered them. They hadn't reported in for several horayons and no sign of their comm signals had been detected either. Until a few moments ago, he feared the worst. How there could even be a Se'leth ship in this system was something he would be looking into shortly. Once they returned to their base on Q'emt'la, he would personally find out who was manning the sensor grid and see if the computer systems that monitored the conduits had been offline or not.

But that was moot right now. He had a precise lock on Ranger An'Arka's signal. Their descent into the atmosphere produced the expected response. Ship's sensors had been on maximum to determine where the Se'leth ship was located. A recent upgrade had allowed them to detect known Se'leth cloaking frequencies. Apparently, this Terran cloaking frequency was different because the signal kept fading in and out. Nonetheless, he quickly determined it was a mid-sized vessel. He was sure of that. The Se'leth must have detected their uncloaked ship, thus leading to their swift departure. Leader Sa'Par watched his display screen as his ship's sensors attempted to trace the Terran ship's trajectory. It was leaving the area at just under local supersonic speed.

Leader Sa'Par's had no intention of investigating further or pursuing the Se'leth ship until he retrieved his rangers. The helmsman set them down near the patrol craft. The forward scanner recorded no energy signatures at all. It was evident the patrol craft had been severely damaged. Disturbingly, only a single life sign was detected, too. As they closed in, the vidscreen showed one motionless body. Sa'Par already mourned the loss of his dead crewman. Sub-commander Ja'Ning, standing next to the Sa'Par, felt the same loss as he observed the scene. An'Arka stood motionless as the craft descended onto his position.

Their ranger was quickly brought onboard. Without ceremony, he reported directly to Sa'Par and Ja'Ning. "Second Tier Ranger An'Arka, reporting, Leader," he stated.

Sa'Par briefly noted his ranger's state of undress. "Proceed."

"A Se'leth craft is operating here. How that is possible, I can't say. It has a nearly full crew complement. Two of their raiders destroyed our craft. Ranger Ba'yad was killed in the attack. The Se'leth have removed the memory crystals from our craft but will find nothing of value in them."

Sa'Par nodded. Any memory module that was removed without the proper command codes would instantly burn out their signal pathways, rendering data on them inaccessible, if not completely unreadable.

"Your uniform." Sa'Par said.

"I was captured and put into restraints. They staked me to the ground. They wished to leave me to die but two of their party later released me and fled."

"Released?" The surprise was evident in Sub-commander Ja'Ning's voice. He looked first at Sa'Par than back to An'Arka.

"It is most unusual. Two Se'leth, who appear to be a two and a one shedling, told me they were not with the ship. I believe it is so, since they were not wearing the same clothing as the crew. It was most odd. I have never seen a one shedling Terran before. I did not know they traveled with their young. They retrieved my utility belt and assisted me. They fled into the vegetation after I released my bonds, perhaps seeking their own ship. They appeared to be… concerned about my capture."

Leader Sa'Par was more than surprised to hear that. He was sure it was considered treason for a Se'leth to help a Telkan. Perhaps he didn't know Se'leth that well after all.

Ja'Ning had been looking at the nearby displays as An'Arka had given Leader Sa'Par his report. He spoke now, loud enough for both of them to hear. "Sensors detect no other ships. There are no known Se'leth outposts on M'jas'la. That would be impossible anyway. We are well into our space and three conduits from any of their known outposts or colonies."

An'Arka spoke the obvious. "Then they are still on foot. Sub-commander Ja'Ning, scan for Se'leth life signs."

Leader Sa'Par nodded agreement to Ja'Ning. Then to An'Arka. "You will need a uniform and food. You have performed your duty well. We will search for them after Ba'yad has been retrieved and you are rested."

In short order, the dead ranger was brought onboard and wrapped in a burial sheath. The fibers would bind tightly within minutes to seal him off from the life support system. The smell of his decaying body would otherwise quickly fill the craft. An'Arka's wounds were tended to. Thereafter he quickly ate, then performed a deep sleep meditation for several minutes. Its effects would last for hours before he needed a full sleep period. Soon enough he was refreshed and dressed properly. Moments later the *Mu'Anelko* lifted off, with scans tuned specifically for Se'leth life signs.

Both Naylon and Tann continued to listen intently. It had been quite a while since the sound of the nearby ship had ceased.

"We can't wait here any longer. Let's go," Naylon decided.

The narrow confines of their hiding place made it difficult to scoot out backwards. Both were standing several moments later, dusting themselves off. Naylon was the first to see the movement out of the corner of his eye. Tann was the first to raise his hands. Instantly, Naylon recognized that hiding had been irrelevant. Did he really think the Telkans wouldn't be able to find them, he chided himself.

An'Arka knew that since he now had command of the Se'leth language he was considered extra valuable. The effects of the RNA injections would take several revolutions to wear off. After they returned to Q'emt'la, he would be removed from patrol duty and put into service in the Surveillance guild for as long as he retained knowledge of their language.

Ranger An'Arka emerged from behind rangers Os'Taga and Th'Gan. At first, neither Naylon nor Tann recognized him because he was clothed. But it was obvious who it was when he spoke to them in Empire Spanish. "You will come with us. Do not attempt to flee or you will be killed," he told them.

Leader Sa'Par had given specific orders to not kill their captives. Despite that, it was difficult for rangers Os'Taga and Th'Gan to comply. Ranger Ba'yad had been unceremoniously killed and they were ready to return the favor. But their training and service to the Ascendency were paramount. To disobey orders would be impossible. But neither Naylon nor Tann knew their orders. They had no intention of running.

Chapter 30

Soldat Ocio didn't have to wait long before Llarena returned. When he did, it was with a dark chocolate toasted-coconut cookie. It was one of the few pleasures they had aboard their little vessel and her personal favorite. She broke off a piece and handed it to him.

"Thanks," she told him.

He nodded an acknowledgement as he popped it into his mouth. "How are our 'guests'?" he asked.

"Haven't heard a peep. It's not fair for us to eat and not them. I don't know why they're not pounding on the door demanding a meal. I would," she said.

Llarena placed his ear against the door briefly. "I don't hear anything," he whispered.

"Maybe they're asleep," she told him.

Llarena shook his head. "It's not late enough for that."

Ocio didn't like the implication of that statement. She swallowed the last bit of the cookie, then dusted off her hands. She withdrew her stun pistol and thumbed the safety. "Open it," she told him harshly.

He unlocked the door, then pressed the open button. The door slid open. "That-that's impossible! I know they were in there!" Llarena stated.

Ocio palmed her comm. "Commander Selaye, we have a problem."

Both soldats were standing in front of the captain's desk in his ready room. No one had spoken for several minutes. The ship's activity log was being looked through by all of them on three separate displays. It had taken all of five minutes to search the small vessel. When no trace of the two was found, it was obvious to conclude they had somehow gotten off the ship. But when? Back in the clearing, they had had to leave in a hurry. It must have happened before then. It was the only answer the captain could come up with right now. But still how had they escaped undetected?

"I've got something. The starboard airlock was activated just before we took off to avoid that Telkan vessel," Llarena said.

Ocio shook her head. "No way. They would have had to know the airlock door code! When did you call me to take over for you?"

"Around 1800 hours," Llarena told her.

The captain had already found out that Llarena had left his post due to the regulator's erratic reading. He had given previous orders that it was to be taken care of immediately if it happened again. As far as he was concerned, Llarena was in the clear for that reason alone.

"Then the only time they could have escaped is after you left. The door was locked, right?" she asked.

Llarena nodded quickly. At least he thought it was.

Ocio nodded as well. "It was locked when I arrived," she added.

"Which was how long after Llarena left his post?" the captain asked.

"A few minutes at most."

The cabin doors were designed to be locked from the inside or the outside. The entire crew knew how to override the locks. Their detainees were obviously quite clever. They had figured out the cabin lock code along with the airlock door code. The captain pushed the display away. This inquiry was irrelevant. Posting internal guards had never been something he had ever had to do before on any of his command flights. Indeed, finding mysterious Terrans on a planet they shouldn't have been on certainly wasn't an expected development either! This whole series of events was bizarre and becoming more so by the hour.

The captain activated his comm. "Commander, scan for that patrol ship again. If it's gone, we're returning to the ranger craft location. Report when you're ready." He looked up at the two soldats who were as baffled at their disappearance as was he. He shook his head. He had no grounds to even reprimand either of them. "Dismissed," he said decidedly.

Half an hour later, the *Cortés Libre* landed in the exact spot they had left earlier. Just prior to touch down, scans of the area revealed neither Telkan nor Terran life signs. Clearly, their staked captive Telkan was missing. Lieutenant Navar exited their craft with soldats Barcega, Agrida and Urret in tow. They quickly fanned out and scanned the immediate area with portable biosign detectors. As they suspected, there were none. But they had to be sure.

"Lieutenant," Agrida called out to Navar.

"What is it?"

"The dead Telkan is missing, too."

"That Telkan ship must have recovered him. They do that, you know."

Navar visually surveyed the area where they had staked the Telkan. He found the cut rope and the pole used to hold the Telkan's arms tied behind his neck. He picked up one of the manacles. He hadn't seen markings like that on metal for quite a while. It took a moment for him to realize it could have only been caused by a molecular disrupter. It was technology only the Telkans were known to have. He activated his hand scanner and checked the display. The residual energy signature on the metal indicated it was indeed Telkan. The myriad Terran footprints in the area made it impossible to discern if their 'guests' had been involved. Nonetheless, he assumed they had. The lieutenant called the ship to report their findings.

"Over here," Urret told him when Navar was done speaking with Selaye.

The three men quickly made their way to Urret. He was facing down slope with his sensor in hand. "There's a faint infrared signature leading that way," he said as he pointed.

The men spread out to look for broken branches in the underbrush and more footprints. Agrida found footprints almost immediately. "Over here," he called out.

They each inspected the prints. Two sets led away from the clearing toward the river. Navar wondered where the other set was. The Telkan ones. These were clearly Terran. Their boot prints were distinct. He had been sure their 'guests' had released the Telkan prisoner and that all had fled in the same direction. But the footprints suggested otherwise. He had originally assumed the Telkan scout ship had picked everyone up. Had they split up on purpose?

Lieutenant Navar reported in again after their assessment. They were ordered to return to the ship straight away. Minutes later, after having scanned further for any other signs of the Telkan ship, they were certain it wasn't anywhere nearby.

From the engine room display console, Llarena watched the vids being taken of Navar's party outside the ship. Clearly, it had been a mistake to not have had all the external cameras in record mode. That oversight had been rectified. He decided he was quite lucky to have escaped a good ass-chewing for having somehow lost their detainees. He watched as the ship's computers interpreted the myriad scans they were running on the area. His conversation with Naylon kept running itself in his head. Naylon's strange talk about an alternate universe and their odd conversation about some sort of alternate history kept repeating itself over and over in his head. What if there's a place where we aren't at war with the Telkans! The very thought of it seemed totally impossible.

But what if it were true?

Chapter 31

The chime on the comm next to Kestin sounded. "I'll be right back," he told Darreth after he answered it. "Someone needs my assistance. It'll only be a few minutes. I'll lock the door on my way out."

Darreth had nothing to do except think. He mused over an interesting detail no one had ever discussed. All of the pirates who had been captured and taken back to Andakar for questioning had met unusual fates. This last year alone two had simply disappeared and one had died mysteriously, although he heard it was of natural causes. Another had supposedly been taken to Earth and one had been deported to Ormi, the most hostile planet with respect to climate of all the Inhabs. Until this moment Darreth hadn't been interested in what that implied, if anything. His job was merely to pilot the ships that would prevent boardings. In the case of an actual boarding, his people would capture whoever they could and bring them back to Andakar for questioning, along with recovering any stolen pharmas.

Now that he thought about it, it was obvious someone wanted the captured pirates off Andakar as quickly as possible. Maybe before they talked to the wrong people. Corporate lawyers never televised trials. The mass viewing of a trial was deemed to be of no interest to the public. Nonetheless, he knew they got quick sentencing. Since every one of them had died or simply 'been removed' shortly after their trials, it was becoming obvious someone was playing a part in it. It was an easy leap of logic to assume Inandra was deeply involved.

Kestin returned much more quickly than Darreth expected. "Well, can you do it?" Darreth asked him. As far as he knew the disk was his only possible link to find Naylon and Tann, and he wasn't about to let it out of his sight.

Kestin glanced at the reprocomp in the corner. It was capable of replicating virtually anything. The disc could easily be copied.

Darreth looked in the same direction. Curious, he stood, went to the corner and observed the machine. He knew what it was. The label on the front proved it. "This is a reprocomp," he said. *An LR-44*, he thought. *I'm not familiar with that particular model but any lab of this size would have one.* In fact, given what he'd seen in the lab this model was probably the most sophisticated one in all of Siaron province. "You can do it," Darreth said, accusingly.

Darreth refused to leave the lab despite feeling supremely sleepy. He sat on a stool beside Kestin as they waited for the reprocomp to complete its task. Darreth finally couldn't stand it any more. He was about to pass out.

"You look awful," Kestin told him.

"I didn't sleep well last night."

"Look, no one's going to come in here." He looked at his office door. "I can opaque the windows in there. The couch is quite comfortable. I've slept on it many times."

"Maybe a nap," Darreth told him. He yawned profusely.

"I'm not going anywhere," Kestin assured him. They both went to his office. "I'll wake you when the reprocomp is done," he said as he pressed an icon on his desk surface. The windows instantly darkened.

Deep in thought, Kestin pressed the button on the doorframe and his office door slid shut. He would never have thought it possible to be handed something like this object, or be presented this kind of opportunity. Intensely curious about it, he peered into the top window of the reprocomp, watching the duplicate object forming in the open space below. It was assembling atom by molecule, and would be essentially identical to the original device once it was complete. The timer was still counting down. The duplicate would be done in another half hour.

The couch was unbelievably comfortable, Darreth discovered. He didn't even remember falling asleep after his head hit the decorative pillow.

Kestin looked back at his closed office door. He knew he shouldn't do it but he had to. Darreth, he decided, had no idea how important this object was to science. He had to figure out some way to prevent the man from taking the original away. It was impossible to ignore the imperative almost screaming at him. His hands started sweating. It was obvious what he had to do. The Lieutenant Commander's request to duplicate the object had sounded terribly illicit. Clearly, the man needed to use it for a secret project. Despite not wanting to be caught up in anything criminal he had to make sure the object wouldn't be lost. In his mind, unlocking the mystery of this object, perhaps unraveling what the unknown language was on its surface, was of paramount importance. The paper he could produce about it would be talked about for centuries. Kestin paced the lab as he thought about it. He glanced back at his office ever so often. Darreth was surely out cold.

The speaker icon on the flimsy to his right beeped, calling his attention. The reprocomp was done. Immediately, he retrieved the duplicate device from the machine and placed it in the scanning chamber he'd first used on the original. A few minutes later his comparison of the duplicate with the recorded information from the original assured him it was identical, except this one was made from materials derived from his universe. There might be one million atoms difference but that wasn't enough to bother with. As far as he was concerned, the coil was identical to the original and would activate whatever it was supposed to trigger.

He returned to the reprocomp and pressed an icon on the front panel. Duplicate number two started taking shape within thirty seconds.

Kestin placed the first duplicate under an optical scanner for further analysis. A microscopic scan of the odd spiral writing on the casing was of no help in determining its origin or use. He was sure it was writing, yet nothing in any language database he had access to had any reference to the symbols. Unfortunately, language wasn't his area of expertise. He knew that would have to remain a mystery in the short run.

He heard the reprocomp beep again. *Thunder*, he thought. Time was flying by and he had only begun to do a detailed analysis of the object.

Turning to the reprocomp yet again, he pulled the duplicate and the original from the machine and set them on the counter next to it. He retrieved the first duplicate and placed it on the right. Lined up, he noted visually they were all identical. The one on the left was the original so he placed it in a container and sealed it.

The door to his office slid open. He saw Darreth stifling a yawn.

"How long was I out?" Darreth asked.

"Nearly an hour," Kestin told him.

Darreth spied the two discs side by side. "You were able to duplicate it!" He heaved a sigh of relief.

"The two dupes are nearly identical to the original."

"Two? Nearly?"

"I'm not worried about a few million atoms difference."

"What's this about two?" Darreth said sternly.

"I, uh, went to the liberty of making a second one."

"I didn't ask for two of them," Darreth warned.

"I really think the original should stay here. It's extremely valuable. I'd hate to see it get lost," Kestin told him as straight forward and sincerely as he could.

"What are you getting at?" Darreth asked suspiciously.

"Only that you leave the original with me temporarily while you use the other two I made for you."

Darreth immediately shook his head. "What if the dupes don't work?"

Kestin was expecting that. He retrieved the original from the case. He brought up the spectral analysis of the original one he did before Darreth went to take his nap. He placed one of the duplicates in the scanner and performed a fresh scan. Syncing the two resultant graphs they matched precisely. As Kestin indicated though, they both were different only in the minutest way. It was impossible to get any more precision or better tolerance than the several million atoms difference both showed. "As you can see they're essentially perfect copies. They should perform as you expect. I'm merely suggesting the original stay here while you use the other ones. After all, one doesn't come by something like this object every day."

There was a short silence while Darreth mulled that over. "How about you keep a duplicate and I keep the original," he offered.

"You must understand, Lieutenant Commander, this object represents a scientific discovery of monumental proportion. Nothing like this has ever been found in the entire history of mankind. Surely, you can understand how important that is." He let that sink in, then continued. "I'm not going to ask you what you need the devices for, but it's obvious you need two. I'm merely suggesting since the original is an ancient alien artifact it should stay here. What if it gets lost or broken? It's irreplaceable. It's the only one that exhibits that anomaly of not belonging to our quantum universe. That alone makes it worth preserving."

"You're sure they're identical?" Darreth asked, desperation in his voice.

"That reprocomp is the best that's ever been manufactured. You saw the analysis yourself."

Darreth was sure it was a bad idea, but he wasn't stupid. The scans showed the duplicated discs were as identical as they could possibly be to the original. Plus, there was no indication the coil had been affected in any way through the duplication process. He took a deep breath. "You better keep it safe. I'm coming back for it after I'm done." In the back of his mind, he was sure he should kick himself for this. But his brain was fogged from lack of a good night's sleep and he couldn't find it within himself to say no.

Kestin was relieved beyond measure. "You can be sure it will not only not leave the lab, but it will be kept in a containment field that only I have the code for." He placed the object back in the sealed container and had Darreth accompany him to his office. The wall to his left consisted of twenty drawers, all of which would only open with his code. He input the code and the top leftmost drawer opened. He placed the sealed container in it and closed the drawer. He carefully and deliberately made sure Darreth watched him enter his code again. He tugged on the drawer. I was certainly sealed, Darreth noted.

Rehl and Darreth stood in the kitchen of Darreth's bungalow looking at the two 'keycards' Dr. Dryter had made. A holo-pic Kestin had made of the original was displayed on a flimsy next to the box where the devices were resting.

"Do you think this ornamentation is a language?" Rehl asked as he held the object up to the light.

"We figured it is."

"Only three people know these exist, right?"

Darreth nodded. "You, me and Dryter."

"Good." Rehl looked extremely nervous.

"Why the agit?" Darreth asked.

"Do you have any idea how difficult it was to get transport for us?"

"Yes, I do. It was extremely difficult."

"I'll probably lose my commission," Rehl murmured.

Darreth nodded. "And mine, too. But it would be far worse if I told anyone about that alien disc thing. Getting my brother and my boyfriend back is more important than my job right now. I know you're risking a lot to help me. You can back out. You-you don't have to do this," he fumbled for the words, hoping Rehl wouldn't say no.

Rehl snorted. "Fruck no. I'm with you. Besides, if what you say is true you're going to need all the help you can get. We'll hire a lawyer when this is all over. Maybe your dad can get us a good one, huh?"

Darreth sighed loudly, then looked over at the holo-mask Rehl had left on the couch. Used strictly for theater productions, the device, when worn correctly, could temporarily make anyone's face look like someone else's. They were illegal to use outside the theater districts because of that. Rehl's wife knew an actor in a local troop who had one. He said he'd let Rehl borrow it for a prank as long as no one in 'authority' found out about it.

Twenty-year-old Hoit Roonyun's shift was rapidly coming to an end at the Chendra spaceport's main embarkation terminal. She had processed well over two hundred people through her turnstile in the last hour. Jasterkin Festival Days were coming up on Ajica Prima and people were looking forward to reunions with their families who were off-world. She looked at the chronometer again, noting she had ten minutes left before Briull took her place. He couldn't get there soon enough, she thought.

Rehl and his companion approached Hoit. Following them was a skycap pushing an a-grav sled with their belongings on it. The skycap told the sled to go to the proper bay and left. Rehl handed Hoit his identification flimsy and the authorization to use one of the spaceport's shuttles for the trip to Rylerra. With the holo-mask firmly in place, Darreth handed his ID and flimsy to her as well, being careful to stand directly under the overhead lights. This close to an actual set of eyes, the mask wasn't as effective as it was when an audience looked toward someone wearing one at a distance.

"Festival?" Hoit asked Rehl, sounding a bit bored.

"Of course," he told her.

Hoit didn't so much as look at Darreth's face.

"Enjoy yourselves," Hoit said. "Next," she said to the couple behind them.

Rehl and Darreth quickly continued on their way. From here on everything was automated except for getting their luggage on board. Rehl's pilot's pass required them to proceed down a non-passenger terminal walkway to the awaiting shuttlecrafts. It took another half hour to be processed through the next checkpoint and have their bags loaded on board the *Andakar Navigator*. They were the only two aboard the eight-passenger ship. Twenty minutes after that Rehl was running through the take-off sequence. Eighteen minutes later, the sky was black and the convex curvature of Andakar's atmosphere was far below them.

"Hey, turn that thing off. You look ugly," Rehl said.

Darreth spoke an alphanumeric code aloud to de-energize the holo-mask. He un-strapped it and set the inert mask on the empty seat behind him. "I'm in real trouble this time," he said.

Rehl was equally in trouble. He knew they would eventually be discovered. "But it's for a good cause, isn't it?"

Darreth sure hoped so.

They both logged in to the nav display. Darreth felt a lot safer in the captain's spot, flying solo. Yet, it was a welcome relief Rehl said he'd join him and pilot the ship for at least the first leg of the journey.

The shuttle headed to where they would be able to wrinkle a wedge. There. The red X at the center of the display was slowly growing larger. Soon enough its shape turned into a frame with a dot in it, indicating they were rapidly approaching an insertion point for Rylerra, not Ajica Prime as stated in their flight plan. That part wasn't an issue. Rehl knew two ways to change the photronic copy of the flight plan to make it look like someone had screwed up, rather than it look like he had lied about it. In fact, the comm buoy for all of today's flights had already been sent to Rylerra Space Operations Command, which included their flight. Their arrival would be registered for Rylerra, not Ajica Prime. Only, they wouldn't actually arrive at the designated spaceport.

Darreth woke Rehl from his slumber. It was only an hour before they would be entering normal space again. Rehl shaved and entered the sonic shower for a few minutes. Refreshed, he took note of the coffee Darreth had made. He had some of it during a quick breakfast.

Darreth took a quick shower too, then donned his gear. He had already checked his backpack several times, but went over some of the equipment in the outer pouches again just to be sure. They both had ample rations for a week, plenty of sensor equipment to help them locate Naylon and Tann, warm clothing and hand weapons. They had no idea what to expect, but Darreth had to rely on his hope that wherever his brother and Naylon were they were alive and able to be rescued. The worst-case scenario would be he and Rehl would cross over the barrier to wherever it actually let to, and find them both dead. If so, the trip would take a lot less time than he envisioned. Regardless, no matter what happened next he was sure he and Rehl would be in heaps of trouble when it was all over.

Leaving the wedge was totally uneventful this time. There were no ships in the vicinity. The telemetry system computed their final vector for sub-orbital entry but Darreth conveniently ignored it. In the pilot seat now, he called up the file containing the coordinates of the cavern and veered thousands of kilometers from normal entry into Rylerran airspace. Within minutes, they were totally off the sensor net that monitored approaching traffic, making them invisible to planetary authorities.

Although they were off the sensor grid, their contrail would be a dead giveaway as to their location. As they descended further into warmer and denser air the trail finally started to peter out, offering them better cover. Soon enough, they were over familiar terrain. Darreth remembered the configuration of the far peaks. The nav displayed their descent vector and automatically plotted a course to the dry riverbed where Darreth's shuttle had ended up. They touched down moments later.

"Scans show no activity anywhere nearby," Rehl announced.

"I guess they really were done with their investigation," Darreth replied to that bit of news.

With descent procedures completed, Rehl pressed the icon that opened the side exit door. The air pressure had been slowly equalizing and now cool air flooded the interior of the craft. Both lifted their packs by the straps and, once outside, they assisted each other in putting them onto their backs. The only sound they heard was a faint ticking sound of the craft's skin cooling, then their footsteps crunching across the gravel and sand of the riverbed.

Darreth pulled out a lantern as they reached the cavern entrance. Immediately they noted a force shield generator placed across its maw.

Rehl looked at the field emitters. They were spaced vertically on thin rails that had been drilled into the rock. He recognized the make and model. "This shouldn't take long," Rehl told him with a grin. He pulled out a vidPAD and touched an icon on the display. Within ten seconds, the vidPAD discovered the frequency used by the generator. He touched another icon and waited for the program to break the encryption code. Two minutes later, the force shield was deactivated.

"They shouldn't have bothered," Darreth said with a grin. Rehl was particularly good at disassembling and decoding photronic technology.

They took a few moments to allow their eyes to adjust to the dark while playing their light beams all over the cavern. It was obvious there had been many people here recently. The dirt floor was covered with fresh boot tracks. Piles of equipment had been left in various places around the rim of the cavern. Both shafts that led away from them were covered with boot tracks, too.

"Which way?" Rehl asked.

"It's this one. The other one goes nowhere."

Paper-thin light films had been attached to the ceiling of the shaft at three-meter intervals. Rehl found the power supply module and touched the activate icon. They quickly illuminated to full intensity, providing an even soft glow along the entire shaft. Both switched off their lights and stowed them.

They proceeded at a swift pace down that corridor and quickly arrived at the interior cavern. Light films had been adhered to quite a few of the boulders all around them, some of which had been wrapped around freestanding ones. The most obvious item in the cavern was the large rectangular object in its center. Darreth saw it fully illuminated for the first time. The rock was clearly not part of this cavern. It was distinctly made of reddish granite, not the brown and white limestone the cavern appeared to have been carved from by natural forces.

"This is it," Darreth said as he pointed.

"No kidding." Rehl pointed to the cylindrical shaft inside the object. "Hey, I can't see through it." He had leaned forward and noted the bizarre play of light along the interior.

"Yeah, that's what we noted, too. And, apparently, that's the way. Ready?"

"Yep. Get your lantern. I'm going to deactivate the light films." He switched his lantern on, as did Darreth.

"Got the device?" Darreth asked.

Rehl pulled his out of the side cargo pocket of his pants. Darreth did the same. Neither had any idea how to use them so simply held on to them as they went through the tunnel.

Neither of them expected the vertigo that accompanied crossing the barrier. Although their flight training had included simulators, and actual experience had provided examples of real vertigo, this was totally different. Rehl instantly felt sick to his stomach and leaned up against the smooth rock once out of the cylinder on the other side. Darreth closed his eyes and dropped to his knees. It took both about fifteen seconds to recover.

"What the hell was that?" Rehl asked as he shook his head.

"I have no idea," Darreth responded. Several minutes later both were satisfied they hadn't been injured, just disoriented.

Now that both of them had sufficiently recovered, they surveyed their surroundings. It looked like they never left.

"I don't get it," Rehl said.

"Don't get what?"

"This is the same cavern. I thought we were supposed to be 'somewhere else'."

"We are somewhere else. This is some sort of alternate cavern. In a different quantum universe."

But Rehl noted right away that this cavern was decidedly different. Both saw the wide opening in the far wall. Sunlight was streaming into the cavern. Plus, it was significantly warmer than before. Both played their lantern beams around. They were satisfied they were alone and that no light films were anywhere to be seen, which proved they were no longer in 'their' cave'.

As they looked around, Darreth noted footprints leading toward the corridor they had just taken to get into the cavern. Both men followed the trail in the dirt and continued for only ten meters before Darreth stopped. "Something's wrong," he said.

"What?"

"There are two sets of prints. But one is going away and the same one is coming back."

"Yeah. So?"

"Do you see another set?"

They aimed their lights in the dirt for another couple of meters. "No, I only see those two."

"That means someone went back to the entrance but came back this way. They didn't leave that way."

Rehl scanned the floor, noting any other clues. "Looks like no one has come this way for a very, very long time."

"Which means they both may have gone another way." They returned to the inner cavern that contained the rectangular monolith. Darreth pointed toward the crack in the cavern wall. Rehl nodded agreement. There they noted several sets of footprints that clearly went toward the open crack in the wall.

"Well, this is definitely where they both went," Rehl said.

Both men went through the open crack, noting their surroundings. It was evident it was warm outside. In addition, a river rushed almost directly below them. Rehl took out his scanning equipment, as did Darreth. Both scanned the full EM spectrum for biosigns or transmissions. While doing so, Darreth tried several times to raise Naylon via his neural implant. No return signal came through. Rehl did the same and got no response either.

"Anything?" Darreth asked him as he looked at Rehl's vidPAD.

"Just background radiation." He looked past his display. "Hey, what's that?" Rehl said.

"Looks like something recently slid down there."

Darreth stepped forward as much as he dared on the slippery slope. "It ends at the water's edge."

Rehl looked at Darreth. "You think they...?"

Darreth nodded. "Looks like it."

Darreth shaded his eyes while surveying the river as it rushed past. "Until we know otherwise, I still have to assume they're both alive. So, we go downriver."

The vegetation all around them made it difficult to see ahead of them. That's where the scanning equipment they had with them came in handy. A scan of the area down slope to their right indicated the plants were at best half as tall and much more scattered. Carefully picking their way down the treacherous slope they came to a much flatter area. Sure enough, the bushes thinned out considerably, allowing them to zigzag their way in the general direction the river was running.

"Still nothing," Rehl told him after his fifth scan. But while they were stopped, Darreth saw a single footprint in the sand. He pointed, greatly relieved they had at least something to go on. *I recognize that tread*, he thought. He was sure of it. Tann was alive.

"I assumed they both slid down that slope back there and were in the river. Looks like Naylon was the one who fell. We have to assume that Tann went looking for him," Darreth told Rehl.

Rehl nodded at that assessment. "I'm getting a faint energy signature now. Residual only."

Darreth's scanner was in navigation mode, still mapping out their best route. He immediately switched the display to the same mode Rehl was using. "Bearing is 42 degrees, range is… what does your scanner read?"

"Eleven hundred meters."

"Same. Weapons."

They stopped, pulled out their stunners and continued on their way.

Ten minutes later, they arrived at the location where Rehl found the greatest concentration of residual energy.

"A ship definitely landed here. But I can't get a match on the energy signature. It's not in the database," Rehl said.

Darreth looked at the reading while Rehl attempted to coax the scanner to cull something out of the data. It kept coming up with nothing discernable. "Whoever it was clearly uses a different type of engine and propulsion system than we do. No surprise there. We're not even in our universe. It could be anyone or anything," he reported.

"Look. Footprints." Rehl pointed.

"Does that look human to you?" Darreth asked.

"No… but these do!"

"They come from that direction. Here. Looks like they were followed by these larger… animals… whatever." Darreth mused over his choice of the word 'animals'. He was entertaining the idea they weren't animals but rather aliens. After all, there were three back on 'their' Rylerra right now.

"Let's see. I count two sets of clearly human footprints," Rehl said. "But these are so odd-looking I can't tell how many of the… other ones there are."

"Looks like at least two sets. Maybe more. This doesn't look good at all," Darreth replied.

Rehl scanned the area again where something had landed. Again, it was fruitless. The only thing they could discern was all sets of footprints led to where a ship obviously had been, then went no further. Obviously, they all took off in the ship.

"What's this?" Rehl said.

"What?"

"Another signature. It's pretty far away. Several kilometers in that direction." He pointed. "This one's different."

"Maybe Rylerra is an alien inhab on this side of the tunnel."

"And maybe they were rescued," Rehl offered. "The larger footprints look a lot like the alien ones we found in the cavern. They have the same long and narrow shape. Maybe in this dimension the place is crawling with them."

"Let's hope they were rescued and not captured," Darreth replied. His stress level just went up a couple of notches anyway.

Captain Pacudas and Commander Selaye studied the readout. The scan was clear. There were two Terran bio signs headed their way. They weren't there a minute ago, but they certainly were now. The captain felt confident they had found their missing guests after all.

Chapter 32

Naylon and Tann were led at gunpoint to an entrance on the side of the large Telkan ship. Naylon instantly recognized it as a military vessel despite it being totally alien. That was bad. Now they were really caught up in this war. There was nothing they could do. They certainly weren't going to run while weapons were trained on them.

Two Telkans, also fully armed, were just inside the outer door of the airlock, backing up as Naylon and Tann stepped in, aiming weapons squarely at them. Os'Taga and Th'Gan remained outside pointing sensor equipment all around, searching for anyone else they might have missed. An'Arka followed behind Naylon and Tann until they were completely inside the long narrow airlock compartment. He pointed at their packs, indicating they were to be removed. Both of them complied immediately. An'Arka stuffed them both into a storage container. Os'Taga and Th'Gan quickly followed him inside and the door was closed. Five Telkans and two humans occupied the compartment in close quarters. Tann was terrified into total silence. He was literally surrounded by fierce-looking and well-armed alien creatures. He was sure at any minute they would both be very dead.

The outer airlock door was curiously semi-transparent. Three long opaque beams within the door reinforced it horizontally. They were motioned to sit down on unexpectedly soft cushions along the sides of the airlock compartment. Seconds later, after Os'Taga spoke something unintelligible, they saw the ground swiftly fall away as the vessel took to the air. Their vertical motion was quickly replaced with a rapid horizontal one.

A door at the other side of the compartment where they had been sitting opened and they were motioned to go into the interior of the craft. Impossible-to-read writing was all over the walls, appearing to Naylon to have been written from top to bottom. It seemed more of an adornment than instructions or warnings because there was so much of it. Tann noted it right away, too. Swirls, dots, small segments, and wavy lines, etched into surfaces everywhere. It looked primitive, but sophisticated at the same time.

Naylon expected the interior of the ship to be dark and evil looking. It was nothing of the sort. It was brightly lit. Metallic objects were brightly colored. The interior was spotless. There wasn't so much as a smudge on any of the brightly colored walls of the wide corridors they were led down. They passed two open rooms, one of which looked like a recreation room, and the other appeared to be a large galley. Curiously, two distinct smells found their way to his nose as they passed. Both were pleasant.

Two of the Telkans who had helped capture them, plus An'Arka, continued to lead them to the end of the corridor, then to the right. The other two left in a hurry when a comm signal was received by one of them. They were led to two individual small rooms. These were distinctly cells, Naylon noted. The only furnishings were a short bed with a thin bare mattress and what looked like a toilet recessed into an alcove. Next to the alcove was a recessed area with what looked like a sink in it. A small cup was next to it in a recess where a spigot protruded. They were ushered into the rooms and the doors were sealed. Once the doors shut, the overhead illumination faded until what remained was a small red pinpoint of light. There were no windows or other light sources. The door was sealed so tightly no light issued from under it.

Their cells were side-by-side. Naylon hadn't had an opportunity to say anything to Tann about their predicament. He yelled it instead, "Don't agit, Tann. I'll think of something."

He didn't hear a reply.

With their Terran prisoners now onboard, the *Mu'Anelko*'s sublight engines were energized. Second Tier Engineer Ba'Tekta activated the conduit detection system and chose the closest one less than one AU from the planet's orbit. He touched the surface of the screen in front of him, sliding a finger against the dark glass. The display connected their coordinates with the entrance, locking them in to the nav computer. The ship slowly altered its vector until it was aimed directly at its mouth.

The *Mu'Anelko's* destination was this star's sister known as Jop'Kav. Once the conduit opening was reached, it would be a matter of a few hours before they arrived back to their base on the waterworld in that system. A world the Telkans had settled only seventeen revolutions previous. A much prized world because of its planetary ocean and abundant life, it was one of four jewels of the Ascendency. The warm waters culled genetic memories of the Telkan past when they too slid through waters such as those. For that reason alone, it was well known as a choice duty station.

Leader Sa'Par and Ranger An'Arka stood in front of the viewscreen at the science station on the bridge of the *Mu'Anelko*. The screen was split in two. An infrared image of the two holding cells where their prisoners were being kept for the time being was displayed. Naylon was just sitting on the bunk. Tann was feeling every inch of the walls, looking for something. An'Arka emitted a chuckle. He knew the Terran's search for a way out would be fruitless.

"The taller one is called Naylon. The other is called Tann," An'Arka told Sa'Par.

"They are the ones who helped you escape?"

"They are."

"Curious."

"Indeed. As I reported before, their clothing is not the same as the others. I conclude they are not military. They may be colonists."

Sa'Par's nose moved from side to side, the Telkan way of indicating a negative. "Our scans of M'jas'la have indicated no Terrans have ever colonized the planet. I'm not certain how they could have arrived here without our knowledge." He hesitated. "Terrans have strayed this far from their space," he added, musing. "We will have to double patrols of this planet and request a speed up of colonization."

"It may be a rogue scout ship looking for intelligence. It has happened before. Certainly not this far from their known territory. Perhaps they're on their way to Q'emt'la and just stopped here briefly. After all M'jas'la isn't as well occupied by our people as is Q'emt'la."

Leader Sa'Par was privy to intelligence his Second Tier Ranger was not. The closest Terran outpost was twenty-five light years from this system. None of the mapped warp conduits ran between this system and any in Terran space. In fact, there were only three known conduits that terminated into Terran occupied space. Was it possible the Terrans had some sort of new stealth technology they were as yet unaware of? Was it possible a warp conduit somehow terminated into this system that was as yet undetected? Discovering how the Terrans had managed to get here was paramount. Questioning their prisoners would be the first order of business once they arrived.

Naylon kept himself occupied in the almost-pitch-dark cell by doing pushups and sit-ups. Lots of them. He did twenty, rested, then twenty more, then rested even longer. After a short while, he did some more. Tann occupied himself by masturbating. Twice. He felt considerably better afterward. Now, all alone in the dark with nothing else do, there wasn't much else to occupy his time except to sleep.

Meals were marked by a short time when the lights were raised. Two guards brought each of them a tray with lots of unidentifiable vegetables and some sort of gelatinous mass in a bowl, along with eating utensils. Naylon figured the gelatinous mass might be the equivalent of a protein product. It smelled delicious. At least they weren't being mistreated, he noticed. After the first meal, Naylon simply put his tray on the floor, not having any idea when his jailers might be back to collect it. They returned what seemed like a half hour later. The guard took his tray then pointed to one of the walls of the cell. He handed Naylon a small vial of orange liquid. The guard left, with Naylon staring at the vial then the wall, not sure what to make of what he had in his hand. As the lights dimmed again, a small section of the previously plain wall illuminated. It was a built-in display screen. A bald shirtless Terran male, or what Naylon thought was one, was pantomiming to open the tube, pour the liquid into his mouth, swish it around, then spit it into the sink. Naylon opened the tube and briefly took a whiff. It smelled vaguely like bananas. He hesitated, then realized that without a toothbrush, this may be the only way for him to freshen his mouth. The vid ended and the wall went black. Naylon tossed back the liquid and swished. Instantly, his mouth was awash in several flavors. Bananas, blackberries, then something completely unidentifiable but vaguely like cinnamon. He spit the liquid down the sink, then sat the empty vial next to it. He was being sequestered, but not mistreated. It made no sense. He was sure he was considered a prisoner of war. Why was he being treated so well, he wondered, though assuredly thankful.

At least one sleep period passed. Naylon hadn't heard any screams or odd noises, so had to trust Tann was okay and wasn't being mistreated either. Finally, the lights rose and stayed on, but no one arrived to open the doors. Several times he heard footsteps on the other side of the door when he placed his ear against it. He figured they had been in flight, but to where?

Hours later the door unceremoniously slid opened. The same two guards, along with An'Arka stood there. Tann was with them already.

Naylon was motioned to exit the cell. The cell had been rather warm and he had been shirtless for quite some time. He took it from the bed and donned it quickly, following them. Tann wasn't being restrained, nor was he. Apparently, the guards, all being much larger than them were enough to assure they would comply.

"Are you okay?" Naylon asked him.

Tann gulped and nodded. "What are they going to do with us?"

"Can't hurt to ask," he told Tann. Then to An'Arka, "An'Arka, where are you taking us?"

An'Arka didn't answer right away. He appeared to be listening to something they couldn't hear. Presently, though he answered Naylon. "You are on Q'emt'la. You will be taken to Minister Ne'Uanju for questioning."

"What is Q'emt'la?"

"A Held World of the Ascendency."

"Which is where?"

An'Arka's standing orders were to simply shuttle his prisoners to the interrogation chamber and return to his ship. Nonetheless, he knew it wouldn't hurt to show them who was in charge. "Q'emt'la orbits the sister star."

Naylon wasn't sure what a sister star was, then almost immediately realized that based on the amount of time they had spent in the cells, they couldn't be too terribly far from Rylerra. "Is this the waterworld that circles the yellow star near where we were taken prisoner?"

"Our Held World," was An'Arka's simply reply.

Naylon turned to Tann. "I think we're back on Andakar."

Tann fully comprehended what was going on now. "Yeah," he agreed sadly. "But it's not our Andakar."

Naylon noticed that no matter where they had been taken on the ship it was well lit. All of the corridors had brightly colored walls. The ship was considerably larger than the Terran one, too. The only thing that was odd was the strange sour odor in the air now, totally unlike the one they had smelled previously. Perhaps it was the Telkans. Could their atmospheric controls not scrub their body odor out? Maybe they didn't want that to happen. Perhaps they communicated by odor.

A dock had been attached to the airlock where they were being led. It had rows of windows along the sides and ceiling, letting in the sunlight. As they were being led through it, both of them were able to observe their surroundings. They had landed on a pad in an evident spaceport near a shoreline. To their right was a mountain range. Something about the mountains looked familiar, but Naylon hadn't focused his attention on it just yet. Nearby was a skyline of several tall buildings, all highly ornamented and shining in the sun with brilliant colors. Everywhere they looked it seemed even the simplest item was highly ornamented with what looked like writing or designs. That included the uniforms the aliens wore outside the docking corridor.

A tall piece of unidentifiable equipment blocked Naylon's view of the mountains briefly. As they passed it, he looked again.

"Tann, does that peak over there look familiar?"

"That's Ytok Peak in the Patoria Mountains. This *is* Andakar!"

"Like you said though, it's not our Andakar."

The dock connected them with a windowless shuttle. From there, only An'Arka led them to it where they were instructed to stand with their backs against flat metal panels. Almost immediately after stepping up on them Naylon noted his feet appeared to be stuck to the surface. As soon as he put his hands to his sides his back seemed to be attracted to the panel too and he could no longer move. Tann was stuck steadfast as well. *Localized high gravity fields*, Naylon thought. *Thunder, these beings are seriously advanced!* The shuttle ride was short. As soon as the side door opened, the panel's gravity fields were deactivated. Both of them were finally able to move freely.

Two Telkans who appeared to be in non-military clothing approached and spoke to An'Arka briefly. Naylon noted both wore bright yellow flowing robes adorned with embroidered designs and what appeared to be the ornamental writing he'd seen all over the ship that brought them here. Naylon and Tann merely observed the interaction. An'Arka continued with the two new aliens, speaking to them in their language at intervals along the way. They continued to be led down several plush corridors in the building where they had been taken.

Eventually they came to a wide ramp. They passed by only two other Telkans along the way, both of who stopped and stared at them as they passed. The second time it happened Naylon stared back. He could discern no emotion on its face. Eventually, they were led into a semi-circular corridor with several closed doors along the walls. To the right were double doors. An'Arka waved his hand in front of a sensor and the doors slid open. The other two Telkans behind them stayed there. An'Arka motioned for Naylon and Tann to go ahead of him. They emerged into a spacious room with noticeable adornments on the walls. Art. Lots of it. In two corners were plants, too. The room looked like the den of a home rather than something found on a military base, if this were indeed a military base.

Behind a desk at the far end of the room sat a large imposing Telkan. Naylon knew right away they had been sent to see someone in authority. Perhaps the minister An'Arka spoke of earlier. This one was wearing a sleeveless shirt that appeared to have no obvious zippers, catches or buttons along the front. He observed the band around the Telkan's bare upper arm. It had three bright gold medals on it, arranged in a triangle. He decided it was a rank insignia.

"Minister Ne'Uanju," An'Arka told Naylon.

The minister spoke to An'Arka for a moment.

"He told me you are prisoners of the Telkan Ascendency."

"No kidding," Tann said.

Naylon looked at Tann briefly then back to An'Arka. "Tell him we are not Terrans."

There was a brief exchange between the two Telkans. Ne'Uanju pressed an icon on the flat display in front of him. He spoke, then a computerized voice translated for him into Empire Spanish.

"You are Terran, yet you say you are not. Why do you even attempt to deceive me with that ridiculous statement?"

Naylon hoped the translator worked both ways. "What I meant to say, sir, is we were not with the group of Terran's on the planet where we were taken prisoner. We weren't supposed to be there at all. We are not your enemies. They are."

There was another brief exchange between An'Arka and Ne'Uanju. Ne'Uanju spoke directly to Naylon.

"M'jas'la is a Telkan Held World. How did you get there?"

"M'jas'la?" Tann asked Naylon.

"My people call it Rylerra," Naylon told the minister.

More words between Ne'Uanju and An'Arka.

"Repeat that name," An'Arka told Naylon.

"Ry-ler-ra," Naylon said slowly.

Ne'Uanju spoke to his desktop computer, looking for that word in the database. There was no result to his inquiry.

"You are lying," Ne'Uanju told him.

"No, your database doesn't have that name in it because we're not from your universe. We don't belong here. We arrived on… M'jas'la accidentally through some sort of-of dimensional tunnel. It's in a cavern on that planet. We took refuge there and went through it, not knowing we would end up… here."

It took a moment for An'Arka to process what Naylon had said. Once he understood what Naylon was describing he chuckled noticeably. Naylon heard it as a wheezing sound.

But Ne'Uanju was immediately keenly interested. "The gateway?" he said aloud.

"Sir?" An'Arka asked.

"From the Time Before."

An'Arka was quite familiar with the Time Before story. It was the nearly universal tale told to Telkan children about their culture. More legend than history, it nonetheless told of the Great Loss.

Two thousand years ago, their people had achieved space travel only to encounter a deadly alien race shortly thereafter. The race's name had long ago been lost. One version of the legend held they were called the K'ell. There was very little actually known about them except that they had superior weapons and technology, and were uninterested in not much more than hunting alien races. At the hands of the K'ell, many people had died and much knowledge about their very own history had been lost. That was because the K'ell had been very effective in their dealing with Telkans they had come across: they simply wiped them out and destroyed their technology. Slowly but surely, the K'ell drew ever closer to the Telkan homeworld until a last stand was made by a group of exploration ships that hadn't yet been destroyed. A classic Trojan horse gift had been given to the K'ell in an attempt to appease them. The gift of a biological weapon. As far as the Telkan people knew their weapon must have done exactly what they intended since within months not a single K'ell was ever seen again.

The Telkans had been successful in preventing the annihilation of their species. That was the fortunate part. The unfortunate legacy was much more devastating. The last stand had come too late. Their struggle against the K'ell had done irreparable damage to their civilization. Their interplanetary economy had been shattered, preventing much more than trying to survive. A nine hundred year Dark Age befell Telkan civilization. It took another three hundred years for the Telkan race to re-emerge from their homeworld star system once space flight was rediscovered. From that point in their history, they once again followed their natural biological tendency, which was to explore and gather knowledge.

Three of their outlying worlds, each with small populations, were found and brought back into the collective fold. Hundreds of years later, the Terran Empire confronted them. By that time, the Telkans had colonized dozens of worlds spanning fifty light years in every direction, and had unified their long-separated cultures into a single huge collective called the Telkan Ascendency. Until encountering the Terrans, they had never come across any alien spacefaring culture although they had come across the devastated K'ell homeworld, which they immediately judged off-limits to any Telkan.

The gateway was one story in the overall ancient Time Before legend. In the story, B'rint, the sole survivor of a scientific team on one of the first expeditions to a now unknown double-star system, told a bizarre tale of a mysterious cavern. Within the cavern lay an inexplicable stone with a tunnel in it. The tunnel led to another dimension which one could cross over to and then return from. With so many double and triple star systems near the Telkan homeworld, no one could be sure if the story had merit since no trace of a so-called gateway had ever been discovered. No one knew how the gateway had gotten there, but it was said the exploration team had discovered how it worked quite by accident. Most of the details were lost, but some remained. The gateway was in a cavern on a temperate world. The tunnel to the gateway went deep into a mountain. At the other end of the gateway was a world very much like the one they came from. Unfortunately, shortly after that discovery, the K'ell had discovered the expedition and killed almost everyone. The legend didn't detail whether the K'ell had ever found the cavern or not. Most likely, they didn't though because of their tendency to simply wipe out Telkan settlements or outposts.

As far as Ne'Uanju was concerned, the collected stories of the Time Before were either totally fabricated, had been greatly embellished or were nothing like what had actually occurred during that awful time. But one thing he was sure of: it was impossible this Terran had ever heard the legend. Which meant he knew of a real gateway.

Ne'Uanju motioned for An'Arka to come near. "Do you know of the story about the gateway in the Time Before?"

"My clan hails from Haj'ret'sa, Minister Ne'Uanju. Our tradition doesn't tell of a gateway."

The Minister gave An'Arka a mini-summary, emphasizing the double-star system setting and the temperate world where it was located.

An'Arka's first thought was there were Terran prisoners to interrogate. There were Terrans still on M'jas'la that needed to be rounded up and eliminated. Indeed, these two still needed to be properly processed. Perhaps the Minister was tired and wasn't thinking clearly. An'Arka hesitated before answering. "It is a legend. Of a time long ago. Before the now time."

"Yet this Terran knows the story. Leave us. I will trust the computer to provide a proper translation. If there is something unclear I will call you back."

An'Arka squeezed a fist in front of his chest in compliance and left the room.

The chairs Naylon and Tann were sitting in were not designed for human anatomy. They were too concave and provided no support for their backs. Ne'Uanju noticed Tann was squirming quite a bit.

"I am Ne'Uanju, First Minister of this base. You are prisoners of the Telkan Ascendency," he reiterated to Naylon.

"We are well aware we are prisoners. Your people already made that clear by capturing us. But you've all got this wrong. We were not with those Terrans. They used their injection on us just like they did to your crewman."

Ne'Uanju considered that for a moment. He knew all about the RNA injections the Terrans used. It was common for the Terrans to inject themselves and each other with such drugs for various purposes. He was also aware the language injections only lasted several revolutions at most. That was why An'Arka would be extra valuable for as long as he retained their language. The Minister ignored that last comment for the moment. "What is this 'tunnel' of which you spoke?"

"Only that it's a sort of rock structure with an opening in it. We found it in a cavern. We, uh, crashed on Rylerra in our dimension and accidentally went through it. We don't belong here. If you let us go, we'll simply go back. You can pretend you never met us." Naylon knew his request would be denied but it didn't hurt to try asking.

"Tell me more about the tunnel."

"That's all we know." He certainly wasn't going to tell Ne'Uanju about the devices that allowed them through. They had no way back without them. Perhaps the minister didn't know about them. Otherwise, wouldn't that have been one of his first questions? But Naylon was suspicious of this line of questioning already. What significance did it have with the creature?

"You know about the tunnel?"

"It is known among my people," the minister replied.

"Then you already know where it is. We don't."

Ne'Uanju was used to dealing with Terrans. They were tricky, full of guile, wily, and had lots of energy. They were unusually intelligent, which explained how they had been able to fill an enormous volume of space with their people. It wasn't until the Terrans first encountered a Telkan colony on R'kinth'la that the Telkans knew the extent of their deceptive capabilities. The first encounter with Terrans was taken as a major scientific discovery. Telkan civilization was not a naturally war-like one. Shortly after the first encounter, an agent from their race came to speak with the R'kinth'la First Prime. It took weeks to discern the Terran language. The Telkan interpreters took great pains to understand it. They were excited beyond belief that they had finally encountered another spacefaring race, and one that seemed determined as well to understand them. The Terran language was very linear and was entirely derived from a very small range of vocal sounds. It was finally deciphered once that fact was recognized. Shortly thereafter, it was firmly understood that the Terrans' only interest was for the

Telkans to leave their colony world! If they didn't leave, the Terrans would forcibly remove the Telkans. Barring that, they would kill each and every one of them.

At least the Terrans weren't like the K'ell, who had killed and destroyed at will. This species gave fair warning.

Never mind that Telkans had occupied the planet for twenty-five revolutions. The Terrans wanted R'kinth'la and they were going to get it, or else. Unfortunately, negotiations to avoid a conflict failed. The Terrans tried several different methods to rid R'kinth'la of Telkan occupation. Those attempts failed. It was mainly due to the fact that Telkan science was at least evenly matched to the Terran war machine. Several other factors caused the Terrans to fail. They were at the far edge of their space and had no back up. Telkan ships tended to be nearly twice as large as Terran ones. The sheer destructive power of the weaponry that came standard on even a Telkan scout ship prevented the Terrans from being able accomplish their mission.

A brief lull in tensions was only due to the Terrans regrouping, re-arming and bringing reinforcements. But the Telkans had been ready. A gauntlet had been thrown down, which quickly brought an end to the attempt by the Terrans to remove them. Out of eighteen warships the Terrans had brought, only one survived. Only a single Telkan ship was destroyed. After the debris scattered enough to safely traverse the system, the entrances to the warp conduits in the R'kinth'la system that crossed into Terran-held space were mined and placed off limits to all Telkan traffic.

A continuous series of Terran encounters ended tragically for the Terrans. Not knowing warp conduits could be mined, the Terrans lost fifteen ships before they got through and then went back to report that tactic. It was because of the huge losses on the Terran side that the Telkans discovered just how tenacious they were. Regardless, R'kinth'la had been safe for an extremely long time.

Ne'Uanju could count four sheddings that had elapsed since that first encounter with the Terrans. Prisoners had been taken, their culture had been studied, and their worlds had been mapped through the use of interrogation and some incursions into their space. A few Terrans had been dissected, some had been mercifully killed, and others had been unceremoniously dumped from airlocks when they got away on prisoner ships and left guards dead. Few Telkans had gone missing;

fewer still had made it back alive to Telkan occupied space after having been captured. Regardless, enough was now known of their species. They were devious creatures.

By default that included the one called Naylon.

Yet somehow, Minister Ne'Uanju knew this one was different. He had a young one of his species with him. Terran military units never traveled with their young. As An'Arka had determined, the two were not dressed as they would expect those in military units to be dressed, nor did they have any of the weaponry known to be manufactured by Terrans. He had been given a full report on their genetic profile and their personal effects before the prisoners arrived in his office. Yes, they were Terran, but something was all wrong about these two. Maybe the one named Naylon wasn't lying.

"If you came through the gateway then how do you not know where it is?" Ne'Uanju inquired.

Naylon noted the use of the word 'gateway' instead of tunnel. It was evident they referred to is as such. He told the minister how he had fallen into the river and ultimately captured by the Terrans. That Tann had come looking for him and been captured as well.

Tann was feeling faint. He hadn't eaten or drunk any water for hours. The ridiculous questioning Ne'Uanju was asking about the tunnel was beginning to irritate him, too. He had to interject himself into the conversation. "Please, Minister. I'm very thirsty. Can I have some water?"

Ne'Uanju was familiar with how Terrans were somewhat fragile. Their skin was far thinner than their own. Terrans dehydrated much more quickly than did their species. The Minister was unsure how Terrans could have survived long enough as a species to achieve space flight without a water bladder behind their lungs.

The Minister pressed an icon on the desktop display "Ranger J'selnof, the prisoners require sustenance," he said in his native language. "Assign them to the keeping place. I will see them later on. See to it they are not harmed in any way. I have a great need for these two."

Chapter 33

Naylon and Tann were taken away in an air transport pod. The entire top of the pod was covered yet transparent. They were not allowed to sit, but rather were instructed to hold onto metal bars for support while the pilot flew them to another facility. It was even more apparent they were on Andakar once they rose into the air. Both of them were equally astonished to discover they were also on the south end of Koehkelko bay. The Patoria Mountains were to the east, the crescent shape of the bay was completely evident and the gentle lapping of the waves on the sandy shore was totally familiar. But Tokaias was nowhere to be seen. Instead, they saw a scattering of smaller interconnected buildings, all were hexagonal in shape and brightly colored. The town, which is what it seemed to be to Naylon, reminded him of a sprawling open-air hive.

Both Naylon and Tann mentally took in all the details during their short journey away from the spaceport to the nearest cluster of low-rise buildings. Once they landed, they were quickly motioned to debark and were sent through a windowless corridor. Halfway down, they came to an alcove were they were instructed to remove their clothing. At first Naylon objected, but the guard quickly indicated this wasn't negotiable.

Tann got down to his underwear, then he stopped. The Telkan next to him motioned for him to remove it all. Tann already felt quite vulnerable. Reluctantly, he shed everything in front of the huge hulking alien creatures, feeling even more vulnerable now that he was completely naked. Luckily, it was quite warm in the corridor. It would have been even more uncomfortable if it hadn't been.

Their clothing was pushed into a pile by one of the Telkans near the alcove. A trapdoor opened and all of it disappeared. One of the aliens pointed to painted footprints on the floor. Naylon and Tann stood side by side on two sets. A red laser played across each of them, wrapping itself around their bodies. Seconds later a panel opened on the wall. Two gray one-piece tissue-thin jumpsuits were pulled out and handed to each of them. Naylon recognized right away they were to put them on, which they did. They were as soft as cotton with nothing more complicated than a zipper that went from the crotch to the neck, he noticed, as he stepped into it. It was cut short at mid-thigh and was sleeveless. Felt slippers were given to them and they both put them on. Tann felt a little better at being clothed again, but not by much. Moments later, they were herded to the end of the corridor where they both smelled food.

Amazingly, there were four humans males, wearing the same gray jumpsuits, standing at the end of the corridor through an opened door. They were ushered through the door, which immediately slid shut.

"Who are you?" the tallest man asked Naylon in impeccable Empire Spanish. He was clean shaven as were the rest of the men.

"Dr. Naylon Ress," Naylon told him. "Who are you?"

"Special Ranger Rogerto Tomús. These are some of my men, Nolo Gonjas, Sedeto Confón, and Férío Atore." He pointed to them as he called off their names. "Why do you have a… child with you?" He looked at Tann.

"Get serious," Tann told him bluntly.

"We're, uh, lost," Naylon told him.

"I don't think so. We're in a Telkan prisoner of war facility."

The smell of food was beginning to make Tann extremely hungry. "Water. I need a drink of water really badly."

"Nolo. Get them water. We were just about to sit for our meal. You will sit with us," he said in a concerned tone.

Tann downed over a liter of water, while Naylon drank almost as much. Naylon then surveyed their enclosure. It was a two-story high hexagonal-shaped open room. He estimated the diameter at around twenty meters. Although there were only six people there at the moment, the place could easily hold five times that many. Along the edges of the circular common area were eight sleeping alcoves, each with four beds and adjacent toilet facilities. Their enclosure looked vaguely like a large dormitory. But there were no windows anywhere, no interior doors, and no furniture except for a table with chairs near another alcove. It was clearly a food dispensary, complete with a place to put dirty dishes and trays. What was most interesting about the interior of the place was how elaborately designed everything was. It was as ornate as the rest of the Telkan facilities they had already seen. Table and chair legs were curved and graceful looking. Bright colorful walls surrounded them. Except for the outfits everyone was wearing, which were grey, all of the textiles in the room were brightly colored with intricate weaves. The Telkan script that Naylon had seen in the ship, which had brought them to the planet's surface, was everywhere, although here it vaguely resembled Islamic artwork he had seen in vids. It was as if this alien culture didn't understand what a prison was supposed to look like.

He was given a tray. He stood with the other men in front of the self-serve cabinets and selected several non-descript items. Nothing looked familiar but each item in bowls had a distinct smell. Chicken here. Vegetables there. A sauce over there. Perhaps that jelly-looking substance was really watermelon. Naylon couldn't tell from looking, but it sure smelled like it.

Sedeto saw Tann's look of bewilderment, too. "Don't try to identify anything by sight. They can't exactly reproduce what we eat. You'll only be able to identify it by the aroma."

"They made this food?"

"Of course. Telkan abominations."

Abominations? What does he mean by that, Tann wondered. *I'm eating whether he likes it or not.*

Eventually everyone had something on their trays and they sat.

"Who are you people?" Naylon asked them as they all ate.

Rogerto spoke up. "My crew was on a survey mission in the Ojen system. As you know it is claimed by both sides. A Telkan Destroyer discovered us. Our sensors were down when it happened. We had… shall I say, a power problem. We fought bravely nonetheless. We holed up in the engine room when the ship was disabled. It was only a matter of time before they scanned the compartment and found us. Turns out we were the only ones who survived the assault. Our best guess is we've been here for approximately a Terran year. It's impossible to say for sure since we have no access to timepieces and are only randomly let out into the sunlight. We know only that we're being held on Q'emt'la. You're the first Terrans we've seen since our capture."

Most of what Rogerto said was impossible to follow. "You've been held for a year?" Naylon asked.

"Give or take a couple of weeks. We didn't start keeping track for a while after we were captured. They don't interact much with us. We do think they're constantly observing us though."

Naylon noted it was becoming troublesome keeping all the names straight. Until a few days ago, he'd only known this planet as Andakar. Now it was Q'emt'la to the Telkans and these men, while it was Ozol to the Terrans they had encountered on Rylerra. The reason was obvious. This planet was unknown to the prisoners before they had been taken here. Thus, they would use only the name for the planet the Telkans used. The other military men back on 'Rylerra' had just made up the name for identification purposes only. After all, they had never been there either.

"They've not interrogated you?" Naylon asked.

"Of course they have. What Telkan wouldn't? We offered them the usual blather to keep them from discovering what it was we were doing. They found out anyway. Now, Dr. Ress. Where did they capture you?" Rogerto asked.

"On Déstica." He deliberately used the name Captain Pacudas had told him.

"What is Déstica?"

"I mean M'jas'la. The other Terrans are calling it Déstica. Well, their captain is calling it that."

"Other Terrans?" The men all looked at each other.

"Maybe they're looking for you," Naylon offered.

"There are other Terrans nearby? How did they get past the Telkan patrols, much less all the mines? We are deep inside Telkan space."

"What mines?" Naylon asked.

"The conduits into Telkan space are all mined. We're nowhere near the border. What was your ship name?"

"Conduits?" Tann asked. He wasn't answered.

Naylon answered Rogerto instead. "We didn't come here with the Terrans on Déstica."

All of this was terribly confusing to Sedeto. "The Telkans brought you here from their space?"

"What conduits?" Tann asked again.

"Naylon, what are children doing on military vessels nowadays. Did orders change recently?"

"Wait, wait. Hold it," Naylon said. He too was becoming confused now. The men didn't have much information to go on and were speculating. "Tann is not a child. He's my friend. We didn't get here because of a one of your military ships. We weren't brought here from

Telkan space. Both of us are from this planet... just, not in this... dimension." He figured that wouldn't go over so well.

He was wrong. It got a rousing round of laughter from the entire group. Rogerto slapped Naylon on the back. "That was a good one. You're from here! From another dimension. That is supremely rich. I had almost forgotten how to laugh." He totally dismissed what Naylon had said as the truth.

"I was born in Tokaias," Tann told them boldly.

Fério spoke up now. "Tokaias. Is that a colony?"

"It's the name of the city that's supposed to be on this bay... but isn't. Naylon, you're going to have to explain it to them."

"Later. What's this about a conduit?" Naylon asked them now. "What did you mean by them being mined?"

Rogerto looked at him curiously. "Surely you are aware the conduits that connect Telkan with Terran space are mined. They've been mined for decades. I assumed you had gotten through somehow," Rogerto told them.

"But what are they?" Tann repeated.

Rogerto crossed his arms across his chest. He wasn't used to being questioned, especially so vehemently, by a youngster. "They are the natural wormholes used as starlanes; the means by which all of our ships travel from star to star. Perhaps you use a different name on your homeworld."

"Did you say 'natural'?" Naylon asked.

"Of course. All stars have them. You are not military. Perhaps you have never had the need to know about them if you don't travel from star to star."

Tann's mind was in overdrive. Naturally occurring starlanes? If that were the case, how was it possible he had never heard of such a thing? "Where are they?" he asked.

"None of us have the coordinates for the ones in this system, of course. But it's very obvious where some of them are due to the neutronic mines and sensor grids at their mouths."

Naylon looked at Tann. This was certainly a revelation. As far as Naylon knew the main difference between this dimension and their own was that here history took a turn on Earth long ago. Yet, there were other subtle differences as well. Like the fact that humans had encountered an alien species. And they were at war with each other.

Rylerra was warmer in this dimension than in their own. There was another other semi-sentient species called Taskers being used as laborers. He wondered if these naturally occurring conduits that folded spacetime existed in his own dimension. If they did, wouldn't the Consortium have exploited them for their own end? It was worth finding out more. He could only hope they did in fact exist in his dimension. "You use these conduits used to travel between stars?" Naylon asked Rogerto.

"As do the Telkans."

"How do you, er, know where they're located? The ones that aren't mined."

"All ships have a standard conduit detection system. The conduits emit a discernable stream of vunian radiation. All we have to do is line up in the beam and blast them at the precise point with the can opener. They're all stable and follow the foldlines of spacetime."

"Can opener? What's vunian radiation?" Tann asked.

Sedeto answered for him. "I was chief navigator aboard our vessel. I can tell you about it later. Now, we eat."

Rogerto told Naylon and Tann that the interior lights were extinguished shortly after twilight every night. The lights had just been doused. Now only red lights glowed throughout the enclosure, making ominous looking shadows. Naylon and Tann had already selected one of the empty sleeping chambers to bed down in. Rogerto's men stayed together in one of the other chambers, while Rogerto occupied one by himself.

Tann sat on Naylon's cot next to him, speaking Lingua in low tones. The Telkans wouldn't have a clue what was being said if they were being recorded. Nor did they want the other prisoners to know what they were saying.

"Spacetime conduits!" Tann said. "Have you ever heard of such a thing?"

"Never. I'm sure even Darreth has never heard of such a thing either," Naylon told him.

"Did you hear Sedeto laugh when I described how we use plasma engines to wrinkle wedges of spacetime?" Tann asked.

"That's because he couldn't believe how much energy we expend doing so. They use nothing more than a sublight engine to get to the mouth of one of those conduits, then follow the beam of energy it emits. We have to find out how they do it. That is, if the things exist in our dimension," Naylon said.

"Why?"

"Do you have any idea how many credits we'd make if we brought that kind of tech back? Just the fuel savings alone would be worth a fortune. I can already see what this is going to do for our planet."

"Back? You think we're getting out of here?" Tann was desperately holding back sheer terror. Naylon could tell from Tann's trembling voice.

Naylon slid his hand down Tann's back, then held him closely in a tight hug. "We have to. Otherwise, we're dead." Naylon knew he shouldn't have used that particular phrase. In the dim red light, Naylon could see the glint in Tann's eyes from tears. "Don't agit. We'll get out of here. I promise," Naylon said firmly as he wiped one off Tann's cheek.

Sedeto had been very careful. He had taken off his slippers before he snuck over toward the Naylon and Tann's sleeping chamber. He stopped just outside the alcove opening, his back against the wall, and listened. The large common area could echo sounds very easily if he wasn't completely quiet. Rogerto had decided there was something odd about the two new prisoners. He was satisfied they were Terran, but they had virtually no knowledge of the Empire, its political or military structure, nor how people traversed the stars. The bizarre description the younger one had given them about how their ship essentially was stationary and they made spacetime move instead, was utterly preposterous. That alone made him suspicious. He was almost convinced they were plants by the Telkans in an attempt to pry more information out of them. Sedeto was aware that the Telkans were not the best interrogators. Their culture deplored torture and they had an almost pathological distaste for the use of force. But they had been quite successful in keeping he and his crewmates isolated and contained.

Telkan technological superiority was to be commended, he had thought on several occasions, although it had also successfully prevented any of them from escaping. But this new turn of events may be exactly what they needed to find some leverage. He was sure Naylon and his young companion were being used to keep them off-guard. He wasn't sure how, but he was going to find out. Sedeto had volunteered to sneak up on the two new prisoners and listen. Anything they said to each other might be helpful to them all.

Sedeto stood as still as he could. The two new prisoners were speaking to each other loud enough for him to hear everything, yet he couldn't discern a single word either was saying. None of it made any sense until he heard Tann say his name. That was the only understandable word.

Sedeto was from Ateli, one of the closest worlds to Earth. The culture on Ateli was greatly mixed. The inhabitants not only spoke Empire Spanish but two other Empire languages. He spoke one of them fluently, and had a relatively good command of the other one. But this language bested his ear. No matter how hard he tried he couldn't make out anything they were saying. *Who are these people*, he wondered.

The next morning the lights rose slowly until they were fully illuminated. Rogerto stood at their door and woke them.

"The guards will be here for an inspection after breakfast. I recommend you shower and shave before they get here." He left abruptly.

Naylon and Tann both shed their thin outfits and stepped into the shower. Each sleeping chamber had its own shower with four individual heads. Tann took one opposite Naylon. On the wall was a dispenser for something that seemed to be soap, although it didn't lather and had no smell. An actual water shower. Naylon hadn't been in one of those for quite a while. It seemed so… primitive. Towels and shaving equipment had been provided, too. Naylon wasn't sure whether he was in a prison or a hotel.

The men had already assembled at the breakfast table after choosing items from the dispenser. Tann and Naylon both again sniffed at each unidentifiable item, chose several, then returned to the table with them.

"Sleep well?" Rogerto asked.

"I don't think I moved the entire night," Naylon replied.

"Get used to it. We think the food has drugs in it," Rogerto confided.

After listening to Sedeto's report last night, Rogerto decided further attempts to listen to Naylon and Tann would be useless, as they would probably use the same incomprehensible language. But they would keep up the casual questioning, especially of the young one. He seemed the most vulnerable of the two and more apt to let something of value slip.

Moments after they had finished their meal they heard a voice overhead in Empire Spanish say, 'Stand by for inspection'.

"This is where we stand outside our rooms," Nolo told them. "It'll be over in a few minutes."

The main door opened and four Telkans entered the common area wearing full uniforms, and with weapons drawn. They scattered and inspected the rooms. The Telkans then scanned each man in turn with some sort of device. It was impossible for Naylon to discern what they were doing.

The door the Telkans came in was still open. Naylon wondered why no one tried to make a run for it. Maybe they had before. He and Tann hadn't been there long enough for him to establish that. Perhaps there was some sort of energy barrier across it. Regardless, there was no way to escape down the corridor. There were two Telkans at the far end standing against another set of doors, looking their way, along with another single one who was halfway down the corridor. That one was coming toward them.

As the Telkan drew nearer, Naylon saw he was in full uniform as well. The closer he got the more Naylon was sure he recognized him. When the alien entered their main chamber, he was sure it was An'Arka.

It was. An'Arka spoke briefly with one of the inspection team, showing him something on a flat screen device he was carrying. He approached Naylon. "You will come with me."

"To where?"

"To see Minister Ne'Uanju."

"Why?"

"Orders."

"Tann comes with me," Naylon told him.

An'Arka looked at him briefly, then spoke a single word. "No."

Tann heard all of it since he was standing next to Naylon. "I'm going with him," he stated boldly. Two of the guards several meters from An'Arka heard the exchange. They didn't understand the words, but it was obvious some sort of defiance was taking place. They approached, then stood next to An'Arka with their weapons at the ready. Naylon reached out and squeezed Tann's shoulder. "I won't be long," he said encouragingly.

Minister Ne'Uanju didn't care to be awake so early. Since his assignment monitoring the Terran prisoners, he had had to alter his normal sleeping patterns somewhat to accommodate theirs. Telkan physiology was adapted to a thirty-five and a half hour rotation. Terrans were adapted to a much shorter one. He would never get used to having to time shift every second day.

The prisoners they had taken from the Terran vessel nearly a revolution ago had provided plenty of intelligence. Within three months, the prisoners had provided enough information to determine the strength of nearby Terran forces. He knew Terrans needed lots of mental stimulation or they got bored. It was a simple matter to bore them for weeks at a time, then force them to exchange information for mental stimulation. It worked on all their prisoners. He was aware their technique for extracting information was not what the Terrans used. Terrans were ruthless with their Telkan charges. Some of their people had been found dismembered, disemboweled or had sustained permanent injuries, all in the Terran quest to get information they wanted. The Telkan pain threshold was tremendously high, they rarely felt bored and they had a natural tendency to not talk unless absolutely necessary. Their species couldn't have been more different in that respect.

But the new prisoners could potentially provide useful information. If it were true what the Terran had told him then the most valuable discovery, perhaps of all time, lay on M'jas'la. Confirmation of part of the lost Telkan past may actually have been nearby all this time!

Naylon sat on the uncomfortable chair directly in front of the minister. An'Arka stood to his side. Neither had spoken since he had been led into the room. In fact, Naylon thought they had both slipped into a catatonic state. When he moved to adjust his position, he noted both An'Arka and the minister watched his every move with their eyes. Naylon decided the silence might be because each was analyzing him, trying to discern something with a sense he lacked. Finally, after several minutes of the bizarre silence, the minister spoke.

"You will tell us where the gateway is located on M'jas'la," he said through the translation computer. *Sort and sweet, and certainly directly to the point*, Naylon thought. He decided he could play their game, too. He counted to twenty before responding. "What will you do with Tann?"

The minister leaned backward slightly after the translation was complete. Naylon didn't answer his question, proving this one was intelligent and concerned about his companion's fate. That was a good sign. Many times when he had interrogated a Terran, they spoke the most vile words and had erratic emotional responses. It added to the wonder the minister had about these creatures. Many of them were nearly psychotic at times. He noted they hardly ever spoke to each other that way, but he had seen and heard of Terran prisoner fights to prove it was always under the surface of their character. The need to struggle seemed programmed into their genes.

"Your companion will be kept until you provide the location of the gateway."

"I do not know the location of the gateway. And why do you want to know where it is?"

A snorting sound came from the alien's mouth. He looked directly into Naylon's eyes this time. "I will ask the questions. You will provide the answers. If not, you will be kept in the prisoner hold. If you wish to end your days as a prisoner, so be it. Be aware you will be provided with no sunlight, no exercise, no companionship and no diversions until which time you have provided the answers I request."

Naylon instantly assessed the situation. He had no intention of spending the rest of his life in a cell for nothing more than being caught by them! If they were kept with the other prisoners for any length of time it would be quite evident they were both not from any Terran world, and could be used as pawns in their war. In addition, it would be impossible for him to pretend for very long that he were not gay. In the back of his mind, Naylon was aware that could very easily mean his life would be at stake in their power struggle. There was Tann to consider, too. Tann was straight and young. He was also very good looking. At least Naylon thought so. It would only be a matter of time before the other Terran prisoners decided to have their way with him. After all, there was no sign of any women prisoners. Tann could hold his own, but not against more than one of them. They could easily overpower him. Terran or human, everyone needed 'companionship'. Even the Telkans apparently knew that. He wondered what the Terrans back in the holding area were doing about that after being held for so long, and instantly regretted leaving Tann alone.

But there was something else that matter most. A way out. The minister had actually provided him with such an opportunity. One he might not ever get again. The minister needed information. If he pretended he had it, it might be the only way off the planet. The plan formed in his head within seconds.

"Minister Ne'Uanju," Naylon began. "I accept your request. I don't have the exact coordinates of the gateway. I will need my companion to assist me in determining its location. He has a vital piece of equipment that helps us detect the presence of the gateway. Only he is trained to use it. All of our belongings were taken from us. We can't scan for it again without our equipment. He was the one who found it in the first place." There, he made it seem as though Tann was vital for the mission.

Naylon waited for the translation to complete.

An'Arka and the minister spoke to each other for several minutes before the minister returned his attention to Naylon. "If you are lying your end will not be swift."

The minister, although trained in the ways of the military command on their homeworld, was otherwise a metal weaver. It required extreme concentration, lots of patience and a gentle touch to produce his art. The brilliant colors that metal weaving produced was highly revered on every Telkan Held World. His required duty with the service had forced him to put his art on hold.

The Terrans had not yet discovered the true nature of Telkan culture. A façade had been carefully invented and choreographed specifically for interaction with Terrans. Being an extremely creative species it was only natural that such a façade would be generated. The minister knew their superior height and weight was to their advantage in many ways, especially psychologically. Those who had to interact with Terrans had been thoroughly trained to use that. The use of language was of special importance as well, since Terrans did not use scent in their day-to-day interactions. In that respect, the minister had always considered Terrans limited in their range of communication. No wonder they could be so easily intimidated. Yet, it took just the right kind of personality to determine what particular psychological technique to use on a specific Terran. Outright use of authority usually worked at first. If not, they would simply work their way through the Scale of Superiority. With this one, the first level worked just fine. But the minister was careful. Always in the back of his mind he continued to tell himself how clever they really were. Clever enough to deceive, if it benefited them.

Naylon was returned to the holding area immediately after his request. He was brought to the double doors, which slid open at a voice command by one of his Telkan guards. He walked in and the doors unceremoniously shut behind him. Naylon looked around. No one was in the immediate area. He heard voices coming from his and Tann's sleeping alcove. When he approached, he noted all four Terrans were standing around Tann. At first Naylon was concerned that his fear had come true about them having had their way with him. But as he looked in, he noted the situation was calm and everyone had their clothes on.

Naylon heard Rogerto emit a laugh, then the men noted Naylon's presence.

"Ah, Naylon is returned to us, unscathed, I hope. Did you have fun with them?" Rogerto asked.

"Uh, what's going on in here?" Naylon replied.

"We're having a conference," Rogerto told him. "Tann has told us all the details about how you arrived here."

Naylon hoped Tann had enough presence of mind to not divulge their real story. If he had done so, becoming pawns in their long war would become a reality much faster than he bargained for.

"And…"

"As before, I do not believe a word of it!" Rogerto emitted a guffaw this time. "Whoever heard of a ship standing still and moving spacetime around it. It is a very inventive story!"

"But it's true," Tann said.

"That's enough, Tann. Why are you lying about how we got here?" Naylon wanted to deflect the men's attention from Tann as soon as he could.

"What?" Tann said, quite confused.

"I said that's enough," he said quite sternly.

"It's okay, Naylon," Rogerto told him. "He provided an amusing tale of your adventures. None of us think it's true, but I will tell you this. He'll provide plenty of amusement for our captors. They don't understand irony or humor very well. They will take a lot of time to determine if he's telling the truth, then eventually become exasperated with him. I suggest you provide more such stories, too. Once you run out of them the real interrogation will begin. Before that happens though, we want to know how you got into the clutches of our enemy."

Rogerto's inquiry of what the Telkans asked Naylon lasted only ten minutes. Naylon made sure Rogerto didn't get any information that might be helpful. He certainly didn't divulge anything about the gateway issue that Ne'Uanju was so adamant about.

The men dispersed, leaving Tann and Naylon alone.

"What did you tell them?" Naylon whispered.

"Don't agit. I didn't tell them anything about how we really got here. As far as they know we were shot down over some planet while we were on our way to one of their outlying worlds."

"But you don't know the names of any of their worlds."

"It didn't matter. I told them I was asleep when the shooting started and I didn't know where we were at the time."

Férío Atore mentally went over the detailed description of the engine Tann had described. The very concept of bypassing naturally occurring spacetime conduits and warping through space wherever one wanted was incredibly intriguing. Of course, that idea had been around for a very long time. Unfortunately, a power supply such as what the young one had described to run a warp engine had never been developed. The unfathomable distances between stars never made such a technology a reality. Férío would know. He had been working on engines systems for a very long time. At first, he was sure the boy had simply made up such a bizarre concept as 'wedges' to deflect their attention from their real reason for being held prisoner. His suspicions about the two were mounting. That suspicion was on hold right now as he determined if Tann might actually be right. It might very well be possible to use a plasma-fusion engine to make at least a small portion of spacetime move around a ship. The monetary and energy cost would be enormous, as Rogerto had astutely determined, but who would care? The strategic advantage such a discovery would provide to Terran forces would be enormous!

Perhaps the boy was a genius. Perhaps they had been testing one of their engines when they got caught. If that were so, it might mean the technology was now in Telkan hands. Férío stopped his train of thought before he let his worst-case fears cascade out of control. There was much he didn't know about what was going on in the Empire right now. They had been held for so long much could have changed.

During the middle of their midday meal, the doors of the main holding chamber doors slid open. Two Telkan guards stepped in and the doors shut. Again, they were in full military uniform and held weapons. They merely stood, watching the men as they finished eating. Rogerto pushed his empty plate aside, dusted his hands off, then approached the guards. He stood in front of them with his arms crossed. "Well, what is it this time?"

The guards said nothing in return. After all, they didn't speak Empire Spanish.

The doors slid open again. It was An'Arka. "Naylon. Tann. You will come with me."

Naylon stood up, as did Tann from the table. They looked at each other. Rogerto stepped aside and looked at them as well. "Special treatment?" he asked.

Naylon answered Rogerto before he approached An'Arka. "I seriously doubt it. I'm sure my pack of lies didn't take."

"They've become frustrated with you more quickly than I expected," Rogerto said in return.

Both Naylon and Tann were led down the corridor. Tann turned to see the rest of the men staring at them before the doors slid shut.

Instead of being led to Minister Ne'Uanju, they were taken down a different corridor, then to a small room where another Telkan guard was standing against the far wall. The only thing in the room other than the guard was a table with a pile of clothing and gear on it. An overhead light illuminated everything. Immediately Naylon recognized his pack then one of his boots.

An'Arka was still standing behind them. "Your belongings."

Naylon didn't hesitate. This was too good to be true. He pulled on the zipper of the outfit he was wearing. "Hurry up, Tann. We're getting out of here," he said in Lingua.

"What?"

"We're going back to Rylerra. Change as quickly as you can."

"How do you know?"

"Trust me," Naylon said.

Both of them were out of the thin prisoner uniforms within seconds. Tann dug through the clothing to find his things. Everything was there, including the belongings from their packs. Within minutes they were both fully clothed and sitting on the floor putting on their boots. Naylon couldn't believe the luck. The minister actually believed him! Somehow the gateway was more important than keeping them prisoner. But he couldn't figure out why. Then it struck him. The aliens in the cavern in their universe were Telkans. Maybe Ne'Uanju knew about them. Perhaps he knew they had gone through the tunnel or gateway, as he called it. Were the Telkans back on Rylerra looking for them? Is that why they happened to be there? Was their culture so old or continuous that they kept records of their missing companions or relatives? He knew the mummified Telkans in the cavern had been there for an extremely long time. Perhaps centuries. He knew next to nothing about this civilization, so could only speculate that the minister needed to retrieve them. Regardless of the reason, they were being released! It meant they had a fighting chance to get back to Rylerra and ultimately to their universe.

Naylon stood when he was finished, adjusted his shirt, then unzipped one of the compartments of the pack. There lay the disk-shaped object that brought them to this universe. Since it was still there, Naylon realized one very important thing. Ne'Uanju may have known there were ancient dead Telkans in the cavern, but he had no idea how to get to them or what the objects were used for. So far, his luck was holding out. He immediately took Tann's pack and looked for the disc in there, too. It was there as well. Naylon could only smile at their profound good luck.

Chapter 34

Navar and Urret hurriedly re-boarded the ship while the captain and Selaye continued to watch the scanner on the bridge. Whoever they were tracking was headed directly toward them. The captain called Lieutenant Navar onto the bridge.

"This is impossible, sir. Our scans showed nothing just a few minutes ago," Navar told him.

"They might have been picked up by the Telkans and taken out of scanner range, then dropped back off. They're headed this way and show no sign of detecting us. Otherwise, they surely wouldn't still be steadily coming in this direction. Have Urret and Agrida wait for them. Use the stealth shields. Stun them only. I do not want them dead."

Navar was greatly pleased at this turn of events. "Yes, sir." He turned and left the bridge. Urret and Agrida were waiting in the corridor and grinned once they got their orders. They quickly gathered together the equipment they needed and left the ship.

The captain then ordered Commander Selaye to take the ship a kilometer to the south at the lowest possible altitude so as not to be seen. He wanted to make sure they were nowhere nearby in case the Telkans also decided to return, too.

Urret and Agrida found a spot some distance from the ship before it took off. They stopped and took a bearing on the two approaching targets. They set up the stealth shields again and waited for their quarry to come into view. They looked at each other with great surprise when Darreth and Rehl came out from the vegetation into the open. These Terrans were definitely not their former 'guests'! It wasn't their place to ponder what was going on, yet Agrida did just that. Where were all these Terrans coming from? He was sure they were light years behind enemy lines and far from any other Terrans. Urret tapped on Agrida's shoulder then aimed his weapon. Agrida nodded an okay and aimed his as well. Darreth and Rehl had no idea they had been hit. They were on the ground and passed out within fifteen microseconds of each other.

Agrida disabled the stealth shield, then placed the generators into their bag and zipped it up. He carried it over to the two unconscious Terrans. He looked over at Urret, who was scanning the immediate area. No Terran or Telkan life signs or energy signatures of any kind were nearby. Good, they were totally alone now.

"Captain, Agrida here. All clear. Our guests are asleep. But get this. They're not Naylon and Tann. I say again. They're not Naylon and Tann."

Captain Pacudas, Commander Selaye and Lieutenant Navar were standing together on the bridge, looking at the readout, which was being relayed from Urret's scanner, and heard Agrida's report. All three of them looked at each other in astonishment.

Doctor Renarde had Darreth and Rehl strapped to the med tables in the infirmary. The observation room next door was crowded with men as they discussed what might be happening on this out-of-the-way planet. Darreth and Rehl's effects had been pulled from their packs. Everything was on top of a table. Their weapons had been removed. Commander Selaye casually looked at one of the discs and observed its iridescent color. All of the Terrans they had come across so far had one. It was impossible to discern their use, yet they had already determined the objects emitted no energy of any kind. They were essentially inert. Maybe they signified their clan or family. That's all he could guess as he dropped it to the table. He had decided the scanning equipment didn't appear to be all that sophisticated. When energized, one of the screens displayed a menu of choices. Pacudas, standing next to his commander, scrutinized the words. He recognized none of them.

"I assume this is the same language?" the captain asked Selaye.

Selaye looked out to the corridor at Urret. "Where's Ocio?"

"She's behind me. Why?"

"Have her come in here."

Daníl came in. Selaye had her look at the words on the screen. It was just her luck she had a relative who had married an Anglan years ago. She had been briefly fascinated with her in-law's first language and had spent a few hours learning a few phrases just for fun. This, on the other hand, was nothing but seriousness and she wasn't at all happy to be considered an expert. "Sir, I don't know this language. Like I said before, I only know a few words. This looks the same so I'll say yes. Will that be all, sir?"

"For now," the captain interjected, noting her tone.

Renarde's voice came over the speaker that connected the observation room to the infirmary. "Captain."

Pacudas looked up through the observation room window to see Renarde pointing to Darreth. He was moving his head from side to side.

"Ah, we'll find out right away," the captain told everyone in the room. The men and one woman moved out of the observation room and made way for the captain to get into the infirmary.

"Un-strap him," Pacudas said to the doctor.

The doctor and Urret went to each side of Darreth and untied his arms and legs. Darreth groaned then shook his head again as he opened his eyes. Immediately, he could tell he was in a sickbay of some sort.

"Who are you," Pacudas asked him.

"Huh?" Darreth responded. *Maybe I didn't hear the question right*, he thought. "What did you say?" He swung his legs over the side of the table as he sat up. It was immediately obvious this was a highly sophisticated ship. "Who are you people?" he asked.

Pacudas stepped forward. "Lingua?" he asked. At this point, he knew the word to use.

Darreth saw that Rehl was either passed out or dead on the other table. The look of alarm on his face was evident to everyone. "What the hell did you do to him! If he's dead, you'll pay. I swear you'll pay!"

The doctor was at the ready. He touched the cylinder to Darreth's neck before he knew it. It took a few seconds for the sedative to kick in. Doctor Renarde pointed to Urret who stepped behind Darreth. They both caught him as he fell backward onto the table.

Several hours later Darreth woke up. The only people in the room this time were Rehl who was already awake, and the doctor.

"Good, you're back with us. The captain will see you both," the doctor said.

"What the hell did you do to me?" Darreth said angrily as he sat up. He closed his mouth as soon as he said it. He was acutely aware he wasn't speaking Lingua.

"We're speaking something called Empire Spanish," Rehl told him.

"What?"

"Banned tech," Rehl offered.

"Huh?" Darreth shook his head. It was the most bizarre feeling knowing he was speaking a language he had no memory of learning.

"The doctor over there told me they used an RNA injection on us so we could speak their language."

"What the fruck for?"

"Because these people don't speak Lingua."

Rehl's explanation was cut short when Captain Pacudas entered the room. Darreth noted the man's uniform right away.

"More Terrans on the Telkan side. This is very interesting. Who are you men?" the captain said to Darreth.

"Who are you?" Darreth demanded.

"I am the captain of this vessel. My name is Pacudas. But I will ask the questions. If you don't answer me you will be dealt with accordingly."

The doctor looked up at the captain. *That was rather harsh*, Renarde thought. He, too, was fully aware the men had committed no crime other than perhaps not knowing the Empire's language. And that wasn't a crime as far as he knew. So far, even the other two Terrans they had discovered couldn't be considered collaborators either. So, that crime didn't fit either.

"My name's Darreth."

Rehl held up a hand and half-heartedly waved at the captain. "Rehl."

"Darreth and Rehl. Where are your companions?"

"We're alone."

"I think not. Naylon and Tann won't get far."

Darreth's instant noticeable reaction was exactly what Pacudas was hoping for.

"So, you do know them. Where are they?"

Darreth looked at Rehl. It was obvious the captain knew them and had contact with them. 'They won't get far' meant they were alive! But why did these men even know about them in the first place? Had they been captured and later escaped? As concerned with their safety as he was, Darreth calmed himself. What mattered most was they were alive.

"We're here to find them. They got lost from our party." He didn't know how much to give away, but his concern was overwhelming.

"Four Terrans on this stinking Telkan world and no ship. I want to know how you got here. I also want to know where your friends are. In fact, I want to know why you're working with the Telkans."

"I have no idea what you're talking about," Darreth told him.

At that moment Tasker Vas walked by the open doorway.

"Holy fruck!" Darreth was sitting on the med table. He slid off and unconsciously backed into it. He didn't get far since it was firmly bolted to the deck plating.

The captain was momentarily taken aback at Darreth's reaction. Rehl reacted the same way, instinctively reaching for a now non-existent pistol that should have been at his hip.

Tasker Vas simply continued on his way without even looking into the room.

"What was that?" Rehl asked.

The doctor was closest to him. "Tasker Vas," he said flatly.

The blank look on both Rehl's and Darreth's face told the captain everything he needed to know now. Clearly, all of these men were not from Empire-held space. Otherwise they would be well aware what a Tasker was.

Darreth and Rehl were both given a meal and water. The doctor insisted. He then asked the captain for a private audience in his ready room.

"Captain. These men have violated no Empire laws. The only question we have is why they're behind enemy lines."

"There's something very odd about this little band of Terrans. I intend to get to the bottom of it."

"But sir, we're already days late getting to our objective. How are we going to explain it to…"

The captain cut him off. "Doctor, I will ask you to not question my orders."

"Of course not, sir. I'm merely pointing out we've already lost the two men we found earlier and are behind looking for a way out of here.

The longer we stay put the more likely we'll be detected by the Telkans. Do we want to risk that?"

The captain leaned back in his chair. The doctor had a point, but there was important intelligence here that might change the course of the war as far as he was concerned.

"Doctor, I certainly do not have to answer to you."

"No sir. You do not."

Regardless, Pacudas explained himself. After all, his doctor wasn't being insubordinate, just concerned. "Clearly these men are somehow outside the influence of the Empire and under some sort of influence of the Ascendency."

The doctor realized he had the captain's confidence back. He sat in front of the man's desk. "Yes, clearly something is going on here that has no precedent I'm aware of."

"Exactly. I have every intention of completing our mission. But there's important intelligence to gather here. I've been doing some thinking. I believe the Telkans here have embarked on some sort of breeding experiment to create agents loyal to Ascendency interests. We very well may have stumbled on it."

Despite the lack of clear-cut evidence for that conclusion, the doctor couldn't exactly dispute the captain's speculation. Perhaps the Telkans had attempted to breed Terrans. Maybe that's the reason for the tech he had found buried in three of them. Or perhaps it was for control purposes. The explanation Naylon had given them could have been a ruse useful to deflect their attention away from the real reason they were on this planet.

Pacudas continued. "The other men. Darreth and Rehl. Perhaps they were sent to find Naylon and Tann. It is entirely possible the first two escaped the breeding colony and are fugitives. I intend to find out. Bring them in here."

"Before I do that there's something else you should know about those two." When Darreth and Rehl had been unconscious, the doctor had scanned their bodies, too. He discovered the two new men both had tech inside their heads. Clearly, only the adults had them. He had decided to use the highest resolution the scanner was capable of. The image he had taken of the nexus under Darreth's shoulder blade was extremely telling. On it, he had discovered an extremely tiny line of writing. It was barely discernable since the ship's scanner wasn't designed to read at that resolution, but he could make out enough of it. It contained two lines. Both were composed mostly of numbers. Numbers used on Earth and all the worlds of the Empire. He also found a distinct D, an L, and a G. Wherever the tech came from it was it wasn't Telkan in origin.

When the doctor was finished with his report, Pacudas nodded. "That adds to my conclusion. Some sort of breeding experiment is going on here. What you've discovered tells me rogue Terrans may be involved, too. I intend to get to the bottom of this-this house of horrors as soon as I can."

The doctor sat with Darreth and Rehl as they ate. "The captain will see you again once you've finished your meal…. The young one. Tann. How did he escape." Actually, he only knew of one specific incident where an 'escape' had occurred: from their ship. On the other hand, he was actually asking Darreth how he might have escaped the so-far unknown breeding colony.

Of course Darreth had no idea how Tann had escaped. Nor how Naylon had either. "Why wouldn't he?" he responded. He tried to sound as mysterious as he could, then decided to turn the questions back to the doctor instead. "Doctor, where are you from?"

"Upila."

"What's Upila?"

"My homeworld, of course."

"Where is this Upila?" Darreth was trying for any information he could get.

"Five conduits from Earth in the direction of Hydra."

Darreth had no idea what that meant although he was familiar with a constellation called Hydra as seen from the Sol system.

"Of course you wouldn't know Upila. You've never been in Empire space, have you?"

"Nope, can't say I have."

Perhaps the captain is right, Renarde thought.

Commander Selaye entered the mess area. "If they're done, the captain will see them now."

Darreth and Rehl sat in front of Pacudas' desk, while the commander stood behind it. The captain was working only on an assumption at this point. While he questioned his two captives, he was having Lieutenant Navar run continuous scans outside. No sign of further Telkan activity had been detected so far. He intended to keep it that way. In addition, using his assumption he ordered scans at the highest possible bandwidth to look for further Terran biosigns. If this were indeed a breeding planet, surely others would turn up somewhere.

The captain leaned back. "I'm concerned I may have started our... relationship on the wrong foot. We are as interested in finding your companions as you are. We too would like to see them returned to your colony."

Darreth noted that. *He thinks we're from some colony? On this planet?* Darreth decided to play the captain to get more information. He took a wild stab. "Which colony? The one here or the one on the other world." Both the captain and Selaye reacted and Darreth noticed. He wasn't expecting to get another clue so quickly. *So, there might be several colonies nearby*, Darreth thought. "You know there's another one circling the other star in this system," Darreth added, trying to pry as many clues out of the man as he could.

Pacudas was aware that scans had so far indicated the other world in this double star system had a significant Telkan presence. Was that where Naylon and Tann had gone back to, or were returned to? The captain couldn't tell so far. They were just missing. Regardless, he'd get to the bottom of this great big mystery and he would get to it before the day was out.

Chapter 35

Lieutenant Navar took a seat in front of the scanner screens on the bridge while the captain and the commander continued questioning Darreth and Rehl.

The biosign scanner had so far continued to read zero. But the aerial activity scanner suddenly jumped. Immediately, Navar read the vector to determine if the object was powered or simply a meteor. He determined the vector was indeed a powered flight object within twenty seconds. Meteors didn't slow down, then change directions. His first order was to activate their stealth shield. He then activated the comm. "Captain, the Telkans are back."

The captain shook his head and frowned in frustration. "We will continue our, er, discussion later," he told Darreth. "In the meantime, you will both accompany me to the bridge." He intended to have his new guests assist him in identifying their newest target.

Darreth and Rehl were ushered to the back of the bridge while the captain took his chair. Ocio kept watch on them. Darreth's pulse quickened. Within minutes, the ship was off the screen, most likely having landed.

"The ship stays here," the captain announced. "We don't want them to detect any movement on our part. Lieutenant Navar, the ship landed three point two kilometers away. Darreth, take a look at that display screen."

"Why me?"

"I think you can identify it for us. Their engines have specific energy signatures," the captain told him.

"And, that's supposed to help me identify it how?"

Rehl shook his head. This was almost comical if it weren't serious. "You realize this is fruitless," he told Pacudas. "We have no idea what you're talking about."

Navar came forward and observed the readout. He turned to Darreth, prodding him anyway. "What do you make of this?"

"I make nothing of it. If you think I'm going to be able to identify it you're out of luck."

Pacudas had now determined, based on nothing more than intuition, that Darreth and Rehl were telling the truth. They didn't give away anything in their body language that could be construed as knowing anything. He didn't need a scanner to determine that.

"Lieutenant Navar," Pacudas said. "Take a fire team and see what we're up against this time. If you find our previous guests, you are to capture them and bring them back here. Alive. If there are only a few Telkans, take them out. If there are too many to handle with just your team, call for reinforcements. Once you return, we're leaving this planet."

"Yes, sir." The lieutenant left the bridge.

The captain faced Darreth and Rehl. He pressed the comm. "Llarena. Report to the bridge and take our guests to the spare quarters."

Darreth was greatly concerned now. The captain intended to take off while they were still onboard!

Efren felt his hands shaking as he took the men to the exact same quarters that Naylon and Tann had occupied before they had disappeared. He pressed the button next to the doorframe. He ushered the two men inside, then stepped in himself. He made a show of making sure the door was securely closed.

"You must let me join you," Efren whispered.

"What?" Rehl asked, greatly surprised at Efren's sudden emotional plea.

"I want to join your group. Wherever they're hiding I can make sure no one is found."

"What makes you think we're with any group?"

"You must believe me. I was one of the guards when Naylon and the boy were aboard our craft."

"What happened to them?" was Darreth's immediate response.

"They escaped. Most likely because of me."

"Were they okay?"

"In what way?"

"Were they hurt or injured?"

"No. We didn't harm them. It's the captain's fault they were even onboard our ship in the first place. All of us were surprised to find any Terrans on this planet. After all, we're far from the Empire."

"What Empire?" Rehl asked.

"You really don't know. Neither did they. I want to get out of here. Can you help me?"

Darreth realized this might be their way off the ship. "Not until you explain what's going on here."

"Look, I don't have much time."

"Just a few questions. First of all, who are the Telkans?"

"Our enemy, of course. They've been so for three decades."

"The big aliens with six appendages?"

"Four, like us. They cut the short ones off at birth. We think they're non-functional. Like an appendix."

Rehl looked at Darreth at that news.

"And this Empire of yours. What the hell is it?"

Efren quickly summarized everything as Darreth and Rehl both shot question after question at him. Within five minutes they had heard enough.

"Naylon kept saying history was different where you are from," Efren said. "If that's true, I welcome it. I may be nothing more than a soldat, but I know this war will not be ending in my lifetime. That much is obvious to anyone, even a civilian. I would welcome a fresh start on your planet. That way, I can live to have my children fight in a war that's winnable."

Darreth sat down on the small cot as he tried to absorb what Efren had told him. He had purposely not made mention of the tunnel in the cavern. From what he'd gathered from the scant information Efren had told him, Darreth concluded he and Rehl had somehow stumbled on a parallel universe only slightly different from their own.

"You'll have to help us off the ship," Rehl said.

Efren nodded. "Where is *your* ship?"

Darreth answered instead, hoping Rehl wouldn't contradict him. He had an idea but needed a ruse. "It's, uh, some distance from here."

"I knew it!" Efren shot back triumphantly. "You must have an extremely efficient cloak. Look, I have to get out into the corridor before anyone realizes I'm in here." He immediately started for the door.

"Wait. Why are we being kept prisoner? We've not done anything," Darreth asked.

"You are well behind enemy lines. It makes no sense you could be here for any other reason than because you're Telkan collaborators." The silence was deafening. "The captain believes you may be part of some sort of Telkan breeding colony," Efren added.

"How did he come to that conclusion?" Rehl asked derisively.

"I don't know. It's just what I heard from the commander." Efren looked at them both. "You're not, are you?"

"We're here to get our friends back and that's all. We had no idea there were Telkans on this planet. No idea, I tell you. In fact, it's a far greater surprise to find you here."

"Desperate times, Darreth. Desperate times. We volunteered for this mission. I was extremely lucky to be picked. It was for the Empire. My Empire."

Darreth stood. "Then why do you want to defect?"

Efren looked angry as he stood toe-to-toe with Darreth. "I realize you are new to our language, but do not ever use that word again if you want me to help you."

Rehl started forward but Darreth held his hand up. "Sorry, bad choice of words. I apologize." *Amazing*, Darreth thought. *The man is loyal to his Empire yet he's sick of his personal situation. The luck!*

"I'll help you off the ship if you will take me to a world that has never heard of the Telkan threat," Efren added.

"I guarantee you this, soldat Llarena. If you can get us out of here and we can get our friends back in one piece, and if we're still alive, I guarantee you will come back with us to a world that has never, ever heard the word Telkan." He looked at Rehl who was nodding vigorously.

"Captain, look," Commander Selaye said. He was peering out the front view port, then back to the LADAR image. Low black clouds had been drifting overhead for about a half hour.

Captain Pacudas checked image then looked outside again. "Contact them."

Selaye nodded. He pressed the comm badge on his wrist. "Selaye to Navar. Report."

It took several seconds before Lieutenant Navar reported in. "*The weather's taken a turn for the worse. It's raining pretty heavily where we are.*"

"Stand by." Then to the captain, "Should we recall them until it stops?"

Pacudas continued to look out the view port. Several drops of rain had already started to hit it. The captain didn't miss a beat. "No. If Darreth and Rehl's friends were on that ship, I want them returned to us as soon as they're within range. The rain should provide enough cover to prevent their fire team from being too easily detected."

Llarena called for Ocio to relieve him an hour later. His first task was to man his station in the engine room. At his console, he logged in to the scanning system on the bridge. Working quickly, he replayed the logs of the last several hour's readings at high speed to make sure there was nothing close by being monitored outside the ship. It was a simple matter to input a string of code to tell the system to ignore any movement closer than a kilometer. No one on the bridge would be aware he had done so.

As he worked on inputting the code in such a way as to prevent detection, he continued to mull over what had recently transpired. As he had told Darreth, he willingly volunteered for this mission. It was for the greater glory of the Empire and he was proud to have been picked. But Naylon's description of a world, even an entire universe, no matter what that even meant, which had never heard of Telkans, had weighed heavily in his mind ever since he'd heard it. For his entire life he had lived in a constant state of semi-fear. His entire life! He had never actually acclimated to it. In fact, being a trained military man had exacerbated his general feeling of dismay instead of diminishing it. He was sick of it. He was so sick of feeling that way it was the main reason he had volunteered for this mission. He felt the intent was that their discoveries on this side of the conduit would result in a decided victory once and for all. Instead, their successful passage through a violent star system and onto this planet had upped the ante. Landing here had only provided him with fresh lingering fear instead of the opposite. Unfortunately, his collective military training and experience had yet to provide him with a sufficient reason to completely shed that fear. Clearly, the Telkans continued to be a technologically superior force. They were physically stronger and had far more endurance than any Terran he knew. They were longer-lived creatures too, and thus able to sustain the war for, who knew, possibly even centuries! Yet, Naylon and his young companion's impossible appearance on this world gave him a glimmer of hope. There were worlds somewhere, wherever they might be, that were outside the reach of an endless and un-winnable war. And now, while he plotted to help release two Terrans who had done nothing more than simply be on this planet, he realized one more important thing. The captain had defied orders. Pacudas had decided to interrogate these men, who were completely innocent of plotting against the Empire or thwarting anything the Empire was doing in space or on any world, instead of continuing on with their mission. That in itself was reason enough to do what he was doing. No, he admitted to himself, he wasn't privy to everything that had transpired between Naylon and the captain. Nor with Darreth and his friend Rehl. So, maybe there was something he was missing. But he was sure Naylon had also told the captain that where he was from there were no Telkans.

Armed with all of that, he worked even faster. Now, he switched to the internal sensor array configuration screen. It was a simple matter to disable the airlock door sensors. They had been activated by default after Naylon and Tann had disappeared. He made sure they were disabled for only an hour. He input a sub-routine that would keep the log file's timer going despite the lack of input.

Minutes later he went to the observation room where Darreth and Rehl's effects were still strewn all over the tabletop. Their weapons were missing, but that was all he was sure were gone. The rest of it he stuffed randomly into their packs. He rounded up Tasker Ebit, handed him the packs and told him to place them in the airlock. Tasker Ebit complied immediately.

Breathing hard from the adrenaline surging inside him, he quickly returned to his quarters, threw a few of his effects into a backpack, then returned to the corridor and placed it in the airlock. Tasker Ebit had done his task since the two other packs were there already.

"Ocio," he said casually, as he came up on her. She was literally sitting on the floor now outside Darreth and Rehl's quarters. She quickly stood up. "Why were you on the floor?"

She looked down the corridor, then whispered to Efren, "Because I'm bored as hell. This is ridiculous. Why is the captain doing this?"

Efren placed his index finger against his lips. He feigned surprise at what she had said for even more effect. "Don't let anyone hear you say that."

She shook her head, somewhat exasperated Llarena wouldn't show her sympathy. "I'm turning in. I'll relieve you later. Is it raining yet?"

He nodded. "Just started."

She spent a few minutes in the galley. Efren could hear her. Eventually, he noted the noises in there ceased. She was completely out of earshot now. He went to the end of the corridor, in full view of the airlock. No one was present. None of the Taskers were nearby right now. It was now or never. He returned to the quarters and pressed the door lock button. The door slid open. Both Darreth and Rehl, who had been sitting on the lower bunk, stood.

Efren whispered, "Quickly. I've worked out a way to get you out of here."

"We'll be caught," Darreth responded in the same whispering voice.

Efren shook his head. "I think not."

Darreth looked at Rehl. "Let's go!"

Chapter 36

"The door won't shut," Tann told Naylon. He looked at the doorframe again. Naylon stood next to him and observed as well. Although the small room had been his cell on the flight from Rylerra to Andakar, this time it was his quarters. Naylon's quarters were next to his, as before, too.

"Mine won't shut either."

Tann lowered his voice. "Why aren't they keeping us prisoner this time?"

"I have no idea. There's no reason they should trust us." Naylon was beginning to see patterns in the Telkans that spoke of their culture. His hand rested on a highly ornamented section of wall that separated their two doors. He ran it along the surface. It would make no sense to put this kind of ornamentation on a warship, since gold was a particularly heavy metal, but he could swear the raised characters written all up and down the wall were gilded.

Tann watched him. "What?"

"Have you noticed how much detailed ornamentation is all over everything? It's like this isn't primarily a military vessel, but rather was converted to be one." It was rhetorical. He didn't expect an answer.

Tann looked up and down the corridor. Although they had been left alone, there were two Telkan guards standing in the middle of it, blocking their way. They didn't move. In fact, although Tann could discern that they had eyelids, neither of them had so much as blinked. Naylon and Tann's every move were being carefully watched. The Telkans' eyes gave away their constant vigilance. Wandering around the ship wasn't going to happen.

Tann noticed movement behind the guards. It was An'Arka. The two guards moved aside to let him through. An'Arka stopped several meters from them.

"I thought we were prisoners," Naylon immediately told him.

"It is a…," An'Arka seemed to be grasping for the correct word. "gesture of our goodwill that you be allowed the comfort of freedom while we return to where we captured you." An'Arka lowered his voice considerably, despite knowing that none of the others could possibly understand him. "Minister Ne'Uanju thinks you will find the gateway. I do not believe him."

Naylon wondered for an instant if this was some sort of ploy. Already he was plotting how they were going to get away. So far, he'd had little success in coming up with a surefire plan once they were back on Rylerra. "You know I have a communications array inside me, right?" Naylon told him.

"Scans of your body have determined an intelligent processor is inside you."

"It has an ocular display. I can see output directly in my brain." He pointed to his right eye. "I can adjust the scanner to detect the power output of the gateway. It has an unusual energy signature. That's how we found it. It was emitting some strange signals, so we went to investigate. Then we use these," he dug through his pack and held up one of the discs, "to activate it." It was terribly risky but he had to pull the device out. After all, they had to know the devices were in there. He had no idea if An'Arka would believe him. And it was a completely different story than what he'd given the minister.

"Observer Ba'Jinja has already gone through your belongings. He determined those objects have no inputs or outputs. They can not assist you in determining anything."

Tann kept his mouth shut, realizing that Naylon was feeding the alien a whole host of lies. *Maybe this is part of his plan*, he thought.

"Well, it's true," Naylon told him. Indeed, it was true. The devices, in a way, would help them. To escape, that is.

"We will arrive shortly. You will rest." An'Arka turned to leave. The two guards at the end of the corridor separated briefly to let him pass, then returned to their positions.

Tann sat in Naylon's cell next to him. They were quiet for a moment. "Good one," he said, referring to Naylon's cover story. There was a slight grin on his face. "What do you think they'll do with those guys they have prisoner back on Andakar, er, Q'emt'la."

"I have no idea. I really don't care either. Really. This time I really don't care." He was still feeling quite sorry about having tried to rescue An'Arka.

Tann was quiet for a moment, thinking about their fate. "How are we going to get away? We don't know where the cavern is."

"I'm still working on that. But at least we have those discs. If they hadn't returned them, we'd have no way back for sure."

The one thing Efren was unable to provide was rain gear. There was none onboard because they weren't prepared to encounter a rainy environment. Regardless, he had located some plastic sheeting that would work as a good substitute. The men quietly entered the inner airlock. Efren pressed the door code and it closed.

As quietly as possible the men unfolded the sheets, tore holes in them and donned them like ponchos. It wasn't pretty and the makeshift ponchos only came down to their waists, but it was the only thing they had. They quickly went through their backpacks, checking what was inside and exchanging gear as needed. With everything accounted for, except their weapons, they zipped up the compartments.

Efren handed each of them a pair of infrared glasses and showed them how they were activated. Each slipped them on. Efren lowered the lights then opened the outer airlock door.

The captain was still in his ready room. The commander had the bridge. Efren knew they would be monitoring communications with the fire team and not focused on what was going on inside the ship.

The raindrops looked like greenish-white streaks as they steadily came down. Darreth adjusted the glasses slightly as they stepped out into the rain. The raindrops fell noisily against the makeshift ponchos. Darreth swung his pack around and pulled out the scanner he used earlier before they were stunned. The log contained enough data to help them assess the correct direction to proceed. It had recorded their tracks in five second increments, along with their direction of travel. Efren showed him how to adjust the goggles so he could read its display more clearly. With a clear view of both the scanner's log and the terrain they headed out. Amazingly, Darreth realized they were not more than a few kilometers from the cavern. Barring an accident or the rain not abating, they might make it in a few hours, not days as he had feared.

It didn't really matter though. He was sure they'd be caught long before they got there.

"What," Tann said. Naylon was staring at him like he wanted to say something.

"You've held up pretty well during all of this."

Tann looked away. "I pretty much remember crying in front of you."

"So?"

"It's embarrassing."

"Embarrassed is better than dead. And we're not dead yet."

"But we could be."

"Don't even talk like that."

"Well, what are we gonna do when we land?"

"We're gonna fake it until we get to the cavern. If we get to it, that is."

Naylon realized they had both dozed off. Both of them had fallen asleep side-by-side on the lower cot. How long they had been out, he wasn't sure. But noises at the end of the corridor woke him. Both stretched and relieved themselves before An'Arka appeared in their doorway.

"We have arrived on M'jas'la. Gather your belongings and accompany me to the food preparation area. You will eat and drink before you exit the ship."

"You didn't say we. You aren't coming with us?" Naylon asked.

"I will monitor your progress from the ship. Others will go with you."

"Others?"

An'Arka stepped aside. He pointed to the two guards who had been standing watch at the end of the corridor. Perhaps all this time the guards had been observing them, attempting to discern their intentions or their resolve. Nonetheless, Naylon was surprised An'Arka wasn't going with them.

"Uh, it's going to be difficult to talk with them. We don't speak your language," Naylon told him.

"I will be in constant communication with them and you from the ship." He pressed what looked like a large button to each of their necks. Within seconds, both felt an odd sensation as the devices pierced their flesh, and latched themselves through their dermis, apparently with some sort of anesthetic, since neither felt pain. "They will monitor your location and provide a means to communicate with you. Do not attempt to remove them. You will be… harmed."

Both of them placed their hands on the devices and tugged anyway. They weren't coming off any time soon without ripping the skin and leaving a nasty wound.

Naylon and Tann took their packs and followed the three Telkans to what amounted to their galley. They were handed trays and given three brown fist-sized bars, each of what looked and smelled like compressed berries and nuts. They sat while the Telkans stood by the table observing them silently. Naylon sniffed at, then bit into the semi-soft bar. It tasted like nuts and berries too, complete with crunch. Tann noticed that at the first bite and devoured the meal.

Done with the bars, they both downed large containers of water. They were ushered to a room before the airlock where a considerable amount of talk ensued between their two Telkan guards and a communications device on the wall.

"Something's wrong," Naylon whispered as they sat on a bench against the bulkhead watching the Telkans.

"Yeah, but what," Tann replied warily.

One of the Telkan guards had activated a large screen. It was split into quadrants. Only the top left one was a visual image of the outside of the ship, the rest were rows of data that constantly streamed down the screen and graphs of various things they had no idea how to interpret. But the visual image was obvious. Outside, it was dark and raining. Naylon couldn't exactly tell what had been discussed earlier, but could tell they were doing a general sensor sweep of the area. Finally, one of the Telkans pointed to three glowing dots on the screen. The image was zoomed in. Topographical markings were obvious on the screen now. The Telkans had a map of the area! It would be an invaluable aid for them if only he could download it. But what was more important was he was able to discern that they had been discussing the three moving blips. What were they? Animals? Terrans? Naylon couldn't tell. If they were people, why were they moving about in the dark and rain?

More conversation with the Telkan at the other end of the communicator resulted in one of Naylon and Tann's guards opening a panel on one of the bulkheads. He pulled out two rifle-like weapons, which they both shouldered. This was in addition to the smaller, pistol-shaped weapons holstered around their massive waists.

Naylon watched their every move. Although they were concerned with the three moving blips, and that extra weapons had come out, they were still about to exit the ship anyway.

The guard that hadn't gathered the weapons opened a trunk near one of the other bulkheads and pulled out what looked like simple ponchos. Four of them were removed, and two given to Naylon and Tann. The ponchos were far too big to fit them, so Naylon motioned for something to tie them around their bodies. The guard complied by cutting a length of black cord for both of them from a spool under a table. They donned the coverings, secured them over their packs, then tied them around their waists.

The communications device on Naylon and Tann's neck activated. A curious-sounding hollow voice presented itself in his left ear. It was An'Arka. *"Do'yukya will lead. You and Tann will proceed after him. Behind you will be Ta'Norat. As you have seen there is a group of Terrans headed toward the mountain range near here. They are deliberate in their movements despite the weather conditions. Do'yukya will see that they do not arrive at their destination. The devices on your necks will track your movements. Do not attempt to flee. We will find you if you do."*

Naylon spoke to Tann in Lingua. "Terrans. I bet they detected this ship."

Tann shook his head. "This is not good. It's just not good at all," he said angrily. He wasn't looking forward to being captured by Pacudas and his men again.

With their two charges in tow, the Telkan guards opened the outer airlock door. Both Naylon and Tann were given rectangular strips of what looked like opaque film. Do'yukya pantomimed for them to press the ends to their temples, while covering their eyes with the devices. Naylon did so and realized the device was effectively some sort of infrared viewing plate. Regardless, Naylon didn't like it that they were going out into the rain. He didn't look forward to getting soaked. Nonetheless, the raingear did its job, the viewing film provided an amazingly clear view of their passage in the dark, and the rain tapered off within fifteen minutes.

Efren, Darreth and Rehl continued their trek several meters from riverbank, effectively backtracking the way Darreth and Rehl had come earlier. The gently sloping bank was quite sandy. Most of the runoff from the now gently falling rain was running in rivulets toward the river. They had to be careful to avoid stepping directly into one of the channels, which resulted in a considerable amount of jumping and hopping as they continued onward.

"The Telkan ship is that way," Efren pointed to his right. "Our ship is back that way about a kilometer. Our objective is in that direction." He pointed straight ahead.

"Where's your fire team?" Darreth asked.

"I don't know."

"You don't know?"

"They're using stealth shielding. This sensor isn't equipped to read a stealth shield."

Abruptly, Darreth halted in mid-stride. "All this time you knew that?"

"Although this can't detect a stealth shield energy signature it can detect movement."

"Even cloaked movement?"

"Perhaps not."

"Perhaps not?" Rehl said, quite alarmed.

"We are as close to the river as we can be. There is a ridge of rocks to our left. They have no idea we're out here. We're relying on our own stealth measures to prevent us from being caught."

"You call that stealth? I can't believe this! We're going to be captured, if not killed," Darreth told him firmly.

Efren would have none of it. "Look, this was as good of a plan as I could come up with. How far have we gotten so far and not been detected?"

Darreth didn't say anything in return.

"Where do your tracks lead?" Efren asked.

Darreth looked down at the display, then pointed.

"Let's go," Efren said.

The rain abruptly ended, making their surroundings quiet in an eerie sort of way. That was just fine with Darreth now, but it was too late for his thoroughly soaked trousers. Nonetheless, it stayed nearly pitch black because of the clouds and the complete lack of any artificial light sources except for the various sensor equipment they had on them. The goggles were quite effective in piercing the inky blackness though, providing plenty of noiseless illumination, which made their journey easy and somewhat simple despite the low bushy vegetation.

Rehl was the first to notice the terrain becoming steeper, which indicated they were close to their objective. A few moments later, they were carefully negotiating scree and talus as they made their way to the crack in the rock wall.

Lieutenant Navar couldn't believe the luck. They had made extremely good time to their position despite the gear they had, the darkness and the rain. His scanner showed two Telkan biosigns coming directly toward them. They showed no signs of slowing down or changing direction. As far as he was concerned, they had still not been detected. Although they weren't particularly scanning for Terran biosigns, the scanner's sensor indicated more movement than what he was scanning for. After he switched to a broader biosign range, he realized two Terrans were in tow as well. Good, that meant their two previous guests were most likely with them. Perhaps the captain had been right in his intuition. Apparently, their previous guests had been working with these Telkans after all!

Navar pecked out a message into the comm strapped to his forearm to Urret. He didn't want to risk even whispering to him. Soldats Urret and Agrida were with him. They quietly released the safeties on their projectile weapons. It had long been known that simple projectiles, tipped with explosive sulphur compounds were extremely deadly to Telkans. No energy weapons were needed here.

The stealth shield had been activated at the last possible minute so they could find the best place to stop and find cover. A small mound of rocks sticking up from the sandy soil was in the perfect location. Dead ahead were the Telkans and the two Terrans. Behind them was the looming rise of the short mountain range they appeared to be headed toward. Navar pecked out another message. 'Less than one minute until target reaches us.'

Do'yukya, who was in front of Naylon and Tann, stopped abruptly. The scanner he had in his hand flashed a warning. A stealth shield had just activated not more than one hundred metyons ahead of them. He held up his arm in a universal motion, which meant 'stop moving right now'. Naylon instinctively went to one knee, as did Tann. Ta'Norat went past the two and observed the sensor. They whispered to each other briefly. Ta'Norat turned around and motioned for Naylon and Tann to turn around. He pointed to a thick tangle of bushes and had them flatten themselves against the ground behind them. He returned to Do'yukya. Do'yukya opened a flap on one of the compartments on his utility belt and pulled out a different scanner. He rotated a virtual dial until it signaled a lock had been fixed on the stealth shield's frequency. He pressed the center button. Nothing perceptible happened from his end.

Urret and Agrida watched their scanners. They had noted the two previously moving Telkan biosigns, along with the two Terran ones, had stopped thirty-three meters from their position. Navar was getting nervous. There was no way they could have been detected. He felt irritated because the dark and obstructions were going to prevent him from getting a good shot, now that they had ceased moving. He checked one of the stealth shield generators. The display showed it was working perfectly. At that very moment, the display went dark.

In the infrared display over their eyes the stealth shield's energy field always looked like a barely perceptible reddish aurora when it was this dark. As soon as the display shut off, so did the aurora. Instantly, Navar realized their position had been compromised. How that was possible, he couldn't imagine. As far as he knew, their stealth shield was not detectable by Telkan technology. Apparently, he was mistaken.

Do'yukya raised his weapon and aimed. Within a millisecond, the cannon's computer found the heat signature of two bodies. Unfortunately, there was a considerable amount of rock between him and his targets. He pressed the trigger anyway.

The energy blast hit less than a second after the failure of the stealth shield. It came as quite a surprise to the three Terrans. Fortunately, the infrared goggles had an automatic limiter on them. The blast, directly against the rocks they were hiding behind, would have been bright enough to overload them, blinding them in the process. Instead, they went opaque. All three were thrown backward.

Agrida landed on his back and didn't move. Navar shook his head. The blast had made his ears ring something awful. Urret had landed next to Agrida. He slowly rose up to his knees, then realized he was a target by doing so, and dropped to the ground immediately. Although Navar couldn't hear much of anything, he had enough of his wits about him to activate the motion detector sensor. One target was coming directly toward them. Navar had the barrel of his projectile weapon in the crack between the two larger rocks on purpose. He only needed to reposition it and set the targeting computer. That took two seconds. He pressed the trigger. Do'yukya had no chance to take cover. A moment later, a searing hot projectile exploded several centimeters inside his body. It caused him to issue a loud roar before he slumped over and stopped moving.

Ta'Norat had already opened the comm channel back at the ship. The sounds of the firefight and the sensor data were being transmitted to An'Arka. Already An'Arka was assembling a small team as back up.

Naylon pulled Tann close to him and spoke directly into his ear. "Go. Back up and crawl straight back. Don't get up. Just crawl."

Tann immediately complied. It was almost impossible to determine where to go though. It was still nearly pitch black, even with the night vision visor. He crashed head on into a bush, which dislodged the visor from his face. Naylon ran right into his muddy boots. Tann fought to get the visor back in front of his eyes then moved the bush's thin branches aside. He scooted over to the right and continued to crawl. The adrenaline surging through him threatened to overwhelm him as he scraped his knees and abraded his hands as he went. From his ground level view, a wall loomed up ahead. He raised his head several centimeters and realized it was nothing more than a pile of rocks. He scooted around them. Breathlessly, Naylon was right behind him. He took cover right next to Tann, and turned his body to face the firefight head on in an attempt to make himself as small a target as possible.

Urret had recovered enough from the blast to check on Agrida. He pressed his ear against the man's chest while pressing his forefinger against his neck. Nothing. Angered beyond control, Urret scrambled to aim his weapon ahead of them toward where Navar had fired. He didn't even bother with the tracking sensor. He managed to get off a hail of rounds.

Urret only saw the distant flash before the second blast slammed into the boulder in front of him. It had enough force to send rock shards through the crack between the rocks, scraping the barrel of Navar's weapon and raining rocky hail all over them. A thin sharp shard of rock pierced the side of Urret's face. Immediately, he clamped his hand against the wound. He was sure it had missed his jugular, but already he could feel blood oozing out in front of his right ear. Trying to stem the flow of blood was proving to be extremely difficult. He needed to fire his weapon but found he couldn't remember how to do so. Within seconds he felt so faint he dropped his head to the wet earth, trying to ward off the feeling dizziness. It was doing no good. The spinning sensation was growing more intense. "Can't... fire," he said to Navar just before he passed out.

Navar pressed the comm on his forearm and spoke rapidly. "Captain, we were discovered. They somehow disabled our stealth shield before we knew it. Agrida's dead. Urret's wounded and might be dead any minute. Only one Telkan biosign left. I think we got one of them. Need backup. Fast!"

Pacudas heard the plea from Selaye's station to his right. He snapped his fingers. Selaye relayed that to soldat Lazcún who was already suited up with Zapante and Barcega.

There was no way they were going to take the ship in. All of them would be discovered if they did that. It would be up to them to hurry in as quickly as they could on foot. Zapante wasn't so sure they'd be able to make a difference, given how far they were from the fighting.

Ta'Norat kept the comm channel open while he continued to fire on his target. He was entirely focused on the fighting and had almost forgotten about the two Terrans who he had been guarding. Knowing they had no weapons and were unfamiliar with the territory, he wasn't too concerned with their whereabouts just now. Regardless, if they were stupid enough to attempt to escape during the weapons fire, they would be wounded or killed. If they somehow managed to get away, a simple scan of the area would turn them up very quickly.

Efren stopped dead in his tracks. Off to their right were flashes of light followed by the sound of weapons fire moments later.

"Weapons!" Darreth stated.

"But whose?" Rehl asked.

Efren aimed his sensor toward the flashes. He continued to tweak the readout until he found what he was looking for. "Terrans. At least three. And… one Telkan. The Terrans are in two groups. They might have the Telkan surrounded. But I'm not sure. The two groups are too far apart. I don't know what to make of this."

Rehl didn't want to state the obvious. After all, the initial weapons fire was already finished. Anyone could have been killed so far. "I'm betting it's your fire team. They've engaged the Telkans."

They continued to stand still for a few more moments, listening. Then, continuous firing went on for nearly ten seconds.

Efren aimed the sensor again, trying to discern more of what kind of activity was going on below them. Darreth and Rehl looked on as well. Moments later the second Telkan biosign faded. All that remained were two Terran signs, which were further away and a separate one closer by. None of them were moving about. Perhaps they were all still taking cover, Efren surmised. "No Telkans. We should investigate," he told them.

Rehl quickly grabbed Darreth's arm. He shook his head no. Darreth shook his in rebuttal, countering Rehl's refusal. "Those two Terran biosigns might be Naylon and Tann. We have to at least find out."

Rehl let go of Darreth's arm just as fast.

The firing abruptly ceased. Tann unplugged his ears. Naylon did the same. They both listened. They only heard wind. Naylon lifted his head up and adjusted the night vision visor. The visor showed two sprawled out glowing patches ahead of him. He shifted his position and saw that one of them was clearly a Telkan laying on its side. The other one didn't move either.

He quickly ducked back down. "I think they're dead."

"What?"

"Both of our guards have been killed."

"What about whoever was firing on us?"

"There's no way to know."

"Maybe we can get the Telkan weapons," Tann said.

"Good idea. But I'm not even going to attempt it until we're sure whoever was shooting at us has either left or is dead."

"What's that sound?" Tann asked.

"What sound?"

"That one."

Naylon held his breath. It was faint but they both distinctly heard it again.

"Help!"

"Someone's calling for help!" Tann exclaimed as he tensed up. "It might be one of the crew on board the ship that captured us."

Naylon tapped on the back of Tann's hand. "We're going nowhere. It could be a trick to get us out in the open."

Tann gulped. "I'm not moving."

Rehl stopped in his tracks. "Did you hear that?"

Efren cupped his ear. There it was again. A cry for help. Efren couldn't quite tell who it was, but it was certainly someone from his ship since it was in Empire Spanish. He glanced at the comm on his forearm. He didn't dare activate it. As far as he could tell, no one knew they were off the ship. If he dared answer he, and by default Darreth and Rehl, would be discovered for sure. He scanned the area again. There were still three distinct Terran biosigns. Two were much further away. One was much closer to them, most likely the one who yelled out.

He had to make a choice and make it now. "Hello!" He called out.

Instantly, Darreth was alarmed. He grabbed Efren's shoulder and loudly whispered. "Why did you do that?"

"That's a call from one of the crew."

"But they don't know you're gone."

"Don't you think I know that?"

"Then why did you call out?"

"Like I said, defection is not a word you will use in my presence."

Darreth was fuming. They were extremely close to the cavern. Now this.

"Did you hear that?" Naylon whispered.

"Yeah. Someone yelled out 'hello'."

"Damn. I wish we had some sort of scanner to determine who's out there."

It was at that moment a voice stirred in both of Naylon's ears. It wasn't Tann's.

"Naylon. Are you there?"

It took a full second before Naylon registered the 'sound' because it hadn't from outside his head. And it was in Lingua so it couldn't have come from the comm device the Telkans had attached to his neck.

He subvocalized it as loudly as he could without actually shouting, *"Darreth!?"*

"Naylon! Is Tann with you?"

"He's right here with me. Where are you? How did you find us?" Naylon was having difficulty hearing the complete sentences due to no repeaters being involved in the comm transmission. His brain filled in some of the syllables.

"Never mind that right now. Are you two okay?"

"We are. We're hiding out. There was a firefight. We're okay though."

Then out loud to Tann. "You're not going to believe this. Darreth is out there. He found us!"

Tann's mouth dropped open in surprise.

"Rehl! The other biosigns are Naylon and Tann. We found them. By thunder, we found them!" He grabbed Rehl by the shoulders and hugged him.

Efren looked at the two of them. "How do you know it's them?"

"Because I'm talking to them right now."

Efren was aware that Naylon had some sort of tech in side of him, but wasn't sure exactly what it was. He gathered now that it was a comm device.

"Over here!" Navar called out.

"It's Llarena," Efren shouted back. "Don't shoot."

Naylon and Tann were close enough to hear voices up ahead of them, but not close enough to make out whether it was a conversation or just shouting.

Naylon took a chance. *"What's going on, Darreth? Where are you?"*

"We're approximately one hundred meters from your twelve."

Naylon relayed the information to Tann.

"Stay put until we're sure the area is secure."

"There might still be Telkans nearby," Naylon warned.

"None are near here. No biosigns." Darreth realized at that moment he'd not ever seen one of them alive.

"According to Darreth our guards are definitely dead," Naylon told Tann.

At this point Naylon was wondering why he hadn't heard even a warning from An'Arka. He was sure all the communication he was creating, along with the firefight, would have had them coming in record time. Perhaps they had their own stealth technology undetectable by anyone with scanners. That thought alone was keeping Naylon on edge.

Darreth, Rehl and Efren made a direct approach to Lieutenant Navar. When they reached him, he was clutching his thigh. He had already made a tourniquet and had tied it just above his knee.

"Llarena. How did you get here so quickly? Why are they with you?"

"I can't explain it right now. Let me see your comm."

Navar held out his arm. Llarena found the latch that held it and removed it from Navar's arm. He carefully laid it flat on the ground, picked up a rock, then smashed it.

"What in hell? Why did you do that?"

"So you won't call the ship."

Next, Efren pulled the hand weapon from Urret and Agrida's utility belts and handed them to Darreth. Darreth passed one to Rehl. He then un-strapped the comms from their wrists and tossed them away as well.

Navar winced as he attempted to move his leg. "Lazcún will be here any minute with reinforcements. You will be court-martialed for this!"

"No one will be court-martialed for anything." He played his light across Navar's bloody pant leg. It looked awful. He turned to Darreth and Rehl.

It was obvious to the Lieutenant they were leaving. Without him. "What are you doing," Navar demanded.

"Getting out of here." Then to Darreth, "Call your friends."

Darreth had already done so using his internal comm. Naylon and Tann were making a beeline toward them. Darreth took the lantern from Efren and pointed it toward them as Naylon and Tann hurried toward them, past both dead Telkans.

"Cover him," Darreth told Rehl. Rehl quickly assessed how the weapon he had been given worked and pointed it at Navar. Darreth left the group and went to the other side of the boulder the Lieutenant was leaning back on.

It was a moment Naylon didn't think he'd be experiencing again. In the instant he saw Darreth the many days of the fear of the unknown melted away. They ran toward each other those last several steps, stopped, then held on to each other in a tight embrace. Tann was a split second behind Naylon. The three of them wrapped arms around each other, tears welling out of everyone's eyes. Naylon quickly wiped his away. Tearful reunions would have to wait. They were nowhere near out of danger yet.

"This way," Darreth told them. "One of the men from Efren's ship is hurt."

"You know Efren?" Naylon asked, greatly surprised.

"We were captured by the same men who captured you. He helped Rehl and me escape from his ship."

Naylon and Tann looked at each other briefly. "Rehl's with you?" Naylon asked, incredulous.

"I couldn't have done this otherwise."

They quickly returned to the others. Rehl quickly greeted the two but couldn't do more than that due to covering the Lieutenant.

Navar was still wincing in pain. "You have to help me, Llarena."

"No, you already said Lazcún is on his way. I'm leaving with these men." He turned to Naylon and Tann. "Good to see you both again. I trust your time with the Telkans was… interesting."

Naylon looked at Efren, not sure what to make of that statement. "We were taken prisoner." He turned to Darreth and spoke in Lingua. He didn't want the Telkans to understand what he was saying through the comm still implanted in his neck. "The Telkans let us go because they know about the tunnel in the cavern. They wanted us to find it for them. They know it's some sort of dimensional device."

"Fruck!" Darreth was greatly concerned now.

Naylon continued. "If you know how to get there, we have to go now. The Telkans on the ship that brought us back are already after us. They can track us with these things in our necks. We have to hurry! You do know how to find the tunnel, right?"

Darreth pointed. "It's about a half kilometer that way."

"That's all?" Naylon asked. "We've got to go now! The Telkans are very efficient at everything."

Navar was fuming as the men started to leave. "We'll find you, Llarena. When we do, you will be summarily shot. Do you hear me? I will ask to pull the trigger myself!"

Efren was already several steps away but he halted upon hearing that. Darreth tried to get him to continue on but knew it would do no good.

Efren went back and looked Navar in the eye as he pointed his finger at the officer. He spoke with conviction although he still had only Darreth's word for what he was about to say. "I am sick of this endless war. You know it will never end. All of us know that. All of us! You know it more than anyone. Where I'm going neither you nor anyone on the ship will find us. Ever."

He quickly returned to Darreth and the rest of the entourage. "You said you had a ship. Why are you discussing a cavern?"

"We, uh, have to find the cavern to get to the ship. Trust me, we're all getting away from here as fast as we can. Scan for Terrans and Telkans."

Everyone adjusted their night vision goggles. Efren activated the scanner. He wasn't happy about the reading. Three Terran biosigns were already headed toward them from one direction and six Telkans from the other. "We have to move quickly. If I can detect them, they can detect us."

"Thunder!" Darreth exclaimed after looking at the screen. "That way." They went as quickly as they could in complete silence, no one realizing that Darreth and Naylon were holding a conversation.

As they hurriedly headed toward the cavern Tann barraged his brother with questions. "How did you get here? How did you know what happened to us? We barely understood what happened ourselves. It's because of those discs, isn't it?"

"Exactly." He explained how he had also found one.

It was Naylon's turn to talk but he used his implant. *"Darreth, I missed you so much. I was sure we would never see each other again."*

"I had no choice but to come back for you. It's a long story, but trust me when I say a lot has gone on since you and Tann were lost."

Talking quickly while picking through the darkness, they gave each other a recap of what had happened to them both since Naylon and Tann had disappeared. The common element that surprised them both was how Efren had turned so easily against his own people. The war had more casualties than the Terrans were aware of.

Twenty minutes later, they reached the second to last track point in Darreth's scanner. Everyone was huffing and puffing as they had had to make their way in complete darkness with no trail whatsoever. It was terribly treacherous trying to find their way back while stopping periodically to determine if the second fire team was on their trail or whether they were indeed attempting to rescue Navar first. Apparently, they were not the team's primary target after all, since the three moving blips on Efren's screen continued to stay at a lower elevation. It seemed the Terrans intended to retrieve their men or engage the Telkans.

Darreth was the last to go through the opening into the huge quiet cavern. The abrupt change of venue was a welcome relief to their journey, which had been completely out in the open. The utter pitch-blackness caused all of their night vision devices to no longer function though. Rehl had been the first one to go in. He activated his lantern. With that, he found the other lantern they had left behind. Its warm even glow barely cast enough light to fill the cavern. In the very center of the huge expanse lay the gateway.

Darreth had expected Naylon and Tann to no longer have the disc devices that had brought them here. But during his conversation with Naylon, he had discovered they still had theirs, and how they had gotten hold of them in the first place. He had told Naylon how Kestin had duplicated the one he had. But now there was a problem. They were one short.

"Rehl. You go first. Take Tann with you. Then you come back and bring the disc that brought Tann through."

"You think that'll work?"

"It better or we're going to have a problem."

"I don't look forward to this," Rehl said.

"Why?" Tann asked.

"I got some serious vertigo when we came this way. I'm going to get it a few more times."

"Fruck. I forgot about that," Tann murmured.

"Go," Darreth told them.

"Where does that tunnel go?" Efren asked as he pointed a light into the interior of the smooth cylindrical opening.

"To where we came from. Back to our universe."

"And to your ship?"

"That, too. Go back to the opening and take another reading. Make sure no one's coming."

Efren went back to the crack. The sky was starting to turn a soft gray. He pointed the scanner outside. It produced no reading, Terran or Telkan. "It's clear. I get nothing from here."

"Good."

"Ready Tann?" Rehl asked.

"I guess." He pulled out the disc from his pack, held it firmly in his hand and followed Rehl. Seconds later, they disappeared.

Unexpectedly, a shaft of light illuminated part of the rectangular rock. The three remaining men looked back toward the jagged vertical opening. Dawn. As quickly as the light beam shone it disappeared, hidden by morning clouds.

Darreth looked back down the empty tunnel. "What's taking him so long?"

Chapter 37

Rehl stumbled from the other end of the tunnel into pitch blackness. Tann, directly behind, ran right into him. He couldn't get through fast enough.

As quickly as he could, despite the disorientation, Rehl found the little square depression on his lantern and touched it. The beam instantly widened, casting a much larger and more intense light around them.

Both of them fell to their knees, breathing hard and gagging.

Tann shook his head. "Why does that happen?"

Rehl held onto the outside of the tunnel's rock wall and stood. "Maybe we aren't biologically suited to be slipping between universes."

Tann felt like he was going to retch but the sensation started to subside before it got too bad. He slowly got to his feet and leaned against the rock face, too.

"Here, give me your disc," Rehl told him.

Tann handed it to him.

"Fruck, you have to go back again," Tann said, glad it wasn't him.

"Will you be okay?"

Tann still felt dizzy, but the intense feeling of the transition was fading even more now. Regardless, Tann had a metallic taste in his mouth. He smacked his lips a few times, trying to get rid of it. He nodded. "Go get 'em."

Rehl pulled out a second lantern from his pack, activated it and set the end on the closest flat surface. "More light for you," he told Tann. He pressed the dispersion button until it widened as far as it would go. "Here goes," he said. He stooped until he got just to the barrier, then went down onto his knees.

"What are you doing," Tann asked.

"In case I pass out."

Rehl secured the discs in his pack, then crawled as fast as he could through the tunnel. He wasn't wasting any time.

"Something's wrong," Darreth said. More than ten minutes had passed since Rehl and Tann had left. That had given him enough time though to fill in the rest for Naylon about what had transpired after they had gone missing. The majority of it was through their internal comm so Efren wouldn't hear a lot of it.

Everyone had been watching the tunnel, waiting for Rehl to return. Efren had been taking readings at the crack in the cavern wall every couple of minutes, scanning for errant biosigns. So far, nothing had come their way.

Darreth heard a scuffling in the tunnel. He aimed his light into it. Rehl's head emerged, then his entire body, from the strange grey shimmering.

Rehl crawled the rest of the way and stopped. "Help me up. You have no idea how intense that is."

Despite Efren and Darreth on each arm, Rehl could barely stand up.

"Is something wrong over there?"

"No."

"What took you so long?"

"Darreth, I've been gone, what, a minute?"

Darreth looked at Naylon. "Maybe the tunnel causes some sort of time shift." Then to Rehl, "Where's the disc?"

Rehl leaned against the entrance of the tunnel and pulled his pack off. Out came the extra disc. Darreth took it from him and handed it to Efren. "Here. Hold this and don't let go or you won't make it through."

"Get ready," Rehl told them. "That dizziness gets worse the more times you do this."

Seconds later they were all on the other side with Tann. This time Rehl vomited before nearly passing out.

The shuttle was exactly where they had left it. Efren looked all around as they made their way out of the other end of the cave to the dry riverbed. The first thing he noticed was how cold it was. How bizarre it was that all they had done was walk through a tunnel. It nearly made him retch, and now everything was different.

Once they reached the ship, Darreth spoke to the security system from his internal comm. The back end of the shuttle opened and let them inside. Everyone discarded their gear while the shuttle sealed for spaceflight. Rehl activated the ventilation system to warm the cabin up. It was just above freezing outside and only slightly higher inside the craft.

Efren took a seat behind Rehl and strapped in as he watched Rehl power up the rest of the systems along with the engines. "What is this language?" he asked. He pointed to a label on the wall next to him.

Tann told him. "Lingua. You're going to have to learn it. No one here speaks Empire Spanish."

Efren didn't like the sound of that.

"Z plus one kilometer," Darreth spoke to the engine system. The ship slowly rose from the stony riverbed and sailed silently into the air. At a point exactly one kilometer above the surface, it halted. Rehl had already activated the scanner.

"Clear. We're good for orbital injection."

"System, nav on," Darreth told the ship. His visual field instantly changed to a clear 360-degree view of the surrounding area. Calculations for the shortest distance into orbit were made six microseconds later. A red line, curving away slightly to the left, projected onto the field. Seconds later the sublight engines kicked in and the nose of the craft pointed slightly upward. Two minutes later, they were clear of 99% of Rylerra's atmosphere.

"Autopilot on," Darreth said. The visual nav field collapsed and the almost claustrophobic surroundings of reality presented itself.

"How long before we reach your world?" Efren asked.

"Andakar is four days away," Naylon responded as he unbuckled the shoulder straps and headed for the food dispenser cubbyhole.

Tann was quick to respond, too. "Darreth. Maybe Efren knows where a conduit is."

"Conduit?"

The next hour, over coffee and snacks, was a long and involved discussion by Efren as he described the naturally occurring conduits between star systems. But did they exist in their universe? Efren quickly discovered that the detection system normally used on all starships he was acquainted with simply didn't exist on this one. Efren was terribly anxious when he learned that Tann had discovered all this because of some Terran prisoners. Prisoners that the Telkans had on the very planet they were headed toward, only in his dimension.

"Any idea who they might be?" Tann asked.

"There are over five million soldats on various missions and in billets across the empire. It is impossible for me to know who they are. And they may not be the only ones either. Entire ships have simply gone missing."

The mood was somber for several moments.

Tann was the first to break the silence. "What if Efren can figure out a way to detect the conduits anyway."

Rehl looked at him. "I don't see how that would be possible."

"It would give me something useful to do," Efren offered.

"I'll show you the sensors we use but you're not going to be able to read any of them. They're all labeled in our language and use our measurement system," Rehl told him.

"Then you will interpret them for me."

For the next two hours Rehl and Darreth both went over the various sensor equipment used aboard the shuttle, explained how the propulsion system functioned and how the nav field enveloped the pilot with a full view of the trajectory they were flying.

"Your sensory equipment appears to be quite old," Efren said at one point.

"This is state-of-the art," Rehl shot back.

"State-of-the-art for your civilization, but not for mine. War accelerates invention. You've told me your culture doesn't engage in warfare. That may explain why this equipment seems to be lacking."

Darreth was completely taken aback at Efren's assessment of the ship. As far as he was concerned, this vessel was one of the finest passenger-class ships on Andakar.

Regardless of what he considered primitive equipment Efren continued to ask questions about the sensors. Eventually, he came to the conclusion that he might be able to use one of the wide-spectrum radiation detectors along with the long-range dark matter detector, and combine their outputs to another display.

"I'm unfamiliar with this equipment, but the waveforms conform to standard ones I'm used to viewing. Here, tune this display to the upper range," Efren told Rehl.

Efren watched the output on a third display, asked which controls manipulated the output, then fine-tuned the resulting graph himself. He was watching for the x and y-axis of one of the detectors to cross as two waveforms came together. He was sure they would work as a crude detector for the presence of the two conduits they had already mapped in this star system. It took another twenty minutes before he felt comfortable with the displays. But something seemed to prevent the sensor sweeps from allowing the waveforms to cross.

"Huh," Efren said. "I'm sure you've explained this to me enough for it to work. Maybe I missed something." He asked a dozen questions of both Rehl and Darreth, mostly about the precise function of the two detectors. Both of them had to refer to the maintenance manual flimsies for most of the answers. Finally, Efren realized why the waveforms wouldn't cross.

"Look. See what happens when I vary this along the y-axis? There. It skips over the reading altogether. Your equipment is not at fault. That can only be caused by a filter. It would prevent the display from showing where the waves cross."

"Prevent it?" Rehl asked.

Efren nodded. "We need to remove the filter."

Rehl consulted a maintenance flimsy. "The circuit that has the filter in it is integrated into the sensor."

Efren shook his head. "This ship may be less sophisticated than what I'm used to, but it is clearly advanced enough for you to prevent the filter from functioning. I'm sure of it. Ask the maintenance computer to bypass it."

"I'll try." Then to it he spoke in Lingua, "System maintenance computer, activate."

"*Working.*"

Rehl took the flimsy and set it down on the nav console in front of him. He zoomed in on the circuit Efren was sure was the cause of the problem. "Diagnostic of sensor circuit J11, junction H7886. Describe this filter."

"*The quantum node filter at that junction is designed to mask phantom radiation uniquely found at the 23 angstrom wavelength.*"

"What phantom radiation?" Rehl asked.

"Command not recognized."

"Damn."

Darreth translated while Rehl interrogated the computer.

Efren shook his head. "That's no 'phantom'. It's vunian radiation. It signals the mouth of a conduit! It's exactly what we're trying to detect. That filter is preventing you from finding it, much less see it." He looked disgusted. "Why would anyone design such a filter?"

Everyone looked at each other. Darreth shrugged his shoulders. Naylon was the only person who responded. "Maybe the Consort doesn't want anyone to know about the conduits. And maybe this could all just wait to be figured out after we've reached Andakar. It's just a few days from here, using a way we know that works. Can't this wait until we're safely back home?"

"Are you kidding?" Tann exclaimed. "I don't know how you guys can stand it. I'm ready to get home *now*. Efren already figured out a way to get us back faster than normal. You have to at least help him get inside that conduit."

Darreth thought about it for a moment then shrugged his shoulders. "It can't hurt to try. After all, it's still hours to the wedge insertion point."

Both Darreth and Rehl spent the next hour culling information from the maintenance computer and from the flimsies. Their objective was to bypass the filter. It didn't look promising until Rehl located and isolated the quantum code that ran the sensor circuit.

"Thunder! This line of code activates the filter. It can be deactivated." He pointed while Darreth looked on.

"Can it be that easy?" Darreth replied.

"There's no way it could be that easy," Tann offered, looking over his shoulder.

"Let's see. Efren, you watch your display. I'll tell the computer what to do," Darreth told him.

Several minutes later, the circuit display flashed red at the junction where the filter had been deactivated. Peripheral circuits took over to receive and process the input from the bypassed filter. Efren continued to watch the display. Finally, the two waveforms crossed as he expected. He zoomed in to look more closely.

"This waveform is exactly what we look for, but without the proper scale I can't be positive."

Efren instructed Darreth to dim the interior lights. He zoomed the display to 10X, then started a sensor sweep thirty degrees from Kaskalon's north magnetic pole and continued outward. A green dot flashed briefly as the sweep continued. Efren wasn't sure because the display was nothing like a standard conduit detection system, but the waveform at the bottom of the screen was what he was expecting.

"There it is. The entrance to your conduit is there," Efren announced. The fact that their efforts had resulted in nothing more than a brief green dot flashing on the screen was a major letdown.

Darreth spoke to the nav computer, then translated for Efren. "The coordinates indicate the conduit is two hours from here at maximum sublight. Now how do we get inside it?"

Joll Zenatel decided that Manager Raxi had paid him enough to be away from his normal job hauling cargo to Andakar and bringing finished goods back to Rylerra. Ever since the shuttle in the riverbed had taken off from the surface he and his co-pilot had followed just outside normal sensor range. And, if they happened to stray into the shuttle's sensor net, their transponder would show them to be a standard cargo ship anyway. Nothing unusual about that.

Joll's assignment had been to report back the moment anyone entered the shuttle. The data Zelin had obtained led him to believe it had managed an unauthorized landing on Rylerra. The Rylerran shuttle identification satellite network had plenty of holes in it, but had successfully tracked its landing. And he had an in which allowed him to follow the data stream.

Joll was in the pilot's seat. "They've changed headings. Where do you suspect they're going now?"

Co-pilot Thal Asrattem looked puzzled as he looked at the projected coordinates his display was showing. "I have no idea. Follow them anyway."

"Look at that. Their vector will take them far outside the normal transport routes to Andakar. They're taking a high orbit outside the ecliptic."

"Why would they do that?" Thal knew Eratil and Kaskalon orbited within six degrees of each other. Making a heading outside the ecliptic would require hours more of time and plenty more fuel than normally used to achieve enough distance to wrinkle a wedge of spacetime, then get back to the ecliptic once they arrived in Eratil space.

"Beats me, but they are."

"Guess it's time to send another message to Raxi."

Efren had been working on a way to pry open the conduit non-stop. Naylon had to hand it to him. Efren could have easily not done a thing. They could have wrinkled a wedge along the ecliptic like normal, and been home in a few days. But for some reason Efren was determined to work on the issue. He seemed to think if they could detect the conduit, they could also open and slip inside it as well.

Tann was sitting next to Efren discussing it with him. "You use that Tetra-G substance in this resonance chamber, right?" Efren said, pointing to a schematic of the engine system.

"Right. It ignites into a plasma and powers a fusion engine. The fusion engine provides enough power to spin up the drive that wrinkles a wedge of spacetime."

"All that energy used for nothing."

"Nothing? I wouldn't say that. We use it to travel between stars!"

"But the amount of energy used is enormous. You run out every 20 light years! No wonder you have so few settled worlds."

The discussion of their propulsion system had elicited a tremendous amount of discussion amongst the men about their two civilizations and their use of technology. Efren had finally accepted that although he'd been lucky enough to stumble onto an alternate universe of star farers, they seemed to be way behind in star travel technology. It alternately amused him as well as made him anxious.

"Hand me that other flimsy," Efren said, pointing.

Tann pulled the forward shield deflector system maintenance flimsy onto the console surface. Efren traced some of the energy conduit pathways, asking Tann to translate the schematic for him. It was slow going because of the delays and miscommunications he had to deal with. But he finally managed enough understanding of the circuitry to announce his findings.

"Darreth, you can vary the energy flow to the engine any time you need to, right?"

"Of course."

"Good. Can you tune the sublight engine output to 9050 gigajoules?"

"That high? The sublight engine's nominal output is only 8000 gigajoules."

"That's how high it needs to be to pry open the end of the conduit. You won't need the wedge engine at all."

Rehl worked on the calculation. "How long does it need to be at that level?"

"Eight point three seconds, then power down to two hundred seventy gigajoules for the rest of the time."

"We'll have one point five three seconds to spare before the failsafe will kick in and shut off the engine. Otherwise, you can be sure we'll be dead in space."

"Then we need to make sure the computer will provide the cutoff…. I can't believe this primitive ship had everything needed to not only find the conduit, but to enter it, and yet no one's ever done this before," Efren stated.

Tann was looking out the port side window, trying to discern if that cargo ship they'd detected several hours ago during a routine sensor sweep was still there. Darreth was suspicious of it because it was trailing them off the ecliptic. That alone was a highly unusual maneuver for that type of vessel. He couldn't see a thing against the background stars. "Frucking Consort," he whispered to himself.

Both Joll and Thal continued to tail the shuttle after sending their report back to Raxi's office. Their orders still stood. Continue to follow the shuttle, then wrinkle a wedge directly after them. Raxi wanted to make sure Inandra knew he was completing his end of the deal. They would send a report directly to her when they reached Andakar space. Although the ship was far off the ecliptic, they both assumed it was headed to Andakar anyway.

Joll continued to watch his display while Thal worked on the computations. One moment the shuttle was there, the next it seemed to wink out of existence without so much as a warning. In fact, the only indication the ship had done anything was that it had accelerated only slightly before it simply disappeared.

"What the...," Joll exclaimed. He commanded several other sensors to zoom in to the coordinates of the suddenly missing shuttle. When none of them showed him what he wanted, he replayed the last five seconds of sensor data. It was exactly as the visual field sensor had indicated. The shuttle simply disappeared.

"Thal, we have a problem."

Thal looked up from his calculation display. Joll pressed an icon to display what he had recorded on Thal's nav screen.

"That's impossible," Thal said. He was well aware an entire series of events had to take place before a wedge could be created. An intense magnetic field was always generated. The engine's plasma resonance chamber always emitted a bright visual and microwave flare, and several other sensors would have indicated a huge energy surge. In addition, a graviton pulse would have been recorded. None of those events had taken place. They saw only a focused beam of neutronic plasma emitted from the forward deflector array, acceleration at extreme sublight speed for eighty-eight microseconds, then the shuttle simply disappeared.

"The boss is not going to like this," Joll told Thal.

"Well, at least the sensor log proves we didn't just lose them."

"It worked!" Rehl exclaimed.

"Of course it worked," Efren said, matter-of-factly.

"How long will we be in the conduit?" Darreth asked.

"According to your system map, the star you call Eratil is 1639 local AU from our entry point. In approximately sixteen hours the conduit will empty us into that star's north polar magnetic field."

"Sixteen hours? That's all?" Rehl asked.

Efren shrugged his shoulders and nodded. "I assume the engine shut down to nominal at the proper time?"

Rehl looked down at his display again. "With six microseconds to spare."

"Good, the sublight engines are all you need to keep the ship moving through the conduit. The ship will be 'flowing' through it, as it were."

"With a minimal amount of energy use," Darreth noted out loud. He looked at Rehl. "Do you have any idea what this means? This is going to change star flight forever. No more reliance on endless supplies of Tetra-G. Just a neutronic beam from the deflector to pry open the conduit, a super high burst from the sublight engines, then throttle back to a ridiculously low level of output until we dump out at the other end."

"We still don't know why that filter circuit was ever designed into the sensor array," Rehl offered.

Tann stood up and rested his forearms across the back of Rehl's compression chair. "Maybe the Consort really thought that was a phantom signal. Maybe they had no idea what it was."

Naylon chimed in this time. "Or maybe they really did know that naturally occurring warp conduits exist, but wanted everyone to be totally reliant on their production of Tetra-G. After all, where is the only production facility? On Triton. In the Sol system. They have total control over star flight."

Darreth didn't say it out loud. *Well, they still have control over production but they don't have total control anymore.*

Chapter 38

Yarosay Bex, shift manager at Andakar's primary navigation control space station, was alerted just before lunch. Yarosay turned to the traffic controlwoman seated along the main floor of the large room. There were twelve men and women on duty this shift. Each sat in front of a large screen, watching as computers logged and tracked traffic from all across the solar system. Their task was to be the human eyes to supplement the automated logs.

Anta Garruti was one of two young women watching her screen. Her specific duty was to watch for objects not coming from the ecliptic. Comets, stray asteroids and other cosmic debris were always being sucked into Eratil's gravity well and could vector in from any trajectory. She monitored such objects before they could become a nuisance or a danger to normal traffic.

Yarosay looked at the readout. "This doesn't look right."

"That's why I called you over. There was a weird delta band tachyon surge just before the object came into sensor range."

As they continued to monitor the readout, a transponder code suddenly appeared on the screen. "That's a ship," Yarosay exclaimed.

"And it's way outside the starlanes," Anta noted.

"Indeed it is," Yarosay said, gathering himself. It wouldn't do for a manager to seem in a dither. "Designation?"

Anta pressed a glowing strip on the dark surface of the panel in front of her to connect the readout to the ship registry database. There was an immediate match. "It's the *Andakar Navigator*."

"So, it's the errant Lieutenant Commander." Yarosay had received the alert from the *Guardian* space station's Captain of the Guard the day after the shuttle missed its landing on Agica Prime. A quick check determined that Lieutenant Commander Takaramyus, along with a companion had gone missing.

"I'll place the call to the officer of the day onboard the *Guardian*. They'll take care of this. In the meantime, let that ship know we're aware of its presence," he told her.

Two officers stood behind the thick transparent barrier at landing deck C aboard the *Guardian*. They were Squadron Master Yoon Wakanabe and space station Manager General Anz Tlor. Once the ship was powered down, the officers waited for them to exit the shuttle and come through the airlock into their area.

"Am I glad to be here," Tann exclaimed heavily once he was off the ship.

"Me, too," Naylon said under his breath.

After being contacted by navigation control for approach instructions, Rehl had contacted the *Guardian* officer of the day and told him who he had on board. But Naylon was quite anxious about what was next. There had been much discussion about his rescuers' fates. When Darreth and Rehl saw Tlor and Wakanabe waiting as they disembarked, they were sure they were in serious trouble. After all, Darreth had defied a direct order and left Andakar. Rehl was in as much legal trouble as well for being his accomplice for obtaining the ship and filing a false flight plan. Neither expected to see Siloy, along with two lawyers standing next to the two officers. Darreth knew one of the lawyers and recognized the other one only in passing. It was completely unexpected seeing them there since he had no idea word had gotten to the ground so quickly about their return. How his father had managed to get two of the finest provincial lawyers to accompany him so quickly was the big question in Darreth's mind.

The first thing Siloy did was to grab his son Tann and hug him as tightly as he could. He wiped away several tears after he let go. "Are you all right? What is this thing?" He said as he pulled himself away.

Tann told him a communications and tracking device had been attached to both he and Naylon by aliens but that was about as far as he got before his father grabbed him again and hugged him even harder.

"We're going to need a surgeon to remove these things," Naylon told Siloy.

"Who are you?" Wakanabe asked Efren. He noted right away that Efren wore a military uniform of some sort.

Efren knew he was being spoken to and recognized an officer when he saw one. He snapped to attention and gave a salute. Darreth had already let him know they would most likely be greeted by at least one higher-ranking person.

Darreth responded for him. "He's soldat Efren Llarena of the *Cortés Libre*. He's the reason why Rehl and I got Naylon and Tann back alive."

"Soldat?"

"A soldier. He's in his people's military. He only speaks Empire Spanish."

"What's Empire Spanish?" Wakanabe asked.

"This is Empire Spanish." He gave Efren a recap of the people who had greeted them, introduced him to his father, and told him they would be taken to the mess hall shortly. They were all in desperate need of a good meal.

Everyone around the four men and Tann were astonished to hear them speaking a language not spoken on Andakar or any Inhab for that matter. Siloy was sure he had never heard his son speak that language either.

Darreth watched everyone's reactions then switched back to Lingua. "I'll explain in a few minutes, sir, but first," he said to the captain, "what charges have been brought against Rehl and me."

"You'll both find out shortly. The adjutant is waiting for you to be cleared."

Clearance was granted in due time, whereupon they were all escorted into an interior room for questioning. A small meal was brought in for each of them since they didn't end up in the mess hall after all.

"You have a lot of explaining to do, son," Siloy said gravely to his son, after they had finished eating.

The two lawyers were already preparing a case for their defense and were there to record everything they said.

"For the record," the captain began, "you, Lieutenant Commander James-Po have been charged with disobedience of a lawful order. You deliberately jumped off the planet against a direct order. In addition, Lieutenant Commander Takaramyus, you've been charged with the theft of corporate property. The deliberate filing of a false flight plan is secondary."

Both Darreth and Rehl looked at each other with a grin on their faces. They both knew that when this inquiry was over, there would be a few more important things to discuss other than these charges.

Efren had been sitting silently next to him. It had been at Darreth's request since there was no one other than their tiny group of four who would be able to help him understand anything that was going on.

Darreth cleared his throat. "I think it's much more important for all of you to understand who this man is to my left. Once Lieutenant Commander Takaramyus and I have finished explaining everything, it will become very clear we did what we did for the purpose of planetary security. In addition, I intend to bring charges of attempted murder against our planetary director, conspiracy to murder, and treason to the planetary interests of Andakar."

A deafening silence rippled through the room.

The ensuing rapid-fire discussion lasted three and a half hours, with breaks for the bathroom and for translations both to and for Efren. Everyone present felt exhausted.

"I move to drop all charges," Manager General Tlor blurted out. Even so, he could barely believe half of what had been told. The facts of the matter would be accepted as long as those who had been involved in spying on the planetary director's office would come forward and present their evidence. He had already motioned to make sure all of them would have immunity from this point forward before they even uttered a single word about it to authorities. More than the accusation that Inandra Alarr was working directly against Andakar's interests, along with the attempted murder of one of his officers, was their guest from Rylerra, or Déstica as it had been dubbed in Empire Spanish. What were they to do with the man? For the time being, no one had a clue; the implication of an alternate dimension had thrown everyone into a whirlwind.

Tlor was in a bit of a quandary about Rylerra's planetary director, Rish Illigan. Could he trust him? Was he in cahoots with Alarr? There was no way to know for sure. He himself was already on board with Siloy, having been briefed a week ago about Inandra and her malevolent intentions. These added accusations sealed it for him. Whatever reservation he might have had about what role he was to play in gaining independence for Andakar had melted away hours ago. He had clearly allied himself with the correct side.

The angle Darreth had presented about Zelin Raxi and his relationship with Alarr was troublesome. Manager Raxi was clearly a man they couldn't trust. Andakar had no jurisdiction to detain or extradite anyone from Rylerra. And although corporate law extended to all its Citizens, it was slightly different than Andakar's due to the different interests that existed there.

While Manager General Tlor mulled over his own quandary, Siloy realized he had one of his own. "Our, uh, guest needs to learn Lingua as quickly as he can. I'm sure his version of the language is quite different from the Spanish that's spoken on our side, for lack of a better phrase, so unfortunately a translation device is most likely going to be of limited use or out of the question. It is certainly not going to be a pleasant experience for him since we don't have this Pelinex RNA drug, nor will we ever have such a drug. Nonetheless, it is extraordinarily important that he be questioned further."

Darreth responded right away. "If you want to question him, there are four of us here who can translate for him. That should be a lot quicker than waiting for him to learn our language. Even so, he'll have to learn Lingua no matter what. He's certainly not going back."

"But," Darreth continued. "It's far more important that the non-military people in this room," he looked at all four of the lawyers, "be held accountable for anything that's been said so far."

"Agreed," Siloy said. "As of this minute all of your notes are sealed." He looked at the lawyers. "Nothing on any vidPAD that's been recorded will leave this station. You are not to discuss these issues with anyone."

There was an immediate protest from one of the captain's adjutants, but it was quickly quashed.

Siloy looked at his two lawyers. "You will be paid for your time. But as you can see, this information is far more important to be kept from the public until which time we can determine the actual threat to our planet, and discover who's really involved."

Siloy held out his hand to each of them, palm up. Each of the lawyers pressed an icon on their vidPAD screens and a small flat disc came out of the side. Each was handed to Siloy. Effectively, Siloy had the only transcript of the proceedings. He slid them over to Tlor.

Tlor looked at him. "These will be kept safe," he said, his face unsympathetic to the look of protest the lawyers still had on theirs.

Chapter 39

Siloy, Darreth, Rehl and Squadron Master Wakanabe sat in the Manager General's plush office. Naylon and Tann had already been sent planetside hours earlier after the Telkan tracking devices were removed. The five men had just finished discussing a very grave issue: that of arresting the planetary director.

"Unless we get Naylon's discussion group members to talk, we won't be able to hold her for very long," Darreth offered.

"I'm more concerned with what Consortium authorities on Earth are going to do. Word will reach there in only a couple of weeks if we succeed," Wakanabe responded.

The Manager General leaned back in his chair. A slight grin crossed his face. "No need to agit. I have a plan. It's going to involve a lot of people, but I can trust them to carry out my request even though they're not military."

Nomid Jattison, Tamik Sil, and Benja Ometo were the Chief and two of the vice-managers of Tokaias's civic police department. Born on Andakar, and all from third generation families, they were completely loyal to their planet's interests. Tlor, along with Siloy, placed a conference holocall to them on a totally secure line and gave them the long and involved story behind why they needed to arrest Director Alarr. The plan was completely without precedent, of course. Their collective issue with complying with the request was the enormous political problem they would have when it came time to renew their contracts with the department. But as Tlor explained, they would be immune to the ramifications. They not only planned to sever all communications with Earth Central Command computers at a strategic time, they had a much longer range plan to prevent any interference with decisions made on Andakar.

The FTL comm Inandra received from Zelin arrived nearly twenty-six hours after Darreth and the rest returned from Rylerra.

"Director Alarr," he began in the vid. He never spoke to her that way in a personal communication. She noted this right away. "I haven't seen you for quite some time now and miss you terribly. I look forward to seeing you again just as soon as my duties allow me to do so. In the meantime, there's something you've neglected to do for me. That would be a grossly overdue credit transfer. I complied with your request with regard to a certain provincial manager's son, yet you've not provided me with just compensation. I know you desire to do so. I do not want there to be a mistaken communication sent directly to said provincial manager's department. I would not like this mistaken communication to end up in an incorrect person's vidPAD either. I look forward to the credit transfer on the next comm buoy. Have a stellar day!"

If her secretary hadn't been right outside her door, she would have screamed at the screen. Instead, she clamped her jaw and pursed her lips while screaming epithets at him in her mind. How dare he make demands on her. As far as she was concerned she shouldn't have to pay him since he was supposed to have assured that Darreth, along with his brother and those two from the museum, would burn up in Rylerra's atmosphere. But that hadn't happened. In fact, she had already heard that he and one of the other lieutenant commanders had finally been found and were on the *Guardian* right now. Every step of the way, Darreth's seemingly charmed life had eluded her best attempts to stop him. But she still had something he did not. She had the law on her side. Knowing Darreth had deliberately left the planet despite direct orders to stay grounded, and had returned, left him open for immediate arrest. She intended to be there when the arrest was made.

"Cial," Inandra spoke to the comm to her secretary.

"*Yes, director,*" the woman responded.

"I need to book a shuttle to the *Guardian* right away. Clear my schedule for the rest of the day, too. And put me through to Chief Jattison. He's the head of the Tokaias civic police department. He will be accompanying me."

"*Yes ma'am.*"

Chief Jattison had never taken an acting class. However, he had an excellent poker face. Briefly, he wondered if Director Alarr had ever played poker, then dismissed the thought. He still had a few details to work out on how to best handle her arrest without drawing too much attention to the department. Once word got out, it would be all over the newsfeeds. Inandra's invitation, rather demand, that he accompany her to the *Guardian* provided him with the perfect opportunity. It couldn't have been more flawlessly timed. He was extremely lucky her comm arrived after Tlor and Siloy's.

Inandra arrived at the private shuttle launch arena in the late afternoon. The Chief and his two vice-managers had a flimsy sealed with two lawyers' signatures and secured so it couldn't be altered once it was presented.

Chief Jattison was absolutely amazed that Manager General Tlor was such a good coordinator. He hadn't been completely convinced the man would be up to such a task. Once he saw how calm and prepared Tlor was, he had a newfound respect for him and the military. Indeed, if all went as planned, Tlor intended to carry out his long-range plan as soon as their shuttle was launched from the ground. They would reach the *Guardian* space station forty-five minutes later, give or take two minutes. By that time, Tlor intended to have shut down all FTL comm buoys and grounded all ships bound for any Inhab other than Rylerra. Next, all security codes any computer used for communications back to Earth would be changed. How long this total blackout was going to be sustained was anyone's guess. But the objective was to delay outworld knowledge of Inandra's arrest as long as possible. The second and most important strategic decision was to place a demand on Earth Central Command. The demand would be on a secure outgoing FTL buoy. It would be another step in what was going to be a long and possibly arduous journey toward true independence. Now that it was clear their Planetary Director was actively involved in not only a murderous plot, but was working directly against their planetary interests, it became obvious they had little choice but to accelerate events. He, too, was glad he was fully on board with the decision.

In the last several hours, the majority of the members of Naylon's discussion group had been contacted and had agreed to testify against Inandra. Their testimony would make a solid case against her. They would be given immunity because of the egregious nature of the evidence. Several other items were already being worked on. The first was to announce a whirlwind election campaign. All of the provincial managers were unanimous. They intended to support the election of Siloy as their president. Some still held reservations about it, yet knew their support of him would result in the swiftest possible breaking of formal ties.

And it was very, very simple. Andakar had a military. Earth had not much more than a planetary security detail scattered mostly throughout seven Inhabs. Andakar had everything to gain and little to lose in making a sweeping demand to be heard as an independent entity and not as an arm of the Consortium. After all, they had some of the most valuable exports in the Consortium's sphere of influence.

The tactical and strategic plans, all laid out now were bold, decisive and extremely dangerous. It was going to be difficult and it was most likely going to be messy no matter the ultimate outcome. But they were decisions whose time had come. The tide had turned.

Siloy had already decided he would have Tlor's contract changed. He would no longer be a Manager General. He would be 'promoted', as it were, and become the station's first Commander General. In essence, he would be a true military General, the leader of the Andakar Space Navy and not beholden to the Consortium in any contractual way except for what he deemed necessary to continue the smooth running of their service to his planet.

Chief Jattison was first to exit the shuttle once it arrived in Docking Bay D onboard the *Guardian*. Inandra was next, followed by the two vice-managers. Inandra, not usually attentive to such things, had noticed the strange tension onboard the shuttle. She twice mentioned that the men were being inordinately quiet, but didn't receive much of a response.

When Tlor and Siloy both greeted the arriving party, Inandra was quite surprised. She was sure Siloy was still planetside. She was sure she had always received the latest on his whereabouts. There had been the communiqué she intercepted from the Southland Provincial Manager about Siloy's impending arrival in the provincial administrative center that very day. His schedule had even shown the meeting time. For the first time in at least a year, she felt inexplicably vulnerable.

"Manager General Tlor, Chief Council James-Po, I have urgent business to discuss," she said as formally as she could muster. "In fact, this business has to do with your son," she said, directly facing Siloy. Funny, he never seemed so imposing before.

"Ah, you must be here to bring kind words about his safe return from Rylerra; and that he found my younger son and Darreth's boyfriend."

"What?" She was only aware that Darreth and Rehl had returned. That Naylon and Siloy's young son had been found, much less returned, had been carefully kept from public or private consumption at this point.

"He and Lieutenant Commander Takaramyus found them on Rylerra. In fact, they were nearby all that time. It's just they were, uh, not capable of communicating with us directly. You are here to thank my son for being a hero, correct?" he said, smiling pleasantly.

The condescending tone Siloy used infuriated her. "It is unfortunate, Chief Councilor, that you've chosen to disregard a regulation the Manager General of this station helped to put into place."

"Director Alarr, whatever are you talking about?" he asked her.

This was too much. She was going to end his smarmy attitude right now. "You are clearly aware of the directive I'm speaking of. Your son," she continued, icicles forming on every word, "was expressly ordered to stay planetside while an investigation was being conducted into his conduct on Rylerra. He chose to violate that directive and his companion helped him. They are both in direct violation of corporate law." She turned to Chief Jattison and held out her hand. "The flimsy."

The Chief looked up briefly at Tlor, then to Siloy. He placed his hands to his sides.

"Chief?" she said at his unexpected inaction, her eyes searching.

Jattison did nothing. Inandra very nearly stamped her foot on the deck. Tlor reached into the pocket of his right sleeve and extracted a flimsy rod. He pressed the tip and it unfurled. He looked down at it as he read aloud. "Director Alarr, you are hereby detained. You will relinquish your right to return planetside. The charges against you for this detention are as follows: attempted murder, conspiracy to murder, unlawful depletion of the treasuries of the following provinces: Siaron, West Litok, Nooms, Kehail and Naxon. Additional charges are unlawful contact with pharma pirates and the continuous willful neglect of your duties as Planetary Director."

For only the second time in her life, Inandra was speechless.

PART III

Chapter 40

It had been recognized over a dozen generations ago that there were a plethora of planets in space. There were multiple problems with that discovery though. Far too many surveyed planets weren't inside a habitable zone, or had orbits far too eccentric to allow for colonization. The vast majority of them were simply too far from Earth to be economically viable even if they were ideal.

Deep Sky Mining carefully analyzed all candidate planets for their potential profit-making resources. Of those, it had turned out Venekir was only barely worth its weight in infrastructure. Profits were difficult to come by due to its lack of abundant amounts of bauxite, much less hematite. Aluminum and steel had always been the materials of choice when it came to construction. They were simply not easily accessible on Venekir.

Worse was the method used to find ideal planets. It was deemed far too expensive to send human reconnaissance to learn whether a planet was worth the effort of Deep Sky's long reach. Thus, automated survey ships did the work. Once the ships returned, the data were analyzed. If there was even one dissenting vote on the Supreme Board of Directors, the planet was simply crossed off as worthless. One such star system designated simply as HN 490003 had been struck from consideration long ago. The amount of radiation the star emitted was deemed far too great despite finding a terrestrial-sized moon in its habitable zone.

This wasn't an issue for Anoon Tilshar who had conveniently been 'killed' in an accident years previously.

The undercurrent of dissent ebbed and flowed as it always had during the long tenure of control over which Deep Sky Mining had on every aspect of life. Despite life having always been good, freedom of movement had always been an issue. Sure, it was possible to travel freely amongst Inhabs. Being born on one world and living one's life on another had never been the problem. It was just that the Consortium told everyone where they would live. Thus, the number of Citizens who weren't necessarily happy with their adopted world was growing longer and longer with each passing decade.

This restriction of movement was purely economic. The fuel with which to move about amongst the stars was tightly controlled because there was only one source of ore containing significant quantities of the mineral used to synthesize Tetra-G. In addition, the main way to make sure Inhab economies worked at peak efficiency meant people couldn't just live and work where and when they pleased, but rather as the Consortium needed them. Thus, each Inhab had a strictly planned economy. Virtually all of the movement of humanity from the Sol system was due to the need for job skills not found on an Inhab.

The Consortium had held such a long tenure and kept the grumbling at a minimum because no one wanted for material goods. Ever. Under their watch, every Inhab had sustained a slow and steady economic expansion. Reasons to change what had worked so well were purely academic at the top levels of the Consortium. 'All for one and one for all' had been the watchword of every business for hundreds of years. Resources had always been where they were needed when were needed. There was never a restriction on where resources were taken. Only people. Some of those people were totally fed up with being told where to go and where they had to live.

Always on the lookout for some opportunity to make a difference, Anoon's untimely 'demise' allowed him to renounce his Citizenship and join the New Worlds Alliance. All of the people who joined the group had 'died' or 'disappeared'. All had renounced their Citizenship and contribution to the Consort, indeed to civilization as everyone knew it. That meant no going back.

Located on the desert moon of HN 490003's second planet, their settlement was dubbed Ethlacos. Consisting of a growing band of ex-patriots, they had had only a loose structure and nebulous objectives until Anoon had joined them. Almost at once, he became their de facto leader, mainly due to his ability to set goals and instill a sense of purpose in nearly everyone.

The more people learned, word-of-mouth, of Ethlacos, the more came. And finally, enough credits had been pooled to purchase a much-needed tunnel borer. After it was assembled and put into place at the bottom of a meteor crater in the northern hemisphere, a proper expansion of the settlement, named Rakaris Rim, took place. Making sure the majority of the settlement was underground would help prevent detection in the short term if, for some bizarre reason, the Consortium Supreme Board of Directors decided to send another probe to visit their star system.

Six months after Anoon's arrival he discovered he might indeed be the right person at the right time in history to make their dream become a reality for all of his followers. It was all due to a closely guarded secret. Ethlacos was the only other source in all of known space that had a recoverable concentration of Tetra-G. The discovery of the ore came quite by accident during the expansion of their settlement. The discovery totally changed how the occupants of Rakaris Rim viewed themselves. Suddenly, their goals weren't so elusive. And now, instead of having to 'appropriate' Tetra-G, they might ultimately be able to make it themselves. Data on how to process the ore was easily obtained. The right equipment to further refine and store it could be made by operations robots. All they needed now was more money with which to lure others to their cause. They also needed to expand their settlement in the exact opposite direction!

With time on their side and a source of high-grade ore ready for exploitation, their aim was totally renewed. Eventually, transactions for the purchase of Tetra-G using the normal channels would be halted. But only if they had the capability to properly refine enough ore.

Andakar, only thirty-four light years away, and with its rich sources of lucrative pharmas, held the perfect way to help fund their operation. Desperation was a powerful motivator. And their desperation was enough to continue to 'appropriate' pharmas as needed, even if it meant some people might not receive them who had already paid for them. It wasn't like Andakar was without the means to replace them.

More than a few well-chosen number of the more expensive pharmas had been stolen over the years, converted into black market credits, which had helped continue to expand their operation. Limited mining had already produced dozens of tons of raw ore. A small amount of refined Tetra-G was easily produced. But what they needed was a full-blown smelter. That would take at least a year, at minimum, to build. Yet building such a plant underground was impossible. And, at this point, they couldn't risk exposure aboveground. They had already become a menace. Exposure would bring immediate repercussions.

So far, no one had found their base of operations. Ethlacos, and thus their tiny settlement of Rakaris Rim were safe. Indeed, Atriel, its sun was a dim main sequence star of no major interest either. And, despite Andakar having what amounted to a working military, Anoon knew they couldn't be everywhere all the time. Space was simply too huge. In addition, there were always those who could be bribed to provide much needed information. Such as who was piloting ships from the *Guardian* space station. When those ships left. Which pharma freighters would be escorted. What was being shipped, and to where. Important and timely information led to proof of loyalty. Proof of loyalty led to a one-way ticket out of the clutches of the Consort. Although life was very good even to those on Andakar, the chance to break away from a benevolent taskmaster had a powerful allure.

Despite having a pretty good idea how to go about financing their colony, no one, not even Anoon, could have anticipated that Andakar would up and arrest their planetary director, much less demand independence from the Consortium. His source of information, strategically working in one of the largest spaceports in Tokaias, had never even alluded to such a move. It was clearly a well-kept secret, just like theirs. This news would turn the tide for Ethlacos. If his personal musings served him correctly, he had what amounted to a deal which Andakar couldn't turn down.

All that needed to happen next were successful negotiations.

Chapter 41

Corren Grusics, First Executive of the Deep Sky Mining Consortium Supreme Board of Directors, pressed the back icon on the screen to watch the last part of the vid again. It was filled with information that simply couldn't be true.

> 'We regret to inform you that Director Alarr has been detained by the Manager General on the Guardian space station. Reasons given were grave and serious, one of which was attempted murder. But there's more. Chief Councilor James-Po, in collusion with every provincial manager on Andakar, has declared a state of emergency along with a demand for immediate independence from all Consortium provisional business ties and taxes. Calls for a political election are being discussed by a large number of rather influential people. Sir, this is an extremely dangerous and volatile situation. No one here in the Planetary Director's office is sure whether we will be detained or arrested for similar made-up charges. Please advise as soon as possible. Also, you should be aware that the aliens discovered in the cavern at 44.971N/-116.283W on Rylerra appeared to have come through some sort of dimensional gateway. We know this now because of two Space Navy pilots and two other Andakar Citizens who have been across this gateway and have returned. In fact, they came back with a human who they claim is from an alternate universe and is quite familiar with the creatures found in the cavern. Sir, these recent events are completely without precedent. We request you send an immediate response team. We can't risk another transmission for the foreseeable future.'

The vid abruptly ended, but the metadata accompanying the message stayed on the screen along with the coordinates of the cavern mentioned on Rylerra. It was highly unusual to receive a vidcomm directly from a Planetary Director's staff member. Moreover, Corren couldn't believe what he had heard. The Manager General of the space station had detained their Planetary Director? Attempted murder? Andakar was demanding independence? A person from an alternate universe? It was not only absurd, it was completely laughable! And had the Chief Councilor gone mad? How could the CEOs of the dozens of large businesses on Andakar be calling for a political election? Had they all gone mute? He'd heard not a single word from any of them. All of them had impossible-to-break ties with half a dozen worlds or more, including some of the largest corporations on Earth. This was simply the most bizarre vid he'd ever received.

Corren's agitation was so great he stood and glanced at the table to his right where the brandy decanter begged askance. But that could wait. He needed to get into action immediately. He pressed an icon on his desk surface. The desktop background changed to display the names and locations of the rest of the Executives. Quickly, he pressed the icon for Second Executive Jafar Rohita. Despite Jafar being six hours ahead and it was nearing eleven o'clock his time, Corren was sure he'd be able to get the man.

Jafar's security system answered. The virtual agent asked why the call was being placed. Corren merely spoke his security code and the agent's face dissolved. Moments later Jafar appeared on-screen, wiping sleep from his eyes.

"Corren, why the top security?"

"Watch this vid. You are not going to believe what's happened." He pressed another icon on the desktop and the vid played for Jafar.

At that moment, Jafar received another top priority communication. Trying to decide which was more important, he chose to place Corren's vid on hold and muted him, telling him so, while scanning the tags on the new vid. Only thirty seconds into the vid he stopped it, went to the very beginning, then unmuted Corren.

"Corren, what in blazes is going on here? Look at this!" The vid was from the Planetary Director on Alkunos.

'Jafar, we've just received several clandestine communications from Andakar. Local officials have arrested Director Alarr! Offworld communications and transport has been halted. Halted, do you hear! Assets have all been frozen access to quantum computer channels to discover why this is happening have been locked out. Locked out! This is impossible. I demand to know why this has happened and why we have no access to Andakar.'

Jafar halted the vid. Corren's mouth was tight with frustration as Jafar continued to play the vid he had received from Director Alarr's office.

"How did this vid make it to Earth?" Jafar asked.

"Perr Volkis, the PD of Jerrin II sent it."

"Yes, yes. That, I know. I mean how did it arrive? Communication has been halted from Andakar," Jafar asked again, now wide-awake.

"It appears Director Alarr's office had an open encrypted channel that wasn't closed off during their blackout."

The look on Jafar's face was of incredulity at what he'd seen in the last several minutes. "I'll call an emergency session of the full Supreme Board of Executives."

"That's going to be difficult. Two are on Luna. Abela is on Mars and two here have non-negotiable schedules for the next week," Corren told him as he looked back to the calendar on his desktop. "Regardless, Abela will be able to attend. She's wrapping up her meeting there anyway."

"Agreed. I can go, too. She should be contacted immediately. It won't be the quickest meeting in the world, but it will happen. In the meantime, I suggest we find a way to contact Director Alarr's staff."

"I'm sending a comm buoy today but it will only make it a few days before us. The fastest transport to Andakar will take twenty-one days," Corren said.

"This is bad, really bad," Jafar fretted.

"It's probably worse than bad," Corren fumed. "More than six weeks will have passed before anyone from Earth can arrive to find out what's going on there. That gives those-those insurrectionists on Andakar plenty of time to organize themselves and consolidate power. Simply put, it means they'll be ready for us."

Corren barely slept that night wondering how he was going to manage this unprecedented issue. The number of meetings and trips he'd have to cancel was going to be very difficult to do. Nonetheless, it would have to be done. The next morning during breakfast Corren was surprised to find another vid awaiting him. This one was from Siloy. It was a demand that he come to Andakar immediately. The slightest grin crossed Corren's face as he forwarded the vid to the rest of the Executives who he had already booked for passage to Andakar. The grin was because he had finally determined precisely how he was going to handle this disruption of business.

The words rebellion and traitor kept running through his mind as he watched the vid over and over while finishing his breakfast. He had never even considered the possibility of something like this happening before today, but then wondered how it could have been so long overdue. Hadn't history been full of rebellions? Factions splitting off from existing powers? One power overthrowing another? Corporations had spun off entire divisions, merged, only to split again many times. Yet, in every case he'd ever been witness to either legally or economically, it had always been accompanied by lawyers, newly elected or assigned boards, and new by-laws. Business had run smoothly for centuries. This was totally different. An entire planet simply up and decided for itself how it was going to go about doing business!

The Citizen file on Siloy James-Po wasn't large. Only three point six terabytes. The majority of it was reference to the vid record of the decade or so when he was a popular entertainer. That was before he was on the local planetary council. Corren was completely uninterested in his entertainment record. It was his dramatic rise to the rank of Chief Councilor that was of most interest to him. His extreme popularity made him a beloved figure. Opposing a highly regarded native would be difficult at best. That was surely going to add to Corren's troubles once he arrived, he was sure of it. He saved the file for later once they were outbound to Andakar. Then he'd learn all about Siloy James-Po. Every man had his weaknesses.

Corren's first assistant had already cleared his schedule for the next several months. Such a complete clearing of his schedule was entirely unheard of, but simply couldn't be avoided. After all, traveling to the far end of Inhabbed space was not a quick and easy undertaking. The next task was to alert a security detail of twelve men. Corren had already determined he would need a crack team of covert operations people. There was no way he was going to what amounted to a hostile planet, 'invited' or not, without a security team he could trust.

The twelve men, lead by Satto Phanafor, were part of a team who had proven themselves twice during local disturbances, and once when a CEO of a subsidiary of a metals fabrication company in South America had been suspected of underhanded dealings. Not only were the men experts with weapons, they were experts in stealth ops, knew how to sift through databases, and had even used questionable tactics to extract much-needed information from people in ways that were always 'within prescribed law limits'. Corren was sure there was much more going on than what the short communication vids from Andakar had revealed. Getting to the bottom of it and in the fastest way possible would be paramount. Thus, shortly after their arrival on Andakar, perhaps even while he was at a table with Siloy and his cronies, his men would already be dispersed throughout Tokaias looking through computer records, asking the right questions, and making the required scans. Newsvids would be sifted, CEO interviews would be recorded and people would be questioned. Nothing would be left to chance. He had every intention of stopping what he considered a mutiny before he left Andakar.

The next stop was to Mars. Third Executive Abela Senerete had been given all the relevant information via FTL comm buoy and had already reviewed it before their arrival in orbit. Abela was still quite surprised at the news once she boarded their ship.

"Are the rest of them on board?" she asked almost immediately.

Corren had just finished shaking her hand. "Yes indeed. Jafar is here. And Satto."

She cracked a smile. "Good." She knew Satto to be their most loyal special ops team leader. "I'm sure that after we've arrived and they've done their jobs, this misunderstanding, for lack of a better word, will be over before we leave their space."

"I'm certain it will be. As certain as I am First Executive."

Less than six hours after they were underway Corren held the first of his formal meetings with the other directors. Satto attended each meeting, something he'd never been privileged to do before. Usually, he was simply given the information he needed, passed it on to his team, and he led them to do what was needed. This was a highly unusual situation and warranted his attendance.

Before this unusual turn of events, his services had only been needed to make sure that corporate law was adhered to under penalty of incarceration or heavy fine. Adherence to corporate law sometimes required 'special' interviews where a little more than arm-twisting, in a literal sense, was required. In this case, only incarceration was being discussed.

It was during the second week aboard their vessel when Satto received an important communication from Earth. A previously unknown individual named Kestin Dryter on Andakar had much to do with how and why the two Citizens who were employed by the Andakar Space Navy, had gone through the so-called gateway on Rylerra. No one understood what his involvement was so far. One of those Citizens was the son of Chief Councilor Siloy James-Po.

During one of the meetings Corren explained to everyone precisely how the various issues would be handled.

"Jafar, I want you to meet with Satto as often as is necessary to not only find this Dr. Dryter, but to obtain whatever information he has. I want to know how Siloy was involved. There is no way he wasn't. I want you to lead the investigation with him." Satto nodded, as did Jafar.

"Abela, since you know Inandra personally, I want you to handle her release. I suspect it will be a simple matter since there is no planetary law that can legally prevent you from doing so."

Abela gave him a nod in acknowledgement.

"Of course, all of you will be directly involved in the initial meetings with their Chief Councilor. Later I will take their 'guest', this Efren Llarena, to Rylerra. I suspect he knows a lot more about that dimensional gateway than anyone on Andakar or Rylerra is aware of."

"What of the language issue? He doesn't speak any languages we're familiar with," Satto asked.

"I'm sure by this time someone has fed either a language translator bot's memory with his language or he's been taught at least the rudiments of ours."

Satto scanned the last page of the report on Efren. "All of the Citizens and Siloy's pre-Citizen son speak his language, according to the report."

The group read the rest of the report and acknowledged that the language barrier would be the least of their concerns after all.

"Each of us has our assignments. By the time we're done this will be a dead issue and we will not have to hear more about it ever again."

Corren had thought about it a lot. The dimensional gateway would be of extreme importance. All the data, however sketchy it was, pointed to the fact that no one on Rylerra or Andakar had claimed the gateway for anything other than the anomaly it was. On the other hand, he had already determined he would be declaring the object or device, or whatever it was, a Consortium artifact. This status would automatically force discussion of the device and delay any attempt to declare independence by Rylerra, too. He certainly didn't want this infection to spread.

By day seventeen in transit, the events that had been pieced together from the vids and other data they had continued to compile no longer surprised Corren or any of the other men and women who were privy to the twice-daily meetings.

Indeed their tasks had been firmed up and had already been drafted into documentation that would be formally presented to Siloy during the first day of their meeting. Lawyers would be present. Satto would eventually be there to take in everything he could, too. Corren was aware that Satto could read a person better than any computer program he had ever used.

The day before breakout to the Andakar star system Corren had a formal vid prepared. The vid was to be sent directly to the newsfeeds the moment they were clear of electromagnetic interference. In it, he merely pointed out that the dissolution of ties to Earth would lead to tremendous hardship for Andakar, and which would ripple throughout the entire Consortium. His confiding tone told his target audience he was arriving to provide structure and support, or just a 'helping hand', to welcome Andakar back into the fold. In the interest of profit and harmony, economic ties of such long duration and magnitude that all of them shared could not and would not be severed.

He did not discuss anything that would allude to how he intended to make sure no local elected official would be remaining in office once they was done. That would ensure nothing of this nature would never happen again.

Chapter 42

Efren Llarena set the vidPAD down on the tabletop. It was quite unfortunate that Empire Spanish was a different language from the Spanish spoken in this universe. After getting access to much material in various formats of what he discovered was known simply as 'Spanish', he quickly discovered it was as different as Lingua was to him. Sure, there were recognizable phrases here and there, verbs somewhat similar, and dozens of nouns were close, but this Spanish was a dialect which was impossible for him to decipher. It seemed the divergence of the two languages occurred at least a thousand years ago, making this version sufficiently different enough as to be useless to him.

It could have been far worse. He could have ended up in a universe where Spanish had never been spoken. Regardless, it meant none of the automatic translation devices available to him were useful. In addition, RNA learning technology was not only not available, the very mention of it to anyone familiar with it resulted in a lecture about how horrible it was. That was certainly not the case in his experience. How else could he have been able to learn the incredibly complicated navigational skills required for deep space travel? How else could he have been able to learn how to cook the cuisine of three worlds? His sellez casserole was the talk of every person who ever tasted it. The very concept of it being horrible technology angered and disgusted him.

Perhaps the worst possible thing he had learned in the last six weeks about his native culture on Earth in this universe was that the Spanish Empire ceased to exist over a millennium ago. That explained why Naylon had been grilling him about history. In this 'reality' Angla had defeated King Philip's navy and eventually went on to become the global world power for hundreds of years. It was nearly impossible to believe that backwater Angla had become a world-spanning power! The very thought that more than ten centuries of long and illustrious history, a history he was steeped in yet didn't exist here, had caused a sadness nearly impossible to allay. It was all he could do to not break down in tears. Tears he didn't know he had inside him.

But Andakar had a treasure trove of pharmas. Some of which had already been prescribed. His sadness was on hold for now. It didn't provide him with much solace though. For now, he realized that as soon as he no longer used them that sadness might return. Perhaps worse than before.

He stared at the title at the top of the page: Lesson 20, and emitted an audible sigh. He had had no choice but to immerse himself in this frustrating endeavor. He had been alternately annoyed and fascinated learning this way. Frustrated, because he was well aware RNA would have made the ridiculous amount of time he'd spent on these language lessons utterly moot. Indeed, within a few hours he would have been speaking Lingua fluently.

Regardless of the frustration at how slow it was to learn anything here, he was still fascinated with this method of instruction. He had never been forced to learn another language. Indeed, he had never been forced to spend hours of time learning anything as an adult. A simple injection, followed by a two-hour nap, had yielded a treasure trove of new knowledge. But not here. In this universe. On this world. Yet, despite that, he already had relatively decent command of basic grammar, vocabulary, and had participated in twelve two-hour long conversation sessions with his designated Tokaias University linguistics professor. Holographic language interaction was quite simple between lessons. There were pharmas that enhanced memory. He had been taking them, too. They were nothing like RNA but they made his ability to learn seem sharp and clear.

The morning sunlight finally found its way to the top of the table where he was sitting, diverting his attention. The sliding glass door at the balcony had been open, allowing in a steady breeze. It wasn't so humid today. He stood, went to the deck and stopped at the railing, gripping it with both hands as he looked over the west end of the city. His view was from twenty floors up, which provided a view with no obstructions. He had been provided with plush quarters, far more luxurious than his station in life warranted. A small favor for providing them with the secret to space travel. A secret they already had but, oddly enough, didn't. The irony was he had emerged into a universe which had no knowledge of warp conduits yet had mastered the stars. It still surprised and amused him when he thought about it.

Further on was Koehkelko Bay. The bay with barely any tides. He didn't care for it at all. Without a good twice-daily flush of water, like what happened all over Earth, the bay smelled. In fact, he was slowly but surely coming to the conclusion that he had made a supreme mistake in his hasty decision so many weeks ago. The decision to help Naylon and his friends. If he had known then what he knew shortly after his arrival on Andakar, he was sure he wouldn't have done it. How horrible it was that hindsight provided so much information.

It was becoming increasingly more difficult to hide his fundamental disgust with a culture he had no choice but to live in. It took all the military training he had accumulated throughout his short life to hold his tongue when he saw Naylon reach for Darreth's hand, or when the planet's second most famous performer on the vidscreen kissed her partner live on air. But that wasn't the worst of it. He was already aware of the seemingly all-pervasive greed nearly every native of this planet seemed to exude, due to their entire culture being centered around business instead of conquest. Where was the glory in making photronic credits? And, they had no memory of their very own flesh and blood's past. Not a single person he had met and asked could tell him anything about someone they were related to more than five generations ago. That disconnect from their very own culture made him feel claustrophobic. That alone was part of general discourse on the two planets he had lived on and the three others he had visited, albeit only briefly. Comparing notes on ancestors was the fluid that oiled civilized interactions.

That aside, a growing emptiness held sway most of the time. The psychologist assigned to him, who he had grown to admire and be wary of at the same time, had been extracting bits and pieces of grief from him with varying amounts of success before the pharmas had been suggested. He had left everyone behind to escape endless war. Now he felt a tremendous amount of boredom, followed by the knowledge he would never be returning home, followed by periods of elation that he had been brave enough to have done what he had done, followed by his growing antipathy toward the culture he found himself less and less enamored with as time went by. Perhaps all of it was because of the isolation he felt. There were literally only four people he could directly communicate with. And none of them were women. Perhaps the most compelling reason for his loneliness was lack of intimacy with a woman.

After the initial one-week period where he wasn't allowed to leave the *Guardian* space station, several people had interrogated him each and every day. At first, he had been pleased to tell them everything he could: about the Empire, its peoples, the Telkans, how long they had been at war. Everything. Naylon, Darreth and Rehl took time out from their own lives to act as his interpreter. Tann, despite having perfect knowledge of Empire Spanish, had not been among them. He was apparently too young and the far too important juvenile son of a dignitary to be a part of his 'recovery'. That left three people whom he could communicate with directly after all. When it became obvious he knew nothing of importance strategically or tactically, the questions quickly became much more mundane. During that week, he realized Naylon and Darreth weren't just buddies or mere friends. They were a couple. A couple which would have been relegated to the fringes of every society he was aware of. Given that he had no choice other than them to communicate with, he had asked as many questions as he could about their culture. That's when he discovered his view of male-male relationships was considered 'quaint', 'lacking' or 'medieval'. Rehl had made it very clear. It was something that would take time to adjust to, if he ever did. Or wanted to.

Despite himself, he still couldn't shake a profound admiration for all of them for their incredible bravery. He had no idea a gay couple would be so inclined to do what they had done. That one would willingly risk his life for the other. But did this entire culture have to accept same-sex couples as completely and totally normal? There was RNA and therapy that tilted anyone's tendency for same-sex anything in the right direction! This culture defied logic and standards that had been in place for centuries, if not millennia.

His musing over these various issues came to a halt as he mulled over a recent change of events. Apparently, Darreth's father Siloy was leading what he would consider a rebellion. Several rallies had already taken place and an election had been held. Something of great political importance had taken place, but he was completely uninterested in it so far. At least his estimation of the events, what little of them he was able to piece together, led him to believe this was an extremely important if not unprecedented turn of events for this planet. The long tenure of this Consortium, which seemed to run everything, was apparently beginning to lose steam. Efren was surprised it hadn't happened long ago. How could any organization keep its citizens in line without a real military? It seemed impossible. Yet, this civilization only just recently resurrected its military, and only on a miniscule scale. The military berthed in Andakar's orbit was a mere squadron compared to what he was not only familiar with, but had been a part of for his entire adult life. Calling it a military was laughable.

Naylon told him only yesterday that the head of the entire Consortium was coming for a visit and would be arriving in only a few days. He discovered that the man's visit would most likely end with some ugly words, declarations and sanctions, not to mention a lot of lawsuits. Efren wasn't entirely sure he was privy to precisely what was going on, but as far as he knew there was no going back now. Andakar had declared itself independent of the Consortium's all-encompassing economic snare and was striking out on its own. Indeed, the Manager General of the *Guardian* space station had recently been declared a military commander. A small purge of sorts had recently taken place where anyone not loyal to their move toward absolute local rule was allowed to leave their ranks. Apparently, at least one person who had been slipping information to the deposed Planetary Director had been given an ultimatum. Naylon wasn't specific, but it seemed the person would be losing more than his bank account. Much of the political nature of the move toward independence bored him, although he could tell that the entire Andakar economy would probably be in real trouble in the short run. All in all though, it was a situation that he had never had to think about before. He was a military man. *Ex-military now,* he thought with a sigh.

He returned to the table, took a sip from the glass next to the vidPAD and pressed the on icon again. He spoke the heading aloud. "Jorga And Kessen Go To A Party." The words were becoming more and more easy to pronounce. Verbs and nouns more easy to recognize. Except for a few irregular verbs, the majority of them had a single conjugation for each tense, unlike his native language. Stringing them all together into more than just what a two year old would say was becoming a lot simpler. He activated the holographic soundfield and proceeded to listen and respond as the interactive program began again.

Chapter 43

Nolis Imla, Inandra's personal attorney, sat across the table from her down the hall from Inandra's detention cell. Nolis was a smaller woman than Inandra, with a statuesque body and wavy platinum blond hair. But her looks were not what had brought her to the top of her profession. She had one of the most brilliant legal minds on the planet, which was why Inandra had chosen her when she first became Planetary Director. Plus, she was from Earth, and thus Inandra expected her to be sympathetic to her interests.

"Nolis, you will get me out of here by the end of the day," Inandra demanded.

"You know that's impossible," Nolis replied.

"You are my personal attorney, not the Chief Counselor's interrogator."

Nolis rolled her eyes. Inandra was becoming increasingly more difficult to deal with. Her normally calm façade, one Nolis was personally familiar with, had all but disappeared in the last week.

"When have I interrogated you, Madam Director? I am *your* counsel. And a damn good one at that," she reminded her client with a cold hard look.

Inandra fell silent. She was simply angered beyond words that she was still in detention due to an insanely high bail. That alone would result in a monumental lawsuit once she was released, she thought to herself.

Nolis scrolled through the next page on the flimsy she had on the table in front of her. "The second phase of the hearing starts at two tomorrow afternoon, as I just said. I expect you to be on your best behavior."

"What exactly does that mean?"

"It means that although you are angered at this nonsense you have to be careful about what you say and how you go about this," Nolis lectured.

"When does the contingent arrive from Earth?"

"They aren't due for another few days."

"I don't want ambiguous replies," Inandra told her.

Nolis sighed. "Four days."

"Four. Four days," Inandra spoke, somewhat to herself.

Nolis just nodded.

Inandra crossed her arms and pouted like a child. "I will not stand for this."

"Madam Director, I can't make their ships warp through space any faster." *She's really starting to come apart*, Nolis thought, not without some amusement.

Inandra was quiet once again. Her shoulders dropped noticeably. "Is Raxi here?"

"He's in the waiting room."

"We're done."

"No we're not."

"I said we're done," she emphasized, although in a tone that fell well short of her usual haughtiness.

Nolis switched off the flimsy's display and allowed the screen to roll up. She was becoming increasingly exasperated with Inandra's mood swings. Perhaps having Raxi speak with her would calm her down. Otherwise, something from Andakar's extremely large pharmacopoeia might be in order.

Nolis left the chamber. By law, nothing said in detention could be recorded, which was still the case here.

Zelin gave Nolis a tight smile as they passed each other in the hallway. Nolis left the building entirely since she had to prepare for the next day's proceedings. This was only the third time she'd been able to see Inandra since her arrest. Inandra's detention had come as a complete and utter surprise. But once she had read and understood the charges against the Planetary Director, maybe 'shocked' more accurately captured her feelings. Being the woman's attorney didn't mean she couldn't form her own opinions and draw conclusions. She would still defend her to the best of her considerable abilities. Yet, if even one of the charges leveled against Inandra were true it would mean the woman would never hold that post again.

Inandra didn't speak when Zelin entered the tiny room. He noticed right away she was completely different. Her normally overconfident demeanor was almost entirely gone. There were lines on her forehead, something which he didn't remember ever seeing before. He quietly took the chair across the table from her. The black stripe across the top of its blank white surface was the only way to determine that an invisible barrier lay between them. They would be able to speak to each other, but anything crossing the barrier would be vaporized. They both knew that.

"What took you so long to get here?" she demanded.

Haltingly, he told her. "I-I couldn't get away immediately. I had to know how much they... knew."

"The very fact you're here means they know nothing," she retorted icily.

"Clearly," he responded, trying to regain his footing.

"Well?" she barked, making an impatient gesture for him to speak.

"If you're asking me to help in your defense you know it will be quite impossible."

She stared at him.

He wondered if she had become dense all of the sudden. "I'm not an Andakar Citizen. You know I can't come to your defense. If they're smart, and you know they are, they'll discover the payments. They'll know I was... involved."

"Get out," she quietly said.

"I just got here," he huffed. He'd never seen her like this before.

"Go back to Rylerra where you belong. Don't ever come here again." *He's a weakling*, she decided.

"You can't mean that. I came here to provide you with moral support."

"I don't need moral support. What I need is to be out of detention."

He needed to divert her attention. "I heard Corren's on his way," he said.

"Yes."

"I've been in contact with Second Executive Jafar many times. I don't know him personally, but I have a working relationship with him, of sorts." A tic developed under Inandra's left eye. He noticed that. "I-I still have some weight," he added.

She ignored his assertion. "Like you said, Zelin. They'll discover what was going on."

"They need you and they want you to remain PD. Their sole goal will be to get you out of here and put Siloy in here where he belongs. I can be useful in that endeavor."

What an idiot, she thought. "They won't trust you."

"I made a normal landing without so much as a nanosecond of official chatter interfering with my right to see you," he whispered, trying to reassure her.

"Get out," she told him anyway.

Zelin was thankful it was over.

Chapter 44

Anoon Tilshar and Marn Sokarikay, his fiancée and currently his second-in-command, were only two hours from breaking out of the wedge from Ethlacos. Breakout would be one point two AU from Andakar. He expected an escort once they arrived but wasn't exactly sure how they would be received. Actually, he expected explosive decompression to greet them by way of one of Andakar's Space Navy pilots. Thus the state of dress they were both in before that moment could arrive. He and Marn had only just now started putting their clothing back on. She was still bare-chested when he reached out, gently laid her on her back on the cabin's bed, squeezed her hard nipples again and kissed her. Despite her moans of pleasure, it was time to get serious.

After dressing and having the cabin bots clean up the room, both were seated in the pilot and co-pilot's chairs. They both watched the timer count down to one. The forward screen's grey instantly shifted to black. A tenth of a second later the nav system overlaid guide stars. The guidance system computer indicated they were within ten thousand meters of their expected breakout point.

"There's the signal," Marn said. "Three hundred thousand kilometers off starboard. Initializing standard greeting."

Anoon braced himself, hoping to at least see the beam before it destroyed their ship. Unexpectedly, they received a request to input coordinates to the *Guardian* space station. One of the escort ships positioned itself behind them as they made their way toward Andakar. Sure now that they were indeed being welcomed, Anoon started looking forward to this. He knew Andakar was a resort planet. He intended to enjoy some of the planet's offerings sooner rather than later, since he anticipated a quick resolution during his planned meetings.

Anoon and Marn had not been granted the courtesy of passage to the surface. That slight greatly ticked off Anoon, but he understood he needed to work with Siloy. He didn't want to push things too far. They had had to wait over six hours before Siloy and several of his staff came up to the *Guardian*. In attendance too were Rish Illigan, Rylerra's Planetary Director and some of his staff. Anoon had nearly demanded him to be there as well.

"I have something you need and you have something I want," Anoon told Siloy bluntly.

Siloy looked across the table from the man in the conference room. He could have easily made it into orbit hours before, but had delayed it on purpose. He had gone over every scant detail of this man's background. Armed with that, he felt far better about dealing with him. "What might it be that we want?" he asked.

"Marn," Anoon said with a slight gesture to her. She unzipped the bag at her feet and lifted a transparent container up from the floor to the tabletop.

"Rocks," Siloy stated flatly. There was a ripple of laughter around the table.

Marn turned the container. The row of lights and the display were obvious to him and the rest of the council members. "You will note that this container is sealed with a Redetch field," she said.

Siloy was taken aback. There were only two reasons to have rocks sealed in a Redetch field.

Anoon glanced at Marn and immediately upped the stakes for the men at the table. "I will be happy to take anyone you elect back with us to the Atriel system. There they can see for themselves that our outpost on Ethlacos possesses a rather large quantity of kajite."

Everyone around the table looked at each other. It was well-known that kajite was the raw mineral from which Tetra-G was mined. That was what was in the container. It was also just as well known that the raw material was transported in a Redetch field to prevent its radiation from affecting living tissue. The mineral contained far too many heavy elements for open transport.

Once the chatter of this revelation settled down, Anoon continued. "After receiving word that Andakar had arrested, er, detained, its PD and then declared independence, we decided it was time to formally reveal ourselves to you. We did not want, I repeat, *not* want to continue to have to, er, appropriate any more pharmas from your star lanes. It has never been anyone's intention to bring harm to those worlds which needed them." Anoon looked around the table smiling. He hoped he was convincing someone he was being sincere.

Siloy's mind was working fast. He was just about sure that when Corren and his contingent arrived in two day's time one of the first things his lawyers would do would be to restrict Andakar's allotment of Tetra-G. That would be the first thing he would do to make sure their face-to-face meeting would go as he desired. That's why one of the first things he did after his declaration of independence was to order an inventory of every fuel container known to exist anywhere on the planet. So far, it had been determined they had at least a two-month's supply, possibly more. That didn't count supply ships still in the pipeline. Fortunately, the time he felt he had bought immediately quintupled if not sextupled, once Darreth and others had brought to his attention that warp conduits existed between stars.

"I believe there is a far more important matter we need to discuss other than a so-called alternate supply of Tetra-G," Siloy answered. "That would be your contact with our PD."

Anoon leaned back and grinned. "Can you say 'played'?"

Siloy's head tilted slightly, trying to understand his meaning.

"I played her. Plain and simple. I led her to believe she was in my confidence. I received payments from her for bogus information. She was led to believe I would reveal where we were located. But everything's different now. She has rightfully been jailed. You have surprisingly declared outright independence, which is something we were utterly incapable of doing. We have gathered enough evidence to know now that despite your Space Navy's need to, uh, get rid of us, you are on our side."

Siloy snorted. He needed a lot more convincing. "You and your people have shown a distinct lack of responsible leadership in proving that point."

Anoon shook his head. "If you mean those people who might have died as a result of our pharma appropriations, then I truly, truly am sorry. But you know as well as I that most of them would have died anyway. As far as I'm concerned we, uh, lifted only strategically needed pharmas which would not be greatly missed, as well as those which would provide us with what we needed. We did it to further the exact same cause as did you."

Anoon stood now. All eyes were on him. "And I commend you for your amazing bravery. You single-handedly have done something that's never been done before. You removed a singularly corrupt PD. You declared true independence from this-this Consort that's run our lives like eternal parents." Siloy's senses were piqued. He could almost hear venom dripping off every word Anoon spoke regarding the Consortium.

Anoon paused for effect as he looked at everyone present. "I offer you an alliance. You provide us with protection. You have a Space Navy that can prevent the Consort from finding us. From finding our source of kajite. A source for you as well. Our surveys prove a fifty-year supply at present consumption levels for us, Andakar and," he looked at Rish Illigan, "Rylerra. That might not be much, but the survey isn't completed yet. We suspect there's a much greater quantity. But we need more bots to find out. Bots cost money. Andakar is wealthy. Andakar might be willing to help us to help themselves."

Siloy was greatly intrigued with the offer, but was equally concerned with how the man was proposing his deal. "We have no way to process kajite. I'm sure you know this. Our economy is geared almost entirely toward the production of pharmas."

"Not Andakar, sir. Rylerra. We're well aware of the profitable mineral wealth generated on Rylerra, the production facilities and the smelting plants. Its infrastructure is already tuned for processing ore. I offer you a far better deal than I believe you are aware of."

Siloy looked at Rish. He hadn't spoken at all during this entire discussion. Leaning back in his chair, Rish told Anoon exactly what he thought about the man's proposal. "What makes you think we want to have anything to do with your-your deal?"

"Because we believe you will have no choice but to follow Andakar's lead and declare independence alongside them."

"Outrageous." he began. "I have no interest – ."

Siloy held up his hand to stop Rish from speaking. "Rish, I propose an hour recess. We have a lot to think about. You and I have much to discuss before we even consider what Mr. Tilshar has proposed."

Rish exhaled loudly and shook his head.

Siloy sat across from Rish at a table in a private dining room down the corridor from where the negotiations had been taking place. The room was quiet. They were the only two people there. "Rish, how long has it been since you were back on Earth?" he asked.

Rish looked up at Siloy. "Six years, three months and some odd weeks."

"Not that you're counting. You regularly communicate with the Supreme Board of Directors, right?"

"FTL comms are sent about production, profits and other items as are required."

"And you willingly came to Andakar despite us having detained our PD."

"I did because you insisted. You were quite urgent in your request."

"It was because Anoon was quite adamant about you being here. Seems he's been keeping tabs on a lot of us. Which proves there are some disloyal Citizens who have funneled a lot of information to him and his people for quite some time," he said with a grimace.

"Disloyal. That's an interesting word."

"I don't use it lightly either. Loyalty is an extremely important trait in anyone, of course. Loyalty to one's family. Loyalty to one's employer. Loyalty to one's planet. After all, one becomes a Citizen of a planet, not a Citizen of the Consortium."

"Go on."

Siloy leaned forward and pushed his plate out of the way. "Rish, your son and daughter were born on Rylerra. They attend school there. You have ties to Rylerra that are far greater than your ties to Earth. You know it and I know it. They will soon be old enough to be Citizens of Rylerra. You are a Citizen of Earth.

"It's also obvious from our initial meeting with Anoon that he's not stupid. Both of us can see that. He's managed to provide leadership to a band of outcasts. Those loyal to him have literally thrown away their Citizenship to follow him for a-a dream. A dream that's within our reach now. Within their reach…. Within your reach."

"I have no intention of being disloyal like you've chosen to be," he said, his nostrils flaring. The recent election in every province on Andakar was still gnawing at the man. It made no sense that this local official was literally speaking for an entire planet. He looked away, unable to hold Siloy's stare.

"To who?" Siloy said coldly. He was goading Rish. But he could see it in Rish's eyes. He saw it in the meeting. Rish was vacillating. There was more at stake here than a nebulous loyalty to a collection of businesses.

"To... to..." But Rish couldn't complete his statement as he drew in a deep breath. He looked away, then back at Siloy. "How did you know?"

"Because you're far too fair to Rylerra. Your record proves it. Time and again, you've stood up for Rylerra's rights over the interests of the Consortium. I've read the tax revenue reports, seen the profit margin vids, and was told about the deals you've personally brokered. There's enough there to know that your interest lies with your adopted planet and not to Earth Central Planning."

Rish was absolutely amazed Siloy pieced all that together. "No one has ever called me on this. Not even the Supreme Board of Directors."

"Because it's not quite affecting their bottom line just yet. Just as you planned it. How old are you Rish?"

"Sixty-two."

"What will your legacy be when you're replaced?"

Rish was still filled with both anger and amazement. Siloy saw right through him. And here he was talking to a local administrator of another planet about it! "Nothing," he said slowly.

Siloy just looked at him. "This is your chance, man. Now. Leave something behind you can be proud of. Something your children will remember you for."

An hour later, the meeting room was full again. Siloy took his seat next to Rish. Anoon and his fiancée sat to the side. Siloy's lawyers as well as Rish's took their places. Guards stood outside the doors once again, making sure no one could enter and more importantly, hear anything. The long rectangular window at the far end of the room had been black this entire time, but now a tiny portion of the limb of Andakar was viewable 142,000 kilometers below.

"Rish and I have discussed your offer. We've decided we need to see your kajite reserves and do an assay on the sample you brought. If all goes as we expect, we will discuss the next phase of this negotiation. We will, in turn, offer you something far more than just protection." Siloy wanted to hover the nebulous offer in the air for Anoon to ponder. The unspoken offer was to divulge how to by-pass the suppression of the conduit detection circuit in their nav systems. After all, they would need a quick way to get ore to Rylerra if it turned out to be viable.

Anoon took the container from the desktop and slid it toward Rish. "I realize you will not be doing the assay yourself, but may I offer this to you in good faith. I assure you this is a typical sample."

Siloy continued smoothly, "As a good faith gesture as well, one of our pilots, Lieutenant Commander James-Po, will accompany you back to Ethlacos. He'll transport the assay team. Allowing you safe passage away from this star system is contingent on your agreement to cease all pirating operations in our star system."

"You have my word that no more misappropriated pharmas will fall into our hands. I gave orders that no 'pirating' operations were to proceed while I was off-world. None of our ships are currently in any starlane." With that, he offered his hand to Siloy. Siloy shook it after a moment's hesitation.

"We have your word, but you can see we both," Siloy glanced at Rish, "have our lawyers here. We will need your signature on the documents they draw up for this agreement."

"I may not be a formal Inhab Citizen anymore, sir, but I am perfectly willing to sign a monumental agreement such as this. I assure you this arrangement will be favorable for all of us."

"You what?" Darreth exploded.

"I told him you would pilot the shuttle that would follow them to Ethlacos."

"Dad, you're having me trail along with a known pirate over a promise?"

"And a formal signature. I assure you it's all legal. Son, you are in a unique position now. Not only have you and Naylon become some of the most famous people on this planet because of your adventure through that dimensional gateway, you are personally well known to Anoon and his followers. Who better to seal this deal?" He took a sip from his glass of selkwine.

"But they know me as something quite different. I've taken their people into custody. Some of them have died as a result."

"We've worked all that out. This offer of kajite is far more important than people you stopped in the past or how many people might have died as a result of their thoroughly illegal activities. You know what this means if it's true about their ore. Corren Grusics himself will be here very shortly. The first thing I know he'll do is to cut off our fuel supply as a leverage point. Thereafter it will be a matter of determining how well we'll be able to sustain ourselves in the short run. You will be instrumental in making history, son." One of Siloy's famous smiles drew across his face.

Darreth sighed audibly. It was stressful enough that in just a few days he would be signing a formal document with Naylon to make them partners. He and Naylon had already determined exactly how their contract would look. Although they could have simply signed the documents and moved in together, both of them wanted their family and friends present. After all, the public expected it. They had talked about a private ceremony, but that was impossible with their high level profile. Vid would hit the newsgrid. Vid for the entire planet to see? Of their joining? It seemed ridiculous.

Rish Illigan stood in the shuttle bay with Siloy on the *Guardian* space station.

"Tlor has informed me your shuttle's nav system has been converted to detect conduits and that you'll be heading for the closer of the two in our system. The pilot has already been briefed on the procedure to get through it as well. We'll have marker buoys staged on this end within a week for return traffic. The department that will be staging them offered to mark the Kaskalon end at half the cost of the buoys."

"Half?"

"The department head has already assured me he'll write off the other half. Think of it as good will for our neighboring planet. The data about the conduit suppression circuit is being sent along in your shuttle, too. You can have your people start modifying your ships as soon as possible."

"Who else knows about those conduits? It won't take long before every Inhab knows about it," Rish told him.

"So far, only a handful of people even know of the conduits' existence, much less how to modify the nav systems. There aren't more than a dozen and a half people on Andakar who even understand how the nav systems work and all of them are pilots and maintenance crew loyal to Andakar. So, I recommend only those people you can absolutely trust be made aware of the filter and how to circumvent it. It's going to take several more weeks before a replacement command module can be programmed without the suppression circuit. But enough of that," Siloy said with a dismissive wave of the hand. He opened his briefcase and pulled out a rolled up flimsy, which he gave to Rish. A bright purple spot on the casing cylinder was glowing.

"Authorized only?" Rish asked.

"You'll find formal documentation in there, but I'll tell you one of the main points. We formally request extradition of Zelin Raxi and four of his employees. Raxi a mining operations manager…"

"Yes, I know him personally."

"He's an accomplice to Alarr in this corruption case. He ordered my son's vessel to be pursued and disabled. He's at least partially responsible for your sat being destroyed. He also had Darreth and Rehl followed back here when they recently left Rylerra. We suspect he'll talk far more than our PD about this issue."

"Siloy, I truly am sorry this has happened." He lowered his voice and drew himself closer to Siloy. "In a way though I must tell you personally that I'm a little heartened about all of it anyway."

"How so?" Siloy inquired, with a slight tilt of his head.

"This is truly a monumental change of events. Who would have guessed this is how history would turn out? You were right. And I intend to be there. Here. At the beginning of all this. We must make it work," he said firmly.

We, Siloy thought as he smiled broadly. This was quite unexpected. He had no idea the man would say such a thing so quickly after being invited to join their cause. Maybe Rish was far more unhappy than he had suspected. He squeezed the man's hand in a tight handshake, then drew him close for a firm hug. "That's the spirit," he boomed, patting Rish on the back. "I'll inform you about what happens after the executives from the Supreme Board arrive."

Corren sat at the head of the table onboard their ship while he scrolled through the second flimsy, reiterating their courses of action. Flanking him were Jafar, Abela and Satto. Everyone's eyes were on their own copies.

"Jafar, you and Satto will go after Kestin Dryter. He's a key to how the others went through that gateway. I want to know what he knows. Abela, you will meet with Inanda's counsel. Determine exactly what has transpired since she's been in detention. I suspect Siloy will be gloating over his coup. He'll stumble for sure at some point," he said confidently. "I'll give him some time to do that before I head to Rylerra.

"Since the bodies of those aliens are still in cold storage I want see them personally. The holos are not like seeing them yourself.

"I will declare the portal an artifact. That status alone will buy time. The proper documentation has been drawn up?" He looked over at one of the lawyers in attendance. He got a nod. Corren continued. "Illigan's compliance will confirm his continued adherence to corporate law. I will press Efren Llarena for more specifics on what's on the other side of that gateway.

"I will ultimately call for Siloy's surrender after all this is said and done. Afterward, there will be several meetings with CEOs of the major pharmas to make sure I know where their loyalties lie."

The vidcomm screen on the desktop lit up. The duty officer on the ship was calling him. "Sir, you requested I let you know when we're one hour from breakout to Andakar," he reported.

"Acknowledged," he responded curtly. The screen went dark. "As we've previously determined, be prepared for these procedures to take at least two weeks." Then to Jafar, "Any word yet?"

Jafar looked at the message flimsy to his right. "No sir, the latest communication from Earth still shows the rest of the Board is undecided about whether to expand military ship manufacture. They won't even discuss a concerted effort to draw other companies in, much less a division, unless this fact-finding meeting turns up a worst-case scenario."

Corren leaned back in his chair and briefly rubbed his eyes. *It's already a worst-case scenario after all we've looked through*, he thought, already tired. *I guess I'll have to make daily reports back to Earth instead of weekly ones.*

Chapter 45

It was five minutes until insertion to Andakar space. Until now, Corren had spent the majority of his life within twenty-five light years of Earth. Flying out to the fringes of civilized space was not something he cared for at all. He much preferred the boardroom overlooking Hogenakkal Falls any day. But after having gone over such a huge amount of data over the last several weeks, putting aside such things as despising space travel was easy to do. These were clearly the most important series of meetings he would ever facilitate. Once they were completed, he was sure he would go down as the leader with the most foresight of any First Executive in the history of the Consortium. His immediate remedy for these recent actions by Andakar would be talked about for years, if not decades.

Foresight or not, no one was sure whether Andakar might use their Space Navy ships to their own advantage instead of for the good of the Consortium. There were plenty of laws in place, not to mention well-placed directors and managers on their space station to make sure such a thing couldn't possibly happen. Yet Corren was acutely aware their screening process was incomplete on several levels. In addition, no one was sure whether the Space Navy was still in Andakar's control or not. Clearly, the top people should all have been from Earth and not Andakar. How this could have been overlooked made no sense to him, he mused, not realizing how just such a 'colonial-attitude' had utterly failed a thousand years prior.

It was only in the last several days, while not in meetings, that Corren realized precisely why this happened. He was aware that the Consortium, with its multiple layers of divisions and division heads couldn't all be controlled. It didn't matter how many quantum processors were always churning away, crunching exa-quints of data around the clock, working out permutations to supply problems, or providing solutions to staffing issues. It didn't matter how many meetings with CEOs and managers there were, how they were screened, how laws were drawn up or penalties meted out. There were simply too many variables in life and throughout all the interconnected businesses to account for everything. That included how a man would ultimately make the simplest of decisions, how a man might decide what to do after having been vetted in multiple ways, using all available criteria. Or how a simple relationship might change someone's mind and throw out every solution that could have been arrived at. And most importantly, in the last half millennium, no Inhab had the resources to do something like what Andakar had done. That alone was the red flag everyone should have seen. But no one had. Not even him. Although business was run in a strictly regimented way, no one was at war. No one had been for centuries. The total lack of military thinking at the top levels of the Board had ultimately led to this.

It was clearly time to input a whole new set of criteria into the decision-making process.

Corren watched and listened to the preliminary contact with their escorts. He did so simply to determine the tone of what they might be expecting. After five minutes, it was impossible to discern anything other than their breakout was typical. No hostile intent was indicated. But he was also sure it might be impossible to determine anything by simply monitoring a routine entry being discussed by mere space traffic control personnel. Meeting with the Chief Counsel and the others would be a different thing altogether.

Several hours later, after completing a routine landing at the main space station outside Tokaias, it was still impossible to determine whether hostile intent was forthcoming. So far, all contact with planetside personnel had been customary for a contingent of their import. One thing he did note though as he listened in ever so often. He'd never heard Lingua spoken in such a clipped and accented way before. Not everyone spoke that way but a great number of them did. He was unaware such a shift in how Lingua was spoken had occurred.

Assigned quarters were in the huge administration building overlooking Koehkelko bay. Satto's contingent was assigned an entire wing adjacent to his quarters. His first assignment was to plug in to the Andakar planetary net to find Kestin.

Corren, Jafar and Abela would meet with Siloy and his staff in this very building only hours from now.

Corren's group accompanied him to a grandly appointed meeting room. Huge windows overlooked the park where dozens of people strolled. Further on, he could see three long piers running nearly a half-kilometer into the bay. Several large ships and many other much smaller ones were moored alongside two of them. All pointed to the luxuries Andakar Citizens enjoyed.

Siloy, Tokaias' City Manager Kalder Pent, Commander General Anz Tlor from the space station, several provincial managers and six top department heads from Andakar Pharma Enterprises took their seats. Corren noted right away that his group was greatly outnumbered. Regardless, he still had corporate law over them. As Corren observed the natives, he noted with growing awareness that they were all dressed in clothing styles considerably different than what he was used to on Earth. Not really observant of such details before, he noted how he and his contingent wore crisp finely-tailored suits to their seemingly casual apparel. This was an extremely important meeting. But every last one of them was dressed as if they were attending a party, he decided.

Pleasantries were offered along with refreshments before formal business started. Corren's initial meeting with Siloy before they entered the conference room had been brief since both parties had lawyers in tow. Corren had tried to discern the man's true intentions by reading his face. He got nowhere with that. In addition, nothing of a personal nature, much less of an official one had been discussed.

But now the tone was decidedly different.

Corren stood and brought up his main points before Siloy had an opportunity to say anything. "As you know, I am Corren Grusics, First Executive of Deep Sky Mining Consortium. To my left is Second Executive Jafar Rohita. To my right is Third Executive Abela Senerete. Before these meetings are concluded we intend to rectify this illegal severance of business and reconnect all ties that have been disrupted among the Inhabs due to this, er, mistaken notion that independent business operations are possible.

"In addition, a vid has been transmitted to your newsgrid network. It will be aired several times. In it, I have laid out the illegality of what has taken place here. It will become evident in the next several days that it will be impossible for Andakar to provide for itself for more than a few months without outside help and without the input of the Consortium's interconnected web of corporations. You must understand," he paused and looked at everyone in turn, "that the Consortium's network exists for the benefit of not only Andakar and Earth, but all Inhabs.

"I must make it clear that in addition to this unprecedented move on the part of local officials," he looked toward Siloy, "we intend to have Andakar's Planetary Director released before we are completed with these meetings." Looking around smugly, he sat back down to listen to how Siloy and his people would attempt to defend their position.

Interesting opening remarks, Siloy thought as he watched the plump man sit down. He was sure now that Corren was working under a full set of false assumptions. It had been weeks since his invitation had been delivered to the Board on Earth. Siloy felt certain Corren would have fully reviewed every available fact with respect to what had been initiated on Andakar. But apparently, the Executives were only selectively reading the data, or perhaps just ignoring the most important items. Siloy pressed the off icon on the flimsy in front of him. He had no need for any bullet points to indicate the flaws in the man's argument.

"Director Grusics," Siloy nodded to him. "Directors," Siloy nodded to the two others formally. "Welcome to our independent world. Andakar has declared complete independence from the basic ties of the Consortium as have been traditionally recognized. Since our initial declaration, many changes have been made. First of all, we legally detained Inandra Alarr on charges that have been officially laid out in not only vid but documentation, copies of which have been given to your lawyers. Secondly, our operation on the *Guardian* space station is no longer a cost center with respect to the transportation division. It is a fully functional military division which is being used and will continue to be used to maintain order on this planet and to provide for our defense, our defense as an independent planet." He paused momentarily for effect as he looked at each member of the Earth contingent. He wanted Corren to see he was completely serious. He was. His face took on a cold hard look. Corren had been busy congratulating himself on his opening performance. But now he realized it might have been a bit premature. Siloy was a much more formidable opponent than he, at first, had thought.

Siloy continued. "As you will note, despite the initial confusion of the first several weeks, business operations with respect to all Consortium divisions have resumed. It's just that we will be in charge of our relationship with them, not the other way around. I regret you were not informed of our actions before they occurred but we will not be deterred from this course. We intend to continue to be fully independent despite what may be thought otherwise. You will find that there are plenty of CEOs on board with this decision. You will find that Commander General Tlor here," he looked to his left and nodded at the man, "is also on board with this decision. You will find that the majority of the population of this planet has already given their opinion on this matter and are in agreement with the actions taken. You will find that we have not just up and removed all safeguards with respect to business or profits. We have in fact, secured them for our future. A future which reflects a change in the way Andakar will do business with Consortium ventures in this star system.

"The dissolution of the previous ties to Earth have been carefully and legally laid out on the flimsies you have in front of you," he indicated as he pointed to the nearest one. "You will find that the transformation of our Space Navy from a patrol force to a planetary defensive force was not taken lightly, but rather reflects our intention of backing up this policy change with force, if it should ever become necessary," Siloy told them, with an emphasis on the word 'ever', a subtle reminder they would remain ever vigilant. "You will find that you no longer have access to our quantum computer accounting network unless specifically authorized to do so. We will be taken seriously.

"From this day forward you will refer to me as President James-Po. Elections have been held and I have been duly elected as first President of this world."

Immediately, there was not a single person from the Earth contingent not talking. Siloy waited several seconds before calling the room to order.

"How dare you declare yourself 'President'," Corren bleated heatedly.

"Declare? I did not declare myself President," Siloy shot back, a cold look in his eyes. "There was an election which was legally held several weeks ago. 89% of the Citizens of this planet elected me as their first President. I will hold a six-year term. A Constitution is being drawn up as we speak, which will be worked out with the Citizens as we go. We have every intention of making sure this works for the benefit of our Citizens."

"Impossible. You may as well be a dictator!" Corren retorted. The two other Executives nodded their agreement with his assessment.

Siloy was somewhat amused at the man's accusation. He had never considered such a thing. In fact, he wasn't so sure he would actually serve his entire six-year term. Being Chief Counsel was stressful enough. Being elected President had automatically upped his stress level significantly. "First Executive, the data on the election is on the flimsy. You will find the word 'dictator' has not even been hinted at anywhere. To accuse me of being such is simply unprofessional. I would have expected better of you." Siloy shook his head, as if suggesting disapproval of a child.

Corren's mouth opened in astonishment. How dare this man! He hadn't been spoken to in that way for decades. "Chief... ," Corren started.

Siloy held up his hand and shook his head ever so slightly. "President," he corrected.

Corren's mouth tightened slightly before he spoke again. "President James-Po, you are aware that the sale of Tetra-G is tightly controlled. That control comes in various forms, one of which is allocation. I must warn you that this continued charade will result in sanctions. The first of which will be the re-allocation of Tetra-G supplies to Inhabs other than Andakar. Even if business interests on Rylerra purchase those supplies, they will be unable to allow the resale of it here. I'm sure you don't want that to occur," he said, looking straight at Rish. Corren knew that a simple change to the sales network would prevent the purchase of Tetra-G by any of the refueling stations on Andakar.

"You will not do so, Director." Siloy was bluffing. He was perfectly aware this would be the first thing Corren would attempt to do.

Corren nodded to Jafar, who pressed a few icons on the flimsy in front of him. Transmission of the codes to the ship in orbit, then to an FTL comm buoy to Rylerra would be occurring shortly. Siloy knew it was taking place at that moment. He suppressed the grin forming on his face. He knew the man was totally unaware of several important changes in Andakar's favor: that of the discovery of the warp conduits, their new source of Tetra-G and that the Planetary Directory on Rylerra had no intention of complying with the order.

Corren figured Siloy was trying to deceive him, yet decided to play along with him for the moment. *If Siloy wants to hang himself, well, I'll be happy to supply the rope*, he thought. The meeting had just barely begun and he wanted his lawyers to record as many items as they could about Siloy's obviously illegal actions. He leaned back in his chair, linking his stubby fingers together over his protruding stomach. This might turn out to be more fun than he anticipated. He imagined there might be any number of surprises still to come.

"Andakar has already made many changes with many more to come. It is far too late for our actions to be altered," Siloy added for the record.

Chapter 46

The flight to Ethlacos would have required traversing three warp conduits, based on preliminary findings of their locations. But the flight this time was via the normal wedging of spacetime. If the ore turned out to be viable, the secret of those conduits would be divulged.

As a gesture of goodwill on the journey, Marn volunteered to fly as co-pilot with Darreth in exchange for an equally high-level person from the Space Navy. At the end of the flight, all doubts Darreth had about what they were doing had been completely removed. He had enjoyed many hours of conversations with the woman. He found her engaging and quite charming. In addition, she was what he would easily call good looking. She was excited for him that he'd be getting married soon. She spoke several times of her forthcoming marriage, as well.

Darreth's tour of Rakaris Rim proved there were a large number of people who were eager to begin their long-awaited alliance. However, he was greeted by several small groups of hecklers just before his tour of the primary kajite mining shaft. They were not at all pleasant, but he was assured they were in the minority. Darreth felt that was to be expected. After all, his job had been to prevent their survival. How was he to know their ultimate objective? It surprised him he was even inside their stronghold at all. It surprised him even more that events had developed so quickly in the way his father had told him they would.

Darreth watched as a bot lifted a freshly blasted chunk of kajite ore from the floor of the mining shaft. Half a ton was placed in a Redetch field and sealed biometrically with his own retina scan. Proof that their discovery was real and the ore was viable would be realized once the container was returned to Rylerra where it would be thoroughly examined for quality. A 500-gram sample was sealed in a much smaller container. The assay team would conduct a preliminary examination during their voyage back later.

Darreth's new position as liaison allowed him to be privy to many top-level changes that had occurred on Rylerra since Rish Illigan returned home. Even before the Executives from Earth had arrived on Andakar to begin their meeting with his father, he now knew Rish had called several meetings of his own. An election would be held on their planet as well, but it wouldn't be happening for at least nine months. Even so, he already declared that Rylerra was officially allied with Andakar and Ethlacos. Immediately, high level managers protested. Many of them had strong ties to Earth and didn't like being forced to take part in what they considered an insurrection. Those protests were quickly quelled, not by force, but by careful economic reasoning and discussions about the huge profit soon to be made processing kajite ore.

All of the secret meetings and machinations briefly reminded Darreth of how he also had to secretly meet with Kestin Dryter to retrieve the original device that allowed one through the gateway. Darreth's omission about its existence and its secrets had been revealed to his father and those in his chain of command when he presented it to Commander General Tlor. That information brought an ass-chewing like he'd never received before. Directly afterward though that reprimand was expunged from the record. Since the originals and the duplicates were all on the *Guardian* now, Darreth was assigned the task of destroying them except for one original. Under the threat of a lawsuit that would ruin him, Kestin was ordered to talk to no one from the media until a thorough investigation of the data he had culled from the objects could be conducted later.

"We found Kestin," Satto stated, his face not showing any emotion as he entered the room.

Corren had been in the conference room with Siloy and their respective staffers for nearly eight hours that day. He had just finished up a half hour previous. It was exhausting, but necessary to obtain as many facts about their declaration of independence as possible. This news served to refresh him almost immediately.

"And?" Corren said eagerly. His shoulders squaring from their previously slumped position.

"It was exactly as we suspected. Aliens weren't the only thing discovered in that cavern on Rylerra. Each of them had some sort of device that activated the gateway. Siloy's son found one, figured out what it was used for, then sought out Dr. Dryter who successfully duplicated it. That's how they were able to traverse the tunnel into that other dimension. Once they returned to Andakar all of the devices except for one original were destroyed."

"For what reason?"

"He didn't know."

"That wasn't part of the official report about the aliens," Corren nodded. "That must be how they entered our domain. How did you discover that bit of 'information'?"

"We 'legally' used methods at our disposal," Satto told him, barely able to suppress his grin.

"I see," Corren responded, not bothering to hide his.

"One original is on the *Guardian* space station."

"And?"

"We don't have the manpower to get it," Satto said. "Nor can we discover its precise location. Dryter didn't have specifics. But that's irrelevant because he still had the template of the device in his duplicator. We, uh, 'requested' he make two of them."

"What of Kestin?" Corren asked.

Satto hesitated briefly, his tone disingenuous. "Sadly, he had… an accident."

"He won't be found," Corren intoned.

"No sir. He will not."

"Bring the devices to me," Corren ordered excitedly. "I want to see them myself."

"Yes sir."

The next morning's meeting started at eight a.m. local time. Naylon and Efren were to be in attendance this time, at least at first. No one from Satto's team would be present, including Satto himself. Naylon was to act as their translator despite Efren's newfound command of Lingua.

Efren was considerably interested in recent events now that the First Executive and his people were on Andakar. Naylon considered Efren a friend now and saw no reason not to keep him abreast of current events and the details of what was transpiring politically on Andakar. He had learned enough now to be aware that a radical change had taken place. A show of force might be necessary to prove Andakar's intent. That was something he could relate to. But the details had brought him to a much better understanding of the role he played in these events. He had leverage. Surprisingly unexpected leverage. This might be his chance. If the contingent from Earth wanted information from him, he would make a deal with them.

While sitting in the room adjacent to the conference room before they entered, Efren asked intentionally vague lead-in questions. He had been practicing Lingua with Naylon. But not now. He had reverted to Empire Spanish. He knew no one knew his language but was taking no chances. He spoke in hushed tones.

"Executive Grusics is considered an emperor, right?"

Naylon shook his head.

"Then how would you describe him?"

"He's just the head of the Consortium. That's all. Earth is over one hundred light years from here. His influence isn't what he seems to think it is. At least, not to the majority of Andakari Citizens. Personally, I think he's wasting his time."

"Is he the richest man on Earth?"

Naylon shrugged. "If not, he's damn well near it. He didn't get his position without amassing personal as well as planetary wealth."

"So, he's like the rest of the business leaders on Andakar. His focus is on profits."

"I really don't know anything about him personally except that his intention is to bring Andakar back into the fold. He can't seem to accept the reality of what's legally taken place. He seems to be caught up in some sort of conceited belief that no one would dare challenge Consortium authority, at least while he's First Executive." Naylon shook his head at the vanity of it all.

"What about conduit technology? Can't you exchange that for, say, security?" Efren was fishing. He needed to know what Deep Sky executives knew about it.

"I've been told they don't know a thing about conduit detection, much less how to navigate one. You do know they've threatened to cut off our fuel supply unless we capitulate to their demands."

"They would do that?" Efren asked innocently.

"I think they're bluffing. But it's irrelevant. They have no idea we know about the conduits. Using them will provide us with enough time to start producing our own fuel."

"How many conduits have you found?"

"Darreth told me that eight have been found in the systems they've mapped so far. It's going to dramatically change everything. All thanks to you, my friend." Naylon warmly patted Efren on the shoulder.

Yes, thanks to me, Efren thought. *And thank you, Naylon. You've told me exactly what I needed to know.* He hoped the smile on his face looked genuine. He tried extremely hard to make sure it looked that way.

One of the guards who had been stationed outside the main meeting room opened the door and pointed to the two men. Both Naylon and Efren rose and went to the conference room. Three hours later, after Corren asked a myriad of questions of him, Efren was booked passage to Rylerra. Siloy could see no reason why Efren couldn't go there with them, although he had no idea why it would be necessary. Legally, no one on Andakar had any authority over the man.

Naylon and Efren both left the conference room. They were free to go while the high level negotiations resumed after lunch and long into the afternoon, then evening.

"We have no intention of using our Space Navy for anything other than its original purpose," Commander General Tlor stated irritably, for what must have been the fifth time, he thought.

"Yet we have no guarantee of that," Corren replied. "Given the blatant breach of every corporate contract that ties the Inhabs inexorably together, you are in no position to tell us you have no intention of using your-your escort service against Earth."

Escort service, Siloy thought. *He tries to downplay their true use while accusing us of being a threat.* Siloy knew Corren was simply trying to rile his new space station General. No one had even hinted at such a course of action.

Tlor didn't bother to take Corren's bait. "We have nothing in our by-laws that even hints of using it as an offensive force against any Inhab.

We will continue to use our 'escorts' to make sure expensive pharmas get to where they're shipped and when they're needed. Andakar is well-aware of the need for the continuous flow of profits amongst the Inhabs."

"Without the input of your Planetary Director as to the pirates' whereabouts you can't be assured of your success," Corren told the General flippantly.

Commander General Tlor put his fists on the table and leaned forward in a convincingly menacing manner. He was starting to get tired of what appeared to him as unwillingness to comprehend simple statements. "The pharma industries on this planet are secure," he growled. "More secure than they've been in several years. The pirates have not only been dealt with, but their leader has been identified."

"What? Why wasn't this brought to our attention?" Corren asked, quite angered at this sudden news. After all, he'd been on Andakar for several days now and not a hint of this had been given to him.

"That hasn't been the focus of these discussions. As the documentation will attest, it was through no action our planetary director initiated. The facts all point to how she prevented us from learning their identity, their whereabouts or even how they knew where our ships were bound. That has come to an end."

Corren struck a conciliatory tone for only the second time so far. "Third Executive Senerete has requested the bail be reduced so Alarr may be freed pending her trial."

"Mr. President?" Tlor turned to Siloy so he could answer.

"We were coming to that."

"And?"

"This is what will happen, First Executive," Siloy began, glad the issue was finally getting the attention it deserved. So far, Abela had been meeting with her in private. The results of their discussions had not come up yet. But it was moot as far as he was concerned. "She will be granted immediate passage on a ship back to Earth. She will not be tried here despite the charges of attempted murder and planetary treasury looting. We will have nothing further to do with her."

Corren sputtered a surprise. He wasn't at all prepared for such a statement.

Siloy continued. "We have no need for her presence since her duties are no longer required. Several of her staff have already sought other employment. Tev Yannic, on the other hand, will not be allowed to remain on-planet. He's been deemed an accomplice in this matter and has been told to return to his Inhab of origin. He is no longer welcome on Andakar. If either he or former Director Alarr ever return, they will be immediately arrested and the original criminal charges reinstated."

"You can not banish Citizens from a planet, much less a Planetary Director!" Corren blurted, his corpulent face flushing.

"Need I remind you sir. Director Alarr is not a Citizen of Andakar, nor could she ever be, by law. That makes her an undocumented foreigner and unwelcome to stay. Especially after this clear criminal activity was uncovered. Mr. Yannic is a Citizen of Jaren II, not Andakar. He has no long term interests on this Inhab since he is now unemployed."

Corren tapped the tabletop several times with his stubby fingers, gazing at the room's other occupants. He was glad his lawyers were recording every word of this proceeding. "This is all very amusing. Very amusing, indeed. For the last several days you have provided me with evidence for enough violations of corporate law to have you jailed for the rest of your life," he finally said, smiling up at Siloy.

The lawyer to Corren's left touched his arm and shook his head.

Corren pulled his arm away with a hard jerk. "I will have my say," he told the man. Then to Siloy, "Your so-called election has no precedent in planetary colonial history. I do not recognize your presidency, Siloy James-Po. No one on the Supreme Board of Directors does. In fact, as far as we are concerned *you* are the criminal with clear unlawful intent. My lawyers have most of the appropriate documentation already drafted. After having personally witnessed your confession to multiple illegal actions, the case against you will no doubt be swift after formal charges are brought up.

"Keep that in mind while we make our passage to Rylerra to view the artifact and the aliens there. I will be meeting with the planetary director to assess the extent of this-this 'independence infection'. I intend to return in nine days. You will have resigned your position, turned local administration over to alternate local managers, and returned Inandra to her post. I expect you to accompany us back to Earth for a formal trial. If not, there will be severe repercussions. We are done here," he said pompously, heaving himself out of the chair and duck-strutting out of the room.

Chapter 47

Naylon and Darreth had just arrived at Partnership Hall in downtown Tokaias ten minutes previous. The hall had several different formal and informal rooms in it. This particular one was the second largest room in the building and one of the nicely appointed formal ones. It was filled with over two hundred people, which consisted of family and friends, along with journalists wearing head cams. The ceremony was scheduled to start in about an hour. The journalists had discretely interviewed a few random guests, thankfully staying out of the way of most people. Both Darreth and Naylon were still some of the most famous people on the entire planet because of their adventure on Rylerra and couldn't easily say no to their presence. Naylon had mixed feelings that their sudden notoriety hadn't faded enough for this to be a non-event. He couldn't wait for he and Darreth to eventually fade into history. That is, if the populace let them.

Both men had wanted Efren to attend their celebration, but sadly, that hadn't happened. Instead, he was halfway to Rylerra with Corren. Something told Naylon it was probably better Efren wasn't with them. Although Efren refused to say it, Naylon was acutely aware Efren seemed disturbed about the upcoming male-male partnership ceremony. Naylon couldn't understand why it still seemed to cause the man such consternation.

Darreth took his father aside for a moment. "Are you okay, Dad? You don't look well."

Siloy had no intention of divulging the ultimatum Corren had, only hours previously, given him about resigning his post. This day was to be for his son and his soon-to-be new husband. Siloy placed his hands on his son's shoulders, smiling brightly despite the stress. "It was an extremely long day. We'll talk about it later. Good news though. It's been brought to my attention that the ore was viable."

Darreth's face lit up. "Excellent! One of the Rylerran assayers who was with us said the same thing after he tested a small sample. He still wanted an official test done to make sure his methodology wasn't flawed. An interplanetary shuttle is no place to determine such things."

"Well, the deal is firmly sealed now. The first empty ore ships have already been booked for Ethlacos to take delivery of a shipment. I've already had a communication from Director Illigan about that. They've already started the conversion of one of their heavy metal processing facilities to handle the new ore."

Darreth felt a shiver of excitement work its way up his back. "Then it's really happening. The alliance is for real."

"We've even outlined how Ethlacos could restructure their governing system to take full advantage of our mutual strengths."

"We've done that? Why not them?"

"They've been living like pirates for years. Tilshar made the request to have us provide them with some, er, guidance. That's all."

"So, they don't think we're pressuring them."

Siloy sighed. "No, the pressure is on me." *You have no idea how much, son.*

Soon enough, Naylon and Darreth stepped up onto the raised platform. Darreth in his dress blues and Naylon in a crisp, black tunic. Words were exchanged, their kiss drew applause from everyone and they formally signed an actual paper document. Some things hadn't changed in hundreds of years.

Rehl had been assigned to accompany Efren as they made their way to Rylerra. He was extremely disappointed he was missing his best friend's formal signing ceremony, especially with all the hubbub because of their renown. But he knew it would be almost as good seeing it on holovid later when he returned.

Despite having an official translator, Efren had prepared himself well in advance, learning specialized vocabulary necessary for the deal he was going to make. It was during their second day in transit to Rylerra that he stole away to meet with Corren in private.

"Come in Efren. May I call you that?" Corren asked as Efren stood at the door of his quarters.

"Of course. That is my name," Efren responded.

"You're sure you don't want your translator here?"

"I'm sure," he said, enunciating as precisely as he could.

"Come. Sit," Corren told him airily, waving his hand as he turned to pick up a bottle. "I have a particularly excellent brandy I would like you to try."

Efren shook his head, not understanding the somewhat rapid pace of Corren's statement.

Noticing that Efren had not quite understood him, he shortened his request. "Uh, drink?" Corren pointed to the rich brown bottle he held.

Efren's eyes lit up. "Yes. Drink."

Corren poured them both small snifters and the two men sat on an L-shaped couch. Efren took a sip, then placed his glass on the coffee table. He didn't want to bother with small talk, so started right away. He had been on Andakar for far too long as it was to waste any more time. "I have information you want and need. I will give it to you in exchange for something I want."

"I'm sorry?"

"You do not know of a secret."

"I do not know of a secret," Corren repeated, not understanding what that meant.

"Yes. A secret kept from you about star travel. I hear no one talks about it."

Corren shook his head sagely. "There is no secret about it. We have traveled the stars for a very long time."

"My people have a way of traveling between stars that is unknown to you. President James-Po keeps this secret." Efren was trying to stay away from nuanced verb conjugations, sticking with present tense as much as possible.

Corren's mind was racing now, trying to discern what Efren was trying to tell him. "And you will tell me this secret?"

"It is one known to your people but hidden centuries ago."

"Hidden from who?" Corren asked, his curiosity piqued.

"Your fathers hide this secret. For profit."

Profit. Now that was a word that always merited his attention. He sat forward, speaking slowly and as clearly as possible. "What do you want in exchange for this secret?" He motioned with both hands back and forth between Efren and himself.

"To leave Andakar."

"That's all?" he asked cautiously, so as to not misunderstanding Efren's exact meaning. "Just to leave?"

"I wish to live on Earth. I no longer want to live on Andakar."

"Why?" He was sure Efren was about to tell him something about Siloy. Something even more nefarious than what he had learned in the hours of meetings he had already attended.

"Many reasons."

"Does any of this have to do with the new political climate on Andakar?"

"I do not understand 'political climate'."

"Uh, the changes that have happened. Siloy's election. Things like that."

"No. Other things," Efren said plainly, wasting no words.

"Are you sure you don't want your translator?" Corren was beyond curious now and desperately wanted to make sure he was getting the right information.

Efren adamantly shook his head. "No. Rehl can not know what I say. You will promise me to live on Earth," he demanded.

"You don't belong on Andakar anyway. They're traitors. I will grant you passage, er, travel, to Earth. When we return to Andakar I'll tell them you'll no longer live there. I have full authority to grant such a thing."

Efren didn't know the word traitor but he did know belong. "Belong. I belong on Earth," Efren said with a wide smile.

"Precisely," Corren said. "Now, what is this secret?"

Efren had his speech already memorized. The week before he had carefully not told Rehl the reason he wanted to know the exact words for conduit, detection system, and others phrases. And now he had the exact sentences in their proper order, syntax correctly laid out, vocabulary still fresh. He didn't stop until he explained it all.

Corren had a difficult time comprehending all of it. He had never heard of this suppression or filter circuit before. Could it be possible that hundreds of years ago it had been integrated into every nav system for the sole purpose of maximizing profits? Maybe no one knew what that radiation was that was being detected. Whatever the reason, it was certain Andakar was either using the technology or would be very shortly. Efren didn't know, upon inquiry. He only knew that some of the so-called conduits had been mapped. The strategic advantage such knowledge would bring to Andakar's fledgling independence movement would mean that he, and thus Earth, no longer had the upper hand.

This new information was greatly disturbing. Corren had been sure this issue was all sewn up before they left Andakar. Now, he was sure that wasn't so. And he was, at minimum, a month from getting back to Earth with this information. There was every indication, based on Efren's detailed knowledge of how his people traveled space, that he wasn't lying. Corren changed the subject, satisfied he had obtained what information he needed about the conduits. "This gateway you came through. What can you tell me about it?"

"Nothing. I was not aware such a thing existed until I went through it."

Corren ignored Efren's denial of its purpose. "Perhaps you can take me across and we can look."

Efren looked shocked. After all, this chubby, middle-aged man certainly didn't look like the type who would deliberately walk a block, much less want to go through a dimensional gateway. "There is much danger. It is… not smart."

"On the contrary, it's very smart," he said, sound quite full of himself. Corren could have kicked himself for not having studied the intel about the aliens a lot more closely when he first heard about it. After all, it wasn't a business deal, had nothing to do with accounting and had occurred at the far end of Inhabbed Space. During the long trip to Andakar he had studied the details of the mummified aliens, the reports about the mysterious stone structure in the cavern, the role of this Empire Efren belonged to and that they had long been at war with the exact same aliens. There had been hours and hours of vids about it all. Most of the information was nearly impossible to believe. But there was something nagging at Corren. Something had been left out. He was sure of it. Despite the hazards the reports alluded to about the other side of the portal, Corren saw profit. He had convinced himself there were more details than had been reported. After all, not a single person who had traversed the portal was a businessman or understood how business was supposed to be run or developed. He was sure Rylerran Citizens would soon be exploiting the gateway for the profit potential it represented. That much he had already decided before they had disembarked on Andakar. If it were true an entire civilization lay on the other side of the dimensional gateway, aliens or not, it represented a way to secure an even more lasting legacy than he'd already garnered. After all, no one in his universe was at war with the Telkans. A look. Just a look. To see if what was spoken of were really true. After all, what could a mere look hurt?

"You do not have the travel things," Efren said. "They were... broken."

"Travel things?" Corren needed Takaramyus, but there was no way he was going to let the Lieutenant Commander know anything being discussed here.

Efren held the fingers of his hands together, forming a circle. "The travel things to cross the tunnel."

Corren chuckled as he now understood what Efren was saying. "Not to worry, my friend. I have two of them." He stood and motioned for Efren to accompany him. They went to a desk at the end of the room. Corren pressed an icon on its surface and a small opening appeared. Inside were two of the disc-shaped devices.

Efren couldn't believe what he was seeing; his large brown eyes grew wide in surprise. "They said they ... broke them."

Corren chuckled to himself at the way Efren was speaking. The man sounded vaguely like a three year old. "These will work. I've been assured of it."

"Assured?" Efren didn't know that word.

"I have a guarantee," Corren told him smugly, holding one of the discs up victoriously.

Efren involuntarily bit his thumbnail. This was not good, he realized. This man was extremely powerful and was going to do exactly what he wanted. Despite Efren knowing it was exceedingly dangerous, even for a moment, to go across the barrier he nonetheless realized he had become a major player in the man's risky game. A game he had started. After all, he had offered conduit technology to Corren as bait. To gain himself safe passage off Andakar. He needed to get to Earth to start a fresh life. Earth was his home planet. No matter that it was totally different from the Earth he knew. He nonetheless held out hope that living there would provide him with an emotional anchor of sorts, in familiar territory. After all, a place called Spain still existed.

But that would have to wait. There was an exchange, a barter going on here. Unfortunately, Efren realized too late that Corren had not only a greedy look, but a downright hungry one. Efren needed to continue to make sure he got his end of the bargain. Unfortunately, it was only now that he understood the depths of the man's ruthlessness and utter disregard of the advice of others. He felt he should kick himself. The man actually had two of the devices!

Corren noted how distressed Efren appeared to be as he put the disc away and made sure the desktop opening was sealed shut. He snorted. Corren was convinced the emphasis placed on the risks were far too great. It was a ploy. A trick even. After all, anyone could be traded with. An empire. An alien culture. Did it really matter? Everyone had a price. Everyone. *Efren just proved that*, he thought with a haughty smile.

Corren had not spent his entire lifetime working deals, sealing them, and finding more engines to generate more economic wealth for nothing. More than two dozen times during the last twenty years he made sure those people under him who balked knew they would comply with his methods, or else. Corren was supremely grateful Efren had made his decision to defect. It simplified matters greatly, he thought, as he and Efren went to the couch where he raised his brandy in a silent salute before downing the rest of it.

Chapter 48

The ties that bind, Rehl thought. It was only moments before breaking out of the wedge to Rylerra. He felt awkward being aboard an official Consortium starship. After all, as far as he knew he was officially a traitor in their eyes, although no such words had been spoken to him. He had been treated with the respect he deserved given his rank and position as a highly skilled and trained pilot. But that wasn't the reason he was on board. He was representing neither Andakar nor the Space Navy. His official capacity was solely to serve as a translator between Efren and Corren, thus his lack of a uniform. Corren had insisted Rehl come along. Rehl had noted Corren drove a very hard bargain and was extremely persuasive. He wasn't privy to how the meetings had turned out with the man and Darreth's father, but wondered how Siloy had held up. Yet, Siloy himself had recommended this would be an excellent way to keep tabs on Corren. Actually, the flight couldn't have come at a better time: Rehl had some official business with Rylerra's Planetary Director later after the formal meetings had taken place.

"Good to see you, Rish. It's been a very long time. It must be extremely difficult for you on the very edge of Inhabbed space," Corren told the man.

Rish stood with Rehl, Corren, two of Corren's lawyers, Satto, and Efren in the spaceport terminal.

"Yes indeed, First Executive …"

"Corren, Rish. I insist you use my first name," he said magnanimously as they shook hands.

"Yes, yes," Rish fumbled. He was very tired. The time since his initial meetings with Siloy had been a blur of continuous work once he had returned to Rylerra. The long days of constant meetings and preparations for converting one of the ore processing plants had left little time for rest. Plus, he had been extremely busy trying to keep the fact that Rylerra was now allied with Andakar as secret as possible. That fact was still unknown to Corren and his people.

"Yes it has, Corren," Rish replied. "Much has transpired recently." He immediately turned his attention to Efren. "The famous Efren Llarena returns, too."

"Famous?" Efren asked in surprise.

"Extremely," Rish said as he took Efren's hand now and shook it formally.

"He's with us so we may get a firsthand tour of the cavern and that portal," Corren told Rish as they strode from the terminal to the awaiting transports.

"You are aware it's several hours from here," Rish indicated.

"Yes, I read the report."

"Then you know it's of unknown construction and origin."

"That much I am aware. But my friend here will be able to explain much more about it," Corren told him, indicating Efren.

"He knew nothing about it until Commander James-Po and his party went through it."

Corren waved his hand vaguely. It was more of a dismissal than anyone in the group was aware of. "That is of no concern. I believe there's much to be learned about the portal. Much more than is believed so far."

"Well, we can certainly visit the site but we'll be unable to tell you much more than what you'll see with your own eyes."

Corren grinned. "Enough about that. We have meetings to attend to," he said as he took a seat in the open car.

Rish and his lawyers, along with several mining executives were attending their second meeting with Corren and Satto.

After almost an hour of rushed questions and even shorter answers, Corren said, "So, to sum up, Rish, we're here to officially provide you with tools you will need to prevent the so-called independence movement on Andakar from coming to this Inhab. In addition, after going through all the vids and examining the data that has been gathered it would be best if the dimensional portal were declared a Consortium artifact. This status, as you are aware, provides a reservation for full examination by our science team for further exploitation and development as a source of revenue."

"Revenue? We were not aware it would be deemed worthy of tourism," Rish stated with a distinct surprise in his voice.

"That's merely one of the provisions in the directive. That aspect of the portal's value has yet to be determined." He shifted the topic. "Our team will need to examine the alien bodies before they're shipped back to Mars."

"Mars?"

"The exo-biologists there have the latest equipment."

"No need to go to all that trouble, Corren. They've been kept under strict quarantine since their initial examinations. Plus, we've had two other teams come and comb through the data. In fact, Efren has already provided current information about their race. He has had multiple contacts with them. I recommend you send a team of the best people you have to come here. Rylerra would welcome their expertise."

"The lab in Coprates City on Mars has accepted full responsibility once they've been released for shipment," Corren stated flatly.

Rish pursed his lips. This was certainly a one-way meeting, he noticed, laughing to himself nonetheless. He was glad for his multiple discussions with Siloy before Corren's arrival. It wasn't as if he'd never been involved with high-level discussions or negotiations before. This one was particularly egregious though because of the nature of the topic and that Corren would have no other way but his own.

Corren continued to go over the points he'd already laid out. "Efren will be accompanying us to view the portal later today."

"Are you sure that's wise?"

"Why would it not be?"

"What can he offer that hasn't already been officially recorded?" Rish asked reasonably.

Corren was silent for a moment, pondering what Rish could be up to. It was as if the man was trying to prevent his team from discovering something important. "If nothing else he'll get an opportunity to see where he first entered our uh, universe. I understand he's not been back there since he first arrived."

"Of course, sir," Rish said obediently. Silently though, he wondered what Corren's real goal was. He was certain Corren didn't really want to fly a few hours distance only to look at a dirt-floored cavern in Rylerra's outback.

Rehl sat opposite Efren as they both faced inboard in the shuttle transport. Touchdown to the cavern site was less than a half hour. This particular shuttle was quite plush Rehl noted, not realizing Rylerra had such luxurious transports. There were seventeen people on board, including the two of them. Rehl was noting Efren's odd demeanor. The man seemed troubled. He'd barely spoken the entire flight, had responded only when addressed, then returned his unfocused gaze to his lap. Rehl too couldn't figure out why Corren needed Efren on this trip. There was absolutely no information the ex-soldier could provide that he himself couldn't. After all, the reports had been in great detail. But Rehl realized it wasn't up to him. He looked up at the chronometer on the bulkhead. In six hours the trip would be over and they'd be back in the main compound.

Many things were going through Efren's head right now. He had already tried several times to change Corren's mind about going through the gateway. He went so far as to even plot out how he might steal the duplicated devices and destroy them if he could. But he knew that undertaking would be impossible. He didn't dare tell Rehl what had transpired because he was sure he'd lose his ticket to Earth. He didn't want to be implicated in anything underhanded. He couldn't risk that. Not after having made it this far. He also knew it would only be a short jaunt if all went well. If the opportunity presented itself, and Efren was sure it wouldn't, he'd prove to Corren there was nothing to gain by showing him a dark empty cavern on the other side of the portal. That would shut the man up fast, they would return and he could easily say Corren had duped him into going through the gateway if he were questioned about it.

Touchdown was nearly in the same place Darreth's shuttle had landed. It had long since been towed back to a facility where it had been repaired then flown back to Andakar. Now a cordoned off area flanked by automated sensor equipment stood outside the cavern entrance.

Banks of unidentifiable computer and monitoring equipment along with permanent lighting were crammed inside the interior of the entrance cavern.

Rehl strayed from the group for a few moments, placed his index finger on the logon pad of a display panel on one of the pieces of equipment and pressed several icons. *Hmm,* he noted. *Everything's in place, just like Rish said it would be.* He entered the security code. The display responded as he expected. He quickly logged out and returned to the line of men now traveling down the well-lit corridor to the larger room further beyond that contained the portal.

Corren wasn't at all concerned with what he was about to do. No one had any authority to tell him he couldn't examine the portal up close and in any manner he felt necessary. Indeed, he merely needed to announce aloud that the object was a Consortium artifact. It didn't matter that he had never examined any artifact in real life before. It didn't matter that he had clandestinely duplicated the devices he'd need to do a proper examination of it either. After all, Siloy ordered the destruction of most of the devices after it was determined what they actually did. That much he had learned from Rehl upon casual inquiry. As far as he was concerned, they had been as equally valuable as the portal itself.

The rustle of cold weather clothing accompanied hushed voices as the men walked down the corridor. Within minutes, they arrived in the large well-lit room where the anomalous dark polished rectangular rock lay in the very center. Rehl casually looked all around the cavern looking for the charges. There to the left, wrapped around that stalagmite. Another one to the right, behind the power supply for the lighting in that corner. He looked for the other ones. They were all there. Faint glowing pinpoints of light indicated they had power. Rish told him he would face no reprisals. In fact, the plan was Rish's own, as mutually agreed upon by both he and Siloy.

All twelve of them took turns looking at the polished rock. Several of them tentatively looked into the cylindrical opening. Efren and Corren deliberately did not.

Rehl was already bored with this. He already knew analysis of the rock by many people had turned up nothing but mysteries and questions. No one knew how the tunnel to the interior cavern was built, where the rectangular stone had come from, what it was made of despite looking like granite, how long it had existed, how it was powered, and most likely would never find out anything at all about it. Speculation was that it might exist in several dimensions, possibly dozens.

"Anyone hungry?" Rehl offered.

Several of the men quickly took him up on the offer. Rehl maneuvered them away from a direct line of sight of the stone. Three of the men took the small pouches of snack food Rehl offered them. Two others went for water bottles.

Corren watched as the rest of the contingent walked away. He kept one hand on the stone's smooth surface, beckoning Efren along with him. They rounded the portal so as to be out of sight of Rehl and the others. Corren quickly pulled out one of the devices. He handed it to Efren who immediately placed it in a pocket of his jacket. He immediately zipped the pocket up. Corren snapped on his lantern, as did Efren. Efren had already told Corren that they would be needed. Corren peered back at the men. Rehl wasn't looking their way just now. Corren beckoned Efren to walk ahead of him. They went through the tunnel as if to simply get to the other end.

Efren completely forgot about the intense vertigo that accompanied his previous transit. Corren was completely unprepared for it as a result. He fought for composure as he dropped to his knees. He literally crawled the rest of the way through the tunnel, emerging into a well-lit cavern, although the intensity and the color of the lighting were not the same as they had just experienced.

Both were astonished to find themselves face-to-face with two Telkans, weapons drawn, aimed directly at them.

Chapter 49

Rehl upended the bag of westrum mix and finished the rest of it off. He crumbled the bag then wiped his mouth. As he inserted his water bottle into the pouch on his belt at his left hip, he noted that he no longer heard Corren and Efren's hushed tones. He turned and glanced around the large open cavern. They had just moments before gone around the other side of the tunnel. Rehl zipped up his jacket a little more and quickly went to look for them. It was apparent within a millisecond that neither were in the cavern any longer. The fact that they had just been near the tunnel and were now nowhere to be seen instantly told him they had somehow gone through it to the other dimension!

"Where did they go?" Rehl said out loud. He had no idea if their sudden disappearance represented a new method of transfer they hadn't identified before, or if something much more sinister had occurred.

"What is it?" Corren's personal lawyer Dolet Krem asked as he hurried toward Rehl. He had noted the distinct alarm in the Rehl's voice.

"The First Executive and Efren are... gone," Rehl said, again loudly to get everyone else's attention.

"What?" Krem shot back. There was a sudden gasp from nearly everyone as the group quickly gathered in their direction.

"They were just there," Rehl pointed. "Now they're not. But that's impossible. The portal doesn't respond to anything except the discs."

"I just went into that tunnel!" one of the men shot back. He was the only one who had dared step foot in the cylindrical opening and go right up to the odd static-like barrier in its center.

"And you're still here. It's impossible to trigger the portal unless it's properly activated," Rehl told him firmly.

"Then someone must have done so," Krem retorted, overstating the obvious in true lawyer-like fashion.

"The remote controls that could do so were destroyed," Rehl responded immediately. "There's only one left and it's back on the *Guardian*."

"Obviously not. Get them back."

"How?" Rehl demanded. "I don't have a disc."

"You're the security here, you figure it out," the lawyer boomed.

He was indeed the security here. "Everyone. Get out now! Wait for me back in the entrance cavern," Rehl ordered. He began ushering everyone out of the large cavern, his arms spread wide while keeping his eyes on the tunnel ever so often. Once everyone had vacated the cavern Rehl pulled out a small pistol from his pack. It was a good thing he had kept it with him because it was beginning to look like he might need it. He made sure the last person was headed down the corridor, then turned back to the now empty cavern.

He placed his back against the polished surface adjacent to one of the cylindrical openings with his weapon aimed upward and listened for scuffling, crawling sounds, or anything that might indicate something was coming out of the tunnel. Nothing. Finally, he hazarded a fleeting look inside. The cylindrical tunnel was as lifeless as it had been when they first arrived not twenty minutes before. Rehl could only conclude the worst. Frantically, Rehl tried to figure out how this had happened. All but one of the discs had been destroyed, or so he thought. Was it possible it had been stolen? If so, did Efren get hold of it? The man couldn't possibly have known where it was, much less gotten it without help. Even if he had it, how had both he and Corren gone through the tunnel with only one disc? Was it possible they held on to each other? They hadn't even considered that method of transfer before. He quickly concluded there was no way to determine what actually happened. It would take days to find out if the disc was still back on the space station even if he sent a comm buoy right this minute. In a heartbeat, this sudden change of events completely altered how he was going to complete his task.

After determining there was indeed no sign of activity at either end of the mysterious tunnel, Rehl ran as fast as he could back to the entrance cavern. He needed to get a message back to Rish as soon as he could. This little 'event' was going to change how he was going to complete the task he had been assigned by the man. But first, he needed Corren's personal strongman Satto, to help him prove he wasn't responsible for their disappearance.

Corren had never been so frightened in his entire life. One moment he thought he would simply be traversing the portal's tunnel, the next he found he was nearly vomiting from intense vertigo. Worse though were the large powerful-looking aliens aiming weapons at both of them. He knew immediately they were Telkans. They were considerably more imposing looking than any of the descriptions he had read or the vids of the mummified ones he saw.

The look on Efren's face told Corren everything he needed to know. He realized he had made a horrible mistake only seconds before everything went black.

Satto had had to make sure his people were safe and had been more than willing to lead them out of the larger interior chamber. Once the group was all together, he had everyone exit the cavern and wait on the dry riverbed. Nonetheless, he hadn't been pleased at all about being hustled unceremoniously away and was already returning to the cavern when Rehl showed up out of breath. They nearly ran into each other.

"Phanafor, this way," Rehl told him decidedly as he jerked his head back from whence he came. "Where is everyone?"

"Outside."

The look on Rehl's face was all Satto needed to issue his order. "Dolet," Satto called out to Corren's lawyer. "Everyone will return to base now."

"Why?" he asked. "We're not in any danger, are we?" His voice was very shaky.

"No, and I intend to keep it that way. We'll stay and monitor the situation. Have the pilot send a standard rescue team. They'll have weapons and equipment." Satto was obviously preparing for the worst.

Everyone rushed toward the shuttle, now nearly in a panic. This wasn't Earth. Who knew what might happen. This was an alien planet as far as they were concerned, regardless of whether it was an Inhab. They moved quickly, but with all the dignity they could muster.

Satto drew a weapon from his holster and raced back down the corridor with Rehl. Moments later they reached the inner cavern. Both stopped and listened, letting their breathing calm down. Hearing nothing they circled the tunnel several times, searching, wary, weapons at the ready. Rehl had a sensor in his other hand. It turned up nothing, exactly as he suspected.

Satto came up to him to read the display. "He said he wouldn't do it."

"What are you talking about?" Rehl asked.

Satto barely knew Rehl, yet couldn't help himself. He knew Corren could be impetuous when it suited him, but the man had never been this reckless before. After all, no one became First Executive by acting irrationally. Apparently, Satto had grossly underestimated him. "The First Executive used one of the discs to go through the tunnel."

Rehl was sure it had been Efren. "How did he get it?"

"You don't want to know, nor will you. Regardless, it happened. He gave one to Llarena, too."

Rehl was in total disbelief. "Is the man crazy? He knows what we reported. He had no reason to believe otherwise!"

"He said he was only going for a quick look."

"How quick?" Rehl shouted at Satto, furious. "Do you see them yet?" He waved his weapon at the rectangular rock.

Satto didn't respond.

"How long do you intend to wait for them?" Rehl demanded.

Satto looked at his wristcomp. "If they don't return in another hour we're going after them."

"An hour!" Rehl laughed heartily. "Maybe you're going after them but I am not going through that portal again. I couldn't even if I wanted to. I don't have a disc! Even if you do I'm not going with you."

Satto thought about it for a moment. It would take a week, probably even longer, before he would be able to have more of the discs made and sent to Rylerra. The logistics were impossible for a quicker turnaround. "We have an hour. So, we wait. The rescue team will be here shortly after that anyway. Position yourself at the other end of the tunnel and watch," he said briskly. "If you see any sign of movement let me know."

Rehl glanced at one of the charges to his upper left. It was going to be a huge risk if he went ahead with what he needed to do while Satto was there, but he realized he might not have any choice.

"Power?" Satto asked, looking at Rehl's weapon.

Rehl checked the tiny indicator on its side. "Full."

"Good." He pointed for Rehl to stand guard at the other end of the tunnel.

Rehl ever-so-slightly shook his head. Here he was taking orders from someone not in his chain of command. It didn't sit well with him but he could tolerate it for now. Rehl sat on a rock several meters from the end of the opening, keeping watch on the cylindrical interior. He had been there for less than a minute when he heard Satto emit a gasping sound. Almost instantly, he heard a weapon discharge, a clatter, then a dull thud.

Rehl's heart rate skyrocketed. He fought for composure as he tried to hold his breath in check. It wasn't working. He had already stood and pressed himself against the side of the massive block of rock. Slowly, he rounded it and peeked. He could see Satto from the waist up, laying on his side in a heap. Rehl could tell that Satto was quite dead. He listened as he kept very still. Scuffling, then the distinct sound of metal against metal. Obviously, something or someone had emerged from the other end without warning. Satto's sudden demise only made that realization worse. He was next, unless he acted fast. He was nowhere near the corridor. He couldn't make a fast exit. Making a run for it was out of the question. Even if he got to the entrance cavern, it would take several seconds to login to the control panel and run the countdown sequence. There was no way he could make it without being either injured or killed. *Damn it*, he thought.

As quietly as he could he slowly raised his weapon, paying close attention to not make a sound. Hushed voices. They sounded odd, guttural. He was sure it was the Telkan language. There were most likely two, if not more of them. He couldn't tell from here. The voices stopped. He was sure they were assessing the situation, trying to determine if they were alone or not. He already knew the Telkans had sensor equipment. Could they scan through the mysterious rock and detect him? Would their equipment pick up his biosigns through several meters of its solid surface? If so, he was only moments from being very dead.

Footsteps. He leaned forward a tiny bit. Two Telkans. One with his back to Rehl. The other was facing left. Both were examining Satto's body. Neither had any sensor equipment at the ready. He was in the clear so far.

Rehl raised his weapon, aimed and pressed the trigger four times in rapid succession. Both Telkans spun around as they hit the dust. One of them fell directly on top of Satto, making his body flail momentarily like it had sprung alive all the sudden.

Rehl's breathing was in rapid-fire. He sprinted across the cavern and down the corridor as quickly as he could for ten meters, stopped, and pressed his back against the wall. And listened. His ears were ringing slightly from the weapons fire. But he still had plenty of hearing left to determine it was quiet now. Two Telkans. Two discs? Should he chance it? He had to. The odds of there being any more were next to nil. He was sure of it.

He slowly maneuvered himself down the corridor and back into the inner cavern. There was no sign of movement anywhere. The irony was that there were once again three dead bodies in this chamber. Only this time one of them was human.

The seconds tick off. There was still no sign of any other movement. He knew his assessment of the situation was accurate now. If what Satto had said was true, then the two dead Telkans had in their possession the two discs Corren had somehow obtained. He briefly wondered if Kestin had been involved or if the man had somehow contacted Corren. Apparently, the threat of a lawsuit against the man wasn't good enough. Had Corren offered him a full credit account? How else could the other discs have been obtained? Pure speculation. No answers. He ceased that train of thought.

Rehl kept his weapon trained on first one then the other Telkan, along with keeping an eye on the portal, just in case he was horribly wrong about the number of discs being used.

The Telkans were oozing yellow blood from mortal wounds. There. The first one had on a jacket with distinct pouches and zipper compartments. He patted several of them before he felt what seemed like a disc-shaped object. He unzipped the compartment, pulled the device out and let it drop to the dirt. Mustering up even more courage, he looked for the other one on the other alien. It was in a pouch at the creature's waist.

He shook his head. Seizing a rock that had long ago fallen from the roof of the chamber, he hefted it, then savagely smashed both of them. Surprisingly, both were brittle and easily broke. Corren was far smarter than anyone on Andakar had figured. Clearly, he was too smart for his own good. Who knew how many more there were? "Fruck!" Rehl said out loud. Worse though was that the cavern in the alternate universe had been compromised. It was quite obvious that Corren and Efren were lost on the other side of the portal, which the Telkans had clearly been occupying. Since there had been no sign of either of them, Rehl was sure now they had either been captured or killed. He had more than enough impetus to carry out his clandestine mission now.

He immediately activated the imager component of the sensor he had and snapped off dozens of 3Ds of the dead bodies as quickly as he could from various angles. He wanted to have plenty of evidence in his defense for what he was about to do. He made sure the smashed discs were in at least three of the images, too. Two minutes later, he was again sprinting as quickly away from the portal as he could toward the entrance cave.

He went to the console he had checked on when they first arrived, pressed his finger against the logon icon and entered the code. He looked for an options icon. Finding it, he changed one of the parameters. The program had been set to detonate the charges in two hours. That way they would all have been long gone from the cavern when the timer reached zero. He changed the countdown to two minutes. He watched the display for several seconds to make sure it was counting backward, then dashed outside.

The shockwave from the blasts was so massive that it shook the ground and even caused dust to fly out of the entrance. A slab of loose rock above the entrance collapsed in a dusty heap all over the side of the dry riverbed. He didn't have to see any more to know there would be no way any other Telkans would ever find their way through the portal.

Efren awoke with a massive headache in a dark cell. Only a red glow above him on the ceiling allowed him to determine the boundaries of the room. It was devoid of anything except for an alcove that was clearly a bathroom and a pullout bare slab from the wall, which passed as a bed. He sat up, holding his head.

He was nearly apoplectic with rage. Telkans, he spat. For the first time in his life he had been taken captive by them, and without a weapon to defend his honor. On a planet he shouldn't have been goaded into visiting. Once he started thinking about what had transpired, it made sense the cavern would have been guarded. After all, it was a Telkan Held World and they would be very interested in the portal. Idiot, he told himself. It would have been only a matter of time too that Lieutenant Navar would have been found either by his people or by that other team of Telkans. He had tried to convince the man of the dangers! He fumed at not having stood up more forcefully against Corren. In anger, he went to the wall and punched it. While nursing the new pain he had inflicted to his knuckles he was sure he heard Corren yelling somewhere nearby, or was it far away? He couldn't be sure. He had heard Telkan ships were nearly soundproof in their interiors.

"Welcome to Q'emt'la, soldat Llarena," Captain Pacudas said pleasantly as he stood dressed in a grey prisoner uniform in the center of the six-sided room. The men who had survived the Telkan attack months before stood alongside him and Rogerto Tomús's men. "It's been too long." He turned to his Lieutenant. "Navar, I believe you have some unfinished business."

Corren hadn't been so much as introduced to the eight men, but clearly they all knew each other. It was impossible to follow the exchange because it had taken place entirely in Empire Spanish. Nonetheless, the look in the man's eyes who approached Efren was unmistakable.

Lieutenant Navar's eyes squinted as he took aim. "With pleasure," he told the captain before he pulled back his fist and struck Efren squarely on the side of his jaw. Efren fell in a heap, out cold; blood splattering the floor and across his face.

Horrified at the immediate display of violence, Corren braced himself. He was sure he was next.

Epilogue

"The last of the water was drained out three hours ago," Aarón told Chimo.

"Then it's safe to go down now?"

"There's no mud. Just wet sand at the bottom."

"Okay, lower the ladder," Chimo told the other two. Domingo and Goyo lowered the ladder into the gaping hole.

Every week a new section of the quarry was ready for blasting. The odd part of the last one was that it opened up a large hole filled with water. The hole was a meter and a half wide, halfway up the side of the nine-meter high hollow chamber. Plumbing the hole, they discovered that it led to a huge chamber. Galea MarbleWorks had worked the quarry for nearly two generations. It was assumed the marble was solid for several more kilometers. No one had ever reported such a large opening in this rock mass in its entire history.

At first, after the water had been pumped out, Aarón send in a Tasker to investigate the anomaly. But after the discovery of a perfectly rectangular dark object in the dead center of a rather spacious chamber, he decided a Terran needed to investigate further. Since Aarón and Chimo were the owners, they would do the investigating. Both climbed down into the wide pit.

The Taskers had brought down several light panels, which had been placed around the edges of the chamber. Their soft glow evenly illuminated everything. As Aarón and Chimo looked around all they saw were a flat sandy floor and a dark rectangular, finely polished block of stone in the dead center. A cylindrical opening went directly through it from one end to the other. The opening was slightly over three meters in length and had the diameter the height of a man. Aarón peeked in, not understanding how this stone could have gotten here. It was clearly fashioned as if it had been made yesterday and deliberately placed in the dead center of this hollow chamber. As he looked through the cylindrical opening, he noted that halfway through it shimmered oddly. He couldn't see through it all the way.

"Look through there, Chimo. Tell me what you see."

While Chimo looked, Aarón went to the other end of the tunnel and placed a light panel inside the opening, hoping to illuminate the tunnel better. It did no good. Although it was obvious the tunnel went all the way through the block of dark stone neither men could see through its entire length. It defied logic. Aarón stepped back three steps, four, trying to figure out why. His heel caught on something in the shallow layer of sand. He pulled the object out and wiped it on his pant leg. It was disc-shaped, had an orange iridescence and, upon closer inspection, seemed to have some sort of tiny writing etched into its surface. Perhaps it was the illumination from the light panels making the coloration on the disc appear to be swimming. Like it was alive. This item appeared to be brand new, too. Were there more of these objects nearby? He kicked around the sand. His toe struck something. Was it just a large piece of gravel? He swiped it even more with his boot. No, it was another one of the objects.

"Chimo, look at this!" He called his partner over. Chimo went to Aarón and took one of them. He attempted to discern if what appeared to be writing was readable. Was it Empire Spanish, but merely in tiny print?

"Domingo, Goyo. Bring some more light panels," Aarón yelled to the men above.

The men ran back to one of the storage sheds to retrieve several more, returning moments later. Both of them stepped down into the opening with the other men, looking all around. For years they all knew the marble in this quarry to be of extremely high quality. Kilometers long, it was well known to have been a shallow sea millions of years ago, then intruded upon by an upwelling of magma, below which ultimately had cooked the accumulated limestone, turning it into the finest quality marble ever discovered on the planet. There was no way an artificially-made object could have survived the geological changes that had produced this formation.

"How could such a thing have been brought down here?" Domingo wondered aloud.

"I have no idea," Goyo told him, shaking his head. "What is that?" He asked Aarón as he pointed.

He handed Goyo one of the objects. "I found two of them buried in the sand. There may be more," Aarón told Goyo as the man inspected it. They kicked all around the sand. Finally, Aarón found a third one.

Learning nothing new after the third find, Aarón stood at one end of dark rectangular block of stone and looked into the tunnel. He knelt down to inspect the inside surface again. It looked as if it had been polished with one of the fine abrasives used in their finishing rooms. He shoved the two discs into one of his pants pockets, then crawled right up to the center of the tunnel. He reached his hand out and scooted a little closer. The nearer he got, the more transparent the 'barrier' became. He ventured his hand closer still. Suddenly it was as if he had been whirled in a circle extremely quickly. The feeling of vertigo was so swift and strong that he fell over even though he was already squatting down. Once he regained his composure, he quickly crawled headlong to the end of the tunnel opening. Choking weeds blocked his way. In panic, he pushed through them and immediately fell downward almost a meter and a half, landing squarely on his back.

He looked upward, trying to catch his breath. The vertigo, that only moments before made him feel as if he were being twirled in a circle, was slowly fading. Toward his feet was a high rock face. Behind him were hundreds of trees as far as he could see. To his left and right was a curved, leaf strewn path. Aarón turned over and rose up unsteadily onto his hands and knees, his stomach threatening any second to empty the wrong way. What was this place? How could he have emerged onto a wooded footpath when just a moment ago he was dozens of meters below the surface in a quarry and another couple of meters underground inside it?

Voices. He heard voices coming from the right. Someone was coming toward him on the path. Three of the voices were distinct. Now two of them sounded surprised. A man wearing a yellow jumpsuit took his arm and helped him up. He involuntarily accepted the man's assistance. He saw two more men. Everyone had a surprised expression on their faces. All of them were wearing similar outfits. Who were these five people? How did they get here? How did he get here? Where was he?

The vertigo was quickly dissipating, making it easier to get his bearings. Aarón saw that all of the men had patches sewn over their breast pockets with names on them. Names he had never heard of before. There were circular patches on their left sleeves with some sort of design on them. Writing spanned the patches in two lines. All of the words were totally unfamiliar. The first line read 'Xoch Resources, Ltd'. Its font was large and bold. The second line was in a smaller font. It read 'A Division of Deep Sky Cellulosics.' He had no idea what any of those words meant.

People, Places and Things

Aarón Celado	A partner at Galea MarbleWorks
Agica Prime	One of the 14 Consortium-developed Inhabs
Alista Kosovil	One of Naylon's co-workers and best friends. Alista is a paleoclimatologist.
Alitu	The Terran name for Kaskalon
Alkunos	One of the 14 Consortium-developed Inhabs
An'Arka J'selnof	Captured Telkan ranger
Andakar (*on-da-car*)	Pelagic world that orbits Eratil. Andakar's year is .92 Earth years long.
Anoon Tilshar	The leader of the Settled Worlds Alliance on Ethlacos
Anz Tlor, Manager General	The *Guardian* space station head manager and later promoted to Commander General.
ASN	Andakar Space Navy
Atriel	The star that Ethlacos orbits
AU	Astronomical Unit, the distance from a particular planet to its star. For Andakar, an AU is 141.5 million km.

Barcilio Navar, Lt.	Leader of the soldat team aboard the *Cortés Libre*
Ba'Tekta	A Telkan
Ba'Yod	Telkan killed by Urret and Agrida
Benja Ometo	Vice manager, Tokaias civic police
Bov Ghendeed	Previous mining operations manager on Rylerra before Zelin Raxi
Caddo	One of the people in Naylon's discussion group
Chimo Escartín	A partner at Galea MarbleWorks
Consortium, The	Also known as The Consort (a derogatory term). The collection of interconnected corporations that spans the 14 Inhabs. Corporate center is on Earth.
Coprates City	A domed city in Coprates Chasma on Mars
Corren Grusics	First Executive of Deep Sky Mining Consortium
Cortés Libre	A Terran military starship
Daníl Ocio	Soldat and the only female aboard the *Cortés Libre*
Doratzo Ranarde, Dr. (Capt.)	Doctor aboard the *Cortés Libre*
Darreth James-Po, Lt. Cmdr.	Protagonist, 6'2" (1.87m), 185lbs (84 kg), salt/pepper hair, dark brown eyes, Andakar Space Navy pilot. 29.8 Andakar years old (27.4 Earth years).
Deep Sky Mining Consortium	An interconnected group of interstellar businesses that provides everything to the 14 Inhabs
Déstica	Terran name for Rylerra
Domingo Fejos	A worker at Galea MarbleWorks.

Do'Yukya	Naylon and Tann's guard when brought back to M'jas'la from Q'emt'la
Droon	One of the people in Naylon's discussion group
Ebórica 4	Taskers are culled from this planet
Ecca	One of the people in Naylon's discussion group
Efren Llarena	Soldat aboard the *Cortés Libre*
Epo Agrida	Soldat aboard the *Cortés Libre*
Eratil	Andakar's sun and the primary of the Eratil-Kaskalon binary star system. G0 main sequence.
Ethlacos	The desert moon of a planet that orbits the star Atriel
Fério Atore	Terran prisoner on Q'emt'la.
Flimsy	A photronic flat film device similar in function to a book or notepad, but can be rolled up or folded, if needed
Fruck	Lingua for 'fuck'
FTL	Faster Than Light
Galea	A colonized planet in the Spanish Empire. This planet is an Inhab called Xoch in the Consortium.
Goyo Pretel	A worker at Galea MarbleWorks
Grevi Helop	One of the people in Naylon's discussion group
G'San	Telkan scientist
H-180	An 8-person transport shuttle
Hoit Roonyun	Turnstile operator at the Chendra spaceport

Dolet Krem	Corren Grusics's personal lawyer
H'Tor	Telkan scientist
Inandra Alarr	Andakar's Planetary Director
Inhab	The word used for a colonized planet within the Consortium, e.g., 'Andakar is an Inhab'
Ja'Ning	A Telkan
Jao Selaye, Commander	2nd in command aboard the *Cortés Libre*
Jarien Lazcún	Soldat aboard the *Cortés Libre*
Jaron Ress	Naylon's father
Joll Zenatel	Pilot hired by Zelin Raxi to follow Darreth
Juan Barcega	Soldat aboard the *Cortés Libre*
Julun	One of the people in Naylon's discussion group
Kalder Pent	Mayor of Tokaias
Kaskalon	Rylerra's star. The secondary in the Eratil-Kaskalon binary star system. An F2 main sequence.
Kattan	Andakar's single continent. Slightly larger in area than Australia.
K'ell or Kelna'ack	A marauding species that killed Telkans in the distant past
Kella James-Po	Darreth's 17 y.o. sister. Fraternal sister to Tann.
Kals Sanadan	Provincial Manager of Gartenda province
Kattan	The sole continental landmass on Andakar
Kestin Dryter	A physicist who duplicates the disc-shaped devices for Darreth

Kirin Arenti	One of Naylon's discussion group members
Koehkelko Bay	Tokaias is built along this bay
Kyana James-Po	Darreth's mother
Lingua	The primary language throughout the 14 Inhabs. A dialect of English.
Marco Zapante	Soldat aboard the *Cortés Libre*
Marn Sokarikay	Anoon Tilshar's 2nd in command and his fiancée
Merek Soliciellio	He works with Naylon and goes to Rylerra with him
Merrin Takaramyus	Rehl's wife
M'jas'la	Telkan name for Rylerra
Mu'Anelko	Leader Sa'Par's patrol ship
Naram	One of the people in Naylon's discussion group
Dr. Naylon Sente Ress	Protagonist, 6' tall (1.83m), 172 lbs (78 kg). 29 Andakar years old (26.6 Earth years). Ph.D., paleo-microbiology.
Nels Hodofar	Andakar's previous planetary director before Inandra Alarr took that post
Ne'Uanju	Minister on Q'emt'la overseeing the Terran prisoners
Nolo Gonjas	Terran prisoner on Q'emt'la
Nolis Imla	Inandra's lawyer
Nomed Jattison	Tokaias civic police chief
Nona Ice Station	The rescue center on Rylerra
Olton Avela	The man who rescues Darreth and Merek from the cavern on Rylerra

Omley	One of the people in Naylon's discussion group
Orl Ustbe	West Litok Provincial Manager
Os'Taga	A Telkan
Ozol	The name for Andakar coined by Captain Pacudas
PAD	Acronym for 'Personal Access Device'
Patoria Mountains	The mountain chain that overlooks Tokaias on Andakar.
Pelinex	An RNA injection used to allow Telkans to learn Empire Spanish
Pharma	Short for pharmaceuticals. Andakar's main export and derived from its unique sea creatures.
Photronics	The blending of photonic and nano-molecular components, which comprises the foundation of the technology used by the Consortium
Q'emt'la	Telkan name for Andakar
R'kinth'la	A colony planet in the Telkan Ascendency
Rakaris Rim	Pirate settlement on Ethlacos
Rehl Takaramyus	Lieutenant Commander Takaramyus is Darreth's best friend and works with Darreth on the space station
Rodigue Pacudas, Captain	Terran Captain of the shuttle *Cortés Libre*
Rogerto Tomús	Terran prisoner on Q'emt'la
Rylerra	Ice Age world that orbits Kaskalon
Sakirse	The main billeting area where most ASN personnel are stationed planetside
Sa'Par	Leader of the Telkan patrol ship Mu'Anelko

Sat	Short for 'satellite'
Satto Phanafor	Corren Grusics' henchman
Sedeto Confón	Terran prisoner on Q'emt'la
Se'leth	The Telkan word for 'Terran'
Shani Kuhenvik	Newsvid reporter on Rylerra
S'Hith	Telkan scientist
Siaron	Siaron province is one of eleven provinces on Andakar. The administrative center of Tokaias is located here.
Siloy James-Po, Chief Counsel	Darreth's father and Chief of all the provincial managers
Sked	One of the people in Naylon's discussion group
Sopka	One of the people in Naylon's discussion group
Sefana Veoc	Darreth's superior's adjutant and defender during his trial
Tamik Sil	Vice manager, Tokaias civic police
Tann James-Po	Darreth's 17 year old (in Earth years) brother, fraternal brother to Kella
Ta'Norat	Naylon and Tann's guard when brought back to Rylerra
Tasker	Animal-like creatures from Ebórica 4 used as servants throughout the Spanish Empire
Temorrah Ress	Naylon's mother
Telkan / Telkan Ascendency	An alien species at war with the Terrans in the alternate universe. The name of the collective of Telkans.

Terran	The name for 'human' in the alternate universe. Identical in every way with humans. Only the name is different.
Tev Yannic	Inandra's Assistant
Thal Asrattem	Hired by Zelin to follow Darreth off Rylerra (co-pilot)
Th'Gan	A Telkan
Tiso Urret	Soldat aboard the *Cortés Libre*
Tokaias	The administrative center of Siaron province and the largest city on Andakar. Tokaias is equivalent to a capital city.
Traig Maverol	One of the people in Naylon's discussion group
Ulult	One of the 14 Consortium-developed Inhabs
VidPAD	A device similar to a flimsy but with many more inputs and outputs, more memory, and solid in appearance (e.g., can not be rolled up or folded like a flimsy can be)
Xoch	A heavily wooded Inhab. One of the 14 Consortium-developed worlds.
Yarosay Bex	Eratil system traffic control manager
Yason Birovich	Nona Ice Station Rescue Director
Yoon Wakanabe	Darreth's immediate superior. Yoon is a Squadron Master.
Zelin Raxi, Manager	Inandra's lover. A mining manager on Rylerra.

About the Author

Please visit www.mark-kendrick.com for information on the author and his other novels.

ABOUT THE AUTHOR

Please visit www.mark-kendrick.com for information on the author and his other novels.

LaVergne, TN USA
30 December 2010
210641LV00005B/29/P